AFRICAN DAWN
TONY PARK

Quercus

First published in Australia in 2010 by Pan Macmillan
First published in Great Britain in 2011 by Quercus
This paperback edition published in South Africa in 2012 by

Quercus
55 Baker Street
7th Floor, South Block
London
W1U 8EW

A CIP catalogue record for this book is available
from the British Library

ISBN 978 1 78206 245 5

10 9 8 7 6 5 4 3 2

Printed and bound in Great Britain by Clays Ltd, St Ives plc

For Nicola

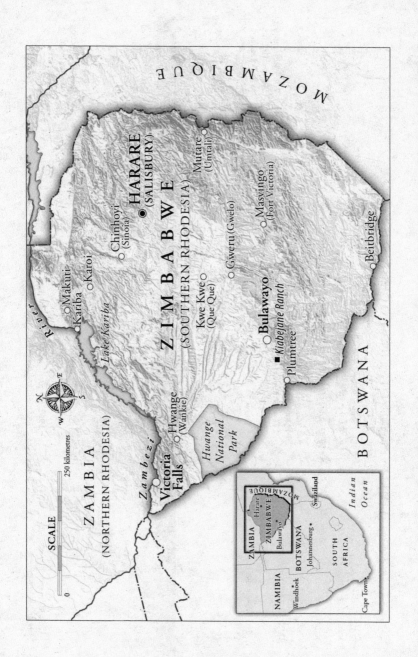

TIMELINE OF EVENTS IN RHODESIA-ZIMBABWE

1890 1900 1910 1920 1930 1940 1950 1960 1970 1980 1990 2000 2001 2002 2003 2004 2005 2006 2007 2008 2009 2010

1890 Cecil Rhodes's Pioneer column moves into Mashonaland and Matabeleland

1893 First Matabele War

1896 Second Matabele War (aka First *Chimurenga*)

1895 British colony of Rhodesia proclaimed

1924 Robert Mugabe born

1958 Zambezi River dammed to form Lake Kariba

1959 Strikes over bus fare increases in Salisbury and Bulawayo

1964 Northern Rhodesia gains independence, renamed Zambia
1964 Second *Chimurenga* (Bush War) begins
1964 Ian Smith elected Prime Minister of Rhodesia

1965 Ian Smith announces Unilateral Declaration of Independence from Great Britain

1981 Gukurahundi crackdown on Ndebele dissidents in Matabeleland begins

2000 Third *Chimurenga* – seizure of white-owned farms begins

1987 ZANU and ZAPU merge to form ZANU–PF

1999 Movement for Democratic Change (MDC) formed

1980 Robert Mugabe elected as Prime Minister (later President) of Zimbabwe

1979 Interim government of Zimbabwe–Rhodesia formed
1979 Lancaster House talks pave way for all party elections

2009 Government of National Unity formed between ZANU–PF and MDC

2008 MDC disputes election results, claiming victory over ZANU–PF

CHARACTER FAMILY TREES

The Quilter-Phippses

Fred Quilter — Sharon Quilter-Phipps

Lara Hamilton
b. 1962

m. 1980

Braedan Quilter-Phipps
b. 1959

Tate Quilter-Phipps
b. 1959

Jessica Quilter-Phipps

Ashley Quilter-Phipps

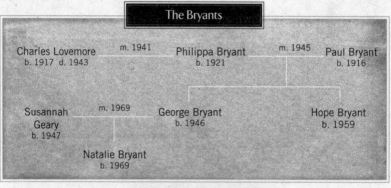

The Bryants

Charles Lovemore
b. 1917 d. 1943

m. 1941

Philippa Bryant
b. 1921

m. 1945

Paul Bryant
b. 1916

Susannah Geary
b. 1947

m. 1969

George Bryant
b. 1946

Hope Bryant
b. 1959

Natalie Bryant
b. 1969

The Ngwenyas

Kenneth Ngwenya
b. 1919

m. 1944

Patricia Ngenwya
b. 1924

Winston Ngwenya
b. 1945
(aka Winston Ndlovu)

Temba Nzou
b. 1950

m. 1980

Thandi Ngwenya
b. 1947

Emmerson Ngwenya
b. 1954
(aka Comrade Beria)

m. 1987

Grace Ngwenya
b. 1954

Naomi Nzou
b. 1982

Patricia Nzou
b. 1984

Tumi Nzou
b. 1986

Sally Ngwenya
b. 1990

Kenneth Ngwenya
b. 1993

GLOSSARY

Baas – Afrikaans for 'boss'. Common form of address for a white man, by a black man, in Rhodesia.

Batonka – Tribe indigenous to the Zambezi valley, displaced to higher ground when the Zambezi River was dammed and the newly formed Lake Kariba started filling in 1958.

British South Africa Police (BSAP) – Originally the police force of Cecil John Rhodes's British South Africa Company, the BSAP retained its name as the police force of Southern Rhodesia (later Rhodesia) until the formation of Zimbabwe in 1980.

Bru – Slang for brother or mate (from Afrikaans).

Bulawayo – Second largest city in Zimbabwe, located in Matabeleland. The name Bulawayo comes from an Ndebele word meaning 'place of slaughter' or 'place where he kills'.

Central Intelligence Organisation (CIO) – The secret police and intelligence service of Rhodesia and, subsequently, Zimbabwe.

Chimurenga – Shona word for 'struggle'. Zimbabwean history identifies at least two *Chimurengas* – the First *Chimurenga* of 1896–97 when the Shona and Ndebele took up arms against white settlers, and the Second *Chimurenga* of 1964–1980 (also known as the Bush War). Some veterans of the liberation struggle described the seizure of white-owned farms from 2000 onwards as the Third *Chimurenga*.

Chimurenga **name** – A nom de guerre adopted by pro-nationalist guerillas during the Second *Chimurenga* (Bush War).

China – Mate, from the Cockney rhyming slang 'China plate'.

Gandanga – Shona word for a guerilla or freedom fighter, also used by white forces (plural: *magandanga*).

Gook – Derogatory term used by US soldiers for Vietnamese civilians or Vietcong fighters during the Vietnam War; subsequently applied to black Rhodesian guerilas by whites. It was probably brought to Africa by American Vietnam veterans who joined the Rhodesian security forces.

Government of National Unity (GNU) – Following disputed presidential elections in March 2008 and protracted negotiations, a GNU was formed on 13 February 2009. The GNU confirmed Robert Mugabe as President of Zimbabwe, and MDC-T leader, Morgan Tsvangirai as Prime Minister, with ministerial posts shared between ZANU–PF and the MDC factions.

Gukurahundi – Shona word meaning 'the rain that washes away the chaff'; the term given to the brutal suppression of the Ndebele people following ZANU's majority showing in the elections which created Zimbabwe. While ostensibly aimed at ZIPRA rebels, military operations by the Zimbabwe army's North Korean-trained 5th Brigade reportedly resulted in the deaths of thousands of civilians.

Harare – Capital of Zimbabwe (formerly Salisbury, Rhodesia).

Joint Operations Command (JOC) – Co-ordinating body overseeing military and security operations in Rhodesia during the war, and subsequently in post-independence Zimbabwe.

K-Car – Killer car, a Rhodesian Air Force Alouette helicopter gunship, usually fitted with a 20 mm cannon.

Karanga – A grouping of the Shona tribe, from the Masvingo (formerly Fort Victoria) area. The Karanga made up the majority of recruits to the Rhodesian African Rifles, the predominantly black regular army battalions of the Rhodesian Army.

Matabele – White colonial pronunciation and spelling of the Ndebele tribe and language.

Matabeleland – The area covering west and south-west Zimbabwe, and the provinces of Matabeleland North and South; home of the Ndebele people.

MDC – Movement for Democratic Change – Main party in opposition to Robert Mugabe's ZANU–PF. The MDC was formed in 1999 by former secretary general of the Zimbabwe Congress of Trade Unions, Morgan Tsvangirai. The party subsequently split into two factions, the MDC-T (headed by Tsvangirai), and MDC-M, lead by Arthur Mutambara.

Mtengesi – Shona word for 'sell-out' – someone who sided with the white government during the Bush War or, later, with the MDC or other opposition to ZANU–PF.

Mugabe, Robert Gabriel (1924–) – Prime Minister, then President of Zimbabwe since 1980.

Muzorewa, Bishop Abel (1925–2010) – Leader of the United African National Council (UANC), and Prime Minister of the short-lived Zimbabwe–Rhodesia, a multiracial government formed in 1979 as part of a doomed internal settlement proposed by Ian Smith.

Ndebele (see *Matabele*) – Second largest tribe in Zimbabwe, descended from the Zulus of South Africa.

Nkomo, Joshua (1917–1999) – Founder and leader of the National Democratic Party, which subsequently became the Zimbabwe African People's Union (ZAPU). Nkomo was Vice President of Zimbabwe from 1987 to 1999 after ZAPU merged with ZANU to form ZANU–PF.

Oke/ouen – Slang for man (from Afrikaans).

Operation Noah – Rescue of wildlife stranded by the damming of the Zambezi River in 1958–1964 to form Lake Kariba. More than six thousand animals were saved by game department officers and volunteers.

Pioneer column – Force raised by Cecil John Rhodes and his British South Africa Company in 1890 to annex parts of modern Zimbabwe before the Germans or Portuguese could lay claim to the territory.

Porks – Derogatory rhyming slang term for Portuguese, from 'pork and cheese'.

Rhodesia – British colony founded by and named after Cecil John Rhodes. The name was officially adopted in 1895 and subsequently changed to Southern Rhodesia. The country renamed itself the Republic of Rhodesia after unilaterally declaring independence from Britain in 1965, following Britain's refusal to grant independence without majority rule. The name was changed, briefly, in 1979 to Zimbabwe–Rhodesia under a multiracial government, then to Zimbabwe in 1980.

Rhodesian African Rifles (RAR) – Regular army unit of the Rhodesian Security Forces consisting of black African soldiers and noncommissioned officers, and white officers.

Rhodesian Front (RF) – Formed in 1962, and headed by Ian Smith from 1964 to 1979, the RF was the governing political party in white-ruled Rhodesia until the forming of the ill-fated transitional government of Zimbabwe–Rhodesia.

Rhodesian Light Infantry (RLI) – All-white regular army unit of the Rhodesian Security Forces.

Salisbury – Capital of Rhodesia (now Harare, Zimbabwe).

Selous Scouts (*Skuz'apo*) – An elite multiracial unit of the Rhodesian Security Forces, named after the big-game hunter Frederick Courteney Selous. Black African Selous Scouts dressed in enemy uniforms and operated in tribal areas, tracking and ambushing guerillas. The scouts boasted the highest kill ratio of any Rhodesian unit.

Shona – The majority tribe of Rhodesia/Zimbabwe.

Sithole, Reverend Ndabaningi (1920–2000) – Founder of the Zimbabwe African National Union (ZANU) in 1963, later overthrown by Robert Mugabe.

Smith, Ian (1919–2007) – Prime Minister of Rhodesia and leader of the Rhodesian Front Party from 1964 to 1979. Smith orchestrated Rhodesia's Unilateral Declaration of Independence from Britain in 1965.

Southern Rhodesia African National Congress – A pro-independence and black majority rule political organisation which lasted from 1957 until it was banned by the white Rhodesian government in late 1958.

Terr – Terrorist; term used by whites for black guerillas/freedom fighters.

ZANLA – **Zimbabwe African National Liberation Army** – The military wing of ZANU. Predominantly Shona, ZANLA's members were trained and advised by communist China and operated during the Bush War from bases in Mozambique.

ZANU – **Zimbabwe African National Union** – Predominantly Shona nationalist political party, founded in 1963.

ZANU–PF – **Zimbabwe African National Union–Popular Front** – Formed in 1987 with the merger of ZANU and ZAPU, ZANU–PF, headed by Robert Mugabe, was the dominant political party in Zimbabwe until the emergence of Morgan Tsvangirai's opposition Movement for Democratic Change.

ZAPU – **Zimbabwe African People's Union** – Predominantly Ndebele nationalist political party.

ZESA – **Zimbabwe Electricity Supply Authority** – Also commonly used slang term for electricity in Zimbabwe.

Zimbabwe, Republic of – Formerly Southern Rhodesia, the

Republic of Rhodesia, and Zimbabwe–Rhodesia, the Republic of Zimbabwe, formed in 1980, takes its name from the Shona-speaking Kingdom of Zimbabwe, which flourished from 1250 to 1450 from its stone-built capital of Great Zimbabwe, near Masvingo (Fort Victoria).

ZIPRA – Zimbabwe People's Revolutionary Army – The military wing of ZAPU. Predominantly Ndebele, ZIPRA's members were trained by Russia and operated from bases in Zambia.

ZUPCO – Zimbabwe United Passenger Company – Bus operator in Zimbabwe.

PART ONE

Rhodesia

CHAPTER 1

Southern Rhodesia, 1959

Makuti learned to swim almost as soon as he learned to walk. He didn't know that he wasn't born to enter the water; he just followed his mother in and did what she did.

The rain had been falling all his short life. Makuti couldn't know it – how could he – but it was not supposed to be like this. It was not meant to pour down so heavily from the skies, at this time of the year. It was not natural.

His first steps were in the mud and he tried as best he could, on his short legs, to keep pace with his mother who was terribly stressed. She walked in circles and Makuti's path was made harder because he had to lift his little feet in and out of the ever-deepening footprints his mother was pounding into the sticky slime.

When she stopped abruptly, Makuti skidded and bumped into her legs. He fell over and, instead of scrambling to his feet, enjoyed the peace of lying there for a moment, wallowing in the cloying mud. When he tried to stand, he slipped and rolled some more, and found that he enjoyed it.

His mother turned and looked down at him. She snorted and stamped her foot. He dragged himself upright again – the brief moment of play over.

Makuti was hungry. Although he was already walking, it would be some time before he was weaned – such was their way – so he sought out the solace and nourishment of his mother's teat. She brushed him aside and, hurt, he stumbled and sloshed after her. The rain started again and spattered his back. He was tired, hungry and cold.

His mother shook her head. She was starving too. The ring of their forlorn footsteps grew shorter each day, as the rain continued to fall and the river continued to rise. In the days before she had given birth, Makuti's mother had exhausted herself climbing higher and higher up a hill, which had now become an island. Although they were safe from the rising waters up here on this rocky outcrop, there was nothing to eat and the new mother was half-crazed with hunger.

Thunder rolled down the valley and lightning ignited the night sky. Makuti's mother walked to the floodwaters' edge and waded in. And Makuti, not knowing any better, plunged in joyfully behind her and started to swim.

'*Bejane!*'

Paul Bryant raised a hand to shield his eyes from the glare of the morning sunshine on the still waters. The lake was the same molten silver as the hazy sky and it was virtually impossible to discern the horizon. Paul pulled the battered pair of binoculars from their worn leather case to see what fourteen-year-old Winston Ngwenya was pointing at.

'Well spotted, Winston. It's a rhino all right.'

'There are two.'

Paul moved the focusing wheel and saw the youngster was correct again. Bobbing behind the first horned head was a little dark blob. 'A calf.'

'Ah, but the mother will be trouble, *baas*.'

'Dad, let me see.'

'Steady, George!' Paul lurched as his son inadvertently shifted the outboard engine's tiller in his haste to catch sight of the swimming black rhinoceroses, but regained his balance. He smiled to show George he hadn't meant to chastise him, just to warn him.

George set the throttle to neutral and the wooden dinghy slowed. Long-limbed and angular, with his father's height and his mother's blonde hair, George had the awkwardness of adolescence and the promise of manhood competing for control of his every move and word. Paul smiled as he handed his son the binoculars.

Winston, kneeling at the bow, reached out a hand to steady his friend, but George brushed it away. 'I'm fine.'

It was amazing what a difference a year could make, Paul thought. Winston's body was filling out quickly and he was almost a man. His voice was breaking and his movements around the boat were self-assured and confident. Bryant thought of the African boy as a second son, almost. He was the firstborn child of his good friend Kenneth, who taught in the black township of Mzilikazi, on the outskirts of Bulawayo, back home in Matabeleland.

Kenneth and his wife, Patricia, had two more children after Winston, a girl and a boy, Thandi and Emmerson. All three of their children were healthy and strong, which was something to give thanks for.

'I see them, Dad,' George said. 'Too bad Mom can't be here.'

Paul nodded. He, too, wished she were here with him, instead of back on the farm, way out near the Bechuanaland border.

'Go, Paul. For God's sake, please go – you're driving me bloody mad,' she'd urged him. They'd tried for a second child after George had been born, back in 1946 after Paul had come back from the war, but Pip had miscarried. Then, thirteen years later, at the age of thirty-nine, she had told him the news that she was expecting what the Afrikaner farmers living in Rhodesia called a *laat lammetjie*.

This, however, was no late lamb. It was a tiny human life that Philippa was carrying. Paul had been adamant that Pip should stop work around the dairy and spend more time indoors resting. They'd had fights over it, but she'd stood up to him, telling him that she would not live her life in fear – not even of another miscarriage. He'd seen in her the same fierce independence and stubbornness she'd shown as a volunteer policewoman during the war, when they'd first met.

When the call had gone out from the Rhodesian Game Department in the early days of Pip's pregnancy for volunteers to help with a massive operation aimed at saving wildlife stranded by the rising waters of the newly created Lake Kariba, they had gone as a family to camp near the growing but still primitive township that had sprung up near the dam construction site.

The three of them had known bugger all about how to save wild animals from drowning when they'd arrived five months earlier, but since then they had learned how to corral and drive impala, kudu and waterbuck into the lake, then shepherd them towards the mainland. They had plucked deadly mambas and irate cobras from waterlogged trees and rescued a host of smaller creatures then transported them by boat to the new banks of the swelling Zambezi River.

One thing Paul had learned from his time working as a volunteer on Operation Noah, as the rescue operation had been dubbed, was that every animal could swim. The problem was that some could not swim as far as others. The rescuers' hearts had soon hardened to the sight of the bloated bodies of dead buck that hadn't made it, or half-eaten remains of animals that had literally fought each other to death.

Earlier in her pregnancy, Pip had come out most days on the boat for an hour or two at least, and proved herself as able and fearless as any of them. Paul was sick with worry about the baby sometimes, but Pip was happy to pull on his old wartime pilot's goggles and a pair of motor-cycle gauntlets and pull a mamba from a tree, or sit in the boat cradling a soaking, shivering baby baboon whose mother had drowned.

Paul had lived in Southern Rhodesia since the end of the war. He'd had few family or prospects to encourage him to return to his native Australia and he'd fallen in love with Pip in 1943, when he'd been based at Khumalo airfield, near Bulawayo, as the adjutant of an aircrew training base. When he'd returned to Africa after being demobbed in 1945, he'd realised he'd also fallen for the continent.

There was a wildness of spirit in Africa that had once existed in Australia but was fast disappearing. Out here, in the wilds of Rho-desia, things were very different. Life was harder in Africa, and it had to be lived on the edge. As such, people seemed to enjoy things more, and live for the day.

Paul had taken Pip back to Bulawayo and the family dairy farm after their first month with Operation Noah, at the same time that George was due to return to school. But as the next school holidays approached, George pleaded with his parents to be allowed to return to Kariba to help out again with the relocation of animals. Paul did not want to go without Pip, but she all but ordered him to take their son back to the growing lake. Paul had been reluctant to leave her alone and heavily pregnant, but if he'd learned one thing in the past sixteen years it was that his diminutive Rhodesian wife was not to be disagreed with. He'd left with George and Winston, promising to be back in plenty of time for the birth, which was still not due for another month.

'Look, Mr Bryant, she is going the wrong way,' Winston said.

Paul saw he was right. 'Head for that island, to the left, George. We've got to try and drive her towards the mainland.'

George nodded, his face set with concentration. The quickest way to the rhino would be to come close around a trio of dying trees that marked what had once been the top of a hill. As they closed on the trees Paul joined Winston at the front of the boat, and both peered ahead looking for submerged trunks that might ground them or tear the bottom out of the boat, which had been designed for waterskiing and fishing rather than rescuing animals.

'Stick!' Winston called, pointing off to starboard. George swung the tiller and the boat glided past the dangerous obstacle.

Paul scanned the nearest tree. 'There's a cobra up there. Make for it, George.'

As George turned again and cut the throttle, allowing the boat to coast up to the top branches of the drowning tree, all three of them looked down at the bottom of the boat to protect their eyes from the potentially blinding venom. Paul took off his Australian Army slouch hat, a souvenir of his war days, and put on his old flying goggles. He reached for a steel pole whose end had been fashioned into a u-shaped hook. Winston cried out and wiped his bare shoulder as a jet of venom lashed his skin.

'Come left,' Paul said. He placed a hand on Winston's neck to stop the boy from looking up, and ducked sideways as the cobra reared in the branch and spat another jet of milky venom towards him. Droplets spattered the goggles' right lens and burned his cheek. Paul reached for the snake. It pulled back and then struck, lightning fast, at the pole, but Paul was able to trap its head against the waterlogged trunk of the tree. 'Pass me the bag, Winston.'

His head still bowed, Winston raised the hessian bag to Paul then took hold of a nearby branch to secure the boat, while Paul grabbed the pinned snake behind the back of its head and thrust the writhing, hissing reptile into the sack.

'Can we go for the rhino now, Dad?'

Winston looked up and laughed at George's deadpan remark.

'Head for the rhinos, George, fast as you can,' Paul said.

Philippa Bryant exhaled and leaned against the hot metal of the Chevrolet *bakkie* as the young African man loaded her paper bags full of groceries into the rear of the vehicle.

'Thank you, Sixpence,' she said, and handed him a few coins.

'Are you all right, madam?' he asked.

'Fine, thank you.' She forced a smile and he walked back into Haddon and Sly. She was actually far from fine. She felt hot, fat, tired and thoroughly sick of being pregnant. She and Paul had been ecstatic about having another baby – at the start – but now she found herself moodily alternating between being annoyed and terrified. It had been many years since her last miscarriage, yet being pregnant again had reopened her old wounds and poured salt into them. At the same time she was full of nervous hope for the baby that kicked inside her.

She regretted ordering Paul to take George to Kariba for the school holidays. She wanted to be there with them, or, if she couldn't have that, she wanted them both back at the farm. Now.

Pip opened the door of the car. 'Bloody hell.' She realised she'd forgotten the bread. She was terribly forgetful these days, and remembered it as a symptom of her first pregnancy. 'I'm too old to be pregnant,' she said out loud as she walked slowly back into the department store. She felt like crying when she found the bakery had just sold its last loaf. Dejected, she turned and headed back out into the street. There was a bakery a block down Fife Street.

The sight of purple jacaranda blossoms cheered her a little. She knew from her time as a volunteer policewoman that this city of Bulawayo sometimes lived up to its Ndebele name, as a place of slaughter. She'd been involved in a couple of murder investigations and several cases of rapes, stabbings and beatings. She herself had been a victim of domestic violence at the hands of her first husband, before she'd met Paul. Fortunately, Charlie had died during the war. Fortunately for him, that is, because she'd decided after a couple of years as a volunteer constable that she would have had him arrested on his return from duty overseas, war hero or not. She knew that the orderly grid of wide, clean-swept streets and the impressive, stately public buildings of Bulawayo were, in some cases, just a façade of order. Pip had seen the grubbier side of the city – the blood, vomit and sewage in the streets of the black townships, and the seamy private lives of the outwardly upstanding members of the white community.

Pip only came to town once every month or so, to shop for what she couldn't grow or make herself. It was a chore at the best of times, but on her own and carrying another person in her belly it really was no fun at all.

'Howzit, Pip?'

She looked up and saw Fred Phipps touching the brim of his hat. Fred farmed in the same district as she and Paul, and they ran into each other at parties once or twice a year. The Bryants and the Quilter-Phippses weren't close friends, but they got on fine. Fred had played in the same rugby team as her first husband, Charlie, and Pip often sensed that he disapproved of her marrying Paul. Word had gotten around town during the war that she and Paul had become an item virtually as soon as she had heard of Charlie's death. Pip didn't care, and she had told anyone who bothered to listen that Charlie had been a bastard, despite receiving a posthumous Military Medal for his actions in the desert in North Africa.

'Fine, Fred, and you?'

'Fine, fine. You must be due soon, hey?'

Pip nodded, and her head felt heavy. She was sick of being asked the same question. 'A month.'

'Sharon's due any day. I'm just busy in town getting some things for when I have to fend for myself on the farm.'

Pip smiled and felt a genuine warmth for the man. She'd heard, ages ago, but had since forgotten, that his wife was pregnant. 'Please give her my best, Fred.'

'I will.' He paused and cocked his head. 'What's that noise?'

Pip heard shouts, and more rhythmic noise, like singing, coming from around the corner. She started walking in the direction of the sound, and Fred, who had been walking in the other direction, turned to follow her. Pip reached the closest corner and saw a group of about forty African men and women holding placards. One read, *Down with unfair bus fares*.

'Bloody *munts*,' Fred said.

Pip turned and looked at him. 'What's all this about?'

'Probably tied up with the bus fare protests in Salisbury. A friend of mine in the police told me they've had to crack a few kaffir skulls up there because the *munts* are complaining about some increases in the UTC bus fares. I mean, why should we whites be subsidising their bloody travel? If a bus company needs to charge more to make ends meet, then who are they to object?'

Pip frowned. Very few African people owned a bicycle, let

alone a motor car and for most of them the bus was the only affordable way to travel. Now that Fred mentioned the Salisbury trouble she did remember reading somewhere that the fare hike meant some Africans were paying up to twenty per cent of their meagre wages on bus tickets.

'Come on, Pip,' Fred said, putting a hand on her arm. 'We'd best get you away from this mob.'

She shrugged off his touch, then turned and gave him a smile to show him she meant him no offence. All the same, Paul was the only man she wanted touching her. And she could look after herself. 'I'm fine, Fred. I'm only going to the bakery.'

Fred looked past her, at the crowd. The group was well dressed – the men in suits and the women in neatly pressed skirts and blouses. A few were singing, and two of the men were walking up and down the street handing out pamphlets of some sort. Most of the pedestrian traffic was white people and they uniformly ignored the Africans and their handouts. A white man stopped to berate the group and tell them to go back to the bloody trees they'd climbed out of.

One of the men handing out flyers had his back to Pip, but he looked very familiar. When he turned around she saw it was Kenneth Ngwenya. Pip ignored Fred's panicked warning cry from behind her, looked both ways, and walked across the street towards the protesters.

'Kenneth!'

The tall Ndebele schoolteacher turned and smiled. He closed the gap between them. 'Hello, Pip, how are you?'

'I'm fine, and you?' He nodded and told her he was well. 'Is this what you do in your school holidays, organise civil disobedience?'

He chuckled. 'It's a peaceful demonstration. The bus companies are holding people to ransom. There have been big demonstrations in Salisbury and I, as an interested community member, wanted to show my support for the people opposed to these increases. We're calling on all African people to boycott the bus services until the companies drop their prices again.'

Pip knew that Kenneth was much more than an interested community member. He was a member of the Southern Rhodesia African National Congress, the dissident pro-black-independence organisation headed by Joshua Nkomo. As a native-born Rhodesian, and the descendant of one of the members of Cecil John Rhodes's Pioneer Column, part of Pip bridled at anyone – African or white – wanting to destabilise the Rhodesian political scene. Rhodesian Africans, in her opinion, were better educated and better treated than any other blacks on the continent. There was agitation for majority rule in countries to their north and Pip, like most other whites, feared what might happen if Britain were to make a blanket decision to give independence too soon to people who were not prepared or educated enough to rule a country themselves. She liked Kenneth, although she found his wife, Patricia, surly to the point of being objectionable. Pip got the feeling that the woman disliked all white people. Kenneth, however, was like Paul – he took people as he found them. Paul often had Kenneth over to the farm for tea or went fishing with him after church on Sundays.

Pip wanted to ask Kenneth more about the demonstration, but their conversation was interrupted by the clanging of a police car's bell. They looked down the street and saw two patrol cars speeding towards them. The cars skidded to a halt and four officers got out of each vehicle, drawing truncheons as they strode towards the protesters.

'Break it up. This is an illegal gathering and you are hereby ordered to disperse,' called Chief Inspector Harold Hayes from the head of the group. Pip cringed. She hadn't seen the bull-necked policeman for years. Hayes had been a sergeant during the war and Pip had been partnered with him for a while. He was an inept, racist bully, and proof that many people in uniform were promoted far above their capabilities simply because they hung around long enough. 'You, move away from that woman!'

Hayes was pointing his truncheon towards Kenneth, but Pip could see the overweight police officer hadn't recognised her yet. 'Chief Inspector . . .'

As Pip started to walk around Kenneth, he put out his arm, as if to tell her not to involve herself. At the same moment two of Hayes's young British South Africa Police constables bolted ahead of their commander, obviously ready to break up the gathering by force if they were given the slightest encouragement.

The protesters had stopped their singing and chanting and looked at each other for guidance. Some stood defiantly facing the oncoming police, but two younger men and a woman started to flee. One of the men, perhaps a student, was looking back over his shoulder at the advancing constable as he ran, and as Pip moved out of Kenneth's protective reach, the man collided with her and she fell over backwards, hitting the ground hard.

'No!' Kenneth yelled.

'He's kicking her, sir!' one of the junior constables cried out as the young man's legs became entangled in Pip's and he dropped to one knee beside her. The policemen raised their batons and charged.

CHAPTER 2

'Come around behind her, George,' Paul Bryant said to his son. George swung the tiller and the boat scribed a wide arc on the silvery surface of the lake. At least it was calm today, Paul thought.

Lake Kariba was still filling, but it was already a monstrous body of water. By the time it reached its capacity, in three to four years, it would be two hundred and twenty kilometres long and up to forty kilometres wide. The huge expanse was already proving treacherous. As well as boats running aground, or having their hulls gashed open by submerged treetops, the freshwater lake was prone to violent storms that whipped up waves of up to a metre. More than a few small boats had capsized and sunk, their crews suffering the same fate as the baboons and monkeys the volunteers were continually finding stranded in branches.

The black rhino and her calf were still swimming steadily towards certain death. Paul reckoned they were paddling towards another stand of trees that were half-submerged. From water level the branches might have looked like an island, but the animals were paddling further out into the lake instead of to the shore, which was also close but out of the rhino's poor field of vision.

'Check, Dad,' George called, and pointed to a fish eagle

executing a shallow dive off to their left. The majestic snowy-headed bird had its talons extended ahead and as it brushed the surface of the water it plucked out a sizeable bream. It beat its long red-brown wings and made for the nearest tree, where it landed and began ripping the fish apart.

The damming of the Zambezi had been a death sentence for thousands of animals, but the rising waters had also provided an unending feast for other creatures. Fish eagles were breeding like crazy and their high-pitched lilting calls were becoming synonymous with any trip to the lake. The lake was being seeded with fish species to provide food for the nation, and a livelihood for the Batonka people who, like the animals that once lived in the valley, had been moved to higher ground.

Some tribespeople had resisted the government's repeated urging to relocate to new resettlement villages, and there had been protests and violence. At Gwembe, on the Northern Rhodesian side of the lake, troops and police had been called in to forcibly relocate some Batonka, but the villagers had rebelled and, armed with spears and clubs, had charged the security forces. Several Batonka had been killed by gunfire.

Paul shielded his eyes against the glare and tracked the rhinos' progress. This was Africa, he told himself. Life and death, predator and prey. Someone always lost while someone – or something – grew fat. If they did somehow manage to steer the rhino cow to the mainland, her tiny calf might still be taken by a crocodile. Like the fish eagle, these prehistoric predators were thriving on the diet served up by the man-made sea. Every crew of volunteers had tales to tell of near misses by the cunning, ruthless *ngwenya*, whose numbers were rising in proportion with the increasing flood level and ever-growing number of animal carcasses.

Paul looked back at George. The motion of the boat through

the hot, still curtain of African air produced enough breeze to ruffle the boy's bushy blond hair. His tanned skin highlighted his mother's blue eyes even more. George would grow into a handsome young man, and Paul almost envied his son being able to come of age in such a fascinating, bounteous and prosperous young country. Paul had lived through the depression in Australia and gone off to war as a young man. The things he'd seen and the friends he had lost during his time in Bomber Command had nearly destroyed him, but meeting Pip had turned his life around. He'd finished the war a better man, back on active service flying twin-engine Mosquito aircraft in a pathfinder unit, and he'd left the Royal Australian Air Force as a highly decorated wing commander. The medals meant nothing to him, though, and his strongest hope was that George and the new baby could live in peace for the rest of their lives.

George grinned back at him.

'Will the electricity from the dam reach Bulawayo, Mr Bryant?' Winston asked.

Paul nodded. Winston had an enquiring mind and was proving to be a good student at the Catholic college he attended in Natal, South Africa. There were few opportunities for higher education for young Africans in Rhodesia, yet in the more liberal provinces of South Africa, at the far extent of the National Party Government's reach, privately funded church schools offered local students and those from other African countries a chance to better themselves, at a price. Paul had tried to give Kenneth money towards Winston's education, but his friend had refused the charity. Instead, Kenneth had agreed that Winston would work at the Bryants' dairy during every school vacation. The other employees on the farm didn't know, but Winston was being paid well over the odds, on the assumption that most of his earnings went towards his school fees. The arrangement allowed Kenneth to retain his dignity and Winston to continue his schooling. Sometimes, especially on the farm, Winston called Paul '*baas*' in order to not flaunt his education or close connection to the boss and his family, but Paul preferred plain old 'mister'.

'The power from the hydro-electricity plant will go into the national grid, so it could end up anywhere, theoretically.'

Winston nodded. 'Then despite the fact that the Batonka and the animals are suffering, this dam is a good thing.'

Paul shrugged. He knew the job of politicians was to make tough decisions – when they had the balls to do so – but all three of them had seen the sad toll of animals killed by the flooding. Paul guessed, too, that Winston's father had some strong views on the forced relocation of the Batonka, which had probably filtered down to his son.

'There are winners and losers,' George interrupted from behind them. 'Some animals, like some people, were smart enough to move to higher ground. The lions mostly moved inland when the waters rose – didn't they, Dad?'

George was right about the lions – on the evidence they'd seen so far – but Paul was uncomfortable with the inference that the Batonka who had resisted relocation were stupid or 'losers' because they were opposed to leaving their ancestral homelands. Personally, having made a home in Rhodesia, Paul couldn't imagine a worse fate than being kicked off the farm by the government and told he would have to live somewhere else. He was about to make the point when Winston pointed out that the rhinos had changed course and were now heading towards them.

'Easy,' Paul cautioned George. 'Come alongside the mother, my boy. She's still heading the wrong way. Let's try and shepherd her.'

George slowed the throttle and it looked as though they would be able to take up a position behind the calf, moving at more or less the same pace as the ponderous swimmers.

'See how the calf is behind its mother,' Paul said to the boys. They were all momentarily entranced by this rare opportunity to come close to an animal that had a justified reputation for unpredictability and fierceness in the wild. 'That's one of their downfalls. White rhino cows make their young walk ahead of them, so they can keep an eye on them, but black rhino babies follow their mothers, which make them more vulnerable to lions and hyenas when they're small.'

'Like the difference between black mothers and white mothers. A black mother carries her *picannin* on her back, and a white woman pushes hers in front with a pram,' Winston said.

Paul and George laughed. 'But, Dad,' George asked, 'isn't it bad for the mother rhino to go ahead of her baby? What if it gets lost?'

'There's a reason for everything in life, George,' Paul said. 'Black rhino live in thick bush and often the mother needs to walk ahead to clear a path for her calf. White rhino live on the grasslands where visibility is better.'

The lesson ended when the rhino stopped.

It took Paul's brain a full two seconds to comprehend what had happened. The rhino's feet must have touched ground on an unseen hilltop beneath the water's surface. It had probably been a rocky kopje, with no trees to give away its position. The water was up to the rhino's chest as she turned and issued a long, loud snort that rippled the lake's shiny surface in front of her. The calf, confused, continued to paddle up beside its mother. Its legs were too short to touch the bottom, and its swimming became instinctively more panicked. Its little head thrashed from side to side as it picked up the shape, size and noise of the approaching boat.

'Cut the throttle! Reverse, George, reverse!'

But they all acted a fraction too slowly. The mother rhino charged.

Each step was boosted by the effect of the water, allowing the cow to surge forward on a near weightless body. When her curved horn splintered the wooden boat just above the waterline, the impact sent Winston toppling over the far side into the water.

Paul crashed to the bottom of the boat and had to roll to one side to escape the wicked point of the rhino's horn. The beast shook her head and grunted and snorted bubbles in the water as she fought to free herself.

As the rhino lowered her head the boat tipped to one side and Paul slid closer to the horn's point. He could hear her grunting and the sound terrified him almost as much as the deadly tip. Water seeped in through the hole she'd created, then poured over the gunwale as she pushed down again, threatening to capsize the small boat.

George revved the engine hard and the outboard screamed. 'It's still in neutral,' Paul called. As Paul got to his knees and started moving aft he saw Winston's arms thrashing in the water. The boy's mouth was open wide in a scream that was drowned out as his head slid below the surface.

Paul crawled to George and reached out, turning the throttle setting to reverse. The boat strained against the rhino, locked in a tug of war. As the great beast finally unhooked her horn the boat surged backwards and Paul used the momentum to help propel himself over the side and into the cool waters of the lake.

When he broke the surface he waved at George to keep going

in reverse. Paul struck out, overarm, for a pale pink palm he saw disappearing below the lake's surface. He duck-dived and groped blindly in the murky waters for Winston. He flailed around him but couldn't feel the young African.

He swam to the surface again and sucked in a lungful of air. George was turning around and had the boat back in forward gear. Paul shook his head, but he didn't have time to warn his son. The rhino was walking in circles on her underwater island, and she shook her head and snorted again when she saw him. Paul wiped the water from his face and eyes. 'Winston!' To lose his friend's son would be like losing his own.

Paul thrashed around in circles until he saw the bubbles. In two fast, hard strokes he was there and diving down again. His outstretched hand brushed something that flicked and groped for him. Paul wrapped his hand around Winston's forearm and felt the boy weakly grasp his in return. He kicked for the surface but Winston seemed stuck. He sensed the boy's panic as he let go of his arm and prised Winston's fingers from his own arm. Paul dived deeper and felt for the problem. Winston's leg was trapped in the fork of a submerged tree. Paul grabbed his foot and untangled the creeper vines that had wrapped around his ankle. He took hold of the young man's limp upper arm and kicked again for the sunshine above.

When he broke free of the water's grasp, Winston was floating motionless beside him.

'Over here,' he spluttered unnecessarily, because George was beside him in the boat in an instant, and reaching over the side to help him. Paul had underestimated George's strength as he felt his son drag Winston almost effortlessly over the gunwale. Paul grabbed the boat and boosted himself aboard. He rolled the unconscious Winston onto his side and checked his airway was clear, then pushed him onto his back and blew into his mouth.

Paul broke from the kiss of life and started pumping the boy's chest.

'Come on.' He lowered his lips again to Winston's and blew in another deep breath. The boy coughed water and began spluttering. Paul rolled him onto his side again and thumped him on the back as Winston continued to cough.

'The rhino, Dad!'

Paul saw, too late, that they had been drifting closer to the cow and her calf while reviving Winston. She lifted her head and blew a challenge at them, then lowered her horn and started her waterborne charge again.

Their rocking movements up and down the boat had caused water to leak in through the hole the rhino had gored in the planking. Paul reached in the bilge for the wartime .303 he brought along for emergencies. This qualified as one, he reckoned, though he had no idea if the round would kill the cow or even slow her. He worked the bolt and as he raised the rifle to his shoulder he saw, in his peripheral vision, George's arm moving in a blur.

The smoking tin canister tumbled through the air, hissing towards the rhino. Suddenly it detonated with a bang as loud as a hand grenade and in a storm of instant lightning that rocked all of their senses to the core. The thunder flash had the same effect on the rhino, which stopped mid-charge and turned away from the painful burst of noise and light. She started swimming and her startled calf paddled slowly behind her.

'Good work, George,' Paul said, clasping his son's shoulder. They'd had three thunder flashes – ex-army hand grenade simulators – in the boat since their last round-up of impala and kudu on an island further south in the lake. The noisy devices were used to scare the antelope into running into a funnel of nets that forced them into the water, where they were made to swim towards shore, or into a *boma* where they could be roped and carried to waiting boats. George had saved the day, and the rhino cow, by his quick thinking. Winston was on his knees, still retching, but apparently not permanently harmed by his own near-death experience.

'Boat,' George said, hiding his red-cheeked flush of pride by pointing towards the oncoming craft that cleaved through the lake's molten metal surface. 'It's Rupert Fothergill, by the look of it.'

Paul cupped his hands either side of his mouth, and yelled, 'Rhino!' His first priority now was to get the two boys back to shore, so they could give Winston time to rest and recover. He pointed to the cow and her calf, hoping Fothergill would take over the shepherding duties, but the ranger's boat ploughed on towards them, its bow riding high until the driver cut the engine and allowed them to coast up to the wallowing dinghy.

Before Paul could explain what they'd been up to, Fothergill held up a hand. 'Paul, I've just received a radio message . . . a friend of yours in Bulawayo, a Doctor Hammond, got through to the ops centre at Kariba by telephone. It's your wife, Paul . . . she's been taken to hospital. It's not good.'

George and Winston sat side by side on a green grassy spit of land in the newly declared Kuburi wilderness area, on the edge of the growing inland sea.

'I wonder what happened to that rhino and her calf.'

Winston lifted the galvanised-tin water bucket and pushed the end of the mopane log deeper into the fire, balancing the bucket again on the newly stoked coals. 'Another man from the camp told me she ran through the township at Mahombekombe, not far from the dam wall, and then up into the hills.'

'Shame,' George said, but his grin at the thought of the rhinos stampeding through the workers' shanties faded when he thought of the animals' plight. 'But her little baby didn't look like he would make it. He was struggling to keep up with her when we left to . . .'

George looked out over the lake and stared at the red ball heading for the water. The sun sank like his spirits. He hated to think of his mother in hospital, in pain, and wondered what had happened to the baby brother or sister she was carrying. He felt his throat constrict and his eyes began to sting. He would not cry, he told himself. He was nearly a man. He felt Winston's hand on his shoulder and looked at him.

'Your mother is a good woman. God will look after her, George. My mother . . . she is angry at everything all the time. She is angry at me, my father, the white people . . .'

George smiled. Patricia Ngwenya's temper was legendary in the district and his mother, who rarely had a bad word to say about anyone, had a favourite word for Winston's mother – insufferable. It was good to have her son here with him, though. George sometimes felt he had missed out, not having a brother of his own, but he and Winston were close enough to be family.

Rupert Fothergill had told George's father, when they'd met out on the lake, that there was a light aircraft leaving Kariba airstrip within the hour for Salisbury, but there was only space on board for one person. 'Go, Dad,' George had said, seeing the indecision further furrow his father's already stricken face.

'We'll take care of the boys until you can send word or organise transport for them,' Fothergill had added.

George didn't feel nearly as brave now as he'd tried to be on the boat. He wanted to be by his mother's side, but at the same time he was scared of finding out what might be wrong with her. He couldn't bear the thought of anything happening to her;

it was easier, he decided, for him to stay here on Operation Noah and act like everything was OK.

'You and your father saved my life today,' Winston said.

George looked at his friend and realised he wasn't the only one who'd been doing some serious thinking. 'You would have done the same for us.'

'Of course,' Winston nodded.

George picked up a stone and tossed it as far out into the water as he could. It landed with a satisfyingly loud *kerplunk*.

'What do you want to do when you leave school?' George asked.

'Me, I am going to join the army.'

George looked at him in surprise. 'I thought you'd become a teacher, like your dad.'

Winston shook his head. 'I'm sure that's what he has planned, but I don't like school enough to want to stay in the classroom for the rest of my life.'

George laughed. 'I know what you mean.' He looked up at Venus, rising bright in the purple twilight, and cocked his ear and held up a finger and pointed towards the far-off call of a lion. When it was still again, he asked, 'Why the army?'

'I want to be a warrior. Your father was in the war; he was a great warrior.'

'He was a pilot.'

'Yes, but he still fought for his country. I wouldn't want to fly an aeroplane, but I would like to be paid to fight. My mother says my father talks too much, and that he should learn to stand up and fight for what he believes in.'

'I asked my dad once about joining the air force,' said George, 'and he told me he would do everything in his power to stop me. He says the war was terrible and that no one should ever have to go through what his generation did.'

'Still, I don't want to be a teacher. Myself, I want to spend my days among warriors, not children. I want to drink beer and have many women. What about you?'

There were hippos honking in a newly created bay, behind and off to their left, but they went quiet when the lion started calling again, closer this time. 'I'd like to be a game ranger. I like it out here in the bush.' He'd also like to be with Susannah Geary, whom he'd seen in church in Bulawayo whenever he was home from school.

'I don't like the bush. But it's good to get away from school, and from the work on the farm. You know, that lion you can hear now . . .'

'Yes?' George said.

'If it comes into camp tonight it's not going to bite you . . .'

'Good.'

'. . . it's going to eat you!'

CHAPTER 3

'Let me see Kenneth Ngwenya,' Paul said to Chief Inspector Harold Hayes.

The police station smelled of sweat and urine. Paul felt as though he wanted to be sick. He hadn't slept and had hardly eaten, save for some gruel-like soup at the hospital. After flying from Kariba to Salisbury he'd hitched a lift to Bulawayo on a delivery van. He'd arrived in Bulawayo late the night before.

Pip was in the intensive care ward. She'd suffered bleeding after her fall, and some cuts and scrapes from the pavement. Kenneth, according to Pip, had tripped as well and then lain on top of her to try to protect her from being trampled by the fleeing demonstrators. But that hadn't stopped the police from arresting him. As soon as he was certain Pip was all right, Paul had come straight to the police station.

'You're not his lawyer, and you're not family, so no dice.' The policeman folded his arms and rested both of his chins on his chest.

Paul glared at Hayes. The two men loathed each other and Paul would have been very happy to live out the rest of his days without ever seeing the fat policeman again. Paul wondered if he'd got the term 'no dice' from an American movie or a crime novel. Either one would have radically improved his knowledge of policing and the law.

'Philippa says Kenneth wasn't trying to assault her at the demonstration, so you've no grounds to hold him in the cells.'

Hayes snorted. 'You've got no grounds, Bryant, to tell me who I can or can't arrest and hold.' He leaned forward over the well-worn timber charge counter. 'You weren't born here, you don't know what these —people are capable of.'

Paul was seething, but forced himself to stay calm. 'No, but my wife was born here and she says there was no assault.'

Hayes stood straight again and shook his head. 'I don't get you two kaffir-lovers.'

Paul clenched his fist. He wanted to lash out and shatter Hayes's nose, but he knew that was exactly what the obese bully wanted him to do. That way he could arrest Paul too.

'A munt knocks your pregnant wife down in the middle of a subversive rally and you come here begging me to let him out of gaol,' continued Hayes. 'Wait a minute. Perhaps this is all a ruse to get me to let him out so that you can *donner* him good, hey?'

'We're not all like you, Hayes. Let me see him.'

'No.'

'She won't make a statement against him. Look, Ngwenya's boy nearly drowned up on Lake Kariba yesterday. He's still up there. You don't want the lad to find out his father's been locked up on trumped-up charges, do you?'

'*Trumped-up*? This is none of your business, or your wife's, Bryant. Special Branch is on the case now, and it's out of my hands.'

'What's their interest in Ngwenya? As I understand it, he and the others were part of a peaceful demonstration over bus fares.'

Hayes snorted. 'You weren't there, I was. If you think that demonstration was about the price of bus tickets you're more naïve than I thought. It's about politics – about them thinking they'd know how to run a country. That's why the Branch is involved.'

'But what's Ngwenya done wrong? If my wife doesn't testify you'll have no grounds to hold him on a charge of assault.'

Hayes smiled. 'I don't care whether he assaulted anyone or not. You see, there's an operation going on right now in Salisbury and Bulawayo. You'll be able to read about it in tomorrow's *Chronicle*. It's called Operation Sunrise. A new dawn.'

Bryant had no idea what Hayes was talking about.

'We're rounding up the rabble and filth who'd sell this fine country of ours out to the communists and the black national-ists. These people think they can bring Rhodesia to a halt by telling honest, hard-working Africans to walk to work rather than catch the bus. All the leaders of the protests have been arrested, and that includes your *friend* Ngwenya. I doubt he'll be filling any young minds with red propaganda for some time.'

'Can I at least see him?'

'No,' Hayes said.

Paul didn't know what else to say. He'd known for years that Kenneth was active in black nationalist politics, but he'd never heard his friend espousing communist propaganda. Far from it, in fact. Kenneth and his fellow agitators wanted one man, one vote – which would mean, of course, black majority rule in a democratic country.

As a schoolteacher, Kenneth was well educated for a black man, having studied teaching at Fort Hare University in South Africa, but this set him apart from the vast majority of black Rhodesians. Even the most liberal whites Paul knew seemed uni-fied in their belief that while majority rule might be inevitable one of these days, it wasn't something to be rushed. There was a need for more Africans to become better educated before they were ready to govern their own affairs.

When Paul had put this view to Kenneth the teacher had retorted that this was condescending, racist rubbish. It was the closest he'd ever seen the bookish teacher come to radicalism. 'Paul,' he'd said, slapping a closed fist into his palm, 'can't you see that this will never happen? Our junior education system might be one of the best in Africa for African people, but as long as we are excluded from higher education and so many professions we will never be given the chance to advance ourselves and take control of our destiny.'

Paul thought of Winston, and the high hopes Kenneth had for his son. He still hadn't worked out when or how he would get back to Kariba to collect the two boys. He hoped they were safe. They were level-headed enough youngsters, but two teenagers together could get up to a good deal of mischief.

'I'll get Kenneth's wife and bring her here. Surely you'll allow her to visit him,' Paul said to the policeman.

Hayes nodded. 'We're not uncivilised, Bryant. I dare say the black communists wouldn't be so accommodating to political prisoners if they were running the country.'

The phone rang and a white constable sitting at a desk behind the charge counter picked up the Bakelite handset. 'Mr Bryant, is it?' the constable interrupted.

'Yes.'

'It's the hospital, sir. Matron says you're to get back there now. It's your wife. She's gone into labour.'

Paul sat by Pip's bedside in the Mater Dei hospital in Hillside until at last her eyelids fluttered and she opened her eyes.

He kissed her cheek.

'Where's George?' she asked, still groggy from the anaesthetic.

'He's fine. Probably having the time of his life up on Kariba with Winston and without me. We have a daughter.'

Doc Hammond had told him the delivery had not been without complications. Pip had lost a lot of blood and had needed a transfusion. According to the doctor, their daughter seemed as healthy as could be expected for a premature baby.

'Oh, yes. I remember now.'

He laughed, but stopped when she tried to join in and he saw her wince.

'Go get her, Paul.'

Paul went out into the corridor and fetched the nurse, who brought the tiny red-faced baby to her mother. Paul plumped the pillow and helped Pip sit up, and the nurse passed her the tightly wrapped bundle. 'Hello.'

'She's beautiful,' Paul said.

'I was so scared.' Pip kissed her baby tenderly.

'Doc Hammond says she's fine and that you'll be fine after some rest.'

Pip looked up into his eyes and blinked a couple of times. 'Not for me and her, Paul . . . It was what happened, before, in the street.'

'It's over now.'

She shook her head. 'You should have seen the hatred in the eyes of those constables as they laid into the crowd, Paul. It was madness. Kenneth tried to protect me, but then people were running by us, over us. It's not over. It's just beginning.'

'It was a demonstration over bus fares, that's all. It got a bit out of hand. It's hardly a civil war, although I have to tell you that things don't look good for Kenneth. He's facing more charges and may end up in gaol.'

Pip rocked her baby gently. 'It's been simmering for years. I don't want her to grow up in a war, Paul.'

'She won't. What are we going to call her?'

'Hope.'

*

It had been, George thought as he walked out of the building, a week for extraordinary names at the Mater Dei Hospital. First there was his little sister, Hope, whose name was quite odd, but not nearly as unusual as the names Mrs Quilter-Phipps had given her new twin sons, Braedan and Tate.

Apparently Braedan had been named by his father after the farm he had grown up on in England, and Mrs Quilter-Phipps had picked Tate because she thought it sounded like the sort of name an American film star might have.

Talk of unusual names aside, George found hospitals quite boring; except for the time he'd had his appendix out and had been allowed to see it after the operation. He was certainly very relieved that his mother was fine, and that the baby was normal, but he couldn't really see the point of sitting at the foot of his mum's bed, with nothing much to say after he'd told her about his adventures on the lake. On his father's orders he'd left out the bits about the rhino goring a hole in the side of the boat and Winston nearly drowning.

He and Winston had been given a lift all the way back to Bulawayo with a motor mechanic. It had been a long, hot drive home and his skin was burned a deep red from sitting in the back of the mechanic's *bakkie* with Winston.

The two days extra he'd spent on the lake with Winston had been two of the best of his life, George thought, as he walked out of the hospital, away from its acrid smells and sick people. He tossed a cricket ball up and down and shuddered as he remembered being sick over the side of the *bakkie*. He'd been embarrassed at the time, but Winston had found it hilarious and had laughed so much there had been tears in his eyes.

They'd stolen a bottle of whisky from near the campfire after the men had all turned in for bed, and drunk half of it as they'd sat on the shore of the lake. Winston had noticed a ripple in the shallows and they'd found a baby crocodile. Egging each other on, George had run into the water and chased it. Winston, not silly enough again to go out into water past his knees, had herded the little reptile back onto the mudflat. George had dived into the silt and grabbed its tail. It had reared back on him and scratched his arm with its tiny teeth, but Winston had been there a split second later and grabbed its snout.

'You saved my life, *boet*,' George had exclaimed drunkenly.

Winston had smiled at him. 'You have never called me brother before.'

'You are . . . you are my brother, Winston,' George had slurred. He'd been drunk, but he'd meant it.

'Then we are even, brother, because you and your father saved me on the lake, but I am in his debt too.'

The crocodile had bucked in their hands, with surprising strength for such a tiny little creature, and George had burst into laughter at Winston's yelp. Soon after, they'd retired, wet and muddy, to their canvas bed-rolls spread out under mosquito nets tied to trees near the water's edge.

They hadn't spoken of their drunken emotions on the trip back, and instead shared a companionable silence brought on by their mutual nausea as the truck rumbled along strip roads and wide tar down to Salisbury. The mechanic had bought them each a cold beer at Sinoia and although George had tried at first to refuse the gesture, he had found that the man was right and that it really did make him feel better.

After they'd passed through Salisbury they'd stopped on a roadside on the way to Gatooma and the boys had slept in the back of the *bakkie* under a big star-studded sky. Driving the last leg back to Bulawayo they'd passed through Gwelo and the high open grasslands of the midlands, dotted with fat cattle.

George had thought about Winston's plan to join the army

when he came of age. George, too, could join up, as the Rhodesian African Rifles, which accounted for the country's permanent military force, was made up of black soldiers and white officers.

'Look.'

Winston, with his keen eyes, had pointed up into the sky as the *bakkie* had raced along at its top speed of fifty miles per hour. George had shielded his eyes and seen the glint of light reflected on shiny bare metal. 'Vampire,' he'd said, immediately identifying the twin tail booms of the British-made jet fighter.

George had watched the silvery jet come in to land at Thornhill Airbase, feeling the vibration of its engine in his chest as it roared low over the waving boys, and he'd made up his mind then and there about what he wanted to do. His father would fight him all the way, of that he was sure, but he didn't care. 'I don't want to join the army. I want to be a pilot.'

'At least you can choose to do that. There are no black pilots in the air force or officers in the army.'

George thought about Winston's comment now as he picked up his pushbike from under the tree in the hospital garden. He started cycling out from the all-white suburb of Hillside towards Mzilikazi Township. Not many whites ventured into the black township, but George went often enough, when he was home on holidays, that he warranted friendly waves and greetings from many of the people he met.

Kenneth and Patricia lived in a two-bedroom brick house, with a tin roof held in place by an assortment of rocks and concrete blocks, behind the school where Kenneth was principal. The house was modest compared to the rambling colonial farmhouse George had been born into, but substantial by African standards, as befitted a man of Kenneth's standing.

Winston had a sister, Thandi, who was a year younger than

George. George hadn't paid much attention to girls up until his thirteenth birthday, but now he found himself thinking about them a lot of the time. Sometimes, when he was alone in his bed in the dorm at school, or home on the farm, he found his body responded to these thoughts.

To his horror, George once got the reaction, down there, in the middle of a church sermon, while he and his mother were standing behind Susannah Geary and her mother. Susannah was named after her mother. Her father had also been in the air force during the war, in bomber command like George's father, except Susannah's dad had been an air gunner. He'd lost the sight in his left eye thanks to a metal splinter from a flak round. He was now a butcher in town.

'Howzit, Thandi,' George muttered as he propped his bicycle against the Ngwenyas' front fence.

'Hello, Georgie Porgie.' Thandi was as tall as George, and try as he might he couldn't help but notice her budding breasts.

'Very funny. Is Winston home?'

'Mmm,' she said, smiling at him. He felt his face start to colour. 'Have you come around to play?'

'I'm too old to play these days, Thandi.' She giggled. He walked past her briskly.

To his even greater consternation, George sometimes thought about Thandi when he was alone in his bed. He fantasised about what she might look like, minus the pink pedal pushers and black sleeveless blouse she often wore. His tummy fluttered as he knocked on the door frame. He heard soft footsteps on the paving stones and was aware of her behind him.

'Why does your face go red when you talk to me, Georgie?' she said quietly.

He couldn't look back at her. He felt his throat constrict, so that he couldn't have said a word even if he could have thought of one. His cheeks burned and he could feel a vein in his temple begin to beat like an African drum.

He coughed. 'Mrs Ngwenya,' he squeaked.

Thandi giggled behind him.

George thought he might catch fire on the spot and burn like the sinner he knew he was. A boy at school had smuggled in some postcards of rather plump European women, either naked or in their underwear, and the older boys at school sometimes joked about the female maids who cleaned the dorms. He knew the term for white men who had sex with black women – 'nanny knockers' they were called. His mother and father were friends with Winston's father, and they tolerated his mother, Patricia, but never in his wildest imagination could George imagine a white man and a black woman together. It just wasn't supposed to happen. They'd been for a holiday the previous year, to Beira in Mozambique, which was a Portuguese colony, and things were different there. George's mother had been to Mozambique once before, but it was a new experience for his father. His father had expressed surprise at the amount of 'intermarriage' in the colony, and his mother had told him it was the way the Portuguese were, and to not talk about such things in front of George. This, of course, had aroused George's interest even more. He'd seen plenty of coloured people growing up, but it was only in the last couple of years, when he'd started taking a keen interest in girls that he started to put the pieces together. Somewhere, somehow – not just in Mozambique but also Rhodesia – some black people and some white people must be making coloured babies.

'What do you want?' Patricia Ngwenya blocked the doorway, arms folded. She wore a white apron over her floral-print dress. She was a formidable woman who was becoming more so, and better able to block a doorway, with each passing year. She scowled at him.

'Afternoon, Mrs Ngwenya.' If she wasn't going to be polite, that didn't give him an excuse not to be. 'I'd like to see Winston, please.'

'Ah, he's not here.'

'But Thandi said –'

'I don't care what she said.' Mrs Ngwenya looked over his shoulder and scowled at her daughter. 'What are you staring at?'

'Nothing, Mama,' she cooed.

Winston's five-year-old brother, Emmerson, toddled up to his mother's legs and peered up at George from behind the stout trunks. 'Hello, Emmerson,' George said.

'I told you, he's not here,' Mrs Ngwenya said, wiping her hands on her apron. 'You must go, now.'

'But –'

'Go, NOW! I don't have time to jump for you, white boy. My husband is in gaol because he tried to help your mother and now I am here with three children to look after and no man. Ah, but I don't even know if the school will let us stay in this house!'

George wouldn't talk back to an adult, but he had to bite his tongue to stop from challenging her. He didn't know exactly what Winston's father had done, and this was the first he'd heard about him being in gaol. The reference to his mother confused him. His father had told him she'd tripped and fallen in the street in Bulawayo.

'Do you know where Winston's gone?'

Mrs Ngwenya shrugged. 'How would I know? That boy, he tells me nothing.' She took a pace back, nearly tripping over little Emmerson, and slammed the door in George's face. George puffed out his cheeks and then spun around in fright when he felt a touch on his shoulder.

Thandi grinned at his shock and subsequent embarrassment. 'I know where he has gone,' she whispered. 'Come with me.'

George followed her to the gate and glanced over his shoulder to see if the fearsome Mrs Ngwenya was still watching. He saw no curtains twitching. 'Is it far?'

Thandi nodded. 'Very.'

He frowned. 'What about my bicycle?'

'You can take it.'

'I can't have you running along behind me.'

Thandi put her hands on her hips. 'You wouldn't dare. You can double me. I'll sit on the handlebars.'

Gosh, thought George, there was probably a law against that. Thandi straddled the front wheel, with her back to him, then wriggled her backside up onto the handlebars. She looked back at him. 'Ready?'

God, no, he thought to himself, but at the same time he felt marvellously excited and naughty and brave. He steadied the bike, and the girl, with a light hand on her hip, then pushed off and leapt onto the saddle. Thandi squealed as they wobbled a bit, but he told her to hush, and after a few hard pumps of his legs they picked up enough momentum for her to stay stable.

He could smell her body as he pedalled. It was a rich, musky scent. Not unpleasant. He'd never been this close to a girl – black or white – in his life. He followed her directions, and although they skirted the edge of the sprawling township, there were enough locals about to take an interest in them. A trio of young men in suits whistled and hooted; an old man smiled; a woman of Mrs Ngwenya's size and vintage shook her head and waved a finger at them.

They left the dusty dirt roads for a stony track and when the going became too rough George reluctantly stopped the bike. Thandi put a hand on his shoulder for support as she eased herself down. '*Eish*. My bottom hurts.'

He felt himself colour again and she laughed. 'Thank you, George. That was fun, wasn't it?'

He nodded, once more unable to speak. Thandi was only twelve, but she never seemed lost for words. George, however, often felt tongue-tied around girls.

'Come,' she said, with an imperious flick of her wrist.

He followed her, pushing the bike by its saddle, and eventually caught up so they were walking side by side. The stunted, rain-starved trees closed in on the track, forcing them to walk closer together.

'Do you know where you're going?' George asked her.

'Always.'

They walked on for a while longer in silence. George started to feel nervous. He hadn't been to this place before. They were outside town, and the shadows were lengthening as the bush around them started to glow in the mellow, golden light. He should be getting back to his mother and father at the hospital. He presumed he and his father would be going out to the farm tonight, but George wanted to make sure Winston was all right first.

'If I take you to Winston, will you do something for me?'

George looked at Thandi and tried to shrug nonchalantly. 'I suppose so, what is it?'

She stopped and he had to reverse the bike a bit when he saw she wasn't going to follow him.

'I don't have any money on me, Thandi.' He saw her eyes flare and knew he'd said the wrong thing. 'I'm sorry, I didn't mean . . .'

She strode off, and this time he had to jog to keep up with her. He wasn't paying attention and the bike veered off the track into a thornbush. He cursed and left it there and ran after her. Each footfall set up a little explosion of dust on the track.

'Thandi! Wait!'

She was running now and he had to sprint hard to catch her. Her legs were long and slender and her stride was fluid like a beautiful female kudu racing from a predator. George chased her, but he wasn't a predator. He had no idea what this game was about, but he felt it was important that Thandi wasn't mad at him.

He caught up with her and when he laid a hand on her shoulder she stopped and turned to face him, her chest heaving. She stared at him and when she reached out her hands he flinched, then stood still. She put her hands behind his neck, drew him to her and kissed him on the mouth.

George thought his heart was going to explode from his body. Her lips were the softest, most delicious thing he'd ever tasted. He had no idea if he should touch her, but one thing he knew was that he never wanted this feeling to end.

It was she who broke the kiss. She wiped her mouth with the back of her hand. 'Oh God. What have I done?' she said. 'My mother would kill me if she knew I'd kissed a *mukiwa*.'

Oddly, he thought his mother might do the same thing to him if she caught him with a black girl, but it didn't seem an appropriate thing to say.

'Thandi? Is that you?'

George looked to the direction the voice was coming from. It was Winston.

'Thandi,' George whispered, 'I –'

'Shush. Winston would kill me, too. We must never speak of this again.'

What did she mean? It was the first time he'd ever kissed a girl and now she was telling him they couldn't talk about it. Did that mean it was never going to happen again, or that he wasn't allowed to tell anyone?

George followed Thandi through the bush. The rocky ground didn't seem to bother her, even though she was barefoot. He thought of the succulent taste of her lips. The sight of her bum in her tight pedal pushers was hypnotising.

'George. You shouldn't have come. I don't want to get you in trouble.' Winston scowled at his sister. She shrugged in reply.

'What's going on, Winston?'

'My father's been arrested and so now I'm running away from home.'

George laughed. He'd run away from home when he was eight, after his mother had scolded him for playing with matches. He'd come home before dusk. 'Only children run away from home.'

'I am not a child. It is why I'm leaving.'

George saw that Winston had collected some clothes and a pot and a couple of utensils in an old blanket, which was spread out on the ground. He had made a fire and was smoking a bream over it. *Sadza*, the thickened mealie-meal porridge that was the staple diet of all Africans, was cooking in the pot on the coals. 'But why?'

'My father has been arrested. My mother says he might be in prison for two years – perhaps more.'

'So,' George said. 'She needs you. You are the man of the house now. You need to look after her and the others.' He looked at Thandi, who rolled her eyes.

'I want to join the army, George. I was serious. They won't take me if they know I am the son of a communist.'

'Your father's not a communist, he's a schoolteacher.'

Winston shook his head. 'I found a book in his bedroom, hidden. It was by Karl Marx. We learned about him in school, in South Africa. The Jesuits say that communism is evil and that they kill Christians in Russia.'

George didn't know about any of that, but he was sure Winston's father was a good man. 'It's not illegal to read books in this country. Come home with us, Winston. It'll be all right. Don't you want to visit your father? He could tell you what's going on.'

Winston clenched his fists. 'I never want to see him again. He has brought shame to us. My mother said that without his income I will have to stop going to school in South Africa. There is nothing for me here in Rhodesia, George, and I am tired of schooling. It is time for me to go and become a man.'

'Go home to your mother, Winston,' George tried again. 'She needs you. I'll come with you. My dad can pay for your school fees. I know he'd want to.'

Winston exploded. 'You don't understand, George! My mother hates your family . . . hates you. She hates the fact that your father helps pay for my education. She says it makes us like beggars. She says one day we black people will run this country, and that all the whites will work for us, or be forced to leave.'

George was shocked. He'd never heard such nonsense before in his life, and he struggled to work out what it was that he or his mother or father might have done to offend Patricia Ngwenya so. He was speechless.

'She is poisoning me . . . and Thandi.'

George looked at Thandi. 'I don't hate white people,' she said to him. He was fairly sure she was telling the truth, after what had happened a few minutes earlier.

Winston exhaled. 'I just want to do the right thing, George, and I don't know what that is. I think the best thing for me to do is to go away from Bulawayo, to somewhere where people do not know me or my family.'

'But what about your education?'

Winston shook his head, and knelt to turn over his fish. 'I

don't want to be a schoolteacher, George. Maybe my mother is right, and that one day Thandi, Emmerson and I will be able to do whatever we want to in life. Until then, I can beg from your father to pay for me to become what my father was, or I can do something for myself.'

'When will I see you again?'

'I don't know. Perhaps never. My mother will be poor with my father in prison. I would be a burden for her.'

'No! Don't go. It isn't fair . . .' It was growing dark and George knew he should be getting back to the hospital. His father had enough to worry about without him going missing. At the same time, he didn't want to leave his friend, or Thandi. It wasn't right that Winston's life should be changed like this.

'Come, George,' Thandi said, and took his hand.

Winston looked at his friend's white fingers intertwined with his sister's, then from George's eyes to Thandi's. He said nothing. George thought he saw hurt there.

'It is time for you to go . . . both of you,' Winston said at last.

Humans had fled from Makuti and his mother when, exhausted, they had touched shore. Makuti's mother had snorted her challenges and tossed her head, but she had been too intent on making for high ground to stop and attack any of the two-legs that fled from her.

When she stopped running, she settled into a plod, not seeming to care whether her tiny calf could keep pace with her or not.

Makuti paused and sniffed the air. The stench was foul: acrid and burning. He had an instinctive fear of fire, inherited from his mother, and she, too, had caught the hated scent. In a valley behind the township was the humans' mountain of refuse.

Wooo-ooop. Wooo-ooop.

Makuti froze at the alien sound that echoed through the valley. His mother trotted away from both, and Makuti gladly followed. There was something terrifying about that sound.

Wooo-ooop. Wooo-ooop.

His mother crashed through a forest of mopane saplings, the new growth from a previous fire. In the valley she would have lived in thorn thickets and dense jessie bush, but these tiny trees with the butterfly-shaped leaves provided scant cover for such a big beast.

Wooo-ooop. Wooo-ooop.

The noise was following them. Makuti's ears were his best defence. Big and out of all proportion to his tiny body, it would be years until he grew into them, but with his naturally poor eyesight, and his hornless head, they were essential to his making it into adulthood alive.

He ran faster, to try to close the gap with his mother, but she only increased her pace. The mournful whooping changed to a high-pitched cackle. Whatever they were, they were laughing at his pathetic attempts to outrun them. Makuti glanced to the side and saw a dapple-coated phantom in the light of the moon, flashing between two tree trunks.

Wooo-ooop, another taunted from behind him, while off to his other flank was a third laughing beast, silvery ropes of drool hanging from its bared fangs. They loped along, and when Makuti saw them his tiny heart beat faster.

He snorted in alarm, but his mother paid no attention. His nostrils were filled with the dust and old ash her great running feet stirred up. He heard them loping along on either side of him and caught their fetid smell on the wind that chased them uphill from the flooded valley. He tried to call another warning, but they were on him before he could draw a breath.

One spotted hyena, the youngest of the three, latched on to

Makuti's stubby tail and yanked him off his rear legs. Another, the big matriarch of the clan, grabbed the little rhino's right ear in her jaws and tore his head to the ground. Makuti wailed in pain and terror as the third beast scurried to join the execution.

Makuti kicked out with his legs and shook his head as they rolled him over. His mother was a disappearing cloud of dust. She wouldn't know of his death until it was too late. Makuti squealed as the queen of the hyenas tore off the top of his ear and wolfed it down as the other one tried to fasten its jaws around his neck. Makuti tried to buck his way out of its reach, but the hyena merely shrieked with joy at his futile protests. The leader closed in again, to end the play and take her share of the meagre meal. Makuti dimly saw the third predator closing in on him before his head was yanked down again by teeth clamped to his good ear. He squealed in agony.

The ground shuddered to the rhythmic sound of great three-toed feet beating a war dance out on the dry earth as Makuti's mother returned for him. Makuti glanced up again in time to see the advancing hyena lifted off its feet and carried sideways in midair. Makuti's mother shook her head and tossed the gored hyena off her horn like a rag doll.

Makuti's mother bellowed and charged again, heading straight for the female who held her son pinned to the ground. The matriarch looked up and snarled, not surrendering her prize so easily. The second hyena, not so brave, tried to flee, but was stomped under Makuti's mother's foot.

The queen of the hyenas dragged little Makuti towards her, taunting his mother to come closer and risk trampling her offspring to death. Makuti's mother paused, tossed her head, then lowered her horn and charged, calling the hyena's bluff.

Makuti could do nothing. It seemed as if the queen might die defending her meal, but just before his mother's hooked horn impaled her, the hyena let go of his ear and bolted off into the night.

His mother paused, near breathless. She snorted and panted for a while, her nostrils flaring and head held high as she tested the air for fresh scent of an enemy. When she was satisfied the hyenas were no longer a threat, she turned and trotted away.

Makuti, bleeding from both ears and sore all over, followed her into the hills.

CHAPTER 4

Rhodesia, 1969

The corporal looked down the long barrel of his FN rifle. He pulled the steel-plated butt deeper into his shoulder. There was no moon, and the river was the colour of his rifle, but its surface still shone enough to allow them to see the boats.

'Now?' whispered the private beside him in Shona, the language they shared in the section when they weren't talking to their white officers.

'Hush, no. Wait until I tell you,' the corporal replied.

'Wait for it . . .' said the white officer needlessly – the black African corporal knew his job well.

There were two rubber boats on the Zambezi River and the corporal could hear the soft splash of the oars in the water. A hippo grunted nearby, the sound echoing down the valley. The corporal sensed the private shifting nervously. He was new to the battalion, and new to the bush.

The terrorists in the boat called themselves freedom fighters; members of the Zimbabwe People's Revolutionary Army, or ZIPRA. The corporal called himself a noncommissioned officer in the 1st Battalion of the Rhodesian African Rifles.

Ironically, culturally and linguistically the corporal probably had more in common with the men in the boat than he did with his comrades strung out in the bush on either side of him. He was an Ndebele, sometimes called the Matabele by the whites, a descendant of the Zulu *impies* that had ranged north and west into Rhodesia from South Africa in the previous century, slaughtering all who dared stand in their way. The ZIPRA men would all be from his home province, as that was where Joshua Nkomo recruited from. By contrast, the majority of the men in the RAR – the Rhodesian African Rifles – were drawn from the Karanga, one of the tribal groupings of the Shona, the traditional rivals of the corporal's people. The Karanga came from the area around Fort Victoria, but some of the men in the boats might very well be from Bulawayo, like the corporal. They might have even gone to school together or played together, but tonight they would try to kill each other.

'If a firefighter fights fires,' the white officer had said to him once, jokingly, 'what does a freedom fighter fight?'

The corporal was smart enough to get the joke, but he had thought long and hard about it the night after, until he decided there was no point thinking about such things. He had a job, and he was good at it. These ZIPRA freedom fighters and their leaders in their political party, ZAPU, the Zimbabwe African People's Union, might talk loud about how they were going to take over Rhodesia, but militarily they were no match for the Rhodesian security forces.

The corporal came from a family who supported ZIPRA, but he had left home as a young man, ashamed by the fact his father had been imprisoned. His youthful decision to join the government's army had been nurtured by his instructors, superiors and peers. Also, he liked being on the winning side. He and the members of his section would win this fight, as they had won all their previous fights, and tomorrow they would eat and drink until they passed out. It was a warrior's life, and it was a good one. He looked through the circle on the flip-up rear sight and aimed at the centre of the black mass of men, who blended in with their boat. It was too far and dark to see their faces. He thought of them not as patriots, heroes or traitors – just as the enemy. Like the terrorists out there in the darkness the corporal also dreamed of a time when black men would be free to occupy any rank or any job in society, but he believed that promotion would come in time, and be awarded on merit, as was the case in the army.

'Fire!'

The corporal squeezed the trigger. There was a splash as the first terr tumbled over the side of the boat, and screams of fear and panic erupted from the enemy. Round after round punctured skin and rubber. The first boat started to sink. He didn't look at the other craft – that was two section's target. The corporal saw an AK-47 raised high out of the water and a head break the surface. He fired again. The lightning of the muzzle flash obscured his target, but when he blinked and looked again there was no sign of man or rifle. He shifted his aim and found another target.

On either side of him was the crack of rifles firing and the occasional whiz of an incoming 7.62mm Russian-made bullet. Further down the line a Bren gun opened fire and sent up a neat line of silver water spouts on the river.

'Forward!' called the officer.

The corporal would have waited a while longer. They had a perfect field of fire, with any living enemy silhouetted against the sheen of the river. Why not stay put and watch for survivors struggling to shore? Any who floated under a boat, or lay in the shallows, would soon be food for the *ngwenya*, the countless crocodiles that lived in the waters of the lower Zambezi. But the officer was an inexperienced *mukiwa* and this was his first contact.

The corporal made a fist with his left hand and pushed his knuckles into the soft earth to raise himself up. He would follow the white man because that was his job. And he was good at it. 'Come,' he said to the private. 'Now we finish the killing.'

Two shapeless lumps, the deflated remains of the boats, bobbed in the shallows. A man floated face up next to one of the rubber carcasses. 'Check for wounded,' the white officer said.

The corporal raised his rifle to his shoulder and fired a shot into the body.

'Damn it, Corporal Ndlovu, I said check for wounded, not fire shots into every body.'

The corporal bobbed his head in acknowledgement, but there was no way he was going to wade out into that river to see if some terr was still breathing. As if to underscore his fear, the water rippled and the private stepped back from the edge of the Zambezi as the jagged ridges of a crocodile's tail momentarily broke the surface.

There was the smell of blood and innards and gunpowder in the air – the odour of war. This had been a one-sided affair so far and that was just fine by the corporal and his men. No one in war seeks a fair fight.

The private knelt beside a man who lay face down in the mud, checking his pulse. 'Sir?' he called to the white lieutenant. 'This man, he is still alive.'

Corporal Ndlovu kept his rifle up to his shoulder and moved to another prone form and kicked it viciously in the ribs. The man was on his back, his eyes wide open. The corporal felt nothing for this man, who had died pursuing a foolish dream. The corporal heard a branch break in the thicket of jessie bush off to their right. He swung his rifle to check it closer, then the fire erupted.

The officer screamed and went down and the private dived behind the body of a terrorist. Ndlovu pumped two quick shots into the bush, in the direction of the muzzle flash. Another AK-47 started firing on automatic, tracer rounds rising high as the untrained marksman forgot to compensate for the weapon's tendency to climb. Ndlovu fired again, then got up.

He ran, dived and crawled to where his officer lay screaming. 'Fire your rifle, boy!' he yelled at the private, who was cowering behind the body of the wounded terrorist. Ndlovu rolled twice, leopard-crawled through the mud and took aim at the muzzle flashes again. He heard a yelp of pain from somewhere in the bush and one of the AKs stopped firing. The rest of the corporal's section had lagged behind when he, the officer and the private had moved forward to check the bodies in the river and on the bank. They were now exposed. Bullets from the living gunman's rifle *phutted* into the mud around him.

The corporal used his elbows and toes to inch backwards until he was within reach of the private. He grabbed the boy by the shoulder and shook him. 'Fire your rifle, I need covering fire!'

The boy looked up, but then his head snapped backwards as a 7.62mm copper-jacketed round drilled a hole through his forehead. The corporal let go of him, slung his own rifle around his neck and rose to his knees. Bullets whizzed by him as he hefted the bleeding, screaming white man over his shoulder. Corporal Ndlovu grunted and pushed himself to his feet and started running along the edge of the Zambezi.

The AK-47 fire followed him, although by now the rest of the section were zeroing in on the lone terrorist. The Bren gun chattered and the FNs slammed away at the jessie bush. Ndlovu's bush hat fell off as he ran. He could see the flashes of his comrades' weapons and heard one of them cheering him on. He would make it.

The hit was like a steel poker being driven through the muscles of his right thigh. He dropped to the ground and the screaming officer's weight drove him hard into the dirt. He looked down at his leg and saw the blood, but he felt no pain. Bullets landed around him. It seemed the gunman was on a mission to kill him, and him alone. Ndlovu grabbed the yoke of the white man's canvas webbing strap and started dragging him through the blood-soaked dirt.

Ndlovu started to feel dizzy as the shock took hold of his body, and he pitched face-forward into the ground. He raised himself on one arm and reached for the officer, but there were other hands around him now, and the gunfire had stopped.

The Zambezi reminded Air Lieutenant George Bryant of the dully shining grey-green skin of a mamba. His Alouette helicopter tracked down the course of the river that divided Rhodesia from Zambia.

'Cyclone seven, cyclone seven, I can hear your approach, over,' an African voice said over the radio, addressing George by the generic call sign for a 7 Squadron helicopter.

George acknowledged the call. He knew the RAR stick's white officer had been wounded so he presumed the man calling the shots was an NCO.

'You are close, I am going to fire a flare, over,' the African soldier said.

George closed one eye as the red firework shot up into the sky and burst open. The incendiary floated slowly towards earth under its parachute as the valley was lit in eerie hues of boiling blood.

George saw the clearing by the river's edge and the flickering forms of men kneeling around others lying in the dirt. George slowed the Alouette and started to bring her in.

'Tracer! Incoming fire,' yelled Goulds, his technician, from the back.

George looked hard right and saw the glowing green blobs arcing at what seemed a ridiculously slow pace straight for him. George heaved on the controls and pulled the helicopter away from the landing zone. The deadly fireflies chased him.

'FAF two, alpha one, we're taking small arms fire, over,' George said into his radio mouthpiece, using his squadron call sign. He kept his voice as calm as he could, despite his racing heart.

'Roger, alpha one,' said the lieutenant back at Kariba Airport, whose military call sign was Forward Air Field – FAF – two. 'Road uplift is en route to the patrol, return to base, over.'

'Roger, FAF two,' George said. He was relieved that someone else was making the decision. Since the Rhodesian Prime Minister, Ian Smith, had unilaterally declared independence from Britain four years earlier, international sanctions had begun to bite. The Rhodesian Air Force's few helicopters were too valuable to put at unnecessary risk. Night flying was tricky enough, but when people were shooting at you it was downright terrifying. 'How far away is the road party, over?'

'Wait one, alpha one.' George circled while he waited for the reply. The lieutenant eventually came back and said the convoy was about an hour away from the patrol. George relayed the message to the man on the ground and asked him if he could hang on that long.

'Negative, cyclone seven,' the man replied, 'one of these men will die before then, over.'

George passed the sergeant's concerns back to Kariba tower.

'What's the situation on the ground, alpha one, over?'

'I still see plenty of muzzle flashes,' said Goulds over the intercom.

George saw the gunfire on the ground. He knew the lieutenant was right and that he should return to base. Instead, he called FAF two and told them the situation was critical and he was going in to complete the hot extraction of the wounded men.

'Jesus,' said Goulds, but George ignored him.

He brought the Alouette around, and the clatter of the rotors attracted the menacing green comets again. He could see muzzle flashes winking on either side as the RAR soldiers and the terrs slugged it out.

George flared the nose of the Alouette and Goulds yelled out 'Taking hits!' as something clanged on the metal skin of the tail boom.

As the wheels of the Alouette touched down, RAR troopers appeared on either side of the cockpit. Goulds was dragging on one end of a poncho and helping the soldiers slide an ashen-faced man across the floor of the cargo area. Goulds took an IV bottle and hooked it to a webbing strap at the rear bulkhead. A burly African sergeant with a radio on his back opened the co-pilot's door and helped a young African man with a blood-soaked bandaged leg up into the vacant seat. The man's uniform sleeve bore the two stripes of a corporal. George looked over his shoulder and saw a third man, shrouded in a green waterproof poncho, being slid into the rear compartment.

'All aboard, skip,' Goulds said into the intercom.

The sergeant raised his hand in a salute as George started lifting off, then the big man was gone, lost in the dust of the Zambezi valley. George heard gunfire and looked around. Goulds had his personal weapon, an Israeli Uzi submachine gun, pointed out the door and was firing back at the tracer that followed them up into the sky and back towards Kariba.

George turned to the soldier beside him, whose face was

illuminated by the ghostly green of the instrument panel. 'Not long now, Corporal,' he yelled over the engine noise. 'We'll have you in hospital in . . .'

The man's eyes must have reflected George's. They stared at each other for long seconds before George had to turn back to the gauges in front of him. When he looked over again, the man was smiling, despite his obvious pain and weakness from blood loss. George held the stick between his knees for a moment and reached across to clasp the hand of his boyhood friend, Winston Ngwenya.

The next morning, after George had been carpeted by the squadron commander for endangering a valuable aircraft, he signed out an open-topped Land Rover and drove from the airport to Kariba Hospital.

On the drive he slowed to let a herd of buffalo cross the road. On the shores of the lake below, a trio of bull elephant were slaking their thirst in the middle of the hot, sticky day. George thought of the time he and Winston had spent on the lake as boys. He still rated it as one of the best times of his life.

This part of the Zambezi Valley might be under water, but Kariba was still a wild, fun place. The lake had filled many years earlier, but much of the wildlife that had walked to high ground or been rescued during Operation Noah still lived around the shores. The town of Kariba had grown from a construction workers' camp to a small but bustling holiday resort. The Rhodesian Riviera boasted hotels and a casino, and a harbour crammed with houseboats. There was even a yacht club. The Zambezi Valley downriver from the dam was a hot spot for terrorist incursions, but for many people, especially those crewing the catamarans out racing on the glittering water below, the war was something that happened to other people.

George parked the Land Rover outside the entrance to the hospital and took off his beret as he walked in and found the right ward. A transistor radio at the nurse's station played a soft, tinny version of a Glen Campbell song about a lonely soldier in Vietnam.

George coughed. 'I'm here to see the men who were admitted early this morning,' he said to a nursing sister in a starched pinafore.

She looked up from the chart she was filling in and raised her eyebrows. 'All right, but not for long, please, the corporal needs some rest.'

George's rubber-soled boots squeaked on the polished linoleum as he walked past the gatekeeper.

The wounded officer was sedated, having been operated on for four hours, but Winston was sitting up in bed, with a white captain and warrant officer dressed in camouflage fatigues standing by his bedside.

The captain turned and nodded a greeting to George. 'Jonty's still unconscious from the operation. Are you a friend?'

'Actually, I've come to see how Corporal Ngwenya's doing,' George said.

The warrant officer, a nuggety man with steel-grey hair, shook his head. 'Ngwenya? Don't you mean Ndlovu, sir?'

George glanced at Winston and saw the moment of panic flash in his eyes. 'Of course, of course. You know these bloody African names, eh? Ngwenya, Ndlovu, they all sound the same to me.'

The captain looked at George like he was a fool, which was probably how he regarded all blue jobs in air force uniform. His eyes dropped to the pilot's wings on his fatigue shirt. 'You're the helicopter pilot?'

George nodded.

To George's surprise the captain extended a hand. 'Thank you. You've changed my opinion of the air force. I always thought you *okes* were more interested in your bloody machines than in human lives. Ndlovu here pulled Jonty out of the fire, but he probably would have died if they'd waited for the road party to get to them. Come back to the camp with us – the beers are on us.'

The captain and his sergeant major said their goodbyes to Ngwenya and stood by the bed waiting for George to follow.

'I might come along later, if that's all right. Still got some paperwork to do back at the airfield. You know how it is . . .'

There was an awkward moment's silence as the captain registered that George wanted to stay awhile and talk to the black corporal. He eventually shrugged and said, 'Suit yourself. Bar'll be open from lunchtime.'

When the army guys left, George sat on the side of Winston's bed and shook his friend's hand again. 'I hope I haven't caused trouble for you.'

Winston shook his head. 'I don't think so, *sir*.'

George laughed. 'I see you got your wish and ended up in the army.'

'You too,' Winston smiled, 'but I thought you wanted to fly Vampires?'

George shrugged. 'Someone's got to do the dirty work, you know . . . picking up you grubby soldiers. I enjoy it, though.'

'I don't enjoy getting shot.' Winston tried to sit up straighter and winced in pain.

'Let me help.' George put his hands under Winston's arms and lifted him a little. 'Better?'

Winston nodded.

'You've changed your name?'

'If I used my real name I'd be dead within a week. If the other men in the battalion knew I was the son of the gaoled *terrorist leader* Kenneth Ngwenya I'd get a bayonet in the belly, and if the comrades from ZIPRA knew I was working for the *kanka* they'd try even harder to kill me when I was next on leave.'

George knew that the terrorists regarded black Rhodesians who worked for the security forces as jackals – *kanka* – and off-duty policemen and soldiers were in danger of being killed in uniform and out of it.

They swapped stories of what they'd been doing these past ten years. George found that after the first few minutes of chatting it seemed as though they'd last been together only yesterday. Winston had left Bulawayo for the capital, Salisbury, and sought out his father's older brother, an old rogue called Joseph. Winston's uncle lived on the edge of the law, running girls and two shebeens in one of the townships on the outskirts of the city. Winston had known that Joseph and Kenneth never spoke, so he had been sure his uncle would take him under his wing until he was old enough to join the army. His uncle had put him to work mopping out blood, beer, vomit and God knew what else from his bars and had rewarded him with a buxom working girl on his sixteenth birthday. Joseph had taken great delight shielding Winston from his hard-working, God-fearing schoolteacher father, and had even invited him to stay on with him in Salisbury instead of joining the army. Despite the good times, however, Winston hadn't been able to see himself spending the rest of his life as a pimp or a pickpocket. He had stayed true to his plan and enlisted in the Rhodesian African Rifles.

'Training at Methuen was hard, but I liked it. The instructors treated us like rubbish, but by the end of it we were men,' he told George, who nodded. Recruit training seemed to be based on the same principles no matter what colour you were or what branch of the services you joined.

They swapped a few tales of good and bad times in the services before Winston finally got around to asking the questions George had expected. 'How is my family . . . How is little Emmerson?'

George could have predicted Winston's main concern would have been his brother. His mother had always been harsh on him, and his father was an imprisoned political enemy of the country Winston served. Thandi was just a girl. George decided not to lie or be evasive. 'He's headed for trouble, Winston. He's ZAPU to the core, and he's been involved in a few street fights with ZANU thugs.'

ZANU, the Zimbabwe African National Union, was the other main black nationalist party in Rhodesia. Its membership was drawn from the Shona, the larger of the two main tribes in the country. Fights between the Ndebele-backed ZAPU and the ZANU cadres were regular and bloody as the two factions battled for supremacy in disputed black areas, while their military wings took on the security forces.

'Your mother doesn't know whether to keep Emmerson locked up at home or to get him a bigger stick. She fills him full of hate for ZANU and Ian Smith and then fusses over him when he comes home with a split head or broken ribs.'

Winston closed his eyes. George knew what he was thinking. If his brother had fallen in with the nationalists – it didn't matter which party – there was a good chance he would end up in one of the military wings. ZAPU's armed force was ZIPRA – who were mostly Ndebeles like Winston and his family – but ZANU had set up its own army, ZANLA – the Zimbabwean African National Liberation Army. The two tribes, the Ndebele and the Shona, and their political and military wings, hated each other almost as much as they hated the whites.

'Good for Emmerson,' Winston said, opening his eyes again

and grinning. 'At least he's sticking with ZAPU and isn't an *mtengisi*.'

George laughed at the self-deprecating joke – Winston had just used the Shona word for 'sell-out', the name given to Africans like him who sided with the government. George didn't tell Winston, but he was scared of Emmerson. Physically, George was still more than a match for the fifteen-year-old, but Emmerson was growing up fast. Thandi had shuddered when she'd told him how she'd seen her little brother almost kick a ZANU cadre to death in a street brawl in Mzilikazi. The way Emmerson looked at George when he visited reminded him of a cobra, its head swaying and its dark eyes entranced with the thought of the coming kill.

'How do you know all this, George?'

'When I'm home on leave my mom gives me mealie meal, milk, eggs, *nyama* and other things to take to your family. Your mom still hates all white people, especially since your father's been in prison so long, but she tolerates me. Sometimes we talk.' The lie, like all good ones, was based on truth. 'My dad put a new roof on Patricia's house last year.'

Winston's eye's narrowed. 'And Thandi?'

'She's in Mozambique, studying.'

The sister walked over, clipboard in hand, and told Winston to open his mouth. The conversation stopped while they waited for Winston's temperature to be read. George gazed out the window. Thandi.

The last time he'd seen her was six months ago, when he was on leave. The time before that had been going on for a year, but every time he saw her it was the same.

George and a few guys from his squadron had piled into two cars and driven nonstop from Salisbury, through the border crossing at Umtali, and then down to the coast at Vilanculos. The first night they'd got drunk in the bar at the Dona Ana and slept on the beach. The next day the rest of the boys hit the bull-fights. George had begged off, saying he had to go visit a friend of his parents. He'd hailed a *chapa* and told the driver of the minibus taxi the address. As he rode he mused about how different things were in Mozambique, how much freer and easier than in Rhodesia. He wouldn't have been caught dead in a kaffir taxi in his homeland.

He'd written to her, but he had no idea if she would be there. Vilanculos was a long way north of Lorenzo Marques, where Thandi was teaching English. She was already fluent in Portuguese.

The beachside bungalows were down-market enough to be affordable and up-market enough, hopefully, to be free of bed-bugs. George walked along a crushed coral footpath flanked by manicured grass. A light breeze stirred the fronds of the tall palm trees that gave the complex its name, Palmeiros. A bell tinkled when he opened the screen door to the reception bungalow.

'*Bom dia*,' he said to the coloured woman behind the counter. She smiled at him, '*Ola*.'

He'd exhausted his Portuguese, but managed to ask her if a Miss Ngwenya was staying in one of the bungalows. No, the woman told him.

George was disappointed, although a part of him also felt relieved. It was odd, he thought, to want something so badly and at the same time to pray it didn't happen. He stood there a moment, weighing his options. He could get a taxi back to the bullfight and quite possibly end up spending the night in gaol, along with some or all of his squadron mates, or he could still check into a bungalow and get a good night's sleep.

What's wrong with me, he asked himself as he dithered in front of the receptionist.

'Senõr?'

George looked at the woman, then pulled out his wallet and asked for a bungalow. She smiled as she counted his money. He took his key and went to his room. It was neat, if a little tired, but it would do him just fine. He kicked off his shoes and shorts and changed into his swimming costume. He left his rucksack in the room and walked outside. The beach was just on the other side of the gravel road that ran in front of the bungalows. The white sand squeaked under his bare feet.

The tide was in and the water an inviting azure blue, but he was cool enough for now with the gentle breeze. He lay down on his back and closed his eyes.

George felt something cold drip on his bare chest beneath his unbuttoned shirt. He lifted his head and opened his eyes. She eclipsed the sun.

'Hello,' she said. 'I thought you'd never get here.'

He raised a hand to his eyes to shield them from the glare, and her features came into focus beneath the black halo of her Afro hairdo. She held two bottles of Dois M beer that dripped condensation onto him. He blinked, then smiled. 'The woman said you hadn't checked in.'

'I hadn't. I've been sitting in the bar down the beach, watching, wondering.'

'If I'd come?'

'Yes.'

'I invited you to come here, didn't I?' he asked. She wore a red bikini top that was visible under a billowy white cheesecloth top. Around her waist was a wrap patterned with some African motif he couldn't make out. It ended at her knees, above her slender legs. Her brothers used to tease her about being too skinny and her mother had told her she'd never get a husband if she didn't eat up.

'I thought you might have had second thoughts,' she said.

He stared up at her and felt the joyous pain seize him. 'I did.'

'But here you are.'

'Here I am.'

She held out one of the bottles. 'Would you like a beer?'

'Afterwards.'

Thandi lay on one of the beds they'd pushed together, face down, naked, her chin propped in her palm as she rested on one elbow. George trailed the wet beer bottle down the ridge of her spine and she shivered and giggled. He lifted the neck of the bottle to her full lips and she tilted her head and sucked greedily.

As she rolled over she spilled some down her chin and onto her breasts. George set the bottle down and kissed the droplets all the way back to her soft, full lips. 'We need some more cold *chibulis* just now. You're making the beer hot.'

She took his head in her hands and kissed him again. George let the bottle slip from his fingers, not caring about the beer that frothed and spilled from the neck, pooling on the floor. For some reason an image of blood in the back of the helicopter came unbidden to his mind. He forced it away – she burned it away with the heat of her mouth, and the one hand that snaked down between their bodies, feeling for him. Again.

Their first time had been four years after that first kiss on the day Winston had run away from home. He'd been confused and excited and ashamed by that kiss, but with Winston gone there had been no excuse to visit Thandi. In the end it was George's mother who had given him the alibi he'd needed to explore a little more every school holidays. No matter what she might have thought of the irascible Patricia Ngwenya, Philippa Bryant had liked Kenneth and had known that his family would struggle while he was in gaol.

George had cycled, heart pounding, to the modest two-room house in Mzilikazi where the Ngwenyas now lived since they'd been evicted from the school principal's quarters. He'd handed the basket of eggs and a note to the surly Patricia then dallied as he pushed his bike up the pathway. When he'd turned a corner he'd been dejected, as Thandi hadn't been home, but a *'Psst'* hissed from around the corner of an abandoned shack led him to her.

It had been a similar routine every couple of months, when term ended. George would return from boarding school and over the long, hot days of his vacation, through the giggles and the tears and the pining, he would learn a little more about this enigmatic, officially untouchable girl, and the female body.

Kenneth had been released from gaol a year after the bus protests and George had thought his world would end. He would have no more need to cycle to the township during his holidays.

It was a confusing time for George. His body was changing and his voice was breaking. He had an interest in all girls, but Thandi was the one he thought about most. At the same time his teachers were warning George and his fellow pupils against the perils of sin and the evils of masturbation. He wasn't exactly sure, still, what constituted a sin, but he'd worked out the second one.

The boys at school made jokes about blacks all the time, and made fun of the cleaning and gardening staff, often playing pranks on them. George joined in, because he didn't want to be different. But he knew he was. He became ashamed of the feelings he had for Thandi, and the things he did when he thought about her.

George had resolved never to see Thandi again when the government went and ruined everything by introducing the Emergency Powers Act. This gave them the power to detain indefinitely anyone they considered acting in a manner contrary to the wellbeing of society. The fledgling African nationalist movements had gained greater popularity after Northern Rhodesia had gained its independence from Britain in 1964 and become the Republic of Zambia. Just across the border to the north was a country run entirely by black people. George could hardly believe it.

After only three years back in the classroom Kenneth Ngwenya was once more arrested and locked up, and George's mother once more ordered him to cycle around to Patricia's place with a basket of food.

It had finally happened when George was sixteen and Thandi fifteen. In the same hidden donga where they had first kissed, by the same stream where Winston had been smoking his fish before his escape, George and Thandi had lain together and become man and woman. And his life had been turned upside down with the wondrous, joyous, terrible pain of forbidden love.

George opened his eyes as Thandi shifted herself on the bed, straddling him. When they'd come in off the beach, their first time in so long had been frantic and they'd clawed greedily at each other. They'd laughed afterwards at how quickly they'd both climaxed. Over the beers and a shared cigarette there'd been small talk, about her studies. He didn't want to talk about the war and she didn't prompt him. They'd lain together for a while, slick bodies entwined. But he wanted more, and so did she. It was one of the things he loved about her. Once was never enough.

He was hard again as she raised herself on her knees, smiling down at him as she lowered herself. Ripe was the word that came to mind when he thought of her like this. Plump lips and breasts, his hands on her arse, she was like some exotic fruit, almost bursting with sweet nectar, ready to be devoured. He could still taste her on his lips, sea salt and her. He closed his eyes again as he felt her take him in, and she slid down on him.

When he opened his eyes he saw she was watching him, gazing intently as she placed her palms on his chest and started to ride him. He matched her thrusts and he knew she wasn't something to be plucked or consumed. She wasn't a holiday treat or a stolen moment of illicit lust. Right here, right now, he knew he wanted to spend the rest of his life in her embrace. He started to raise himself and opened his mouth to speak. 'I –'

She put a finger on his lips. 'Shush.'

There would be time, he told himself. Her lower lip was trembling now and she bit it to still it. George could feel his own orgasm building. He arched his back, pushing up harder into her, and she met him with equal desire. He was mesmerised by her swaying, bouncing breasts and reached for one, drawing the long nipple in. Thandi groaned.

George heard the breath catch in her throat and when he looked up he saw her eyes were closed at last, her mouth half-open. He knew her ways, but also wanted to learn more. He wanted to spend the rest of his life getting to know her. He smiled to himself, but then he saw the first of the tears squeeze from her tightly closed lids. That had never happened before.

Thandi shuddered and the clench of her muscles overwhelmed his control. George was blind to whatever emotion was going on in Thandi's mind as he surrendered to the blissful release.

Afterwards, George lay on his back, still panting slightly. Thandi slid off him and lay on her belly, her face in the pillow. At first he thought she was just exhausted, like him.

He rolled onto his side, propping himself up on one elbow. He trailed a finger down the ridge of her spine. 'Are you OK?'

Thandi was still for a few moments, then she pushed herself up and swung her legs over the side of the bed so she was seated. She looked back at him, over her shoulder. 'We need to talk.'

George saw her eyes were red and the pillow was damp. He'd never seen her cry during sex. He was suddenly filled with dread. 'Can't that wait?'

She shook her head. 'Not this time.'

George swallowed. He knew what he needed to do, what he needed to say to her. 'OK, then I've got something to say. Thandi . . . will you –'

She shook her head quickly. 'Don't say anything more, George. I have to go away.' The ceiling fan squeaked above them, filling the silence. 'For a long time.'

'You're already *away*, Thandi. You live in bloody LM. How much further can you go?'

'A lot further. I'm going overseas.'

'Where to?'

She wiped her eyes with the back of her hand and sniffed. 'It doesn't matter. But it's for a long time. I'll be going to university there. They say I can study medicine. I might be a doctor, George. Can you imagine that? Me, a doctor!'

'Well, you won't be able to practise in Rhodesia. Who'd want to –' He was angry, and he knew he'd said the wrong thing as soon as he'd opened his mouth. He'd come all this way, and conquered his fears and was about to propose to her, and now she said she was going away.

'Who'd want to be treated by a *munt*? A coon? A kaffir? Is that what you meant, George?'

'No. I meant a . . . a woman.'

Thandi sat up and clutched the sheet to her breast. 'Oh, right.

So you're not a racist, just another misogynist male chauvinist pig? We're OK to . . . *fuck* and have babies . . . is that it? But not to treat sick people. I know what you meant. It's all right for a white woman to be a doctor, but not a black woman. You're just like all the rest of them.'

George reached across to the bedside table for his cigarettes. He took one out, lit it and exhaled. 'No. I'm not. And that's my problem. I'm not one of *them*.'

She stood and wrapped the sheet around her while she picked up her strewn clothes. 'Yes you are. You wear their uniform. You fly for the oppressors, you drop frantam fire bombs on people. You defend their evil, racist regime, George. You . . . you of all people.'

Now he was angry. *Oppressor? Racist regime?* Where the hell had all this come from? 'For the record, Thandi, I've never dropped a bomb or napalm on anyone or fired a gun in anger. I fly troops into the valley and I fly sick and wounded out. The last mission I flew was to pick up an African child who'd been run over by a car.'

She pulled on her bikini pants and shrugged on her top. 'This was wrong. I can't see you any more, George, not ever again.'

Christ, he thought, watching her dress was almost as arousing as watching her undress. He realised, with crystal clarity, that he still wanted to be with her. Forever. He ground out the cigarette and stood naked. She kept her back to him, so he moved behind her. Thandi tried to shrug him away, but as his arms closed around her, she let hers fall limp by her side.

'It doesn't have to be like this, Thandi. Look around, here in Vilanculos, in LM . . . black and white people live together, even marry. We could –'

'Don't say it, George. It isn't fair. It couldn't happen.' She kept staring at the door.

He held her tight, willing the courage to come to him. It was easier flying into ground fire. 'We could get married, Thandi. We could live here, in Mozambique.'

She stiffened in his embrace. 'Don't say such things, George. You know your family would never agree to it. My mother would kill me.' She tried to laugh, but it came out more as a convulsion.

'I think my parents would accept it. My father's not Rhodesian and my mother's quite progressive. We could move here. I could transfer to the Portuguese air force. They're doing the same work we are.'

She spun around to face him. 'They're killing the same people your army is, George. Don't you see what's going on? There's a war, George, and we are in it.'

'*I'm* in it. Not you. You'd be safe in LM or wherever we'd be based. The Porks won't let the communists take over Mozambique, Thandi. It's too important to the Portuguese government. Look at all the money they make from their farms; from tourism in the game parks; on the beaches.'

She looked up into his eyes and he was confused when he saw her blink a few times. She closed her lids, but a tear squeezed out. 'George, stop thinking about yourself for a minute. This isn't about you and your family, or even me and my family. I can't marry you. I can't marry a white man who fights for the Rhodesian government or the Mozambique colonial government.'

Thandi placed her palms on his chest and pushed herself out of his arms. She bent to pick up her wrap, tied it around her and walked out the door into the blinding glare of the African sun.

While the nurse filled in Winston's temperature on her chart, the Rolling Stones came on Radio LM and the tinny noise of the

Mozambican pop station reminded George even more of Thandi. Jagger was singing about time being on his side, but George felt the opposite.

'I said thanks, brother, for helping us out in the valley last night. I was being sincere,' Winston said.

'Oh, sorry. I was just thinking.'

Winston nodded. 'About last night?'

'Yes,' George lied.

The nurse walked past, towards the sedated white officer, her shoes squeaking on the polished floor.

'It's changing,' Winston said.

'What do you mean?' George rarely socialised with army guys. According to the papers the security forces were winning the fight against the terrorists hands down. He was interested in Winston's view of the war which, unlike his, was from the ground up.

'Last night they were better organised than usual. They're learning. They know that we watch the likely crossing points, but this time they were ready for us with a counter-ambush. They were too late to save their men in the boats, but the terrs waiting on the Rhodesian side stayed and fought. They attacked us. We,' he gestured at the unconscious officer in the next bed, 'think we're much better than them – smarter, better trained – so we get cocky.'

'They got lucky, that's all,' George said.

Winston shook his head. 'Their kit, their uniforms, their weapons, their drills . . . they're getting better all the time, and more young men from the villages and the townships are leaving to be trained in Zambia, Tanzania, even Russia.'

I have to go away. For a long time . . . I'm going overseas.

George wasn't stupid. He'd known, in his heart, what Thandi had meant. Patricia didn't have the money to send Thandi overseas to study and there was no way her part-time job as an English teacher in LM would have allowed her to save enough to support herself or travel. He knew she barely made ends meet in Mozambique. She'd spouted communist propaganda at him, calling him an oppressor and mouthing off about firebombs. Despite what Winston had said, it wasn't only young black men who were being spirited away to Russia and the left-leaning African nations, it was women as well. Thandi, he was sure, had joined one or the other of the nationalist organisations and they were sending her away for training.

'What else is happening with you, George? Have you got a woman?' Winston asked, changing the subject. Perhaps he thought George didn't believe him about the guerillas' increasing sophistication.

'You remember Susannah Geary?'

Winston looked up at the ceiling, then grinned. 'That blonde girl? The tomboy who used to hang around you when you weren't playing with me and Thandi in the township?'

'That's the one.'

'Ah, she is too skinny that one, George.'

'Not any more, China. We're getting married next month. She's pregnant.'

CHAPTER 5

The war wasn't his affair, but he learned from it. It sharpened his senses and his instincts. He survived, while others around him died.

Sometimes he was surrounded by noise. There were machines in the air and on the ground, and the rattle of gunfire assaulted his sensitive ears. He learned that it was acceptable to run from some fights. But not all.

Makuti's nostrils flared and he smelled the intruder again. Thorns scored intricate patterns through the dried mud on his flanks but barely marked the skin of his thick hide as he trotted towards the Zambezi River. The intruder had crossed sometime in the night, and to add to the insult he'd deposited a fresh load of twig-studded dung on the path Makuti usually used to get to the water.

Makuti defecated and squirted urine in long, strong jets. This was his country and the women hereabouts were his, and his dung and scent were supposed to advise intruders of this and warn them off.

He lifted his head and sniffed again. It was not only the interloper he had to worry about. The river could be a place of death. He'd swum for his life as a baby and nearly drowned when the waters had flooded. He and his mother had lived in the hills above the new lake until he'd grown old enough to move out on his own. The river had lured him, particularly during the long, dry months, and further downstream he'd found it was narrower and less inhabited by the two-legs than the shores of the lake above the huge wall.

But they still appeared here, every now and then, with their attendant bangs and clatters and crashes. He'd learned already to be very wary of them. Others of his kind had died after the strangers had passed through. A huge explosion one night had sent him running like a scared calf to higher ground, but when he'd returned the next morning he'd found an old bull lying maimed, his right front foot missing. The old man was bleeding to death by the time Makuti got there. All he could do was watch while the other rhino died.

The one he was after, however, was very much alive, judging from the freshness of another urine mark Makuti detected. He stopped and swivelled his ears. From the other side of the thicket he heard the intruder's heavy breathing.

Leaves, dust and branches erupted in front of Makuti as the stranger burst from the thick jessie bush. The other male's horn would have pierced Makuti's flank had he not been quick enough to spin inside his own body length. The wicked weapon glanced off him and Makuti pivoted again to meet the next challenge.

Having lost the advantage of surprise, the foreigner paused, lifted his head and snorted.

Makuti was big for his age, but this bull was a brute. Perhaps five or more years older and a couple of hundred kilograms heavier, he was the largest of his kind that Makuti had ever challenged. Except what was becoming very clear to Makuti was that he was the one being challenged by the stranger, not the other way around. The old male had turned the tables in an instant and Makuti felt fear.

He exhaled through his nostrils and tried to square up and make himself look bigger. The other male lowered his head and charged again.

Makuti panicked. He didn't know whether to turn and flee or to stay and fight. His indecision almost killed him. While Makuti hesitated, the older bull dropped his head a fraction more; the two beasts collided and Makuti squealed as the old male's horn hooked up and under his jaw.

Makuti had been hurt in fights before, but never had he been taken so swiftly and so painfully. The horn had pierced the lower left side of his face and Makuti had to shake himself hard to free himself from the driving point. He yelled, the sound similar to that of an elephant trumpeting, as he turned and started to run.

But the intruder was fast, as well as big and strong. He kept pace with Makuti easily and his next thrust caught Makuti in the rear of his right thigh. Makuti's back leg was lifted off the ground by the move and he slid sideways in the cloud of dust they were both creating.

Makuti screamed again. He stumbled towards the river but the next toss of the stranger's head caught him under his other leg and he fell and rolled. A wave of dirt and debris flew up through the grass.

He twisted and turned, struggling to get back up on his feet, and his frantic movements saved his life. The intruder took his time – no more than a second or two – preparing for his killer blow, but when he thrust up with his horn, Makuti's writhing moved his heart out of the weapon's line and the tip merely scored the surface layers of his hide.

Makuti stood and realised there could be no more running. With both legs and his jaw bleeding he would be easily caught again by the interloper, who would run him down and skewer him from the rear. Makuti curled his tail over his arse at the terrible thought and bravely stood his ground.

The older rhino was breathing hard, but he was far from exhausted. He tossed his head, bellowed, and it was all Makuti could do to stay still and not turn and flee again. Makuti had his back to the river now. He hated the water and he never wanted to swim again as long as he lived. He had long since learned that rhinos were not meant to swim.

When the next charge came, Makuti was ready for it. He lowered his head even further than the old bull and when they collided he was as prepared as he could be for the impact. Still, the dust rose from their bodies and the clack of their horns colliding echoed down the length of the lower Zambezi.

Makuti didn't know, couldn't know, that this old *Diceros bicornis* was fighting for his life. He'd been chased from his home across the river in Zambia by men armed with AK-47 assault rifles. These two-legs were not fighting a war among themselves, as they were on Makuti's side of the Zambezi. These men were hunting the black rhinoceros for its horn. The stranger had nowhere else to go, except into Makuti's territory, but the black rhino is not a welcoming, forgiving or sociable creature. He is solitary, aggressive, unpredictable, and, when needs be, a killer.

Makuti thrust back and the intruder parried the blow. The two big males jostled each other through the sands at the river's edge. Makuti felt one of his back feet meet the water and this spurred him back up the beach's incline. He was not going in there.

Both were screaming now, and their high-pitched war cries sent smaller animals around them scurrying back into the grass and bush. None of them wanted to be caught under the feet of these battling titans.

Youth began to tell over experience. Makuti saw a gap and aimed for it. The older bull's reaction had slowed, and Makuti hooked him in the chest, between his two front legs. The thrust was not deep enough to cause fatal damage, but it winded his opponent, who yielded two steps.

Makuti seized the advantage and screamed again as he rammed the bridge of his head under the interloper's chin. He was almost eye to eye with his opponent and he found himself infused with a sense of power and will. This male was big, but Makuti was in his prime. The older bull's footing slipped in the soft sand of the bank, and when Makuti carried on, lifting his knees high, he found he was now perpendicular to his rival.

The old bull was not done yet, however. For Makuti to score another hit he would have to lower his head and disengage from the old bull. When he did, the elder dropped to one front knee and whirled his head around. The viciously fast move drove the point of the intruder's horn into the skin beneath Makuti's eye, almost tearing it out.

Makuti didn't try to pull back. If he had, he would have been blinded. Instead he ignored the pain and let the sharp point continue to score him, right up the side of his head to his shoulder as he lowered his own horn and drove it deep into his opponent's flank, just behind the spot where his left leg met his body.

The old bull yelped, then groaned, and screamed again in pain. Makuti drove on, keeping his horn embedded deep in his enemy's body, even as the blood began to wash over him. It ran into his mouth and misted his eyes. Makuti shook his head, and in doing so shredded his opponent's heart and other vital organs.

Even as the strength and the life flooded from the old bull Makuti turned and started driving him down the slope of the sands. The thrashing grew weaker, and as Makuti graded him into the water the old rhino died, his blood curling and mixing with the waters of the Zambezi.

Bleeding and puffing with exertion, Makuti lowered his head and drank from the river. He was a male. He had learned how to fight. He had won his greatest battle so far. Nothing could take this land from him, or him from it.

Hope Bryant stared at the pieces of metal spread out on the living room rug, her face creased with concentration. She knew this was important – to her father – but she would rather be listening to the Lyons Maid Top 20 on the radio that was playing softly in the background.

She looked over at her mother, who was sitting in her ratty armchair reading a book called *Hold My Hand I'm Dying*. Hope loved reading, but her mother had told her this book was not suitable for children. Hope resolved to sneak a look at it as soon as the opportunity presented itself. Her mother looked over the top of the reading glasses perched on the end of her nose. She rolled her eyes and Hope started to giggle.

'What's so funny?' her father said, setting down his beer on the side table. Dad had a bottle of Lion every evening – just the one. Her mother didn't drink that often, but when she did she had too many 'toots' and started laughing and wanting to dance with her father.

The legs of the side table were made from a pair of impala antlers and the thing gave her the creeps. She'd insisted, a year back, on going on a hunting trip with George and her father. Her mother had tried to stop her, but her father had given in to her, as he usually did. Hope had wished she'd stayed at home. She'd hated the bang of the guns and the sights and smells of the kudu having its skin cut off and its belly slopped out. It was why she wasn't keen on what her dad was making her do now.

'Name the pieces, from left to right. Come on, Hope. You can do it,' her father said.

'Don't badger her, Paul,' Hope's mother said. 'She's not an air force recruit, you know.'

Hope's eyes flicked from parent to parent. She hoped her mother would tell her it didn't matter what the bits of the rifle were called, and that she could listen to the radio for a bit before going to bed. But that didn't happen. Her mother curled her legs up under her and went back to her book. Hope didn't think she could put her legs under her, like her mother did, because her legs were too long. People said she had her mother's hair and eyes, and her father's height and nose. She was only ten, but she was almost as tall as her mother. Her mother said that was nothing to boast about, as she knew pygmies who were taller than her.

'Come on, mate,' her father said. Hope's father was Australian and he still said odd things like that – calling a girl 'mate'. Hope really wanted to visit Australia, as she was fairly sure that they didn't have a war going on there, and that girls didn't need to know how to strip and assemble an FN rifle.

Hope sighed. She knew she needed to get this done. She pointed to the bits, starting from the left. 'Gas plug, gas piston, gas spring, breech cover, breech thingy, and breech thingy slide.'

Her father smiled. 'Very good. Breech block, though, not breech thingy. Now put it back together.'

Just picking up the long steel rod and the spring made her think of the noise of the rifle and the way the kudu had crumpled. She really didn't want to touch this weapon, let alone learn how to fire it, which was going to be the next lesson.

Her father lit a cigarette. 'Did you see Susannah today?' he asked her mother.

Hope slid the piston into the spring.

Her mother looked up again from her book. 'Hmmm. She was in town trying on her dress. They've had to let it out . . . again.'

Hope's father looked down at her, and Hope didn't know whether he was keeping an eye on her as she reassembled the FN rifle, or if he wondered how much he should say about Susannah being pregnant. Hope was sure that her parents were unaware that she knew all about Susannah and babies, but she did, because Susannah's younger sister, Georgina, had been telling everyone in school that she was going to be an aunty soon.

'Well,' her father said, 'what with George having his leave cancelled, it was bound to happen. Did you see Susannah the older?'

Hope's mother frowned. 'Yes. Still the same dour old so-and-so as ever.'

Hope's father cocked his head. 'Still not too pleased, then?'

Hope's mother nodded, but said nothing more.

'Dad,' Hope said, looking up at her father, 'what's a shotgun wedding?'

Her father stared into her eyes and Hope felt her bravado start to waver. She knew very well what a shotgun wedding was – her brother was about to take part in one – and her father could sense that she knew it as well.

Hope's mother put down her book. 'Where did you hear that expression, Hope?'

She shrugged. 'School.'

'Well, it means that two people have to get married because . . . because of circumstances.'

'Don't George and Susannah love each other, Mom?'

Hope's mother looked at her father. 'Of course they do, Hope,' she said.

Hope managed to get the gas piston and spring back into the hole – chamber, it was called – but she knew from her past attempts that getting the gas plug into the end would be difficult. As she fiddled with the plug, depressing the stiff plunger and then trying to turn it at the same time, she wondered if George was in love with someone else.

Like, maybe, Thandi Ngwenya.

It had happened last year, when George had been driving Hope to a friend's birthday party one Sunday.

George'd had to drop some eggs off to cranky old Mrs Ngwenya and he'd told Hope to wait in the car as they pulled up outside the poor little house where the Ngwenyas lived. George had got out and taken the eggs. It was late October, just before the rains came, and it was hellishly hot in the Morris. George hadn't even bothered to park under a tree – not that there were many in the township in any case. It was all red dirt and dust. Hope watched a mangy kaffir dog nuzzling in a pile of rubbish while it scratched itself. A couple of older kids walked past and one of them banged on the side of the car, which made Hope jump. She wasn't scared, but George was taking an awfully long time.

Hot and bored, Hope finally got out of the car and walked up to the doorway. She could hear low voices inside. She should have knocked, but the door was open. She walked inside. The Ngwenyas' furniture was old and frayed and the house, while clean, had very few things in it. The floor was bare concrete, with a worn rug on it. There was a tiny kitchen off the main room. The whole place reminded Hope of a doll's house. She could hear George and as she moved to the doorframe she saw him. And Thandi. She was sitting up on the kitchen bench and she had her legs wrapped around George, who was leaning into her, kissing her. George's shirt was plastered to his back with sweat and Thandi had suddenly lolled her head back and moaned, her eyes half-closed.

Hope turned and, as quietly as she could, crept out of the house then ran back to the car. George was coming out of the house even as she was opening the car door. Her heart pounded. George had been kissing Thandi. A black girl. His face was red as he reefed open his door, climbed in and glared at her.

He said nothing for a while.

'I told you to wait in the car,' he said at last, running a hand through his hair. Tiny beads of perspiration spattered from his fingers.

'I was hot.'

'Did you . . . I mean . . . where were you?'

'In the garden. I was going to walk into the house to look for you, but I got scared.'

He stared at her and they said nothing again for a few moments, until he finally put the car in gear, started the engine and drove off. Hope craned her neck and saw Thandi standing in the doorway, leaning against the frame with her arms folded and staring right at Hope.

'Hope, you've got to get quicker at this.'

Hope was sick of learning about the rifle. She dropped the heavy barrel of the FN down on the carpet and threw the gas plug so that it bounced and rolled under her mother's chair. 'I don't want to play with guns. I don't want to kill any terrorists!'

Her father shook his head. 'It's not playing, my girl, and it's not about killing people. It's about helping your mom if I'm not around and some bad people come to the farm.'

'I'm not scared of black people, Dad, and I don't see why there should be a war. I don't want to fight, and I don't want George to keep going away to the valley where people shoot at him. It's wrong.' She looked at her mother, who was looking at her father.

Her mother put down her book on the side table, reached under her chair and fetched the missing gas plug. She moved to Hope and then knelt on the carpet beside her.

'Hope, your father and I have lived through one war already, and we don't want anything to happen to you – or to George, or to any of us.' As she spoke, her mother pushed the piston down into the chamber and deftly fitted the tricky spring-loaded plug. 'So what your father says is right. If he's away and you and I are left alone, we will need to look after each other.' Her mother dropped the breech block into its slide and slid it home into the grooves in the rear of the rifle. 'No one's talking about killing anyone, but if something does go wrong we might need to be able to defend ourselves.' Her mother slid the breech cover home then snapped the rifle closed.

'Do you understand what I'm saying, Hope?' Her mother yanked back on the cocking handle of the FN and then let it fly forward.

Hope nodded sulkily.

Her mother aimed the rifle at a window and pulled the trigger. The hammer clicked on the empty breech. 'Good. Because I think things are going to get worse in this country before they get better.'

Hope looked up into her mother's eyes. 'My teacher at school said the war the Americans are fighting in Vietnam is wrong. Is our war right?'

Her mother frowned. 'No war is right, but sometimes you have to fight to defend your principles, Hope.'

Hope didn't understand. 'Are our *principles* right?'

Her mother suddenly looked weary. 'I hope so, my girl, I hope so.' Her mother looked away, to her father. 'Pass me the magazine, please Paul. Hope . . . I'm going to teach you how to load bullets into the FN's magazine, all right?'

'Yes, Mom,' Hope said.

CHAPTER 6

Paul Bryant sipped his Lion Lager and leaned against the stout trunk of the massive umbrella thorn tree under which his son had just married a very visibly pregnant Susannah Geary.

It didn't bother him that his son and new daughter-in-law had conceived out of wedlock. It had happened to plenty of blokes he knew in the air force during the war. What did bother him was that at times during the marriage service his son had looked as though he wanted to be somewhere else.

Paul knew some men suffered from wedding-day jitters, although he hadn't. Pip had been his lifesaver. If they hadn't met he probably would have drunk himself to death. Marrying her had been the happiest day of his life.

George was drinking with three of his mates, fellow pilots from 7 Squadron. They'd taken off their blue air force dress tunics, loosened their ties and rolled up their shirtsleeves. Susannah was nursing a gin and tonic, talking to a girlfriend and trying not to glance across at George too often. She was a good-looking girl, and the pregnancy had only made her look prettier, rounding her out and filling out her face. She'd chosen a tight-fitting ivory minidress – which was not only daringly fashionable, but also her way, Paul thought, of saying, 'To hell with it, I don't care who knows.' Susannah senior was talking to Pip, who laughed loudly at something Susannah obviously didn't find so funny. Paul smiled. He loved his wife with all of his heart.

George collected his friends' empties and headed towards the bar table, which brought him past his father.

'Got a minute, mate?' Paul asked.

George looked back at his fellow pilots, one of whom mimed downing a pint with his hand. 'They're not going anywhere,' Paul said. 'They'll find a waiter.'

'Sure, Dad. Sorry. It's like everyone wants a piece of me today.'

Paul nodded. 'Including your wife.'

George looked at Susannah, then back to his father. 'We've got the rest of our lives.'

A band, a trio of guys with bushy sideburns and long hair, were tuning up their electric guitars and testing their microphones. Hope darted in and out of the wedding guests, with ten-year-old Braedan Quilter-Phipps in pursuit of her. She squealed in joy as she narrowly missed bumping into an African waiter carrying a tray of drinks.

'Susannah's a lovely girl, George.'

George called the waiter over and took a beer from the tray. 'Yeah, she is.'

'Do you love her?'

'Of course I do, Dad . . . It's not just because of the baby, if that's what you mean.'

Paul looked at him steadily. 'Was there someone else?'

George sipped his drink. 'Another woman, you mean?'

Paul shrugged.

'I've never brought another woman home, have I?'

'There's no need to be defensive, George.'

George raised the brown bottle of Lion to his lips and swallowed half of it. 'You're telling me I'm not in love with the woman I've just married and who's going to have my baby. *Ag*, I don't need this shit when I'm home on leave, Dad.' George drained the rest of the beer.

Paul sensed he was on the right track, and that something was troubling his son, but he also knew now was not the time to push things. George hadn't spoken to him like that before in his life, but Paul knew well the strains that combat, and relationships, put on a man. George and Susannah were going to be parents, and if either of them had been harbouring second thoughts, it was too late to do anything about it now. George looked away from him, over the crowd, but not at his wife. Paul saw the emptiness in those eyes and as George waved to the waiter he saw something else in his son. Himself.

Paul had battled with the drink after a crash in his Lancaster bomber, in England during the war. While most of his crew had bailed out safely before Paul belly-landed the bomber on an emergency airstrip, his best friend, Will, the flight engineer, had stayed on board with him, refusing Paul's order to jump. When Paul had successfully landed the stricken bomber he'd thought Will had been hard on his heels as he exited the aircraft, but what he hadn't realised was that Will had been wounded. If Paul had stopped to help him out, they both would have been caught in the explosion that had killed Will. Paul had blamed himself for Will's death and, by the time he'd met Pip in Rhodesia, he had been a borderline alcoholic and close to suicidal.

'You know you can talk to me any time, George.'

George had started another beer. He looked at his father blankly.

'About flying . . . being on operations,' Paul said.

George sniffed. 'It's not like your war, Dad. There's no front-line. We're killing our own people. Besides, we're winning and it's not nearly as dangerous as flying a Lancaster or a Mosquito over Germany.'

'Any operational flying's dangerous, George.' Paul had thought of the fight being waged against terrorists in the Zambezi Valley as the Rhodesian Government standing up to communist-backed aggression. He hadn't thought of it as Rhodesians *killing our own people*, but of course his son was right.

George looked back out over the farm, at the far horizon. 'Two days ago I brought in a soldier who'd lost his leg – mortar got him. He bled out on the chopper. Christ, I didn't know the human body could hold so much blood.' George laughed a little, then took another swig. 'And here I am today, getting married.'

Paul nursed his own drink. He wanted to tell George to ease off, but the boy would have to learn in his own time that booze only worked for the symptoms, not the cause. 'Do you remember those rhinos we helped save, on Kariba?'

George looked at him, surprised by the change of subject. 'Sure. The mom and the baby?'

Paul nodded. 'Even though it was dangerous and the cow tried to kill us – remember poor Winston falling overboard and nearly drowning – it was a good thing we did. It was the right thing.'

George lifted his bottle, then seemed to have second thoughts. He swirled it and looked at the frothing contents. 'I see them . . . often. Rhinos, I mean. I sometimes wonder if one of them was the little one from that day. One of the army guys told me he came across a dead one in the valley. It looked like it had trod on a land mine. Someone had hacked off its horn. Why would they do that?'

'Your mother showed me an article the other day about how rhinos are getting nailed in all the countries north of us. Zambia, Tanzania, Kenya . . . They're being killed in their hundreds and their horns sold to the Chinese for medicines.'

George shook his head and went back to his beer. 'Makes you

wonder if it was worth it, saving all those animals if they're just going to get poached for something as stupid as that.'

The band had launched into a cover of Frankie Valli and the Four Seasons's 'Can't Take My Eyes Off You'.

'It was worth it, George. Still is. Go dance with your wife.'

George downed his beer and nodded, then walked away.

Patricia Ngwenya would not have gone to the wedding if her husband hadn't ordered her to be there, a fact she shared with her youngest son, Emmerson.

'But why, Mother?' Emmerson persisted. 'You told me women should be the equal of men.'

'Yes, my son, but this is Africa and some things will take longer to change. Besides, I wanted you to see this place where the Bryants live; how white people live compared to us.'

The minibus taxi dropped them on the main road and Emmerson and his mother walked the three kilometres along the gravel road to the Bryant family's farm. Half-a-dozen times along the way they were coated with dust by cars driven by whites dressed in their Sunday best. Emmerson asked if these people were also going to the wedding and his mother nodded, a look of sheer loathing on her face.

He would rather have been in town, with his friends from the ZAPU youth league. There were rumours of a new party of ZANU boys in town and plans were afoot to welcome them to Matabeleland that night with *knobkerries* and bare knuckles. Emmerson's interest in politics was fuelled by his mother's talks and the books she tried to make him read, but the real attraction of the nationalist struggle for Emmerson was the opportunity to crack some heads.

They crossed a cattle grid and the khaki browns of the bush gave way to a carpet of mown green grass that was being watered by sprinklers. Emmerson stopped and stared. Unlike his older brother, Winston, the runaway, he had never been out to the Bryants' farm, so he was unprepared for what he saw.

'It's like . . . like a paradise,' he said in a hushed voice.

His mother prodded him in the back. 'Move along, Emmerson. If this is a paradise it is a paradise stolen from us. Take a good look at this place, Emmerson. When our people take control of our country this place will be ours.'

'Really?'

'Yes, my son, really. The land belongs to the *povo*, the poor people of our country, not to these rich invaders.'

'And the cars?' Emmerson looked longingly at the Chevrolets and Fords parked on the lawn, and the elderly African in overalls who was washing one. Emmerson decided that when he was older he would have a shiny car, and a man to wash it.

His mother laughed. 'Yes, my son, and the cars. Come. Let us get this over with.'

Emmerson ran his finger around the tight, chaffing collar of his shirt, and when his mother wasn't looking he undid his top button. His trousers were too short for him and he could feel the grass and gravel beneath his feet through a hole in his right shoe. By contrast, all of the whites, young and old, were dressed in fine clothes. Emmerson also wanted to be well dressed. It could all be a reality, according to his mother, when the struggle was over.

Even though he was still considered too young to fight, he had already played a part in the struggle as a *mujiba*, a young lookout. When the older men gathered for their meetings and their war councils, Emmerson and his friends from the youth league were posted on street corners, where they watched out for police patrols. Using an elaborate series of signals they passed messages of warning to each other. Some of the senior men had recently dangled the promise of him travelling out of Rhodesia, to Tanzania or even Russia or East Germany, for training by the comrades overseas. Emmerson looked forward to the day when he would carry a gun instead of leaning on a building watching for passing patrol cars.

'Hello Emmerson!'

He turned at the high-pitched voice and saw Hope Bryant running behind him. She waved at him and he self-consciously raised his hand to her. Hope was being chased by two boys of her own age, who looked exactly the same as each other, though one was a faster runner. The boy in the lead turned his head to glare at Emmerson as he chased after the girl.

'Stay away from them,' his mother said to him. 'We're only here as long as we have to be.'

Emmerson had seen Hope a few times when her mother had occasionally come to visit, to bring food to the family. Emmerson was always happy to have his belly full of beef and milk, and he found it hard to understand why his mother always seemed so surly after Mrs Bryant had visited. In the school holidays it had been Hope's older brother, George, who had brought the provisions, and while his mother also scowled at George, Emmerson had noticed that his big sister, Thandi, had looked forward to the boy's visits. But Thandi was gone now, studying in Mozambique. It was just Emmerson at home these days and he longed for the time when he, too, could leave the house and the township and see some more of the world before returning to fight in the struggle.

Emmerson's gaze rested on a group of white men in air force uniforms. They were laughing and drinking beer and raising their glasses in a toast. Emmerson wondered if they flew jets or helicopters, and how hard it might be to shoot one of them down.

'They celebrate the deaths of our comrades, killed in the name of your freedom, Emmerson,' his mother whispered to him.

'Patricia, how lovely to see you. I'm so glad you could make it,' Mrs Bryant said, striding across the lawn, lifting her feet high so her stiletto heels didn't get stuck in the grass. 'And good to see you, too, Emmerson.'

His mother extended a hand and shook the white woman's, muttering some words of congratulations.

'Do help yourself to food and I'll ask one of the waiters to get you drinks,' Mrs Bryant said.

Mr Bryant and George came over just as Mrs Bryant excused herself, saying she had to go and talk to the cooks about something. Emmerson shook hands with them both and cringed when the older man patted him on his head and told him how tall he was getting. Emmerson knew how tall he was and didn't need some white man remarking on it.

'How's Kenneth doing?' Mr Bryant asked Emmerson's mother.

'Emmerson?'

He turned. It was Hope again, panting slightly after running up from her latest game. He looked at her.

'Don't you want to come and play with us?' Hope asked.

'I am too old for games,' he said to her.

Hope took a couple of paces closer to him and lowered her voice. 'The boys have got an air rifle,' she whispered. 'We're hunting tree squirrels.'

Emmerson's eyes widened. His mother had her back to him and Hope was sidling off, beckoning him with a finger. Emmerson looked around him. He'd never fired a rifle of any kind and the promise of handling any sort of weapon was too good to pass up. 'Mother,' he said. She turned to him. 'I'm going to play with the other children.'

She raised her eyebrows. 'I don't want you getting into trouble, and we will be leaving soon.'

'Ah, let the boy have some fun, Patricia,' Mr Bryant said. 'Go along, son, I'm sure the other kids will be happy to have you along. Hope will look after you, won't you, chicken?'

'Yes Dad,' Hope said with a wave. 'Come on, Emmerson.'

He followed her, lengthening his stride to keep up with her half-skipping, half-running jog. She seemed so happy, always smiling. Emmerson didn't have time to play at anything these days. If he wasn't in school he was hanging around with the youth league and the other *mujibas*. How did these white children have time for games when the country was at war? Did they know nothing of the struggle against them?

Hope slowed her pace until he caught up with her. 'Where's your sister, still in Mozambique?'

Emmerson nodded. 'At university.'

Hope looked at him as though she was going to say something, then faced ahead again. Emmerson saw the two boys – they must be twins, he thought – who had been chasing Hope were now under a tall tree, looking up.

'Give me the gun,' said the slightly fuller, fitter looking one.

'No, you've had a turn, it's my go now,' said his brother.

The bigger twin grabbed the air rifle and reefed it from his brother's hands. When his sibling started to protest he pushed him away with the palm of his hand, raised the rifle and took aim. 'There's one. This is going to be too easy.'

'Braedan, no!' shrieked Hope. 'Don't shoot!'

The boy turned away from his point of aim. 'What's *he* doing with you?'

Hope stopped. 'Emmerson's a friend of my family.'

The boy muttered something Emmerson couldn't hear, but he guessed what it was. He wanted to stride across the lawn and hit the white boy, but he knew what would happen to him if he did that. He said nothing. Emmerson stared, instead, at the air rifle.

'Can Emmerson have a go with the rifle?' Hope asked.

'No way,' the boy said, squinting down the barrel. He pulled the trigger and the lead slug escaped with a *pfft* of air. 'Damn, missed.'

'Ha ha, Braedan,' Hope said. 'You're not such a good shot now.' She turned to Emmerson and looked up at him. 'Can I ask you something?'

Emmerson shrugged.

'Not here,' Hope said, looking around. She walked off towards another knob thorn tree and Emmerson followed her until they were screened from the twins. 'It's about Thandi – and my brother.'

The band had started playing again and people were dancing. Emmerson looked across at the tables laden with food outside the sprawling white farmhouse; the people in their fine clothes were drinking, talking, laughing, dancing, It was another world compared to where he lived.

'I was just wondering . . .' Hope began.

Emmerson looked away from the party to the little blonde girl. 'What? What is this about my sister?'

'Do you think that George *liked* your sister?'

Emmerson shrugged. 'What do you mean *liked*?'

'Ummm, you know . . . loved her?'

'What?' Emmerson was shocked. What was this little girl saying?

'Well, I just wondered, because one day – and please don't tell anyone else this – but I saw them, well . . . kissing.'

Emmerson felt light-headed. He thought of all the things his mother had told him about how the whites had stolen the land from the people of Rhodesia and the rest of Africa, and how they exploited their workers and underpaid them, and forbade people like his father from getting a better education, then locked him in gaol on trumped-up charges. The white settlers were the enemy. Emmerson could not believe that his smart older sister would be involved with a white man in *that* way. It was unbelievable, unthinkable. 'No!'

'Well, I saw –'

Emmerson felt the rage well inside him, the same way it did just before a fight, when he knew that the only way to feel calm again was to punch and hit and kick. 'I don't care what you saw. My sister would never do such a thing. You people . . . you are the enemy.'

'The what? I was just saying I saw my brother kissing your sister – that doesn't sound like they were enemies to me.'

He hated how she skewed his words, this silly little child, how she smiled up at him, mocking him. He reached out and grabbed her arm. 'No!'

'Hey! Get your hands off me.'

'No!' he yelled louder at her.

'Stop it! You're crazy. Ouch.'

'Shut up!' Emmerson grabbed her other arm and shook her, trying to stop her lies.

'Owww! You're . . . hurting . . . me.'

'Hope?'

Emmerson looked over and saw the two boys with the rifle had left their squirrel hunting and were staring at him and the girl.

'Let go of her, you bloody *munt*!' the taller twin yelled.

Hope twisted in his grip and Emmerson released her, shoving her away. As he did so, Hope got her legs entangled in his. She fell to the ground. He looked down at her for a moment, considering reaching down to help her, but she had mocked him and said the most terrible things about his sister. The boy who had insulted him was running towards him. Emmerson sidestepped the fallen girl and, still looking over his shoulder at the boy with the rifle, started to run.

'Stop him! He just attacked Hope!'

Emmerson looked to his front too late. The tall white man in an unbuttoned air force tunic was zipping up his fly, having just urinated behind a hedge. He was heading back to the reception and reached out for the fleeing boy. 'Got you!'

Emmerson lashed out at the man with a fist, but the adult was bigger and heavier than him, and the next thing Emmerson knew he was lying sprawled on the ground with his vision blurred and his ears ringing. He felt the pointed toe of a leather shoe stab into his ribs and he curled into the foetal position.

'Get up, you little black bastard,' the man said to him, grabbing him by the collar.

'He attacked her, he pushed her over,' one of the twin boys was saying to the man, who frogmarched Emmerson back towards the crowd. As he was dragged away Emmerson looked over at Hope, who had her head in her hands and was sobbing. Emmerson hated her for what she had said.

'What happened, Hope?' her mother asked, wiping her daughter's face with a linen serviette.

Hope looked at the grass. She was shaking. No one had ever grabbed her like that or treated her so roughly. 'Nothing . . . I don't know.'

'Why would Emmerson hurt you like that? Did you say something to him?'

Hope couldn't tell her mother what she'd said. George was standing next to their parents, his face grim. He'd said that

Emmerson should be strung up. There was no way Hope could mention Thandi with George there. 'No, Mom. Nothing.'

'He just grabbed you and started hurting you?'

'Pushed her to the ground behind a tree, out of sight of the other kids, according to Harry,' George said. Harry was George's friend who had intercepted Emmerson when he'd tried to run away.

'Hope,' her mother said, crooking her finger under Hope's chin and forcing her to look in her eyes. 'Is there anything else you want to say before I talk to the police?'

The tears sprouted from her eyes. She *couldn't* say anything else. And Emmerson had been like a madman. There was no reason for him to hurt her like he had. 'No, Mom.'

'Jesus,' her mother said, and it was very unlike her to blaspheme. 'These bloody people.'

CHAPTER 7

Kenneth Ngwenya carefully unfolded a pair of black horn-rimmed reading glasses and balanced them gingerly on the bridge of his nose. The Sellotape that held them together scratched and irritated his skin, as always.

He hated having to wear glasses. It was just one more sign that he was getting older, and that he was not the man he had been when he had been brought to Chikurubi Prison six years earlier.

It was rare that he looked forward to coming back to the cell he shared with twelve other men after his two hours of daily exercise in the yard, but today was an exception. The *guti* had set in and the chilled drizzle made him shiver, even indoors. On sunny days the blue above reminded him of what he'd given up, but today's low cloud made him feel that he had no hope of seeing light again.

He dealt with the near-crushing depression the way he always did, through a book. There was something comforting about the tattered, red leather-bound legal textbook. Here in black and white, on its musty pages, was a guide to right and wrong.

Kenneth had been a teacher all his adult life, until his first arrest in 1959, after the bus strike. He'd railed against the assault charge, because he knew from his friend Paul that Philippa had no intention of pursuing it. The prosecution had relied, instead, on the colluded statements of two of the BSAP constables who'd laid into the crowd with their batons. A better lawyer might have saved him from that charge, but he would have still gone to gaol under the Emergency Powers Act. As it happened, he had only served six months, and in that time he had not had a change of heart, but he had had time to think. Violence, he had decided, achieved nothing.

The police, on the day he'd been arrested, had been looking for an excuse to exercise force. Kenneth believed fervently in the idea of passive resistance, which Mahatma Gandhi had used to such great effect in India's quest for independence.

Aaron, one of the other inmates who shared the cell, shuffled in, nodded to Kenneth and lay down on one of the remaining five beds. There were only six beds in the cell, so the dozen men took turns at sleeping on them. Kenneth sat on another and scratched at a bug under his arm as he went back to his reading. It was hard to concentrate. Aaron was the same age as Winston would be now. Kenneth missed his family terribly, but the greatest ache in his heart was the lack of news about his eldest boy.

Kenneth had planned on mounting a search for Winston when he'd been freed from his first stint in prison, but events had conspired against him. Just weeks after he'd enjoyed Christmas at home with what remained of his family, the Southern Rhodesia African National Congress had been banned by the white government. However, on New Year's Day, 1960, a new resistance arose in the form of the National Democratic Party. Patricia joined and Kenneth did likewise, at her urging.

When he thought on it now, he remembered he had been reluctant, scared even. He'd been more concerned with tracking down Winston, but his wife had shamed him into joining the NDP. Kenneth had had a glimpse of life in prison and that had been more than enough for him. The younger men who had been arriving at Chookie, as everyone in Rhodesia called the gaol, these past months spoke of imprisonment as part of the *struggle*, as if the scratchy Chikurubi uniform was a soldier's, not a criminal's, and the prison number a medal of honour. Kenneth couldn't feel that way. All he felt was failure.

The newly formed NDP had organised a protest march in Salisbury and, illegal as the gathering was, thousands of people had turned out to protest against the government's heavy-handed suppression of African political ambitions. But the government was prepared and as the march wound its way down the capital's tree-lined boulevards, an air force aircraft dived from the skies and roared low overhead. Some in the crowd panicked, fearing the aeroplane was about to strafe them with machine-gun bullets, but all that rained from the heavens were leaflets, telling the demonstrators they were taking part in an illegal activity and would be arrested unless they dispersed. The mood of the crowd changed in the face of this aggressive show of strength and some of the younger men began shouting, working the protesters into a pique of anger at the insult. People grabbed rocks and loose bricks. Government buildings were stoned and windows were shattered before the police arrived and broke up the crowd. Arms and legs were beaten, and blood flowed from head wounds as police truncheons restored the white government's version of order.

Kenneth was given leave from his school to address the crowd that gathered in Bulawayo, days later, in defiance of the government's edict that no similar demonstration would be permitted in Southern Rhodesia's second city.

'Friends, please,' Kenneth called into the megaphone, 'we must stay peaceful today. If we sit in the street, arms linked, we say more about our will and our commitment to the bloodless transition of power in this country than we do if we rampage through the street like the police.'

'*Ma*-rubbish!' a young man heckled. Kenneth shielded his eyes and saw the clenched fist of the troublemaker. It was a boy he'd taught just two years earlier. A hooligan.

The crowd had tired of listening to reason and moved off, its ranks swollen by curious onlookers.

'Remember, passive resistance,' Kenneth called into his loud-hailer as the crowd surged towards the centre of the city. Shoppers were hurrying to their automobiles and shopkeepers bringing down their shutters.

'*Zhii!*' the hooligan yelled at the top of his voice.

'*Zhii!*' two others cried out jubilantly, as if discovering the word for the first time.

'*Zhii! Zhii! Zhii!*'

Crush. Pound to dust. Make war not peace. The definitions of the word were nuanced, but they all had one common theme. Violence.

'No!' Kenneth called, but he was drowned out by the chanting of that one hateful word, and the increasing tempo of thousands of feet on the pavements of Bulawayo's once peaceful streets.

The first stone shattered a window at the municipal offices.

'*Zhii!*'

A volley of rocks and bricks followed.

'*Zhii!*'

Platoons splintered from the army of protesters, running down streets and alleys, waving sticks, throwing missiles. The word gave them freedom to vent years of repressed anger, a licence to beat, bash and break down. The target started out as anything of authority, anything that represented the white establishment, but as the vitriol was given free rein, the fury of the storm lashed anything and everything. A beer hall was broken into and young men guzzled from *chigubus* of opaque beer.

A young woman, one of the protesters, screamed as she tripped and was trampled by a rampaging group of youths.

Kenneth bent to help her and had a horrible sense of déjà vu as he remembered stopping to lift Philippa from the street during the bus strike. An elbow cuffed him from behind. Kenneth grabbed the woman by the arm and heaved her to her feet. Patricia was up ahead somewhere, and although she was not stoning or looting, he saw her raised fist and heard her cry. '*Zhii!*'

His wife had ignored him, just as everyone else had. The rip-tide of hatred caught Kenneth and the woman he had rescued and they swirled forward, unable to swim against it. 'Calm down, calm down,' the schoolteacher tried. People laughed at him. One swore at him and told him to fight.

The police were waiting. They stood shoulder to shoulder, blocking Rhodes Avenue, rifles and shotguns raised, just as they'd stood the last time the Ndebele tribesmen had hurled themselves at their ranks, sixty-four years earlier, when they had taken up arms against the settlers.

Kenneth tried to turn back, but it was impossible to move against the crowd. A trio of young boys pushed past him, eager to get to the front ranks and carry out their share of destruction.

'Help me,' he called to one of them.

The boy, aged about fifteen, the same age as his son Emmerson, turned back at him and raised a *knobkerrie* high over his head. '*Zhii!*'

'Come back here at once, boy, and help me with this woman,' Kenneth yelled over the din.

The wild-eyed boy looked at him, and then back at his friends. 'Zhii!' He raised his club again, turned his back on Kenneth and ran off to join the others.

Kenneth's nose and eyes started to burn. When he took a breath his throat and lungs felt as though he'd swallowed a mouthful of needles. He coughed. Around him people were suffering the effects as the cloud of acrid tear gas washed over them. Rather than stopping, though, people continued to stumble forward, jostled by those in the rear ranks who had yet to be affected by the gas.

The noise of the gunfire was muffled by the hundreds of bodies between Kenneth and the police line. It sounded like firecrackers, but there was no mistaking its effect. People slammed into each other as the forward lines of the demonstration fell to the ground. People were screaming in pain and everyone was looking for an exit. Some smashed shop windows and leapt inside over jagged shards of glass. Others turned back.

Kenneth and the woman in his arms were crushed between those behind who were still pushing forward and those at the front who had turned back. He fell. Kenneth felt a kick in the shoulder and then a man was on top of him. Kenneth cursed and rolled the man off him. He was about to berate him when he noticed the hole drilled in the man's forehead. Blood soaked Kenneth's suit jacket. The woman screamed. The man had been tall – too tall – and had been an easy target.

Gunfire continued, and a fresh cloud of tear gas shrouded the crowd. Police in gasmasks charged the line and waded in among the dazed, retching survivors. Kenneth raised his arm to try to protect the woman, and a policeman, mistaking the gesture as a sign of aggression, struck down at him with his truncheon. Kenneth's arm felt as though it had been broken. It hung limp and painful by his side as another policeman grabbed him by his collar and dragged him away. He reached out for the woman, but she was shrieking hysterically as another constable pulled her in the opposite direction.

'Fucking *zhii*,' a policeman said as he slammed his baton into Kenneth's kidneys.

Kenneth adjusted his broken glasses. They'd been trampled by a prison officer during a surprise search of the cell. Kenneth wasn't sure if it had been an accident or a petty show of power by the guard. He prayed Patricia would be able to find him a new pair and bring them on her next visit.

The law was clear on the demonstration. It had been an illegal gathering and the organisers knew this. It had been anything but peaceful – the mob had delighted in venting anger and destroying property. This was wrong. But were the police justified in opening fire?

Eighteen people had been killed on that day in the streets of Bulawayo. Hundreds more had been wounded or injured by bullet and baton. It had been a swift, bloody response to a violent protest. Patricia had been shot in the arm and admitted to hospital. Kenneth had been locked in a police van and taken to prison. He'd been charged, tried and sentenced to fifteen years' imprisonment. The prosecution claimed that he was one of the ringleaders and made much of the fact that he had addressed the mob and that he was a repeat offender, having already done prison time as a result of his first conviction. Patricia had recovered from her wound, but Kenneth was still suffering from that terrible day.

'Good morning, Kenneth, how are you?'

Kenneth looked up and peered over the top of his broken glasses. He smiled at the man they all called the Headmaster. 'Ah, good morning, Robert. I am fine, and you?' Aaron rolled over and pulled a blanket over his head. Sometimes a man just needed to be alone.

'Fine, thank you, Kenneth. May I borrow your textbook on civil law?'

'Of course.' Kenneth stood and selected the volume from the simple wooden shelf that held their communal collection of books. 'Sit a while, if you wish.'

Robert looked back, as if searching for an excuse not to, then finally settled on a bed opposite Kenneth. Robert, another political prisoner being detained under the Emergency Powers Act, was a quiet man who did not seem to make friends easily. He too had been a teacher and had been a voracious reader and studious during his five years of incarceration. Robert taught the less educated inmates how to read and write, and while Kenneth also took classes, there was no questioning the fact that Robert was in charge – the Headmaster.

The NDP had split into two rival factions, the Zimbabwe African People's Union and the Zimbabwe African National Union. This had happened after Kenneth's incarceration, so he hadn't given much thought to the matter of which organisation he should align himself with. Robert was a Shona, a member of the majority tribe of black Rhodesia, and was a senior figure in ZANU, most of whose members were Shona. Kenneth was an Ndebele and most of his people supported ZAPU, which was headed by Joshua Nkomo.

Kenneth knew Joshua Nkomo personally. The giant of a man, a carpenter who had moved through the ranks of the railway union, had been the face of Rhodesian African nationalism until the rise of ZANU. ZANU was headed by the Reverend Ndabaningi Sithole, who, like Joshua, was in prison.

'It was bad news, about the constitutional referendum,' Kenneth said.

Robert nodded. 'Bad, but predictable. The whites have simply cemented their grasp on power.'

'I can't help but think, though, that if more of our people had voted in the last election then we might have advanced our cause some,' Kenneth said. Under the old constitution there were two electoral rolls – A and B. Voter registration was decided by how much property and wealth a man had. The richest were on the A roll, and they elected members of parliament to fifty seats, while those with less wealth, but still men of means, were on the B roll and allocated fifteen seats. There was nothing stopping a black man being on either roll, though in reality very few made the B roll, and fewer still the A.

Robert scoffed. 'No, Kenneth. There was no way we could be seen to be legitimising their patronising, racist system. Even if one or two black men had been elected nothing would have changed.'

Kenneth nodded. Ian Smith advocated a policy of gradual empowerment of African people. His view and the view of his Rhodesian Front party was that not enough blacks were educated or experienced enough to take a greater role in national affairs, and that not enough of them paid tax – hence their lack of representation on the voter rolls. As blacks became better educated and more prosperous over time, they could play a greater role in voting and shaping the country's future. The catch, of course, was that educational and job opportunities for Africans were limited. Also the new constitution, as well as finally proclaiming the rebel state of Rhodesia as a republic, had actually closed off the A roll on the electoral register to any blacks.

Kenneth believed the number one priority for Africans should be education, and that if the white government was serious about gradual empowerment of blacks it would have given all the children in the country, regardless of colour, the same access to schooling and university. This was not the case. Ironically, people such as he and Robert were educating themselves far better inside the grey walls of Chikurubi Prison than they could have done outside. Here they were supplied with books and other study materials from charities and care groups opposed to the Rhodesian government's policies. Kenneth had completed his Masters of Education by correspondence from London University and both he and the Headmaster were now immersed in law degrees.

'What news of the reverend?' Kenneth asked cryptically.

Robert fixed him with his serious eyes and Kenneth wondered if he had overstepped the mark. Kenneth had been courted, casually, by other members of ZANU inside the prison, and the fact that Robert occasionally deigned to talk to him let Kenneth know that he was not regarded as a ZAPU man – which he wasn't – or as an outsider. However, Kenneth was asking about the general secretary of Robert's party and obliquely referring to the Reverend Sithole's increasingly erratic behaviour. The stare went on for a few more seconds and Kenneth experienced a shiver of fear. A fine educator and reserved, studious man the Headmaster might be, but there was something more to him. Something a little frightening.

Yet Kenneth had also seen this senior party cadre in tears. In 1966 Robert's only son, three-year-old Nhamodzenyika, had died of cerebral malaria in Ghana. Robert had pleaded with the prison authorities to let him travel out of Rhodesia to be with his wife, Sally, so that they could bury the little boy together. Robert had sworn he would return and urged the authorities to send armed escorts with him. The government had refused. Robert had been crushed and had only in the past few months resumed his studies.

'You read his confession?' Robert said at last.

Kenneth nodded. He doubted that a single political prisoner inside Chikurubi did not know it word for word. Ndabaningi Sithole had recently become obsessed with the idea of assassinating Ian Smith. He'd managed to get word to some of his supporters outside the gaol and told them to loiter near its walls and await his orders. Sithole had written his plan for Smith's death on scraps of paper and pushed these inside oranges, which he threw over the wall. Unfortunately the security services had infiltrated his support base and Special Branch police officers were instead waiting outside the gaol to catch the oranges.

Sithole had been charged with treason, found guilty and sentenced to death. When asked by the judge if he had anything to say, Sithole had replied: 'My Lord, I wish to publicly disassociate myself in word, thought and deed from any subversive activities, from any terrorist activities, and from any form of violence.'

As a result of his plea, Sithole had been brought back to Chikurubi and placed in isolation, in maximum security, but there was no sign of an imminent execution.

'I have no news about the reverend and it is not my place to undermine him.'

Kenneth nodded again. The subject was closed, although Kenneth could only wonder what was going on behind the scenes in the secret meetings of the ZANU leadership. Other, less tactful members of the party were calling Sithole a coward. The rumour was that he would soon be deposed as leader. The front runners for the post were Herbert Chitepo, the revolutionary army's military commander directing the war from across the border in Zambia, or the man sitting on the bed opposite Kenneth.

Robert forced a smile, and stood. 'Perhaps, Kenneth, you might consider taking a greater role in the struggle, and come join with us. There are already senior men from your people in the ranks of our leadership.'

Kenneth thought about the offer. 'Perhaps. To tell you the truth, I don't believe we serve ourselves well by having two separate parties fighting in the struggle. If we are to govern ourselves it should be a government of unity, not of two different tribes.'

Robert nodded. 'I agree. You'll consider the offer, then?'

The offer? 'I am not a soldier, Robert. I cannot fire a gun and I do not want to learn how.'

The Headmaster pursed his lips as he considered the caveat. 'To tell you the truth, neither am I. I believe you and I, as educators, are on the right path. Our power is in the pen and the book. Our country will need thinkers as well as warriors. Thank you for the book. I will return it soon.'

Exercise time was over and the other inmates from Kenneth's cell were walking down the corridor. Two stepped aside, deferentially, as Robert walked to the door. 'You'll think about what I said?'

'Yes,' Kenneth said.

'Come on, move inside,' a white prison warder called from the hallway. The man stood in the doorway, confronting Robert. 'What are you doing here?'

Robert held up the law textbook, excused himself and walked past the warder.

'Get back to your cell and be quick about it, Mugabe,' the warder said.

CHAPTER 8

Rhodesia, 1979

Natalie Bryant lay on her back on Aunty Hope's bed, looking up at the ceiling. Something was scurrying about in the ceiling and it gave her the creeps. She liked coming to Grandpa Paul and Grandma Pip's house to stay, but it always took her a couple of days to get used to the different sounds and smells of the farm.

Aunty Hope was at university in South Africa, but she would be coming home in a few days and after that Natalie would have to sleep in her dad's old bedroom. But her nanny, Petronella, would have to clean the room first and make up the bed. Natalie thought it was odd, thinking about her dad being a little boy once upon a time.

On Aunty Hope's dressing table there was a picture of Natalie's father standing beside his helicopter, smiling. He looked young and happy. These days, he was away from home most of the time, and he'd missed Natalie's tenth birthday, just the week before. Natalie had cried, even though her mother had told her she should be used to it by now. Her mother was in Salisbury, looking after Grandma Susannah, who was in hospital busy dying, and not before time, according to something she'd overheard her father saying. Dad and Grandma Susannah didn't get on – everyone knew that.

As was her habit, Natalie had already had a good snoop around Aunty Hope's room. There were pictures of Hope and her friends in bikinis on a houseboat at Kariba, a couple of shots of her and Natalie's dad, George, together as kids, and some horse riding ribbons and a tennis trophy. On her dresser, waiting to be framed, were more recent pictures of Hope and her university friends. Hope had long straight blonde hair and Natalie thought she was beautiful. Natalie's hair was wavy and she would ask Aunty Hope how to straighten it when she got home.

Natalie was staying on the farm, near Bulawayo, for her school holidays, and that was fine by her. She loved the farm, although her mother said her grandparents spoiled her rotten. That was fine, too. Grandpa Paul had told her he would take her on a game drive in the morning. There were kudu, wildebeest and zebra on the farm, as well as the dairy cows.

The dogs started barking.

There were four of them – the two ridgebacks, Cleo and Katie, a boerbull called Zilla, and a tiny Jack Russell cross called Bart, who was Natalie's favourite. They were making a terrible racket. Natalie sat up in bed. It was a moonless night and she could see nothing beyond the steel mesh box bolted to the wall outside the window. When she'd first asked Grandma Pip what the mesh was for she'd said it was to keep the baboons out. Aunty Hope later told her it was to stop terrs throwing hand grenades into her bedroom.

Natalie strained her ears and over the noise of the dogs she heard a faint *crump, crump, crump,* like someone jumping on a cardboard box and blowing the air out. Her grandparents were awake and Natalie could hear their voices out in the hallway.

'Natalie!' Grandma Pip called.

Then the world exploded.

*

Winston Ngwenya, who still went by the name of Ndlovu, sat on the log by the smouldering fire in the middle of the kraal and spoke to the village headman in a low voice. He rested the butt of his Russian-made AK-47 assault rifle in the dust between his blackened tennis shoes and took off his floppy bush hat to wipe his brow. Instead of a Rhodesian Army uniform, these days he dressed as a ZIPRA freedom fighter, in East German camouflage. Thunder rolled across the veldt and the horizon was lit by far-off lightning.

'We need food, *baba*,' Winston said to the headman, addressing him respectfully as 'father'.

The headman scoffed. 'Want, want, want. You claim to be of the people and bring grand promises of land and freedom, but you always take from us, never give.'

Winston nodded, understanding the man's frustration. 'You have already given your spare food to other comrades . . . tonight?'

The headman looked at him through narrowed eyes. 'I know nothing of other comrades.'

Winston leaned forward and traced his finger around an elongated oval indentation in the dirt by the fire. When he lifted his AK-47 he pointed to the mark it left – it was exactly the same as the one he had just highlighted. 'I just arrived, old father, but someone else rested his rifle here as well, not too long ago.'

The old man pursed his lips and nodded. 'Why do you not travel together? Why must I give to one group and then again to yours?'

'We travel separately, in small groups, for safety and security. The other group, the ones that were here, do not know of my orders, just as I do not know of theirs. That way, if the *kanka* catch one of us, we cannot tell of what the other is doing.'

The old man bobbed his head. Winston knew he'd heard the story many times before. 'They . . . your *comrades* threatened to kill me if I did not give them food and shelter. What will you threaten me with that I have not heard before?'

Winston smiled at the old man's defiance. No doubt he was harassed as much by the security forces as he was by ZIPRA. There could have even been ZANLA in the area, such was the latter organisation's determination to take over the whole of the country. Winston knew, too, that the freedom fighters' threats were not empty – they enforced their will by beheading chiefs, burying opponents alive, and raping and mutilating women.

'I will not threaten you, and I will not steal from you,' Winston said.

The old man stared at him.

'We are all in the struggle together, old father. My men and I need you, just as you need us to set you free.' He spoke the words with the conviction of a zealot, but he could see that the headman was weary of words and of war.

'What do you want from me?'

'I wish to address your people, to give them some pamphlets, and to explain to them we are here for them . . . for all the people. If my comrades have caused you trouble, or threatened you, I apologise for them. For myself and my men, all we want is some food and somewhere safe to sleep tonight.'

The old man seemed to weigh the words. 'I will do as you ask . . . and perhaps there will be a little mealie meal to spare at the end of your talk. But tell me, how do I know you are not *Skuz'apo*?'

Winston smiled. 'Think about it. I want a bed for the night and a chance to speak to your people of freedom. If I was a Selous Scout, would I want to talk to your village about revolution? Might I not, instead, threaten to kill you, or perhaps beat you and steal from you, so that you might think less of the real comrades?'

Skuz'apo, which in the Shona language meant 'excuse me for being here', was the nickname given by ZANLA and ZIPRA to the hated Selous Scouts, an integrated black and white unit of the Rhodesian security forces consisting of turned terrorists and experienced black soldiers from the Rhodesian African Rifles. The Scouts posed as freedom fighters, made contact with the real terrorists, then either killed them or set them up to be ambushed by other units. They were feared, respected and hated by their enemy. The Selous Scouts boasted the highest kill ratio in the army, and Winston was proud to serve in their ranks. He dressed as a terrorist, but he still fought for the government.

Much had changed in the country since Winston had first donned the uniform of a soldier in the Rhodesian African Rifles. The security forces still bested the terrorists time and again in the field, but whereas the flow of newly trained ZIPRA and ZANLA cadres from across the borders of Zambia and Mozambique seemed never-ending, fewer black Rhodesians could be convinced to join the police or the army. Africans serving the Smith regime were hunted and killed when they were off-duty, and their families were persecuted. Estranged from his own blood relatives by an unbridgeable gulf of time and ideology, Winston fought on more for the comrades in his stick – they were his family now – than for the intractable politics of either side of a society polarised by war. Winston knew he couldn't have changed sides now if he'd wanted to: while *Skuz'apo*'s commanders could see the value in turning an enemy and recruiting him, Winston knew he would have been shot on sight if he'd tried to defect to the guerillas. Besides, he still liked fighting and winning, and the Scouts almost always won.

The old man scratched his chin, but said nothing.

'There is one more thing I need from you, old father,' Winston said.

The man raised his eyebrows.

'You know in which direction the last group of comrades left. I see by the sign their leader left by your fire that they were here not long ago. They will have tried to cover their trail but you and your sons know this area better than they do. If they were of your people they would not have acted as they did. What I want, *baba*, what I *ask* for is that you send a trusted *mujiba* to go to them, to make contact with them, on my behalf.'

'Why?'

'As you see, we are small in number. My masters have given me a mission that I believe would be better served with more comrades. I want to contact these other men and propose that we join forces, to strike a greater blow against the *kanka*.' What Winston really wanted was to track down the band of real terrs, make contact with them, and kill them, that was his mission.

The headman used his bare foot to wipe out both of the marks left by the AK-47 butt plates. 'And what if these other men, who my son may persuade to come to you, are *Skuz'apo*? What will you do then?'

Winston grinned. 'Kill them.' There were no other Selous Scouts operating within fifty miles of the village, so Winston knew the men who had just passed through the village before them were definitely ZIPRA.

Later, after Winston had stood in front of the tired-looking mothers nursing infants from sagging breasts, the wide-eyed juvenile boys, the shyly flirty older girls and the old men of the village and preached his parables of revolution and freedom, the headman came to him and whispered that he had sent his youngest son to make contact with the recently departed comrades. Winston could have asked him why there were no able-bodied young men of fighting age present at his talk, but he knew the answer. They were in the bush, in hiding for fear that they might be recruited and taken away.

Winston lay down in an empty hut with two of his men, leaving the fourth member of their band to stand picket in the shadows outside, watching for the return of the other group. They wouldn't be far off, and Winston hoped their curiosity would get the better of them and they would come back to check out this new group of comrades operating in their territory.

He pulled two curved AK-47 magazines from the canvas pouches on his chest and laid them on the hard polished floor made of dried cow dung mixed with water. The magazines made a good enough pillow and they would be close to hand if he needed them in a hurry.

Acting his part as an impassioned freedom fighter, he'd spoken to the villagers of a utopian world, where all men and women were equal, where land was owned by all, and where people worked for the good of the state and each other. He'd talked of a world where education was free, and available for all, no matter their gender or colour. Ironically, he thought his father would have been proud to hear him say those words.

What if it was true? he wondered. It was all well and good to win every battle, but what would happen if – when – the Smith government and the whites tired of the war?

Winston laid his AK-47 beside him, half on the floor and half-resting against his right thigh, his fingers resting on the pistol grip. He closed his eyes, but just seconds later he was sitting up, fully alert and sliding the magazines back into their pouch. The rumbling echoing back across the night sky to the village was not thunder this time. It was the unmistakable sound of mortar bombs exploding.

The novelty of parachuting was fast wearing off.

Braedan's stick had jumped twice the previous day. It was always the same. The first jump brought on a massive rush, but the second was just plain hard work. Your body was subjected to an adrenaline overdose – from the jump and the shooting – and if you had to do it all over again your legs were like lead as you shuffled towards the door, weighed down with parachute, ammo, FN and kit.

Braedan licked his chapped lips as he watched the ordered patchwork of crops and the grey-brown carpet of untamed bush flash below the aircraft. Although only a lance corporal in the Rhodesian Light Infantry, he was the stick commander, so he was jumping first for the first time. His corporal had twisted an ankle on the second jump yesterday. It was also his first time in charge of the stick, so he had another reason for the dry mouth and the pounding he could feel in his carotid artery.

The Dakota hummed and vibrated around him. They'd loaded in the pre-dawn darkness and the sun was punching gold through a gap in the clouds, still hanging low and menacing. The aircraft lurched and Braedan swallowed hard. It wasn't great weather for jumping, but the nearest choppers were at Wankie. All part of the job, he thought to himself as he mentally prepared for the jump and what might wait for him below. He'd known the risks when he'd joined his country's full-time army as a regular soldier in the all-white RLI, and despite the horrors he'd seen and the friends who had been killed or wounded, he knew this was what he was meant to do in life. He didn't fight for Ian Smith, or the government, or an ideology –

he fought for himself and the *ouens* in the stick lined up behind him. He fought because he was good at it.

The jumpmaster gave the signal to check equipment, and the stick ran their hands over their buckles and straps and gear, calling out the litany of checks that had become ingrained in their minds through training and action. They took these drills seriously – their lives depended on them.

The tiredness had gone now they were getting closer to exiting. Braedan was pumped. The whole stick was. If what had happened on the farm was true, it was terrible. To make it worse, he knew the family.

The jump lights were on red and Braedan shuffled a step closer to the door. When the light flashed green he stepped out into the chill of the slipstream and felt the sickening, exhilarating lurch as he dropped.

'One thousand, two thousand, three thousand,' he screamed. The count was to give the static line time to do its work, but the act of shouting was also a means of keeping focused and of venting some of that adrenaline. He looked up. The lines were twisted. It was the little *okes* who made the best parachutists. They kept their short arms and legs tucked neatly in against their body, but Braedan was pushing six-four, and he was weighed down with muscle. He spun, as usual, on exit. He grabbed the risers and held them apart while he kicked his legs in a pedalling motion.

They'd jumped from less than eight hundred feet. He had fewer than thirty seconds under canopy. Braedan used up most of that kicking the twists out of his lines, and just had time to set himself up for a hard, fast landing. The wind, the remnants of last night's storm, was stiff. He could tell the speed and the direction by the pall of black smoke from the farmhouse. Something reached for his heart and squeezed.

Braedan had turned into the wind, and although he pulled down on his rear risers, to flare the front of the canopy above him, the oncoming breeze was faster than his forward motion, so he was moving backwards when he hit the ground. He executed a back-right landing as best he could, to stop himself from ploughing the field with the barrel of his FN, which was strapped under his harness on his left side. He was arms and legs akimbo, as usual, but he was unhurt. He pulled down on a riser to collapse the chute and stop himself from being dragged along the furrows. Braedan released his straps and rolled out of his harness.

The stick formed up on him and each reported he was OK, with no injuries. They jogged across the uneven ground towards the ominous smoking signal pyre of the Bryant farmhouse. Braedan yanked back on the cocking handle of the FN, chambering a round, and flipped up the rear sight. His weapon was ready for action.

'Someone's moving,' Al Platt, the forward scout, called. 'From the trees, not the house.'

Braedan instinctively pulled the butt of the FN tighter into his shoulder and raised the barrel, but lowered it when he saw it was a woman.

The dawn light showed her silver-blonde hair. She was slight and short and the FN loose at her side looked longer than her. The woman wiped her eyes with the back of her free hand.

'Over here!' she waved. 'Hurry.'

The stick broke into a run.

She planted the butt of the rifle in the grass at her feet and sniffled. 'My granddaughter . . . my husband . . .'

'It's all right, ma'am, we're here to help,' Braedan said. 'Take your time.'

She sniffed again, then glared at him. 'There is *no* time.' She took a deep breath to steady herself. 'My husband is over there,' she pointed to the line of plantation gums. 'He's been hit. Bullet . . . through the left calf. I've patched him up. My granddaughter has been abducted. You have to hurry, she's only ten years old!'

'Shit,' said Al.

Her face was blackened with soot and streaked with dried tears, which started to well again as she said the words.

Braedan silenced Al with a look. 'When, Mrs Bryant? Do you have any idea how many of them there were?' Braedan remembered the house, and the wedding where a black kid had got in trouble for fondling the daughter. It was a short-lived scandal. Mrs Bryant's son was air force. Braedan's recollections were vague, though, as his family had moved to Salisbury when his dad gave up farming and took a job with the Rhodesian Railways. 'Mug's game, farming,' his old man had said.

Philippa closed her eyes for a second, squeezing out the tears. 'An hour ago. We radioed the Agric Alert at three-thirty am. I don't know how many there were . . . four at least, I should think. RPG. Mortar somewhere out there.' She waved in the distance, towards the trees. 'So that'll be another two, I expect.'

Jesus, Braedan thought, they'd been in contact for an hour. The husband – Braedan couldn't remember his name, but recalled he was Australian – must have followed them.

'Mr Bryant . . . we need to see to him, ma'am.'

She blinked as though trying to focus on his face. 'I know you . . .'

Braedan nodded. 'Ja. Yes, ma'am, a long time ago, but . . .' They needed to get going. She was distraught, and in shock.

'Sharon Quilter-Phipps's boy . . . Nate? Tate?'

'Tate's my brother, ma'am. I'm Braedan,' he said quickly. Braedan didn't have time to waste thinking about his useless bunny-hugging brother, waterskiing on Lake Kariba when he wasn't out picking wild flowers in his national parks and wildlife uniform. Joining the parks service had exempted Tate from military service, even though their country was fighting for its bloody survival.

'My husband's over here,' Mrs Bryant said, gathering her wits again and leading them on.

Al and Wally Collins, good men, moved ahead into the trees and took up firing positions behind stout trunks without being told, while Braedan and Andy Hunter, the stick's rifleman-medic, knelt beside the ashen-faced man lying on the ground. He was wearing pyjama bottoms and a cable-knit jersey. The left leg of his pants was ripped open and his leg was bleeding.

Andy introduced himself to Paul Bryant and began to unwrap the bandage his wife had applied. 'Nice work,' he said, looking up at Pip.

'Get me up and get me some trousers, Pip,' Paul said to his wife. 'I'm ready to go after them. Get the Dodge.'

Braedan surveyed the terrain. There was no way they'd be able to follow the gooks in a vehicle. The bush beyond the ploughed lands was too thick.

'Fresh spoor,' Collins called from up ahead. 'The girl's with them, barefoot, and at least one of the gooks is bleeding.'

Andy was re-tightening the bandage. 'You're going to be fine, Mr Bryant. Ma'am,' he said, looking up at Pip, who looked lost, 'I'm going to leave you some painkillers and fresh bandages.'

'I'm coming with you,' Pip said.

'Come,' Braedan said to Andy. 'Mrs Bryant, you need to stay here with your husband, hey. We can move faster on foot by our-selves. You've already radioed for an ambulance, yes?'

She nodded.

'Lekker. We'll move Mr Bryant over there, to the farm shed. You can wait for the ambulance there. Are you OK for ammo?'

Pip looked at him vacantly. Braedan unbuttoned one of the pouches on his chest webbing and pulled out an FN magazine. He handed it to her, and she took it, staring at the camouflage painted tin box of bullets.

Braedan and Andy picked up Paul and carried him to the tin-roofed shed and workshop where the Bryants garaged their tractors. They laid him on a pile of empty mealie bags.

Braedan put his left hand on Mrs Bryant's shoulder. She was a short woman and she seemed almost childlike as she looked up into his eyes. 'Your husband will be fine, Mrs Bryant. Stay here with him.'

She reached for him and gripped his arm, hard. 'Promise me you'll find her.'

'Yes, Mrs Bryant. We will.' Seriously, however, he doubted their chances.

'And if you do find them, Braedan, and she's . . . if they've hurt her . . . kill them for me.'

He nodded. That he most certainly could do, if they caught up with the gang. 'I promise.'

Andy, who carried a radio in addition to his medical supplies, radioed a sitrep to the Dakota that had dropped them and was still orbiting overhead. The Dakota pilot relayed the message and confirmed a civilian ambulance was on its way to the farm, and that two helicopters, including a K-Car, had been scrambled from Wankie.

Braedan and Andy left the Bryants and picked up Platt and Collins as they swept through the plantation. Wankie was more than three hundred kilometres away, so the choppers would be some time arriving. The local police were probably organising a PATU stick, but the Police Anti-Terrorist Unit volunteers would have to be roused from their farms and jobs. For now, Braedan and his men were the only hope the little girl had.

*

Comrade Beria grabbed a handful of the girl's blonde hair and dragged her to her feet. The little bitch kept falling over deliberately, he was sure, to try to slow them.

She screamed into the gag, a bandana Beria had tied tightly around her mouth. He'd fill it with something else as soon as they were safe. She struggled against him and he slapped her across the right side of her face hard enough to nearly knock her down again. He saw the raw terror in her eyes and he grinned. Until he had the settlers' land he would make do with one of their women. They would have to kill her, eventually, which was a pity.

For now, though, they needed to keep moving, and to make matters worse, Comrade Jesus Christ was dying.

Beria had laughed when the youngster had joined them. What a *Chimurenga* name to pick! The boy, who fancied himself an intellectual, said his choice of nom de guerre was ironic, as he did not believe in religion, but he was prepared to die for his cause. Beria had never been religious. When others his age were wasting time in missionary school, Beria was beating ZANU cadres bloody in street brawls and fucking any woman he could find. There was no time for schooling or religion in a time of war. Beria had been fighting all his life. They'd tried to teach him in the juvenile gaol he'd spent time in, but the real lessons to be learned there were breaking and entering and new ways of inflicting pain.

After six months in the boys' training centre, he'd been released to the care of his mother, but with her blessing had spent most of his time on the streets, acting as a lookout for the ZIPRA men, watching for the security forces when they dared enter the township, and fighting the ongoing war against their ZANU enemies.

He'd nearly beaten a ZANU man to death in a brawl in Gwelo.

A few of them had caught the bus from Bulawayo, and the fight had been worth the price of the ticket. Gwelo, in the midlands, was neither fully Ndebele nor fully Shona, which made it territory worth fighting for by both the main parties in the struggle. He'd had to be pulled off the hapless Shona youth, and Comrade Beria hadn't even smelled the tear gas as he'd kicked and kicked at the boy's head. Rather than earning him a reprimand, his tenacity and commitment had propelled him to the front of the line of young men waiting to be sent out of Rhodesia for revolutionary training.

He'd felt the rage several times since then, in shebeen brawls, and even in the camp in Russia, where he'd earned his nickname, Beria, which he'd subsequently kept as his *Chimurenga* name. They all had 'war names' to protect their real identities from the *kanka* and from each other. If a man were captured and tortured by the settlers he couldn't reveal the true identity of his comrades if he didn't know it.

He'd hated Russia, but the communists had taught him how to kill properly. The instructors joked about the black students behind their backs, and when they went into the city, on leave from the camps, the Russian people stared at them as though they were exhibits in a zoo. Beria had learned the Russian word for 'monkey' early on in the year he'd spent in that freezing, grey, dead place. The only warmth in Russia came from between the legs of their women. The men might mock them, but their women soon learned that no pathetic, limp-membered, vodka-swilling Russian could match an African warrior's spear.

There had been a fifteen-year-old girl in Leningrad who had begged for his manhood, but Beria had been disciplined by his instructors when the girl's family found out what she was up to and made a formal complaint. Few citizens had the temerity to complain about anything the military did, but the instructors had seized on the opportunity to beat him, and told him to stay away from Russian children. Beria had taken his punishment, but when next on leave had followed the senior instructor, a sergeant, the man who had called him 'monkey' while beating him, and stuck a knife up under the man's ribs and into his heart when he'd staggered out from a bar. Beria had dragged the huge bear of a sergeant into a darkened alley and held his gloved hand over the man's mouth while he watched the blood flood from him. Beria had pulled off his ski mask so the man could know, in his last minutes, how well his student had learned the art of killing.

The local police had begun an investigation and questioned Beria and the other Rhodesians about the sergeant's death, but the Africans had completed their course and were heading back to the liberation struggle. Nothing came of it.

One of the other instructors, a friendlier, older Russian, had given him the name Beria on the rifle range. 'You are best shot and best student in unarmed combat. You could be great – a killer of the same order as the great Comrade Leventy Beria,' he'd told him.

Beria had cared little for the history of the Russian Revolution that he and the other recruits had been spoon-fed. 'Who is Leventy Beria?' he'd asked the instructor.

The man had grinned. 'Beria was Stalin's right-hand man – head of the secret police. Beria was responsible for elimination of many thousands of enemies of the state. You could be this man.'

Comrade Beria smiled. He liked the name. It was certainly a better name than Jesus Christ, who was now busy dying for his people. They were moving too slowly. 'Hold her,' Beria said to Nighttime Moto. Moto meant 'fire', but there was none of this in this man's body. The man had a squint, and he took the bound girl's arm as if he thought he might break it. '*Hold* her!' Beria grabbed the child's neck and she uttered a muffled squeal as Moto grabbed her harder.

Beria was surrounded by incompetents. He would be better, he thought, acting alone. He slung his AK-47 and moved back to where another of his band was struggling along with Jesus Christ hanging off his shoulder.

Jesus Christ's intestines had begun pushing out of the hole in his gut. The man had stuffed his own floppy bush hat in his mouth to muffle the sound of his crying. Christ was brave, but he was doomed. He looked at Beria with wide, pain-filled eyes. 'Leave him . . . set him down,' Beria said to the man who had been carrying Jesus.

The bearer did as he was told and Jesus winced in renewed pain as he was laid at the foot of a big marula tree. He shook his head and spat the hat from his mouth, his eyes suddenly wide as he saw Beria unsling the AK-47. Beria smiled and shook his head. 'No, comrade,' he said. 'I would not do that to one who is so brave.' He rested the AK against the trunk of the tree. 'Leave us,' he said to the other man. 'Go join the others, keep moving. I am afraid we have to leave the *saviour* here to the mercy of the enemy. They will take you to hospital.'

Jesus moaned. 'They will hang me.'

Beria grabbed the other man under the shoulders and lifted him a little, so that his back was against a tree. 'Shush,' Beria said as the man cried out in pain. 'Perhaps we can come free you from prison. I will personally recommend it to the leaders.'

The boy looked at Beria as if he wanted to believe him.

'Now, close your eyes. Rest.'

Jesus did as he was told, and Beria unsheathed the bone-handled knife at his belt. He put one hand over the wounded man's mouth and with the other, slid the blade up under his rib cage and into his heart. He held Jesus Christ as his body shuddered, until he was still.

Beria wiped the knife, and then his hands, on the dead man's khaki shirt. He took two magazines and a grenade from Jesus's pouches, then tucked the fallen fighter's AK under the crook of his arm. His work done, Beria stuffed the extra magazines in his own webbing, retrieved his rifle and trotted off after the rest of his men. He wasn't sure how many settlers he and his men had killed, but the Bryants' farmhouse, built with the blood and sweat of the *povo*, whose land they had stolen, was burning. Beria had lost a man, but his death would be avenged with the girl's, once he and his men had finished with her.

The girl looked so much like her aunt had at the same age that it made him hard. He'd thought about her often over the years, especially while he did his time in the juvenile prison, of how he would take his revenge on her. He smiled to himself as he ran through the bush.

CHAPTER 9

Natalie was beyond terrified. She screamed into the stinking piece of cloth tied into her mouth as another thorn pierced the soles of her feet. They were on fire, and it felt as though the man who dragged her along was going to rip her arm off each time she stumbled.

The longer they ran through the bush the more time she had to think about what was going to happen to her.

The leader, she didn't know his name, had her again now. He'd snatched her back from the man called Comrade Moto, who had been gentler with her. The two men had talked to each other in Ndebele and Natalie only understood a few words. She'd got the impression Comrade Moto wanted to let her go, but the leader had yelled at him, then snatched Natalie back, hurting her in the process. When she'd tried to mouth something through the gag, to beg him to let her go, he had slapped her on the side of her head and knocked her to the ground again.

It had all been so confusing. She kept hoping it was a nightmare and that any second she'd wake up, but when she looked down at the brightening gold of the grass, when the men stopped to briefly confer about something, she saw the red of her blood on the stalks. This was real. She started to cry again.

Grandma Pip had led her from the bedroom to the farmhouse's safe room. She'd told Natalie to lie on a mattress and had laid another on top of her. Natalie had been too scared to be left alone, smothered like that, but when the next explosion landed close enough to shake the plaster from the ceiling, she did as she was told. The walls of the room were lined with sandbags. Grandma Pip had gone back out into the hall and Natalie could hear her talking on a radio while a gun started firing.

'Pip, get more ammo!' she'd heard Grandpa Paul call out. The gunfire had been scary, but the explosions were worse.

The fourth one landed right on the house. Natalie felt like someone had *klapped* her on both ears at the same time. Something fell on the mattress on top of her. Smoke and dust filled the room. She couldn't hear. She knew she needed to move.

Natalie pushed and wriggled and struggled until she could get out from under the mattress. A layer of plaster dust covered everything and part of the roof was missing. She heard the crackle and felt the heat of a fire taking hold. A rafter beam had fallen across the mattress. Half of the wall between the safe room and her dad's old bedroom had been blown away and the stack of sandbags had fallen over. The ripped hessian of the bags was spilling red dirt like blood on the floor. The air stank of chemicals.

Flames whooshed out in a jet from the kitchen down the corridor.

'Gas!' Grandpa Paul seemed to whisper from beyond the kitchen. As much as she wanted to, Natalie couldn't run down the hallway to the sound of her grandfather because the fire blocked her way.

'Natalie,' she thought she heard her Grandma saying softly.

'Here!' Natalie thought she was yelling as loud as she could, but she could hardly hear her own voice. The flames licked at the carpet that ran down the polished concrete floor of the hallway.

Natalie had no choice but to turn and run down the corridor, towards the back door of the farmhouse. She slipped on a mixture of dust and water running from the bathroom. The back door was locked and she had to reach up to slide the bolt. Her back was starting to sting as the fire leapt from room to room, chasing her through the house. She screamed and this time she heard herself a little better.

Natalie turned the door handle and heaved, but still it wouldn't open. She looked over her shoulder and saw the fire had taken hold of the splintered rafters in the roof. It was moving closer and closer. She rattled and turned and pulled on the doorknob, but it was locked. Behind her, there was more gunfire. She screamed again. She was going to die because she didn't know where the key to the back door was. Natalie banged on the door with her fists.

At her feet was a rubber mat. Natalie dropped to her knees. She could smell cool, clean air coming in a draught from under the door. Behind her, the hallway was filling up with choking smoke. She lifted the mat, thinking Grandma would have left the key under it. There was nothing.

Boom!

Natalie rocked back on her haunches. The door had just shuddered as though someone had kicked it. 'Grandpa Paul! I'm in here!'

Boom!

The door rocked again. 'Hurry!'

A paling splintered and a black hand reached inside.

Natalie screamed.

Comrade Moto froze and raised his AK-47 to his shoulder. The sky was brightening by the minute and the long shadows gave the boy's movement away. The boy was running down the path towards them. 'Halt!' Moto called out.

The boy wore a grubby white singlet and baggy shorts. He was barefoot, skinny and looked to be in his early teens. He stopped and raised his hands. 'Don't shoot!' he called back in Ndebele.

'Bring him here,' Beria said. He stopped and held the girl still. She was becoming more compliant as she learned that disobedience would be dealt with immediately. She was sobbing. Beria was annoyed by the presence of the boy. He was one more witness to the fact that they had taken the white child. He would have to be dealt with.

Moto shoved the boy in the small of his back with the tip of his AK's barrel.

'What do you want?' Comrade Beria asked him.

'I come from the kraal, where you stayed last night, comrade . . . *sah* . . .'

'What of it?'

'My father, the headman, he says there are more comrades in the village. They wish to meet up with you.'

Beria knew of no other freedom fighters operating in the area, but then again, why would he? This band of intruders could be genuine comrades or, of course, they could be the dreaded *Skuz'apo*.

Beria's choice was simple. Now that he knew there was another group of armed men in the kraal, he could link up with them, or he could deliberately head off in a different direction and disappear. He could kill the messenger to ensure no one followed them or knew which way they had headed.

They all looked up at the drone of aero engines above.

Moto raised a hand to his eyes to shield them from the glare of the rising sun. '*Ma-brooka*.'

The nickname for the white soldiers came from the word for little girls' underpants, *brookies*, a reference to the Rhodesian Light Infantry's bush uniform, which usually included short camouflaged shorts. Beria followed the Dakota's track and, along with the others, counted the four parachutes that blossomed in its wake. They were too far away to fire on, and doing so would simply give away their position. The arrival of the RLI airborne troops changed things.

Beria bit his lip and held up a palm as Comrade Moto started to say something. He needed to think. There were only four men in the RLI fireforce stick, but it was not only them they had to be concerned about. If the stick made contact with them, they would call in the spotter aircraft and the K-Cars – the killing cars, as the air force's helicopter gunships were known.

The girl complicated things as well. On one hand, she was slowing them down. Beria could kill her now – releasing her was out of the question as she might be able to identify them at some time in the future. However, as long as they held her – and her tiny bare feet would give her away to even the most inexperienced tracker – the *kanka* would be less likely to drop bombs or spray the bush with 20mm cannon fire. The Botswana border was only about twenty kilometres away. If he could lure the *Mabrooka* into an ambush and dispatch them quickly, he might gain enough time to slip across the border before the security forces could get organised to send more soldiers or police. His chances of eliminating the RLI stick before they could get word to an orbiting command and control plane would be greatly enhanced if they had more firepower. With Jesus dead he was down to five men.

'We move back to the kraal,' Beria told his men. 'If these other *comrades* seem in any way suspicious, we kill them all. Understood?'

He looked at all their faces and each man nodded. The little girl started to cry again. Beria grabbed her by the throat. 'Shut up . . . one word and I kill you.' She blinked away her tears and nodded. Yes, she slowed them down, but she would be their prize once this day was done. And if they were cornered and faced death, then she might be their ticket across the border as a hostage.

Winston roused those of his men who had not been woken by the far-off sound of the mortar explosions and gathered them outside the headman's hut. 'We can't wait,' he whispered to them. 'It sounds like the terrs are revving a farm. We have to go find them and get them before they kill more innocent people.' Each nodded his assent. They were good men, good warriors.

The headman emerged from his hut, wringing his hands. 'My son is not yet back.'

'I know this area,' Winston said to him. 'There is a farm over that way.' He pointed to the east, from where the noise had come.

The headman nodded. 'Will you go join them, in their fight?'

Winston was dressed and ready to kill and he wanted nothing more than to follow the sounds and take the fight to the real terrs. Unless it had changed hands, it would be the Bryant farm – the parents of his friend, George, who had shown him and his family nothing but kindness.

He needed time to think. 'What do you say, old man? Should we join in the killing of the settlers who live over there?'

The headman stared at him for a long second while he worked up the courage to speak his mind. 'Those are good people. I know them. To kill them would be a sin.'

'I could beat or kill you for saying something so traitorous, old man, for siding with the settlers.'

The headman nodded slowly. 'Yes, but you will not.'

'Come,' Winston said to his men. The headman had been can-nier than Winston had given him credit for. 'We will find our comrades and join them in their fight,' he said loud enough for the few villagers who were poking their heads out of their huts to hear him.

He turned and the headman grabbed hold of the sleeve of his shirt. 'Please remember, my son is out there somewhere.'

Winston gently freed his arm from the bony fingers. 'I know. He will be safe. You have my word.'

Winston gave the signal for his men to move out, with Obert, his best tracker, moving ahead of them to scout the way. Once they were well clear of the village, Winston called a halt. He took off his Russian-made pack and opened it. He pulled out a torch with a red filter, and a topographical map of the area. He knew where they were, and what the problem was, but he needed to explain it to his men.

'Gather around,' he said, calling Obert and the others in. 'We are here,' he said, pointing to the cluster of black dots that represented the kraal, between the farming district of Plumtree and the Botswana border. 'The farm the terrorists are attacking is here,' he moved his finger across two grid squares – two kilometres to the east of their current position, 'but we cannot go there now, because it is outside the boundary of our frozen area, by one kilometre. The boundary runs north–south, halfway between us and the farm.'

He looked at the faces of his men to see if they understood the predicament. Each of the three men nodded. A frozen area was a no-go area, marked on the map, which ensured that no other Rhodesian security forces would enter on foot while a Selous Scouts group was operating in that area. No air force aircraft would bomb or strafe the area either.

Obert cocked his head and raised a hand. They all listened, and heard the gunshots. 'FN, but far,' Obert said.

Winston nodded his concurrence. 'We go no further. If the

magandanga come this way, we kill them. We don't want to go any closer to the boundary of the frozen area. There will be PATU farmers looking for black men to kill, and maybe –'

They all looked up at the lightening sky. They watched the Rhodesian Air Force Dakota pass overhead. 'An RLI fireforce,' Winston said. 'That settles it. We must wait here.'

In the distance they heard the crackle of more gunfire. The farmers – perhaps the people he knew – were putting up a fight.

'Bright,' Winston said to his radio operator. 'Send a sitrep. Let headquarters know where we are.'

Wally Collins held up a hand, signalling Braedan and the others in the stick to stop.

Braedan dropped to one knee, raising the barrel of his FN. His heart started beating faster and he watched Wally slowly turn his hand so that his thumb was pointing down. Braedan crawled forward, to where Collins had taken up a fire position behind a stout mopane tree. Braedan looked to where Collins was pointing and, after staring hard through the shroud of butterfly-shaped leaves, he made out the pointed crown of an East German bush hat and the muzzle brake of an AK-47.

The man wasn't moving. If he was a sentry, he was either very calm or he was asleep. 'Cover me,' Braedan whispered. 'Put two in him if he starts to move.'

Collins nodded and peered through the rear sight of his FN.

Braedan eased himself up, skirted right and started circling slowly towards the man. He, too, had his rifle up and ready. He watched the terr over the top of his FN, his finger curled through the trigger guard. He stopped when he trod on a dry twig and it snapped. The man, Braedan could see now, had his back to a tree trunk and his hat pulled low down over his eyes.

Braedan straightened. 'Dead,' he called out to Collins. He

looked around as the rest of the stick moved up. He saw the scuffed leaves of the terrorists' spoor.

Andy knelt by the body and raised a hand to the dead man's throat. 'Still warm. They were here just now.'

'Check his pockets quickly,' Braedan said to the medic. 'Wally, Al, scout ahead a bit, hey, into the *shateen*. They're leaving spoor like *maningi* jumbo.'

'Girl's still with them,' Collins said. He picked up a leaf and examined it. His thumb and forefinger came away red and sticky. 'The poor little thing's feet are bleeding.'

'Bastards. Come on, let's go,' Al said.

'*Ja.*' Braedan looked back and saw Andy had stopped rifling through the dead terrorist's pockets and was now unbuttoning his bush shirt. 'Andy, leave it . . .'

'Check, they knifed this *gandanga*,' Andy said. 'He was dying and instead of leaving him for us to look after him, his bloody Chinas slotted him.'

'These bastards need sorting, one time,' Wally said.

Braedan nodded, but he was impatient to keep moving. The fact they'd abducted a white child told him this bunch of gooks would fight to the death.

'Braedan, check,' Andy said, pointing.

Andy was young, a conscript who'd opted to join the RLI and get his national service over and done with quicker than if he'd signed on to one of the part-time territorial battalions of the Rhodesia Regiment. He was new to the troop and had proved himself a competent medic on the three occasions they'd needed him so far. But he didn't know what he was doing now. He was reaching under the terr's body for something.

'Andy, no!' Braedan yelled, seeing, too late, the topographical map that had attracted the young soldier's attention. No one sat on a map, even if they were dying. 'Down!'

Braedan hit the ground and rolled away, catching a glimpse of Andy crouching there, frozen at first as he heard the spoon fly off the grenade that had been lying under the dead man's backside, along with the tempting prize of the map. Andy started to stand and tried to run, but he tripped over his own feet. The grenade exploded.

'Shit,' Braedan said. He dragged himself to his feet and patted himself down as he ran. His head was ringing and the explosion had sandblasted him with grit, sticks and small rocks, but he was unhurt. Andy, however, was screaming. He was lying face down and clawing at the dirt with his hands, and scrabbling with his feet as though he was trying to crawl away from the pain.

Bright Mpofu double-checked the grid reference on the map and read it out to Winston.

'Yes, that is correct,' Winston said to his radioman, unable to keep the alarm out of his voice. 'What do you mean they say we are not in the frozen area?'

Bright looked worried, and he had good cause to be. 'HQ says we are outside the boundary, and that it is five kilometres to the west, closer to Botswana.'

Winston shook his head. 'This can't be. We radioed the sitrep two days ago, telling them we were moving into this area.'

The Joint Operations Command would be informed by a signal every time a frozen area was proclaimed or changed by the scouts. There was the inherent risk for the scouts, operating as they did dressed as enemy combatants, that they would be shot by mistake by other Rhodesian security force troops. Such catastrophes had happened before, in the early days of these unconventional operations, and the frozen area concept had been introduced to keep other units well away. Winston realised that if headquarters had miscalculated the boundaries of the frozen zone, then any security force units responding to the attack on the farm would also be unaware that there were other friendly troops in their vicinity.

Winston took the radio handset and told the operations officer, a white captain, on the other end of the radio to check the logs because Bright had told the young lieutenant on duty two days previously about their intended move to the kraal in pursuit of a band of ZIPRA terrorists.

'Well, it's not on the log, and not on the map, over,' the captain said. The man sounded defensive, Winston thought. If it were him, he would have been calling for the lieutenant who had failed to note the change in boundaries and demanding an answer.

'Well, get the boundary changed *now* and signal JOC,' Winston insisted. He knew the captain by name, and he was a good man. Despite their differences in rank, he knew he was on firm ground.

'Affirmative. Will do, over.'

'Do it now, now,' Winston added. 'There's a farm being revved not two k's from my position and a Dak just flew over. I suspect the enemy group may be heading my way and for all I know half the RLI will be coming along for the party as well.'

There was a pause on the other end of the radio as the captain grasped the seriousness of the situation. 'OK. I'm contacting JOC right now. Don't worry. We'll sort this thing and deal with whoever stuffed up later. Just as well you contacted us when you did. Suggest you pull back west, just in case, over.'

Winston was just thinking the same thing. It angered him even more to know that if Bright's last message had been received and acted on they could have been ordered to the farm to help. Instead, an RLI fireforce had been activated as soon as the farm was attacked and could very well be heading towards them right now. Winston looked up and saw the Dakota orbiting above them. He didn't have its frequency, but he had to assume that the captain would contact JOC, who would then relay the warning to the RLI troopies on the ground to stop at the border of the frozen area.

'Affirmative,' Winston said to the captain. 'We'll pull back five hundred metres so we're even further inside our boundary. Tell JOC to leave the terrs to us. I strongly suspect they're coming my way, over.'

Bright exhaled a long breath and Winston clapped him on the shoulder. 'Good work. And don't worry, I know you sent the right coordinates in your other message. Thank God they're going to let JOC know where we are; otherwise we might have found ourselves in a contact with our own people.'

The man in charge shoved Natalie in the back and she fell again. Couldn't he see that she could barely walk, let alone run? This time she crashed into a tree and its rough bark tore down the side of her arm.

'Get up!' He grabbed her other arm, but his hands were slippery with sweat. She fell from his grasp and this time her head banged against the tree. A small branch slid painfully between the gag tied around her mouth and the soft skin of her cheek. For a moment she was left hanging there, hooked on the limb.

The man grabbed her again and tried yanking her away from the tree, and in doing so he ripped the gag from her mouth. Natalie felt as though he was going to dislocate her jaw, but all of a sudden her screams were no longer muffled.

'Aaaargh! HELP ME!'

'Stuff something in his fucking mouth,' Braedan said.

Wally looked up at him, his hands red with Andy's blood as

he cut the smoking remains of Andy's camouflage shirt and trousers away from his writhing body.

'Shut him up! I thought I heard something else.'

Andy dragged a hand through the dirt and leaves and shoved two of his fingers in his mouth and bit down on them. Braedan instantly regretted the harsh words he'd used. Andy had heard and understood. Wally tipped a water bottle over the scores of holes that peppered Andy's back and legs, then started shaking antibiotic powder over them. It must have stung because Andy kicked and convulsed and moaned into his fingers.

Braedan looked to where he thought he had heard the noise, his mouth half-open. 'Listen, *ek se*,' he said to Al. 'There. It's the girl! Check the radio, Al.'

Braedan, impatient to get moving, took a few steps towards where he'd heard the scream, rifle up and ready. He looked back at Platt, who had dragged the blood-spattered radio away from Andy and now had the headphones on.

The Dakota that had dropped Braedan and his men had returned to Bulawayo and been replaced by a Lynx, the Rhodesian Air Force's version of a twin-boomed Cessna push-pull aircraft. The Lynx was doubling as a command and control aircraft for the rapidly escalating mission to catch the terrorists, and as a forward air controller for the other air support that was on its way.

'Echo one, echo one, echo one, this is bravo one, radio check, over,' the frustrated pilot said for the fifth time.

The pilot banked and brought his little aircraft down for another low-level pass over the farmhouse and the lands to the west, hoping to spot the soldiers on the ground. He saw an ambulance and three police vehicles, two cars and a truck, pulling up the long gravel driveway. A fair-haired woman was running to meet them. The house was still burning and his prop wash spun the black smoke into a corkscrew as he passed over. The pilot was about to try the RLI men again when he heard another voice using his call sign.

'*This is cyclone seven, alpha one . . . one hundred and fifty kilometres and closing. Any news, over?*'

'Negative alpha one,' the Lynx pilot said. And that was the problem. He recognised the voice of the helicopter pilot and fully understood the man's urgent tone, and his reasons for asking the same question he had asked five minutes ago. It was George Bryant, the CO of 7 Squadron, and it was his ten-year-old daughter who was missing somewhere down there in the bush.

The pilot tried again to contact the RLI stick on the ground. 'Echo one, echo one, echo one, radio check over . . .' He waited a few seconds. 'Echo one, if you are receiving me and unable to transmit you are to hold in place, repeat, hold in place. The boundaries of the frozen zone near your loc have been moved eastwards, I say again, *moved eastwards*. Hold in place and wait for reinforcements.'

The pilot sighed. It was going to be a long morning. Until reinforcements and the helicopters arrived, there was nothing more he could do.

Bright snapped his fingers, and Winston nodded. He'd heard the noise as well. The terrorists were making more noise than a herd of stampeding buffalo. They were running scared.

Winston felt the electric jolt as the adrenaline pumped from his heart to his fingertips. This was what he'd craved as a boy, the life of the warrior, and what he'd gradually come to learn over the past two years was a kind of sentence. He had proved himself, time and again, and learned that he could do this. He could kill. Whether the government of Smith-*i* was right or wrong, or whether the new man being touted as a successor, Bishop Abel Muzorewa, was a strong man or a puppet of the whites did not matter to Winston. He had known no life as an adult other than war.

Winston heard movement in the bush, then saw the white of the boy's singlet. His hand tightened around the pistol grip of his AK-47. 'Stop,' Winston said to the boy, his voice calm but authoritative. The headman's son came to a halt, his chest heaving with ragged breaths, and raised his skinny arms.

'I have the comrades . . .' The boy looked back over his shoulder.

Two men, one with an AK, the other with an RPD light machine gun, materialised from the screen of mopane leaves. The machine gunner kneeled and took up a firing position behind a tree. The other stood with his AK pointed in Winston's general direction, his nostrils flared and his breathing heavy from running or a hard forced march. His uniform shirt was mottled with sweat. These were the real terrorists that Winston and his men had been hunting, and the headman's son had served them up on a platter.

Winston heard muffled sobs and the sound of something falling to the ground. 'Get *up*!' a voice said. Winston licked his lips. He and his men were also behind the cover of an anthill and the stoutest trunks available. The two terrorists had stopped about fifty metres from them with the headman's son, who still stood with his hands up, quavering in the no-man's land between them.

'Which one of you is in charge?' a voice called from behind the two lead men.

Winston saw another flash of white through the bush. His eye was immediately drawn to the face of the terror-stricken child in a torn nightdress stained with blood and dirt. When he'd heard a little girl had been taken he'd felt relieved – Mr and Mrs Bryant were getting old now, and their daughter, Hope, was away most of the year at university. He'd assumed it was another farm that had been revved. But he recognised this girl instantly. George had showed him the photo. This was George's daughter, though he couldn't remember her name. Her abductor was holding her in front of him, as a human shield.

As Winston's eyes travelled higher he saw the Makarov pistol pressed to the child's temple, and the barrel and flash-suppressor of the AK-47 slung across the man's back, protruding above his shoulder.

Winston was in cover, his body mostly behind the tree trunk and his face obscured by a net of heavy, bright-green butterfly-shaped leaves. The terrorist commander couldn't see his face, but Winston could see the other man clearly.

It was his brother.

CHAPTER 10

'It's no good. Bloody radio's *frot*, man,' Al said.

'Shit.' Braedan ran his hand through his sweat-dampened hair. One man down and the radio out, and a little girl disappearing further and further into the bush with every second. He'd passed all his army courses with flying colours and he was one of the youngest lance corporals in the troop. He played rugby for his RLI Commando and he had a reputation for never backing down, for being tough and aggressive on the field. He'd won far more fights than he'd lost and he'd learned how to play the chicks well enough that he scored on every leave. But nothing in his life had prepared him for this.

'What do we do?' Collins asked, looking up at him. 'He's going to do a wheels-up unless we get him to a doc soon.'

Wally Collins was ten years older than Braedan – a good, solid soldier, but he was never going to be promoted. He was relying on Braedan, a twenty year old, to lead him and the rest of them to safety or victory.

Which was worth more – Andy's life or the girl's? Shit, the gooks might have killed her by now, and they had a good lead on Braedan and his men from the start. They were probably halfway to Botswana by now. Braedan looked down at Andy Hunter. The morphine had kicked in, but Andy's back was shredded. His skin was deathly pale.

'He can't walk, not even with help,' Collins said, as if Braedan needed to be reminded of their fellow soldier's condition.

Al stood up from the shattered radio. 'I'll go, man. After the little girl. You and Wally look after Andy.'

That made up Braedan's mind. 'No. There are too many of them, Al. Shit, man, I couldn't live with myself if I sent any of you *okes* on a bloody suicide mission.'

Al nodded, and Braedan saw he was unable to hide his relief. 'Right,' Al said, 'so we all carry Andy back to the farmhouse and wait for the cavalry, *ja*?'

Braedan shook his head. He knelt beside Wally and Andy and took two grenades and two extra magazines from Andy's webbing. He clasped the wounded man on the shoulder. 'Be strong, *boet*. I tune you, you're going to be fine.' He stood and placed the extra munitions in his own pouches. 'Al, you and Wally carry Andy back to the farmhouse.'

'What about you?' Collins asked.

Braedan grinned. 'Myself, I have some work to do.' He turned and jogged away from them, into the bush towards where the terrorists had gone.

Winston blinked away the drop of sweat that rolled down his forehead and into his eye.

'Show yourself and prove who you are,' said his brother, Emmerson Ngwenya.

Winston wanted to believe he was wrong, but George had shown him a photo not only of his daughter but also one of Thandi and Emmerson. It had been taken around 1972 or 1973. George had been vague when Winston had asked him how he'd come to be in possession of the picture. He'd said something about his mother getting a copy from Winston's mother. Winston thought that unless his mother had changed her opinion of the Bryants, then this was highly unlikely. Thandi was smiling, but Emmerson had sneered at the camera, with the arrogance of the youthful rebel.

Whether Emmerson knew whose child he had kidnapped didn't matter – the fact that he would kidnap a little girl for any reason was almost beyond belief. He had seen the atrocities ZANLA and ZIPRA had inflicted on people who sided with the government, but he could only guess what his brother had in store for George's daughter. Was it personal?

Bright looked at him from behind the neighbouring tree, and Winston blinked again. Winston saw Obert, from the corner of his eyes, shifting from foot to foot.

If Winston showed himself to his brother, he was sure Emmerson would recognise him immediately. What would his brother do then? Winston studied the wide eyes, the cruel set of Emmerson's mouth, and saw the way he did nothing to relieve the pressure of the gun on the girl's temple as her tears flowed.

Winston decided to do what he knew his brother would do. He drew a breath and aimed.

Natalie screamed into the gag as the man's blood spurted all over her.

He'd been holding the gun to her head but had relaxed his hold a little when one of his men asked him something. In turning to answer, her abductor had lowered the pistol's barrel. Natalie had squirmed and then the gunfire had started.

The man holding her pitched back as though he'd been slammed in the face with a sledgehammer. He still had his arm around her and she fell back on top of him. He was clutching at his upper body somewhere and blood jetted from him. Natalie could feel it on her back and she screamed again. She rolled over, and blood sprayed into her face. The man yelled in pain as she wriggled on him to try to get to her feet. It wasn't easy with her wrists tied behind her. She saw his gun in the grass, where he'd dropped it. She knew as soon as he could get to it he would shoot her. Even as she rolled to her knees she saw him scrabbling in the dirt for the pistol with one hand, while he held the other to a spot above his right lung. Blood was pumping out between his fingers.

Bullets were zinging and whizzing all around her, but all she wanted to do was get away from that foul man who'd been pushing and shoving and hurting her. There were flashes of fire from the mopane trees in front of her. If these men were shooting at the terrs, they must be army guys, she thought.

Her feet were bloody and pricked with thorns, and not having the use of her arms for balance made running even harder. She tripped and fell, crying and yelling into her gag. A big man stepped from the trees in front of her and she saw his canvas tennis shoes and camouflage trousers. She craned her head to look up at him.

'Come,' he said, motioning her towards him. He was black, and looked like another terrorist. Natalie had no idea what was going on.

The big man raised his rifle to his shoulder and fired another couple of shots, then changed magazines. Natalie got up onto one knee, and then to her feet. She wasn't going to run into the arms of another bad man. She turned to run away from the two sets of warring Africans.

'Get down, girl!' the man yelled. She stopped. Natalie was in the open, with bullets flying all around her. Another man cried out in pain. 'Covering fire!' the big man yelled. The sound of bullets seemed to increase in ferocity as the man ran to her. He wrapped a muscled arm around her and half-lifted, half-dragged her to a large tree. He sat her down. 'I am a friend. I know your father. He is my friend.'

Natalie looked up at him and started to cry. She didn't know how this bloody terr would know her dad, or if he was here to help her or kill her. She was tired and sore and scratched and cut and all she wanted was to go home to Grandma Pip and her mom and dad.

The black man reached a hand out to her and she cringed into the rough bark of the tree. 'I'm not going to hurt you.' He hooked a finger in the gag around her mouth and pulled it free. 'There, is that better?'

She nodded, trembling.

'Winston!' another man called. 'They are running. What shall we do?'

'Leave them, Bright. We have the girl. Jonathan?'

'Here,' called the third member of their stick.

'Obert?'

Winston paused then tried the other man's name again. There was no answer. 'Find him, Bright.'

'All right.'

The man called Winston pulled out a knife from a sheath at his belt.

'No!'

'Hush, little one,' he said to her. 'I'm just going to cut the ties on your wrist. Turn for me. It's all right. I know your father.'

Natalie blinked back her tears and slowly turned. She tensed her whole body, waiting to feel the pointed blade pierce her back at any second. She whimpered as she felt the steel against the inside of her wrists.

'Obert is dead,' the man named Bright called.

Natalie felt the big man pause with the knife. 'Don't hurt me, please!' Thoughts raced through her mind, terrifying her even more . . . *He's going to kill me; please, God, don't let him kill me; he just said he knew my dad so I wouldn't struggle.* Natalie looked over her shoulder, eyes wide with fear.

The big man called to his men, 'Leave him, but get his weapon. We'll pull back to the kraal and call for reinforcements there.'

Someone screamed from the bush. The man called Bright raised his hand and said something, then the gunfire started again.

Natalie saw her chance and leapt up and ran.

'No! Come back!' the man called after her.

Braedan had gone to ground behind a fallen tree when the rounds started coming down range in his direction. It was odd, but he thought he could hear fire going the other way, away from him, from off to his left.

Perhaps the gooks hadn't actually seen him and were just firing blind. He peered around the corner of the log and saw one of them, not thirty metres away. The man was firing an AK, but across Braedan's front, not at him. These guys . . . everyone said they were hopeless soldiers who couldn't shoot straight. Living proof, right before his eyes. The guy was jumpy as hell, too, shifting his weight from one foot to the other.

Just then he heard a high-pitched voice scream '*No!*' Christ, he thought. The girl. She was still alive. What were the bastards doing to her?

Braedan had fired his weapon plenty of times before and he thought he had killed two men; however, other members of his troop had claimed the same kills, so he couldn't be really sure. He put the fidgeting floppy in his sights, drew a breath and squeezed the trigger. The man fell back behind his tree and didn't get up again. There was no doubt about that one.

Braedan knew he couldn't lie here. He heard voices. There were *maningi* gooks – plenty of them – and he knew he had to get up and into the fight.

'*Don't hurt me, please!*' a little girl's voice cried out.

Braedan swallowed hard. They were going to fucking kill or rape a ten-year-old girl. He planted his left fist in the dirt and pushed himself up.

He heard one of the gooks saying something about pulling back to a kraal, but then he drowned out their voices and his own fears with a primal, animalistic yell that came from deep down in his core. Braedan vaulted the dead tree and ran forward, the FN tight in his shoulder as he looked down the barrel for a target.

A young African in a Russian hat turned to stare at the noise he was making. He had an AK in his right hand and raised his left, palm out. 'No, don't shoot. We are –'

Braedan fired twice. The double tap. Both rounds found their mark in the *gandanga*'s chest. The man fell back, blood spewing from his mouth. He saw a flash of white through the dull greens and browns of the trees. Two down. He was fucking invincible. He searched for another target.

'*No, come back,*' called a man with a deep African voice.

'I'm fucking coming for you, cunt,' Braedan said.

Another terr stepped from behind a tree, dropped his rifle and raised his hands. Braedan spun and fired twice. His first shot missed, but the second caught the man in the guts. Braedan ran to him and stood over him; he was writhing in pain.

'No!' the man said.

'Where is she?' Braedan said, his chest heaving from the run, from the adrenaline, from the sheer rush of it all. He was almost there.

'No!' the terrorist said again through his pain. 'We are . . . we are –'

He had no time to waste. He'd seen the girl running. He pointed the barrel of his FN at the man's forehead and finished him off. 'Thanks for coming, China.'

He ran into the bush, following the sound of the little girl's screams.

Winston thought about letting the girl run. She was heading away from where Emmerson and his men had come from, although from the gunfire behind him it sounded as though they were in pursuit. No, he had to get her.

She tripped and screamed and he closed the distance between them in a few long bounds. He didn't waste his time trying to calm her. He drew his knife and reached down for her skinny little wrists. Perhaps if he freed her she might calm down and trust him.

'Noooo!' she shrieked.

'Bastard,' said a voice behind Winston.

Winston turned, knife in hand, and saw the RLI soldier standing there.

'Thank God,' he said, dropping his knife and rifle and spreading his arms wide.

Braedan stood in the clearing, the morning light filtering down through the mopanes, turning the dry grass a beautiful golden yellow.

The little girl was on the ground, her nightdress stained with dirt and blood. Her hands were bound behind her and she was scrambling in the dirt and grass like a centipede, trying to put as much distance as she could between herself and the filthy terr.

The man had spread his arms, like he was Jesus Christ himself, and had the hide to grin at him. 'Bastard,' Braedan said.

'*Thank God*,' the man said.

Braedan was breathing hard out of his nose, like a stallion blowing after a charge. The gook probably thought he'd spend time in gaol, or maybe swap sides, like they'd all heard some of the *magandanga* did. He had the guts to kidnap and try and murder a little girl, but not to stand and fight. The gutless prick started to say something, but Braedan had no time for his words.

He knew what he had to do. There would be no trial for this one, no comfy prison cell, no lawyers for this piece of filth. Sometimes he wondered if it was all worth it. Braedan was young, but he wasn't stupid. He knew the security forces' losses were mounting and the gutless, back-stabbing politicians were already working on a deal to put a criminal in charge of the country. Others were in the business of compromising and taking the path of least resistance.

Not Braedan Quilter-Phipps.

'My brother –' the terr started to say.

'I'm not your fucking brother,' Braedan said. He took aim and put two in the man's black heart.

CHAPTER 11

Tate drove from Kariba to Salisbury for the medal ceremony, mostly because his mother wanted him there, but partly because he was genuinely proud of what his twin brother had done.

Braedan could be a huge pain in the arse sometimes – most of the time – and had always been a hothead and a bully when they were growing up. But Tate had learned how to get on with him. All the same, Braedan's barbed taunts about Tate joining the national parks service because he was too scared to do his army service festered under his skin.

A soldier in starched camouflage fatigues stopped him at the entry to Government House and Tate showed him the invitation to the awards ceremony. He was nodded through and directed to a car park.

Tate could have come in his Parks and Wildlife service uniform – he probably should have for such a formal occasion – but he didn't want to give Braedan an easy opening for yet another jibe about him not being in the military. Instead, he wore a beige body shirt and blue tie, brown flared slacks and a second-hand sports jacket he'd bought from a charity shop. His civilian wardrobe was limited – his pay was abysmal and, besides, he rarely went out *jolling* when he was on leave. Most of his spare time was spent studying by correspondence for a Bachelor of

Science in zoology. He was due to write exams in a month, so his social life had been curtailed even more than usual. He'd never had a steady girlfriend and was still a virgin. It seemed when he was around girls he never knew the right thing to say and few ever gave him a chance to try.

A military band played an awkward cover of an old Beatles song as people dressed in far better clothes than Tate was made their way from the car park across the grass to where a big marquee was set up. Tate took a deep breath, closed his car door and set off.

He found his mother and kissed her hello. He could see Braedan, in his dress greens uniform, standing in a knot of black and white soldiers, laughing out loud at something one of them had said, or more likely something he'd said himself.

'I so wish your father was still alive. He would have loved all this palaver,' his mother said. Even before Tate and Braedan's father had died of a heart attack, their parents had needed to scrimp and save to put the boys through boarding school. With Fred's death, there had been no money to send them to university. She led him to the second row of seating, which was reserved for families of medal recipients. People were taking their seats.

In the first row, off to their right, was the little girl Braedan had saved. Tate recognised Natalie Bryant from her photos in the *Herald*. It had been front-page news when Braedan had rescued her and single-handedly annihilated a terrorist cell near her grandparents' farm. It was chilling, Tate thought, to realise that he and Braedan had been to that same farm, as children, for a party.

Natalie looked sullen and withdrawn, as if she didn't want to be there. The poor thing was probably traumatised, Tate thought, and forced to relive the ordeal every time the news

media wanted another crack at her story. Today's medal ceremony would force her to recall those events all over again. A
newspaper photographer was already taking pictures, his
camera flash bouncing off the bright white roof of the marquee.

George Bryant put an arm around his daughter and whispered something, words of reassurance perhaps, then returned
his gaze to where it had been a moment earlier, straight ahead
and out into the middle distance. He wore the blue dress uniform and rank of a squadron leader in the air force. Tate
recalled reading in the newspaper that the father was a helicopter pilot. A thin blonde woman sat on little Natalie's other
side. That would be Susannah, her mother. Beside her were the
grandparents, Paul and Philippa. He remembered Philippa –
Pip, his mum called her – just as she was now, small, smiling
and full of life. Paul was talking to a man in Tate's row, but further along, and the twang of his Australian accent was still
evident.

The band started to play the Rhodesian national anthem,
'Rise O Voices of Rhodesia' to the tune of Beethoven's 'Ode to
Joy', and everyone stood. Tate was a terrible singer so he
mouthed the words quietly.

While they were singing a tall girl with long straight blonde
hair that reached almost to the waistband of her blue jeans
rushed up the centre aisle between the seats and slipped into a
vacant spot next to Philippa Bryant. Pip paused in her singing
long enough to grab the young woman's arm and kiss her on
the cheek.

Tate looked over at his brother and saw that he, too, had
noticed the attractive late arrival. The young woman made no
pretence of singing the national anthem, but just stood there
with a neutral look on her face. She wore a flimsy cheesecloth
top and when Tate checked her feet he saw she was wearing san-

dals. Most of the other women were aerating the lawn of Government House with high heels.

As the music stopped, the young woman shuffled across in front of Pip and Paul to where Natalie sat. She leaned over and kissed her, then awkwardly regained her seat.

An army colonel invited the crowd to sit and welcomed them to the awards presentation ceremony. He droned on for a few minutes – Tate wasn't interested in what the man had to say – and then introduced the Prime Minister, who was sitting on the podium near the people he was about to honour. Ian Smith, the erect, angular-faced former fighter pilot who was the leader of the ruling Rhodesian Front party and Prime Minister of Rhodesia, got up and moved to the microphone.

'We live in trying times . . .' he began.

Tell us something we don't know, Tate thought, as he switched off again. He was too busy studying the lightly tanned, flawless skin of the girl in the first row. It must be the Bryants' daughter, Hope. He hadn't seen her in, what, ten years? He remembered the wedding, and the pieces started falling into place. That would have been George's wedding, and Hope was his younger sister. She had grown into a beauty.

The Prime Minister was talking about challenges and sacrifice and the forces of good and evil and the need for resolve and courage . . . or something like that. When everyone else started applauding, Tate joined in half-heartedly. Hope sat there with her hands in her lap.

The colonel stepped back up to the podium and started reading the citations for the awards that were to be presented today. There were three black soldiers and two white, a white air force officer and a civilian couple in their mid-sixties. It was a nice mix, Tate thought, and no doubt made a good photo opportunity.

The civilians, it turned out, were farmers from Bindura who

had fought off a terrorist attack and killed two terrs. As each citation was read the recipient stood, marched to the PM, saluted, received his award and then shook hands with Smith while a government photographer snapped two frames. The farming couple didn't salute, but they looked suitably humbled and at the same time impressed to be meeting the iron-willed leader of their country.

Tate really only paid attention when the officer began reading Braedan's citation, and when his brother stood Tate returned his eyes to Hope Bryant and saw she was staring at Braedan. Insanely, Tate felt a stab of jealousy as Hope followed Braedan's movements on the podium. Braedan's citation was the last, perhaps because his award was the highest of those being presented today – the Silver Cross of Rhodesia. Winning the SCR, the country's third highest honour, was a big deal.

The newspaper photographer joined the government snapper for the picture of Ian Smith pinning the medal on Braedan's chest, and when he was done, the audience burst into applause. A couple of people stood and, eventually, the whole crowd of guests was standing and clapping.

Rhodesians, Tate thought, were a pretty reserved bunch and this spontaneity was out of the ordinary. Their country, their white way of life, was under real threat and people desperately needed to hear stories like that of Braedan rescuing the helpless child from the forces of evil.

Tate didn't underestimate what Braedan had done, but in his own mind he questioned the morality of the war, if not the actions of individual soldiers. Hope, he saw, was applauding as loudly and enthusiastically as anyone else in the crowd, but when he glanced at Squadron Leader George Bryant he saw him put his palms together, then leave them like that, as if he were lost in his own silent prayer.

After Braedan shook the Prime Minister's hand he and Smith exchanged a few words, which were drowned out by the rolling thunder of applause. Smith smiled and nodded and Braedan excused himself.

Braedan strode towards little Natalie, knelt down in front of her, so that he was eye to eye with her, then reached to his left breast and unhooked the silver cross he had just been presented. He held it out to her.

Little Natalie shook her head at first, but he said something to her that made her reach out, take it in her hand, then start crying. She wrapped her arms around his neck and the applause began anew as the photographers jostled each other to capture the moment.

Tate looked at Hope. She was palming tears from her eyes and, if he was honest with himself, he also felt something welling up from his chest. His mother clasped his arm and held on tight.

Hope took a glass of champagne from a black waiter bearing a silver tray. She thanked him and he nodded then moved off silently.

She'd never been in the grounds of Government House and she was impressed by the architecture of the official residence, which seemed to be at the same time both simple and imposing. Ian Smith was talking to a ring of acolytes and, to Hope's shame, her father was there too, hanging on the Prime Minister's every word.

The manicured lawns, the ladies in big hats, the smiling but silent African waiters, the platters of fine food and chilled drinks . . . it was all too good to be true. Out there, beyond the walls topped with razor wire, was the real Africa, and it was encroaching closer by the minute.

A raucous laugh caused heads to turn and Hope saw Braedan

Quilter-Phipps holding his own court. More people crowded around him than Smith. There was nothing, in Hope's view, heroic about the struggle between the Rhodesian Security Forces and ZANLA and ZIPRA, but there was a real live hero over there, laughing in between the beers that were being foisted on him by his own entourage of worshippers. Hope had read the newspaper accounts, first in South Africa and then when she returned home to Rhodesia. Braedan, so the papers said, had killed no fewer than seven terrorists, single-handedly, and put two bullets into the heart of the man who held a knife to her niece's throat.

Hope hated the war, and Ian Smith, and the Rhodesian Front, and her people's futile, tragic, costly attempts to hang on to a world that would soon be over and done with. She sipped her champagne and, despite her moralistic revulsion, shuddered when she remembered her first sight of the damage to her family home.

Natalie had been kidnapped from Hope's bedroom. What would have happened, she asked herself yet again, if she had been home from varsity on the night the freedom fighters had attacked? They wouldn't have taken a twenty-year-old woman hostage, they would have killed her. Or worse.

Hope let the cold bubbles fizzle on her tongue as she watched Braedan down a glass of beer. Her most vivid childhood memory of Braedan was of him chasing her and pulling her pigtails at George's wedding, and the business with Emmerson Ngwenya. She felt terrible about what had happened to Emmerson, but he had hurt her and the word was he had run off to join the freedom fighters as soon as he'd been released from the juvenile training centre.

Braedan looked typical RLI. He was young and strong, and his hair was wavy and pushing the boundaries of a military cut.

These men called themselves the invincibles. To Hope, they were just paid killers.

'Hello there . . .'

Hope turned and saw another Braedan Quilter-Phipps. One with slightly longer hair, sideburns and an ill-fitting, slightly scruffy sports coat and flared trousers. 'Oh, hi . . .'

'Tate.'

'Yes, of course. Braedan's twin.'

'Does it show?'

She laughed. Except for the haircuts and the clothes, the boys were still almost identical. She remembered Tate as the smaller of the two, and while he had caught up to his brother in height, he was less stocky than Braedan. She hadn't noticed Tate during the speeches. 'You're not in the army as well?'

Tate sipped a Mazoe orange juice and shook his head. 'No . . . um, parks and wildlife.'

'Don't say it like you're embarrassed about it.'

'No, no. I'm not, but . . .'

The poor thing, Hope thought. He was practically stammering. 'But when you come to something like this, surrounded by men and women in uniform, you start thinking that maybe you should have joined the police, or the army, or the air force or something. Maybe someone like me brings this to your attention and you start to feel the self-doubt, possibly self-loathing again . . .'

'Sheesh.'

She laughed. 'I'm sorry. I'm studying psychology at UCT.'

'Well, you're learning something,' he said, taking another sip of his drink. 'But I don't . . . loathe myself, that is. I just don't fit in.'

Hope put a hand on his arm, surprising herself even as she did so. 'I'm sorry, Tate. I wasn't poking fun at you. And I think it's much better, much more honourable for you to have joined the national parks service rather than the army.'

'Why?' He seemed genuinely puzzled.

'Because I'm against the war. The sooner it's over, the sooner ZAPU and ZANU win, the better,' Hope replied.

Tate looked around, as though he thought there might be CIO agents in trench coats lurking in the bougainvillea. 'Really?'

'Yes.'

'You don't think all us whites will be slaughtered in our beds, or that Mugabe and Nkomo are just stooges of the communists and that, if they win, those of us who survive the bloodbath will be press-ganged onto collective farms or locked up in gulags?'

Hope laughed. 'No. I think Robert Mugabe's a nationalist more than a communist. He's using the Chinese to back his armed struggle – which I also don't agree with – but he'll cut them loose when he takes over the country.'

'I thought Bishop Muzorewa was taking over the country?'

Hope scoffed. 'He's a puppet, Tate. Everyone knows that Smith's hand is so far up the bishop's bum he can hardly say grace by himself.'

Tate looked around again.

'Stop looking for spies. What do you think? You opted out of the army, but do you agree with the war?'

He finished his orange drink and handed it to a passing waiter. Hope had nearly finished her champagne, so Tate took a fresh drink for both of them from the proffered tray. It seemed to her that he was buying time, perhaps trying to think of the right answer, the one that would impress her. She was no stranger to guys coming on to her. There were those that charged at her like a bull at a gate, and those, like Tate, who stumbled over their words as they tried to say what they thought she wanted them to say. She didn't particularly like either type. She liked honesty.

'I don't know of, can't think of, an ideology worth killing for.'

She said nothing, and waited for more, but she was impressed by his opening line.

'I live my life surrounded by the most amazing creatures in what must be the most beautiful surroundings in the world. Yet I often hear the sound of people killing each other. It's spread to the wildlife, too, this cancer. My scouts and I came across a dead rhino just the other day – people are even killing animals now for no good reason. I don't care who runs this country, or what colour they are, as long as they protect the only thing that's still good about it – the bush and the wildlife.'

Hope took a sip of her champagne. That was a little disappointing, she thought. She'd wanted something more spirited.

'I would kill to protect an animal from a poacher, but not for a cause,' Tate said.

That stopped her in her tracks. 'Hang on . . . you're saying animals are more important than people? Would you have stood by and let the freedom fighters kidnap and kill my niece?'

Tate shook his head. 'She was helpless, like this country's animals and the environment they live in. I don't know if I'd be as brave as my brother, tracking those men and killing them to rescue Natalie, but I like to think I would have done anything in my power to stop them. I guess few of us ever get the chance to find out if we've got the guts to put our lives on the line for the things we love.'

'Or people we love.'

He shrugged and looked away from her, back to the sound of laughing. She followed Tate's eyes to the man of the moment, his twin brother.

'Are you staying here long or going straight back to university?'

Hope was distracted. She looked back, from the man with the

military bearing, broad smile and muscle-filled uniform, to the slightly dishevelled version beside her. 'A week or so. I can't go home – it's a mess, and Mom and Dad are staying with neighbours and there's not much room. I'm staying with my brother in Salisbury for a few days. I love little Nat and I want to spend as much time as possible with her after what she's been through. I'm planning on coming back as often as I can – maybe deferring a subject or two at varsity till next semester.'

'I was wondering if you'd like to go to a movie or something while you're here? I have to get back to the valley next week, and I don't get to town that often. But it's all right if you have other things to do . . . I understand you've got family commitments and . . .'

'I'll think about it.' Hope hadn't picked Tate as such a fast mover. Perhaps the shyness and stammering were an act. She knew she really should spend as much time as possible with George and Natalie, but she found Susannah a bit of a pain. She had dressed in her ill-fitting uniform for the ceremony. While Natalie was at school and George away flying, Susannah was a volunteer 'blue bird' who packed parachutes for the military. Her mother, apparently, had done the same job during the Second World War. Susannah had remarked more than once that she thought Hope should have been contributing in some way to the war effort in her university holidays. Hope had given up trying to discuss the absurdity of the war with the conservative, sour-faced woman.

Hope glanced back at where Braedan had been laughing and drinking and saw that he was now walking straight towards her. He had a crooked smile on his face, and he'd undone the top button of his uniform shirt. He fixed his eyes on hers and she found she couldn't look away.

'OK, right,' she registered Tate saying.

'Hope Bryant,' Braedan said.

She lifted her glass. 'Howzit, Braedan. Congratulations on the medal – though I'm glad you moved away from us when you were little. Otherwise I wouldn't have had any hair left.'

Braedan raised his beer in return. 'Well, your hair looks just great to me. Just as well it's not in pigtails, though, or I might want a handful for old times' sake.'

Hope felt her cheeks redden.

'Where's Julie today?' Tate asked.

Braedan looked from Hope to his brother. '*Ag*, she walked out on me, man.'

'Sorry to hear it, she was a nice girl.'

'*Ja*,' Braedan's expression went from mock sad to a broad smile, 'but her roommate was even nicer.'

Tate shook his head.

'You don't approve, *boet*? I can hook you up with Julie, if you like. She needs a shoulder to cry on.'

Any attraction Hope might have felt towards Braedan – in a purely physical sense, because he was indeed a handsome, well-crafted example of the male species – evaporated.

'I can give you the roommate's number as well if you like, Tate.' He grinned. 'How about you, Hope? A few of us are going to the Monomotapa for drinks after this is all over. Fancy coming with?'

Hope smiled. 'I'd rather slit my wrists.'

Braedan laughed and downed his beer, then looked around for a waiter. He snapped his fingers and an African man threaded his way through the crowd towards him. Braedan took a Lion from the tray then, as an afterthought, asked Hope if she wanted a drink.

'I'm fine thanks,' she said. She glanced around to see if there was anyone else nearby that she knew, so she could excuse herself.

'Is Natalie all right?'

'What?' Hope looked back at Braedan and saw his eyes were fixed on her again. 'Oh . . . she's as well as can be expected.'

Braedan nodded. 'It will be hard for her. She'll have some dreams . . . nightmares . . . and she'll keep coming back to what happened. They say it's good to talk to people, to tell people about it. She'll be lucky to have you at home. She told me you were coming to stay with her.'

'And you? Who do you talk to?'

Braedan smiled. 'Come to the Monners tonight and I'll talk to you.'

'Can't,' Hope said.

Braedan nodded. 'I understand, it's better if you're with little Natalie.'

Hope shook her head. 'No, I'm going out with your brother tonight.'

Tate spluttered and raised a hand to his face to cover the orange drink that bubbled from his nostrils. Natalie laid a proprietary hand on Tate's arm and smiled at Braedan, who turned and walked back into the crowd.

CHAPTER 12

Tate felt like the luckiest man alive. He was still a little baffled about how and why Hope had fallen for him, but each time he saw her he felt pure, unadulterated joy at the realisation that she was his. They'd talked for two hours over dinner, after the movie on that first date, and Tate had known he was in love with her right from the start. He'd begged the chief warden to let him take his annual leave earlier than planned so that he could spend time with Hope when she was next able to get back to Salisbury from Cape Town.

Now, two months later, almost to the day Tate was waiting in the small, hot, stuffy terminal at Kariba Airport for Hope to arrive on the Air Rhodesia Viscount. She was actually coming to visit *him*.

He was in his neatest national parks uniform. He had picked a bouquet of wild flame lilies for her and hidden in his Land Rover was the present he would give her tomorrow, for their two-month anniversary. It was an intricately carved stone pendant depicting Nyaminyami, the serpentine river god of the Zambezi. It wasn't expensive – he couldn't afford anything pricey – but he desperately hoped she would like it.

It wasn't only because of his poor pay that he couldn't afford a nicer present for Hope – he'd also started saving for a ring.

Tate couldn't control his smile as he heard the drone of the

Viscount's four engines over the terminal building and saw its shadow flash across the shimmering runway outside. He had it all planned. He was going to take Hope down to Andora Harbour and load his camping gear and the food he'd bought onto a boat he was borrowing from a friend. He was then going to take her across to Tashinga, the main camp of Matusadona National Park.

He still couldn't quite believe she'd agreed to go with him – just the two of them – and while he'd scrounged an extra tent from the same friend, he had high hopes that she might share his with him. How he would ask her, or suggest it, he still had no idea. He'd never had sex, and while he was sure he would know what to do when the moment came, he hadn't a clue how to initiate it.

The only thing Tate was sure of was that he was in love.

Hope wished she were dead. Her head throbbed, her tongue was dry and swollen and she felt another wave of nausea rise up from her body as the Viscount banked hard for its final approach to Kariba.

It wasn't the flight that was making her sick, nor the fact that she'd drunk far too much the night before, although that hadn't helped. No, what was making Hope sick was herself.

Lizette, her Afrikaner friend at varsity, had joked about it. 'Sleep with both of them, hey? Maybe at the same time!'

Hope shook her head. Why, oh why, oh why had she ever agreed to go out with Braedan? She *hated* him. She hated everything about him – what he did for a living, his racist remarks, his politics, his arrogance . . .

She *loved* Tate. He was kind, gentle, innocent, and he was opposed to the war. He worked with Africans and respected their culture, and he looked forward to the day when they would have equal electoral representation and run their own country. He looked forward to working *with* them, he'd told her, not *over* them. He was going to take her camping and introduce her to his friend, an African game scout. They'd kissed, but Tate had been too polite to try anything more.

God, God, God! Hope balled her fists and pushed them into her eyes, as though she could force the images of the night before out of her mind. How, she thought, could she be so bad?

'Are you scared of flying?' said the businessman next to her, interrupting her self-flagellation. He had on a toupee and wore an open-necked shirt showing too much chest hair and a gold medallion.

'No.' He'd tried chatting to her at the beginning of the flight from Salisbury, but she had done her best to ignore him. Perhaps she gave off the vibe of being available. A slut. She hated herself. Why, oh why, oh why had she said yes?

Hope had heard the knock on the door at George and Susannah's air force bungalow, but as it wasn't her home, she didn't get up to answer it. She was bored. She went back to her magazine, ignoring the RBC news on the television, which was just more war and more propaganda. Natalie sat on the floor, dithering over her homework. She was a quiet child, much quieter now than before the attack on her grandparents' farm.

'Susannah!' George called, though there was no answer from the kitchen.

Natalie got up, but instead of answering the door she scuttled down the hallway, in the direction of her bedroom. It wasn't the first time Hope had seen her niece avoid meeting someone, and she could tell it was adding to George and Susannah's concern about their daughter's behaviour.

Hope looked over the top of her magazine and saw her

brother's harrumph. He set his beer down and got up and walked to the door. He had on camouflage trousers and a green T-shirt. He'd been flying during the day, and spoke about as much as his daughter. God, this was boring, Hope thought, even if it was only for a two-night stopover on her way up to Kariba.

'Hello,' she heard George say, with no trace of welcome in his voice.

'Howzit, sir?'

Hope recognised that voice. She stood up and peered around her brother's wide shoulders. There it was, that face again. It was so similar, yet so different to Tate's. Hair the same colour but a little shorter, a little neater; the same lean body, but the muscles better edged, the shirt a little tighter where it should have been. The eyes : . . that was the difference. Tate's were soft and warm like a puppy's; Braedan's were ice, like a cobra's.

'Hope – howzit? I heard you were in town.'

'Come in,' she found herself saying.

George turned and gave her a pained look, which Braedan couldn't see and Hope didn't understand.

'Braedan, Braedan, Braedan!' Natalie emerged from the hallway and ran across the lounge room and threw her arms around the young soldier, her face buried in the crisp white T-shirt above the faded but ironed denim jeans. Braedan bent down a little and picked Natalie up, lifting her until she was eye to eye with him. He grinned.

'Howzit, my girl?'

'She's not your girl,' George said.

They all looked at him. George's cheeks coloured. 'Natalie, get back to your homework. Leave Braedan alone.' He nodded to the soldier, by way of some sort of apology, and Braedan lowered Natalie gently back to the carpet. 'I'll be in the kitchen,' George said to Hope.

'Gosh, sorry,' Hope found herself saying. She had no idea why George had snapped like that. Theirs was a happy family, even with the trauma that Natalie had gone through. Perhaps, Hope thought, her brother blamed himself for Natalie's kidnapping because he was away flying at the time. It was nonsense, but it explained his outburst – that and the fact this was the most animated Hope had seen little Natalie since the kidnapping.

'It's OK,' Braedan said quietly. 'I think I understand.' He prised Natalie's spindly arms from around his waist, then ruffled her hair. 'How about a coolie, hey?' Natalie bobbed her head up and down and ran off to the kitchen to get Braedan a cold soft drink.

'Why are you here, Braedan?' Hope asked.

He shrugged. 'Tate told me you were coming to town. I thought that since you're not from Salisbury and . . . well . . .' he nodded towards the kitchen, 'from what I know of this side of your family they don't exactly *jol* every night, so I thought maybe you'd like some company of your own age.'

Hope folded her arms. 'That's a bit forward, don't you think?'

He shrugged again. 'That's the only direction I know. It's what they teach us in the army. Going backwards is for the gooks.'

The joke was poor, as well as bigoted. Natalie pursed her lips. 'There's no way we're even going for a cup of tea if you're going to preface every sentence with "it's what they teach us in the army".'

Braedan held up his hands. 'OK. I surrender. No army talk. Is that a yes?'

Hope wasn't even sure she knew what the question was. She suddenly felt as though she'd been tricked into agreeing to something slightly underhanded.

Susannah bustled out of the kitchen, wiping her hands on her apron and then fidgeting with her hair. 'Braedan, what a *lovely* surprise. I'm afraid we've just had dinner and it's the cookie's night off, but I can fix you a sandwich or something . . .'

'No, it's fine, thanks, Mrs Bryant. I've had some graze already. I just came around to see Hope.'

'Really?' said Susannah.

Hope saw Susannah's disapproving look.

'You're sure I can't fix you something to eat, Braedan?' Susannah tried.

'You heard the lad, Susannah,' George said, emerging from the kitchen.

'Don't be so rude, George,' Susannah said.

George frowned at his wife.

'I like Braedan,' Natalie said, as though that put an end to the discussion.

Hope felt suddenly like an *Nguni* cow or, worse, a native bride – like something whose ownership is discussed between men. So that was it, she suddenly realised, George was trying to protect her honour. Hope had noticed on past visits that George and Tate seemed to get on very well, particularly when discussing wildlife. George had kept Tate enthralled, and Hope slightly bored, with his tales of rescuing rhinos during Operation Noah, and Tate had gone on and on about the emerging problem of rhino poaching in countries north of Rhodesia. Now it looked like George was trying to lock Hope up, in order to protect her from Tate's evil twin.

'I'll be back in a second, Braedan. Just let me change,' Hope said.

She didn't envy Braedan having to wait there in George's den, but Braedan deserved it; Hope took her time. She brushed her long hair and put on blue eyeshadow and some lipstick. She thought about what to wear while she did her makeup. She was Tate's girlfriend, so she didn't want to dress provocatively. Braedan was in jeans, so they couldn't be going anywhere too smart. She put on her good pair of jeans, but didn't want to wear the same white blouse she'd worn to the medal award ceremony. She rummaged through the suitcase she'd brought with her. Most of her stuff was in the wash and wouldn't be ironed until Susannah's maid came in to work the next morning. The best she could come up with was a red strapless top. So much for not being provocative. Still, she thought, they were only going for a drink.

'Wow,' Braedan said, 'you look great.'

Hope waggled a finger. 'Don't get any ideas, hey. And save your flattery. We're not going to an end-of-school ball, you know. Just a couple of drinks.'

'Don't be late back,' George said.

'Yes, Dad,' Hope said sarcastically.

They walked down the driveway and Hope could feel her older brother's eyes on her all the way. Stuff him, she thought. 'Where's your car?' she asked, looking down the road.

Braedan walked over to an old BSA motorcycle propped on its stand. 'I brought a helmet for you.'

Hope put her hands on her hips and stared at him.

'What?' he asked.

'You presumed I'd agree to come with you.'

Braedan shrugged. 'If you didn't, someone else would have.'

'Oh . . . so where was I on the list?'

Braedan handed her the helmet and, after making him wait a few more heartbeats, she took it and put it on, tucking her hair up inside it as best as she could.

He grinned his lopsided smile at her. 'First.'

She shook her head as he climbed on, then got on behind him, wondering if she shouldn't just take off the helmet, turn around and go back inside. George's attitude annoyed her, though. He was acting like her father – except her father wouldn't have carried on like this – and she hated the way he was rude to the man who had saved Natalie's life. Men, she thought. George thought Braedan was some kind of threat to his position as king of his own little suburban castle.

And Tate? Tate wouldn't know, and he was too considerate to care if she went for a drink with Braedan. In fact, she resolved as Braedan kicked the bike into life, she would tell him.

'Whoa!' Hope screamed. The motorcycle leapt forward so suddenly that Hope had to grab him around the midriff. His body was hard, muscled. There wasn't an ounce of softness on him. He revved the throttle and the poorly muffled engine screamed as he tore up the quiet jacaranda-lined street. That'd give George's neighbours something to talk about, she thought.

Braedan rode too fast and leaned into every corner so that Hope didn't have a chance to release her grip on him. When she peered over his shoulder she saw the speedometer needle edge past sixty miles an hour. God, she thought, if the police didn't stop him he'd kill the pair of them.

'Want me to slow down?' he yelled back at her, reading her mind.

'Would you, if I asked you to?'

He shook his head and revved the bike even harder. Hope held him tight and let out a wild scream of fear and pure joy.

She'd been studying hard and had been looking forward to the break, and to the free and easy lifestyle up on Lake Kariba. Tate's letters had been earnest and heartfelt and he'd been hinting at things that, if she thought too long about them, made her feel a little nervous. She thought she might love him, and had come close to telling him so more than once, but she wasn't ready to get married, settle down and produce babies like a good white Rhodesian girl should.

'Here.' Braedan reached around behind him and Hope involuntarily slithered a little way back on the bike's seat. He wasn't trying to touch her, thank God, but instead reached into the back pocket of his jeans and pulled out a slim, curved pewter hip flask. 'Try some.'

She took it, more so he could return his hand to the handle-bars than because she wanted a drink. The flask was engraved with the powder horn insignia of the Rhodesian Light Infantry. Braedan eased off the throttle, presumably so she could let go of him with her other arm long enough to unscrew the cap.

'Go on . . .' He grinned back at her, then pulled on the brakes as they coasted up to a red robot on Second Street. Off to her left was the orderly neatness of the gardens in Cecil Square, with their palm and jacaranda trees and a host of other immac-ulately groomed shrubs. There was chaos in the countryside outside of Salisbury, but here they were free to ride through the night without a care in the world, while African Rhodesians fought for the right to higher education and young soldiers like Braedan faced death from a bullet or landmine for . . . what? She looked at the flask in her hand again, fingering the engraving.

A Ford pulled up next to them and the middle-aged driver glanced across at them, disapproval plain in his fleeting look. Hope unscrewed the flask and tipped it to her mouth. The brandy burned like fire. She licked her lips and grinned at the driver, who accelerated slowly away from them.

Braedan looked back at her. 'Light's green,' she said.

'I'll go when I'm ready.' He took the flask from her and downed half of it, before passing it back to her. 'Hang on.'

Hope barely had time to recap the flask and grab him again as Braedan mercilessly revved the BSA's engine and let out the clutch.

'Whoo-hooo!' Hope was laughing as they roared past the Ford. The driver honked his horn in annoyance as they overtook him illegally, roaring up his left-hand side. Hope turned and raised two fingers at him.

Braedan cut across to First Street, and then turned into Speke. He stopped the bike amid a line of cars and a few other motorcycles outside a sign for Club Tomorrow. She'd heard of the place but never been into it. She got off the bike and Braedan took the helmet from her. A young white man with short hair was leaning one hand against a shopfront a couple of doors down. Hope heard the deep throb of a bass beat coming from the door to the club, and saw a flight of stairs leading down. It looked like the place was in a basement.

'Is this some troopie dive?' she asked.

'Of course,' he said, grinning. 'Do you want to eat first?'

'No, I ate at George and Susannah's already.'

'Good, eating's cheating.'

'Braedan,' she said, running her fingers through her now dishevelled hair, 'I'm not getting involved in any drinking games and I'm not flying to Kariba tomorrow with a *babelaas*.' She wasn't a good flyer at the best of times, and the last thing she wanted to do was get on a Viscount with a hangover.

'Sure. No problems. I'll pour you home safely.'

She laughed. 'I'm serious, hey?'

'I thought that, until you gave the finger to that *oke* in the Ford. Wait till I tell Tate.'

'You wouldn't dare!'

He grinned, a wide streak of pure mischief. It made her laugh again.

He led her inside and as they walked down the stairs the music grew louder, until she could feel it throbbing in her chest. Inside the club smelled of cigarette smoke, sweat and perfume. The lights were low, but behind the cocktail bar was a long fish tank filled with cichlids. She'd had some of the little brightly coloured tropical fish when she was younger – they'd come from Lake Malawi and Lake Tanganyika. It seemed the place was aiming for an under-the-sea theme, but as they moved past the bar and the dining area, where no one seemed to be sitting, the music hit them full blast and destroyed any illusion of marine tranquillity. A crowd of guys were on the dance floor, in front of the stage, raising their fists in the air. The long-haired members of the band were doing a Queen cover, thrashing their heads as they sang, *We will, we will . . .*

'Fuck you!' yelled the guys in the unison.

Despite herself, Hope smiled. 'I did warn you,' Braedan said.

He pushed his way through the crowd back to the fish tank bar and ordered her a drink.

Braedan downed his beer in one long gulp. 'Drink up.'

'No,' she yelled over the music.

He shrugged and went back to the bar and returned with another beer, which he drank as quickly as the first.

'Are you trying to get drunk as quickly as possible?'

'Yes.'

She shook her head. 'Why?'

'Because I'm with you.'

'Thank you very much. Charming.'

He laughed. 'No, you don't understand. You're beautiful, Hope.'

It hung there between them, and it was as if all the chatter and the music and the singing in the club had stopped. 'Braedan, I'm –'

He held up his hands. 'What I meant was that I can only dance when I've had a few drinks, and as I have to dance with you, I need more beer.'

She shook her head as he went back to the bar. When he was there he turned to look back at her. Hope drained her glass and held it over her head. He smiled and nodded, then threaded his way back with another beer and a glass of champagne for her.

The band were taking a break, after a loud round of applause and cheering, and a DJ stepped up to the stage and put on a record, which encouraged a few girls to move out onto the dance floor as the familiar opening riffs produced a few impromptu cheers.

Braedan handed her the champagne, and although he didn't finish this beer in one gulp, he downed half of it before he spoke again. 'Come. Dance with me.'

'No, caveman.'

'Come.'

'No!'

Braedan finished his third beer and strutted out towards the dance floor. The DJ had put on the Bee Gees' 'Night Fever'. Braedan looked around and grabbed a man's sports jacket from the back of his chair as he passed. Before the man could stop him, Braedan was in the middle of the dance floor doing a John Travolta impersonation. He swung the jacket around over his head and as its owner stood and moved towards him, he flung the jacket back with a 'Thanks, *boet*! Buy you a beer.'

Hope had followed Braedan to the edge of the seething crowd, which applauded and cheered on his moves. She'd worried his stunt with the jacket might degenerate into a fight, but now she was laughing, despite herself.

Braedan held out his hand to her and several pairs of eyes fixed on her. Hope felt her face flush and she shook her head vigorously.

'Go on!' the girl next to her yelled over the music. 'He's *gorgeous*! If you don't want him, I'll have him.'

Braedan had both his hands out, beckoning her. More and more people were clapping and cajoling her to join him. The girl who had offered to step in started swinging her hips and boogying out in Braedan's direction. Hope looked at the other woman, downed her glass of champagne and strode out onto the dance floor. The crowd roared.

Afterwards, hot and breathless, she told him to ask her properly next time if he wanted her to dance with him.

'I will,' he said. 'Drink?'

'Yes. Cane and coke this time, please.'

'Ah, spook and diesel it is, then.' He grinned his boyish, sexy, wicked grin again. Braedan led her back to the bar and they found a spot at the end, away from the crush of people ordering and where they could hold a conversation without having to yell over the music. Over their drinks he asked her about Cape Town, and university, and what she wanted to do with her life.

'Travel, first,' she said. 'Before settling down. What about you?'

'I've already done some travelling.'

'Really? Where?'

'I've been on a few day trips to Mozambique.'

She laughed, although she'd been trying not to talk about the war. 'What will you do when it's over?'

He shrugged. 'I don't know. Farm, maybe, if they'll let us white *ouens* keep some land. One thing's for sure, I'm not letting any gook kick me out of my own country, and I'm not taking the chicken run.'

Hope was surprised. 'So you don't think we'll win?'

'I might be a soldier, but I'm not stupid. Smithy's already sold us down the river by letting Muzorewa take over. The blacks won't be satisfied with the bishop, so it won't end until Mugabe or Nkomo are running the country. We're killing them by the hundreds – the gooks that is – out in the bush, but the men in suits will sign our lives away.'

'But you keep on fighting? Why don't you leave . . . go to South Africa, or overseas?'

Braedan shook his head and drank some beer. 'This is all I know. It's all I'm good at.'

'I hate it . . . the killing, the suffering . . . What? Why are you looking at me like that?'

Braedan drained his drink. 'You think they should win – *kumbaya* and all brotherhood of man bullshit.'

'I think Smith is kidding himself if he thought the blacks were prepared to wait indefinitely for independence. They have right on their side, Braedan. They're the majority of the population and most of them don't have the right to vote.'

'Right? Like the men that kidnapped Natalie. They were right, hey?'

She shook her head. 'They were animals.'

'You'll get no argument from me.'

Hope stared at her drink. Her head was feeling fuzzy. She looked up at him. There was something about him . . . something dangerous. He was staring at her. 'What's it like . . . to kill a man?'

'That's the question you're not supposed to ask and I'm not supposed to answer truthfully.'

'Truthfully?'

'When I shot the man who was holding Natalie, I was higher than anything this can give you,' he held up his glass, 'or morphine, or grass. What's it like?' He set his glass down on the bar and leaned in closer to her. 'I fucking loved it.'

Hope felt a chill run down from the top of her spine to the base. She could feel herself buzzing from the alcohol, but it was more than that. There was something fascinating about this man, something so different from his brother. Her chest felt constricted, almost as if it was hard for her to breathe, and she felt the chill supplanted by a warmth that radiated up to her face. She felt it down low, too, in her core, below the pit of her belly. He held out his hand and slipped off his bar stool. She took it and followed him wordlessly back into the crush of sweating, swinging bodies.

They danced again, and then to the last song of the night. It was an old Frankie Valli and the Four Seasons hit that had been made popular by the Vietnam War movie, *The Deer Hunter*. Braedan held her tight and she rested her head on his shoulder. She could feel his erection. God, she thought to herself, this couldn't be happening.

They hardly spoke a word as they left the club. Hope climbed onto the bike and wrapped her arms around him. Braedan raced through the near-empty streets of Salisbury, but cut the engine to coast up to George and Susannah's home. The house was surrounded by a high wall that George had only recently built. Hope was sure he was scared of Natalie being abducted again, although the chance of that was virtually zero in the city.

Braedan pulled on the brakes and Hope climbed off, taking off her helmet. She knew she should just say goodnight and ring the buzzer to be let in. Instead, she stood there. Braedan kicked down the bike's stand and got off. He came to her and reached out, brushing a strand of hair from her face.

'You're beautiful.'

'Don't, Braedan . . . don't say that.'

'I –'

She put a finger to his lips and he understood. He took her and kissed her, hard, and she opened her mouth to him. She'd felt it since they stopped talking, since he held her on the dance floor. She knew it was wrong, but she was overcome with greed for him.

They moved to the wall and he continued kissing her as he

undid the button of her jeans. The zip came down as he slid his hand into her pants. She was embarrassed at how ready she was for him. He found her and she ground against him as he rubbed and rolled her clitoris between his fingers. His lips on hers muffled the sound of her orgasm.

Hope was breathing hard, unsteady on her feet as he turned her around. She put one hand out, her palm flat on the rough stucco. She reached back with her other as he was pulling his cock out of his jeans. She guided him into her from behind and grunted as he slid inside her.

She reached around her back, wanting to touch him, but at the same time not wanting to see him. He was rough with her, but she didn't care, even as her arm bent and she felt her face pressed against the wall. She needed it to be like this. She wanted to feel as though he had forced her into this, but at the same time she couldn't get enough of him. It was so wrong. Hope felt her second orgasm building inside her and bit her lip to stifle her cry as he grabbed her hips and forced himself deeper inside her.

The Viscount lurched as it hit another updraft, then settled with a screech of rubber on tarmac. Hope opened her eyes. The businessman with the hairpiece was grinning at her.

'See, nothing to worry about. Are you here on holidays?'

She ignored him and stared out the round window. The aircraft slewed around and she could see Tate, in his national parks khakis, standing at the low fence. He had a bouquet of flowers in one hand. He was waving with the other.

Oh God.

Everyone else on the aircraft was eager to get out and start their holiday on the Rhodesian Riviera. There was the promise of waterskiing and sailing on the lake, game viewing, and gambling and partying at the Carribea Bay casino. Hope was the last one to get up and shuffle down the aisle. The heat hit her and sucked the air from her lungs. She felt as though she couldn't breathe.

She walked down the stairs, holding the railing for support, and ignored the hostess's practised smile. Tate high-stepped over the fence and ran across the tarmac and folded her in his arms. Hope started to cry.

'What is it, my girl?'

I'm not your girl, she thought. She'd gone through all the options on the plane. She would say nothing; she would confess all; she would break it off with Tate; she would ask his forgiveness. She still had no idea which one to choose.

'What's wrong?' he asked again as he shepherded her inside the small terminal. The other passengers were milling about, waiting for their bags to be brought in on a trolley pushed by an African porter.

'Nothing. It's just . . .'

'What? Why the tears?'

She would hate herself forever if she kept it a secret from him and she would hate herself more if she told him and it crushed him.

Why had she done it? It was more than the sheer animal attraction of the brother, the pure badness of him. She knew some women fell for the wrong men for whatever self-destructive reason, but it was more than that. It was more than the sex, though God knew it was the most intense couple of orgasms she'd had in her life. She knew, standing there in the stuffy, airless little building that she could not live the life Tate had planned for her.

'Tate, I'm sorry.'

The baggage trolley had just been wheeled in and Tate, recognising her bag, was reaching for it. 'Sorry, what was that?'

She started to cry again and he led her by the hand out into the afternoon sun. 'What's wrong? Tell me?'

'Tate . . . I saw Braedan last night.'

He put her bag down, straightened and just stared at her. She knew she didn't have to say more.

Tate put his hands up to his head and clutched at his hair. 'No.'

'Tate . . .'

'No, no, no . . . this can't be happening.'

She changed her mind again. She could make this work. She *did* want to spend the rest of her life with this beautiful, gentle man. He would be a kind, selfless lover and she would want to make love to him every day until they died, to atone for her sin. 'It was nothing, Tate . . . I'm so sorry. Please forgive me.'

He would, she was sure of it. He would be angry. He might cry. She would be ashamed, but he would forgive her.

Tate turned away from her and walked towards a green open-topped Land Rover. He opened the door, got in and started the engine. Hope picked up her bag and walked slowly towards the vehicle. She began lifting her suitcase to put it in the back, but Tate just stared straight ahead, over the windscreen, which was folded flat on the truck's bonnet. Hope couldn't blame him for being angry and sad, and for not helping. Just as she was about to lower her luggage into the rear of the Land Rover Tate let out the clutch and drove off, out of the airport car park.

Hope sat on her suitcase in the shade of a mopane tree for two hours. She didn't know where or how to contact Tate. She'd never called him: all their communication had been by letter. She knew he was working in the Kuburi wilderness area around Kariba, but that was it.

She cried until there were no more tears. When she was done, and she realised he wasn't coming back to fetch her, Hope went into the terminal to the Air Rhodesia booking desk and asked if there were any seats on the return flight to Salisbury.

The girl checked some paperwork. 'It's busy, but we've got two flights this afternoon – there are some bigwigs in town so they've put on another Viscount. I can get you a seat.' Hope nodded and the reservations clerk handed her a green boarding pass.

Hope went to the payphone in the terminal and fed it some coins. She fished the scrap of paper from her handbag and dialled the number.

'Ja,' said the voice on the other end. It was husky from too much drink and too many cigarettes.

'It's me,' she said.

'Izzit? Oh, right. Howzit? This is a surprise.'

'Yes, well . . . I'll be on the five o'clock flight back to Salisbury. Air Rhodesia, flight 825.'

'I'll be there,' Braedan said.

Hope said nothing more and hung up. She sat in the terminal and watched it fill with sunburned holiday-makers in shorts and sandals, as well as a growing group of military men – some in uniform and others in the neatly pressed, slightly unfashionable clothes of soldiers in civvies.

Two armed soldiers walked in and several others got to their feet as Lieutenant-General Peter Walls entered the building. Hope looked up. The jowly features of the General, the chief of the Rhodesian defence forces, were instantly recognisable from his appearances on TV and in the newspapers. Hope hated him and everything he stood for.

The woman who had served Hope at the ticketing counter made an announcement over a tinny-sounding tannoy calling all passengers with green boarding passes to the gate. Hope checked hers and stood. She saw the General and his aides chatting. He held up a red pass. Hope wondered if he might bully his way onto the first flight, but he and his entourage found themselves seats in the terminal instead.

Hope joined the queue of mostly homeward-bound passengers and looked back over her shoulder, hoping against hope that she might see Tate's national parks Land Rover pull up to the terminal entrance. But he wasn't there. The young couple in front of her were holding hands. Honeymooners, she guessed. The man had a small pistol, a .38 she thought, in a holster on the belt threaded through his shorts. She needed to get out of this screwed-up, self-destructive country of hers. South Africa might be home to one of the world's great evils – apartheid – but at least you didn't need to carry a gun to protect yourself.

Hope handed her boarding pass to the same woman who'd issued it to her.

'Your lucky day, hey? Getting a seat and then getting on the first plane.'

Hope said nothing. She didn't feel very lucky at all.

CHAPTER 13

A young man sat in the bush, in the hills near the tiny settlement of Makuti, seventy kilometres from Kariba. He heard the drone of aero engines and lifted the binoculars to his eyes.

One could see forever, up here on the edge of the escarpment, overlooking the giant lake and the Zambezi Valley. It was little wonder the hotel up the road was named the Clouds' End.

He found the aircraft and saw its four engines. He lowered his binoculars and double-checked the torn page from the Air Rhodesia inflight magazine. It was definitely a Viscount. From his canvas satchel he took the marine distress flare, which had been bought in the boating shop at the Carribea Bay marina. He removed the cap, placed it on the base so the pin was in contact with the striker, then pointed it skywards and slapped the cap hard down on the palm of his left hand.

The green flare whooshed towards heaven.

Emmerson Ngwenya, known to the men who served under him as Comrade Beria, saw the flare, even before his spotter confirmed it. Emmerson felt his heart start to beat faster, but he told himself to remain calm.

He lifted the SA-7 Grail man-portable surface-to-air missile launcher onto his shoulder. He licked his lips. Three months on since the bloody contact with the *Skuz'apo* stick west of Bulawayo this was his reward for orchestrating the annihilation of those jackals. Emmerson had risen in the ranks and the esteem of the senior comrades of ZIPRA when he finally made it back across the border to Zambia.

His tale of survival was already being taught to new recruits to the struggle. Ngwenya, it was said, had recognised the traitors of the feared Selous Scouts as soon as he had seen them and had bravely opened fire. Even though he had been wounded, he had engineered the *Skuz'apo* patrol's demise by cunningly firing on a Rhodesian Light Infantry force that was on its way to link up with the scouts. In the confusion that followed, the *kanka* fired on each other. The white racist regime called it a victory, but everyone in Lusaka knew that the security forces had blundered, that *Skuz'apo* were not invincible, and that Emmerson Ngwenya was a hero.

This Ngwenya, the wide-eyed volunteers were further told, crawled away into the bush from the scene of his brilliant work and hid, bleeding from his wound, in the heart of an old baobab for two days. After that he made his way to a rural store, broke in and liberated a bottle of Dettol and some bandages. A bullet had entered his body, after ricocheting off the wooden stock of his AK-47. Its progress slowed, the round entered below his left clavicle, narrowly missing his brave heart and strong lung, and then lodged beneath the skin of his back. This man Ngwenya, the recruits learned, stripped the bark from a thin mopane stick, then reached around to where he could feel the bullet and sliced his own skin. This fearless lion of a warrior tipped Dettol over the stick and then rammed it into the entry wound and pushed until the bullet came out of the fresh cut on his back. It was said Ngwenya nearly passed out as he tipped the burning liquid into the wound, and if a man had stood behind Ngwenya at that moment he might have seen the antiseptic pouring out of the newly created exit wound.

Emmerson rolled his shoulder, the movement an involuntary reflex. His own brother. That was not part of the story, not part of the legend of Emmerson Ngwenya. The comrades would have suspected him, if they knew that Winston had served in *Skuz'apo*. No matter that Emmerson had tried to kill him. At least his traitorous older brother was dead and Emmerson had had the satisfaction of watching the white man, who he now knew from the Rhodesian newspapers to be Corporal Braedan Quilter-Phipps, shooting Winston without knowing his brother was a member of the security forces. Naturally the government had covered up the affair, but Emmerson wondered if Quilter-Phipps – the same boy who had caused him so much trouble at George Bryant's wedding by yelling out in alarm when he had tried to silence Hope – had been told of his mistake.

Emmerson had planned the attack on the Bryant farm out of revenge, and he had hoped to find Hope Bryant, who had cost him long months of freedom, at home. The child would have been a fitting substitute for her aunt, if his mission had succeeded, but Emmerson had taken solace and satisfaction at the private pain the raid had caused the family.

'*My brother . . .*' Emmerson would forever recall Winston saying, just before the *ma-brooka* troopie shot him. My shame, thought Emmerson.

'There it is,' said the spotter.

Emmerson nodded. He had heard the Viscount approaching, the engines still running hard and hot as it climbed towards the southeast. He was in a perfect position for the shot. The setting sun was behind him, which meant the missile would not inadvertently lock on to it, like a mindless Icarus.

Emmerson took a breath and flicked on the thermal battery.

He peered through the optical sight and found the growing spec of the aircraft. The infra-red seeker locked on almost immediately and Emmerson heard the buzzing tone from the grip stock and saw the green light appear in the optical sight.

'Fire,' said the spotter, another particularly devoted comrade who was known for his willingness to dish out swift and savage beatings to comrades who were found guilty of laziness in training, cowardice in battle or reactionary talk. Emmerson wondered if the younger man's sole purpose on this mission was to make sure Emmerson went through with the firing and didn't get any pangs of doubt about shooting down a civilian airliner.

The hated war criminal General Walls was on board this aircraft, and he was ZIPRA's prime target. Emmerson, like the comrades in Lusaka, knew that the deaths of the civilian passengers would also have tremendous repercussions. White resolve, already weakened by years of war, would crumble, and what was left of the Rhodesian tourism industry would collapse. The puppet Muzorewa would see which was the strongest force in Rhodesia, and it was not his army of black and white jackals. And ZANU, headed by the newly crowned Robert Mugabe, would see who had the biggest balls and the strongest stomach for war.

'Quiet,' Emmerson said, ignoring the spotter. The fool probably wanted to be able to tell his children and grandchildren that he gave the order. Emmerson was too smart to shoot too soon. He tracked the aircraft, waiting for the perfect shot. The tone still sounded and Emmerson knew he had sixty seconds of battery time. Plenty.

Emmerson swivelled as the aircraft climbed high and passed over him. When he was facing towards its right-rear quadrant he depressed the trigger on the grip stock halfway. He heard the gyro inside the missile start to spin up, as the seeker was uncaged. He counted the seconds . . . four, five, six . . .

Emmerson pulled the trigger and the ejector charge fired the missile from the launcher.

Hope was staring out the window, again trying to ignore the passenger next her – this time a matronly woman who'd drunk too much before boarding the aircraft and wanted to tell Hope about her stay on Fothergill Island, one of the larger hilltop islands in Lake Kariba, which boasted a safari lodge and bountiful game.

Hope had taken a seat near the rear of the aircraft, on the right-hand side, and thought she might be able to sleep if she could lean her head against the window. It was pointless, though. She kept replaying every word, every second of her unspoken confession to Tate. He'd known straightaway. Unbidden, Braedan intruded into her gloom. She could still *feel* him, for God's sake. She wanted to cry again, but a bright flashing comet of light caught her eye.

Hope lifted her forehead from the window. The woman next to her was talking about a close encounter with an elephant, but Hope wasn't listening. The light raced towards them.

The two hostesses on board, one white and one black, had just got out of their seats and had started to wheel out the drinks cart. 'Hey!' Hope yelled, waving to one of them. The white woman looked up, mildly annoyed, and Hope saw the heads of a few other passengers ahead of her who turned to look at her.

A man yelled something, but Hope couldn't register what it was before the aeroplane erupted. Hope was thrown against the woman next to her as an explosion opened a hole in the right-hand fuselage wall, three rows in front of her. Chunks of metal blasted through the aircraft's skin and punched out the other side. People were screaming and the cabin was filling with smoke. The hostesses were running down the aisle.

Her ears rang. She looked out her window and saw the right inboard engine was on fire, the propeller not turning. Air was whistling in through the multitude of holes ahead of her. Hope felt something wet on her face. When she touched her forehead and inspected her fingers she saw blood. The woman next to her was screaming. Hope ran her fingers over her face again. She felt no pain, no cuts . . . It took her a few seconds to realise the blood had come from someone else. In front, in the rows near where the bomb had hit, she saw blood running from the top of a man's head, which lolled against his seat rest. The man next to him was out of his seat, screaming to the hostess to find a fire extinguisher.

'Get back in your seats!' the white hostess was saying. The black girl was running to the rear of the aircraft.

Hope felt the aircraft lurch and bank, as if it was sliding sideways out of the air. 'My God, my God,' the woman next to her keened, 'we're going to die!'

Hope put her head in her hands. I deserve to, she thought. Hope looked out the window again and saw the fire had spread further out along the wing and that the other engine had now stopped. The aircraft shuddered.

On the flight deck of the Viscount the pilot radioed a Mayday and told anyone who was listening what he was planning on doing. He knew he had to try to extinguish the fires in the two right-hand engines, and to get the aircraft down as quickly as possible. Ahead he could see wide-open tracts of land.

'Cotton farms,' said his co-pilot.

They were west of Karoi, over the Urungwe tribal trust lands. 'Undercarriage down,' the pilot said, moving his hand to the lever. The landing gear apparently hadn't been affected and there was the reassuring clunk and attendant confirmatory lights to tell him the wheels were down. Thank God for something, he thought. 'Brace, brace, brace,' he said over the aircraft's internal intercom system. There was no time for anything else.

Emmerson Ngwenya watched the Viscount turn and lose altitude. Through the spotter's binoculars he saw smoke trailing from the right wing. The hit had been good.

'Come,' he said to the spotter and the ten-man security detail that had been fanned out around the firing point and had now regrouped around Emmerson. 'We must go to the crash site. We have our orders.'

One of the men raised his AK-47 and cheered. It was too soon to celebrate, Emmerson thought. There would be time for that once he knew the job was done properly. They set off at a jog through the bush.

The aircraft bounced back up into the air as soon as its wheels touched the uneven farmland and Hope's stomach was left behind. *I don't want to die*, she told herself. She grabbed her legs tighter and kept her head down on her lap. *I don't want to die.*

The Viscount settled again and when the wheels touched again they stayed on the ground. Hope felt her spirits soar. They were hurtling along and the aeroplane was jiggling and bouncing, and things were raining down out of some overhead lockers that had popped open, but they were on the ground.

Someone cheered.

Then the aircraft cartwheeled and broke in two.

When Hope regained consciousness she felt as though her head was about to explode. It took her a moment to realise she was upside down. Someone near her groaned. She smelled smoke and started to panic.

She fumbled for the clasp of her seatbelt and before she could think through the consequences she crashed head-first into the overhead locker and crumpled to a heap on the aircraft's ceiling. It was gloomy, partly from the encroaching twilight but also from the pall of sickly smelling smoke that had filled the cabin. It was a mix of oily, chemical smells and, oddly, the odour of cooking meat.

Hope put out a hand and shrieked. It was the woman who'd been sitting next to her. Her head was bent at an unnatural angle. Her skin was cold and her eyes lifeless. 'Help me,' Hope coughed, her lungs suddenly full of the smoke. The woman must have undone her seatbelt too early and had broken her neck.

Hope crawled towards an orange glow. It appeared the entire aircraft had broken in two, somewhere near the rear of the fuselage, not far in front of where Hope had been sitting, near the spot where the bomb – or whatever it was – had gone off. Other people were stirring around her. Someone behind her brushed past. It was a man. He was barefoot and he trod on her hand in his rush to get to the light. 'Ow!' Hope protested. She tried to stand herself, then winced with pain as her right ankle refused to take her weight. She dropped to her knees. The man who had pushed her paused, then turned back to her and offered her his hand.

'Sorry,' he said belatedly. He lifted her to her feet.

'My ankle.'

He draped her arm around his shoulder and together they hobbled out of the cabin and into a vision of hell.

Tate had done what he always did when he needed to think. He had driven out into the bush, away from Kariba and up into the hills near Makuti.

He pulled off the road onto one of the firetrails that criss-crossed the Charara Safari Area. As a local ranger he didn't need signs to tell him which path to take. If only life had been the same, he thought, already thinking of it in the past tense.

The track deteriorated as he climbed higher. He stopped the Land Rover and pulled down on the gear lever with the red knob, engaging low-range four-wheel drive. The engine groaned in protest, but slowly he climbed a flight of naturally eroded rock steps to the top of the hill. The sun was just about to hit the horizon. Somewhere off to the west he saw a pall of smoke rising. Probably some native farmer burning his lands.

Ahead of him he could see a sliver of Lake Kariba. Its waters glowed like lava in the sunset's reflection. Tate switched off the engine, opened the door and started to unlace his right boot.

It wasn't just Braedan and Hope, he told himself as he pulled off his boot and unpeeled his sweaty sock from his foot. The slight breeze on his toes felt nice. Funny, he thought, how he was noticing such things at a time like this. He paused to wipe his eyes with the back of his hand. He hadn't wanted to cry, but the tears streamed out anyway.

Losing the only woman he had ever loved had forced him to contemplate his future. Even if he never saw them again he would be forever tormented by the thought, the mental images, of Braedan and Hope living together, getting married, going on holidays, making love and having children.

He would never be able to give his heart over to another woman, to dissect and dangle in front of his face. That was for sure. And what of his job? The blacks were not going to settle for Abel Muzorewa and Ian Smith in a phoney alliance; Mugabe and Nkomo would fight on, and they would win. The heart had gone out of the whites' war. Rhodesians would never die, as the popular saying went, but more and more of them were moving to South Africa or 'taking the gap' to Australia instead.

When the Africans took over Zimbabwe–Rhodesia, as the country was now known, the whites in government jobs, like Tate, would be expelled or, at best, passed over for promotion and relegated to menial positions. Other rangers had talked of going elsewhere in Africa and getting jobs as safari guides or professional hunters, but Tate didn't like people enough to follow either of those paths. He loved wildlife, and he had made the mistake of loving one woman.

Tate reached behind the Land Rover's seats to the gun rack and lifted out the FN. He grasped the cocking handle with his left hand, yanked it back and then released it, letting the working parts fly forward. At least he would do something right – he didn't want to get a double feed and jam the rifle when he needed it most. He flipped the safety catch to 'fire'.

Tate placed the steel butt plate of the FN in the dirt, beside the open door of the vehicle and, still sitting in the driver's seat, dangled his legs out and inserted the big toe of his right foot into the trigger guard. He leaned forward until the soft skin under his lower jaw was pressed firmly against the rifle's muzzle.

He started to lower his foot and felt the pressure being taken up on the trigger, under his toe.

'Hope,' he said out loud.

Braedan checked his watch again. Hope's flight was late, but there had been no announcement. He went to the bar and ordered a beer while he waited for news about the delay.

A man in shirtsleeves and shorts and long socks walked in, went to the bar and ordered a double Scotch. When the barman served him the man raised the glass, drained it and then ordered another.

Braedan was ready for another beer, so he sauntered over to the bar. He noticed the Scotch drinker was ashen-faced.

'Have you heard the news?' the man asked.

Braedan shook his head.

'The flight from Kariba . . . it's missing.'

Makuti was running, snapping branches and flattening small trees under his tonne of bone and muscle.

He had smelled human, which was cause enough for worry, but when the lights and the smoke had lit up the evening sky he had taken panicked flight in the opposite direction. He hated fire, and the smell of burning was still in his nostrils as he ran.

Makuti huffed and snorted as he climbed higher into the hills and the gradient became steeper. In the past few years he had had to move further and further inland from the lake where he'd been born. There were more humans, more death, more noise than ever before.

He wasn't built for the hills, but he had adapted. The climbing had kept him fit and he had become adept at seeking out the thickest stands of bush, more often than not in deep gullies, which were closer to the habitat he should have been living in, on the floor of the river valley that was now a lake. He'd learned the patterns of the humans as well. He liked to use the tracks they had cleared, for it allowed him to cover greater distance in his nightly feeding forays, and he had learned which pathways were busy and which were often travelled by humans on foot or in their machines.

He sniffed the air. There was more smoke; it was the kind he associated with men and machines. That was not normal for the steep path he made his way onto now, but he needed to climb higher and move deeper into his territory, and quickly. Behind him the sun was setting. He needed to get over the crest of this hill and into the protection of the thicket in the valley beyond. There he would be safe. For now.

Makuti made it to the top of the *gomo* as the glowing red ball was disappearing. He stopped. His eyesight was not good, but his sense of smell was excellent. There was something ahead, a blurred outline of a shape not natural to the land, and that terrible scent again: smoke, sweat and oil – the smell of man.

Tate heard the snort and raised his head. He could feel the circular impression of the tip of the rifle's barrel under his chin.

He'd waited until the sun was just about gone. The setting sun of his own life, he thought, and had enough of a sense of humour left to quietly chastise himself for being so melodramatic.

Tate knew that sound. There, silhouetted against the glow cast up by the disappearing sun, was *Diceros bicornis*. A black rhino bull. The rhino lifted his head and sniffed the air, his body tensed. He knew Tate was there, but Tate knew enough about rhinos to know that the animal probably couldn't see him.

Tate felt a jolt of adrenaline and pure fear zap from his heart out to his fingertips and toes. Odd, he thought. He lifted his toe slightly to release the pressure on the FN's trigger. Odd that his body would produce adrenaline at the moment he was about to end his life. Why be scared of a rhino when he was going to kill himself? He watched the beast for long seconds, seeing its indecision. It wanted to pass, to cross the top of the steep hill it had climbed, but he knew there was something in the way, something potentially dangerous.

He needed to get to the other side of the hill, Tate thought. If he shot himself he'd spook it and it would run back the way it had come, all the way down that bloody great hill. Tate had chosen the crest of this particular hill because of its beauty and inaccessibility. It was the highest for miles around, knife edge at the top, with barely enough flat space to park the Landy. There was a near-sheer drop-off on either side of the roadway. If the rhino wanted to pass him, it would be no more than two or three metres from him.

The rhino sniffed and snorted again, then took a couple of tentative paces forward and stomped the ground with his right front foot.

Tate kept perfectly still. Black rhino were notoriously aggressive and unpredictable. When in doubt, they usually charged. He was half out of the vehicle and any movement he made to get back in and close the door might spur the creature to action.

He gave a snort of his own as he contemplated the ridiculousness of his situation. The rhino heard him, tossed his head and blew more air out of his nostrils. He trotted forward and Tate eased his toe out of the trigger guard as carefully and quickly as he could, and slowly swung his leg back inside the Land Rover.

The rhino charged.

Tate slammed his door closed, although he knew the aluminium panels would be like cardboard to the long wicked horn. He struggled to bring his rifle up to bear, but just as he got it up to his shoulder he saw the bulk of the rhino flash past the bonnet of his vehicle.

He lowered the rifle. Tate's heart was thumping and he could feel the vein in his neck pulsing so hard he thought the blood might explode from it. He'd yet to be this close to one of these magnificent creatures. It could have killed him. He'd thought its reaction would be to come for him, to try to bulldoze him out of the way, but it had seen him, finally, as it closed on him and had veered away at the last second, seeing a way around.

The rhino had conquered his fears and his natural distrust of man, and if he could overcome these instincts then so, too, could Tate. He looked at the rifle in his hands and switched the safety catch back to 'safe'. He opened the door of the Land Rover again and retrieved his shoe and sock, all of a sudden feeling foolish.

While Tate was tying his bootlace the radio crackled to life. It was national parks headquarters at Kariba.

'Tate here, over,' he said.

His boss, the senior ranger, identified himself by his call sign and asked for Tate's location, which he gave. 'Tate, we need you on the ground. A civilian aircraft's gone down, not far from you.'

The bile rose in Tate's throat and he swallowed hard. 'What kind of aircraft, over?'

'A Viscount, en route to Salisbury.'

CHAPTER 14

The girl was eight and her name was Sandra. She'd howled and screamed for her mother and now she sobbed, her head nestled against Hope's breast. Hope winced as the doctor tightened the makeshift bandage – someone's bath towel torn into strips – around her ankle.

'That's the best I can do,' the doctor said as he knelt in front of them.

'I'll be fine,' Hope said.

'The girl?'

Hope shrugged. 'Physically, Sandra's OK, but . . .'

The doctor nodded. He wiped his hands on his blood-stained shirt. 'We're going now. I wish we could take you with us, but we have to move quickly. We'll be back in no time at all.'

'I'll be all right,' Hope said.

He nodded. 'I know you will be.' He lowered his voice to a whisper. 'Between you and me, the women are holding up much better than the men. Keep an eye on the others for me, won't you?'

Hope nodded. She had no idea why the doctor thought she would be any stronger than the other injured survivors. It had been a godsend having a doctor on board. He'd calmed the survivors and organised them, then set about bandaging bleeding heads, splinting a broken leg with a branch cut from a tree at the edge of the cotton field, and relocating a dislocated shoulder.

'Take this.' The doctor held out a snub-nosed revolver and Hope stared blankly at it. 'I found it . . . I think you should keep it, for protection. It'd make me feel better about leaving.' The surviving passengers had discussed their plight and decided that those who were able would set off on foot to try to find a farmhouse or village, or a main road to flag down a passing car.

Reluctantly she took the pistol from him, then laid it beside her in the furrowed dirt. The doctor stood and joined a group of a dozen men and women who were standing in the gloom by the severed tail section of the Viscount, waiting for him. They set off. Hope suddenly felt very afraid.

The hours dragged. An elderly man whose head had been gashed by flying shrapnel from the missile came and sat with Hope and Sandra. The six other injured passengers were all lying or seated nearby, amid the scattered wreckage and piles of bags, which the able-bodied survivors had taken from the baggage hold.

The man sat down next to Hope. 'Do you think the rescue party will be coming soon?'

Hope had no idea. 'I'm sure they won't be long.' The man asked the same question a few minutes later.

Hope nibbled on some peanuts and tried unsuccessfully to get Sandra to eat something. The girl was curled up into the foetal position now under a thin airline blanket, her head pillowed on a backpack. Hope found a bottle of Coca-Cola, which she insisted the confused man drink.

Far off, she heard a dog bark. Hope eased herself away from Sandra. The girl stirred. 'I'll be back in a few minutes – I just need to go check on the others.'

'Can I come with you?' Sandra asked as Hope stood.

'No, my girl. Just sit there. I won't be long. Promise.'

Hope hobbled across to a pile of emergency equipment that had been salvaged from the Viscount. She found a torch and switched it on.

'Don't go far,' a male voice said from the knot of survivors.

'I won't.' She needed to pee, and she was curious about the dog barking. Did that mean someone was on their way? Rescuers perhaps?

Hope found a length of metal tubing, about a metre and a half long, lying in the dirt. It had once served some purpose on the aircraft, but she used it as a walking stick. The uneven ground made walking even harder, and she screwed her eyes shut with the pain of placing her injured foot down at a wrong angle. She walked towards the charred hulk that had been the front half of the aircraft. It was still smoking in places and the smell of it assaulted her. The doctor and a couple of the male survivors had speculated that the Viscount's nosewheel had gone into a drainage ditch that apparently ran across the cotton field, and that this had caused the aircraft to flip.

When Hope rounded the fuselage she wished she'd peed where she was and waited for the rescuers to find her. She dropped to her knees and threw up.

The beam of her torch had picked out three charred black lumps. It had taken her brain a few seconds to realise she was looking at the remains of human beings – people she'd been queuing with just hours before. She raised a hand to her mouth, gagged, then dry-retched. Tears streamed down her cheeks.

Hope climbed to her feet and turned away from the horror. She had to get back to little Sandra. She started to walk, but froze when she heard voices. She listened to the noise on the faint breeze. They were men's voices, and they were speaking an African language.

*

The troop sergeant was issuing his orders as he tightened his parachute harness straps. 'An Air Rhodesia flight's made a forced landing west of Karoi, and we're –'

'The flight from Kariba, right?' Braedan interrupted.

'No, the fucking flight from Moscow,' the sergeant said, his annoyance at being interrupted halfway through his briefing plain.

Braedan shut up and saddled up. Two RLI Fire Force teams and an SAS stick were being scrambled and the troop sergeant and troop commander, a newly graduated lieutenant, would be jumping with Braedan and his stick. It was an indication of the seriousness of the situation. Braedan barely registered the details of the orders. All he could think about was Hope.

'Move it!' the sergeant barked.

Braedan walked across the tarmac towards the rear of the Dakota. The air-traffic control tower was silhouetted by the first pinks of the new day. He bent his head as he entered the hot, oily-smelling prop wash of the aircraft's port engine. He grabbed the ladder and climbed up inside the ageing aircraft.

He told himself that she was alive, and that he would find her.

Tate stood on the Land Rover's brake and clutch pedals as the figure emerged from the darkness into the cone of his headlights and started waving. He'd been briefed to head towards the rough location of the crash site and the drive had given him more time to clear his head and think through what he would do next. People needed his help, and so too, he realised, did Hope. He'd been childish to leave her stranded at the airport. He needed to talk to her, and he needed to confront his bastard of a brother, but all that could wait. For now, he was still praying Hope hadn't been able to get on a flight back to Salisbury so soon.

'Help us!' the man called.

Tate climbed out of the vehicle. The man rushed to him.

'We're survivors from a plane crash. My God, I'm so glad to see you.' More wild-eyed figures emerged from the bush and crowded him. Tate leaned back into the cab and reported to national parks headquarters at Kariba that he had found thirteen of the passengers alive with a range of minor injuries. Nine more people were still at the crash site and they all needed medical attention.

'Roger, Tate,' the senior warden replied. 'The army's on their way to the crash site. Police will meet you at the main road. Take the survivors there and wait for the cops, over.'

'What about going to the crash site? I say again, there are injured people there, over?'

'Negative, Tate. Leave it to the army. Those people have been through hell, man. Get them to safety.'

Tate held the handset and thought about what he should do.

He turned to the dark-haired man who seemed to be the leader of the group of stragglers, some of whom were climbing into the back of his Land Rover in anticipation of their ride to safety. 'Was there a woman on the flight . . . blonde, about five-eight . . . very pretty? Her name is Hope . . .'

The man nodded. 'Hope Bryant.'

Tate gripped the edge of the truck's door for support. 'Is she . . .'

'She's all right. She's got a possible fractured ankle, but Hope's very much alive.'

'Thank God.'

'Do you know her?' the man asked.

Tate paused a moment. 'Yes, she's my girlfriend, and I love her, and I've got to get to her.'

'We should go to the crash site,' the man said, loud enough

for the rest of the survivors to hear. 'It's about six kilometres from here, on a cotton farm.'

'No, Doc!' said another man from the rear of the Land Rover where the group was already crammed in, some having to stand. 'You just heard the radio. The army guys are on their way. Let's get back to Kariba.'

Tate looked at the man, apparently a doctor, who shrugged at him. 'The main road's straight ahead,' Tate said, pointing down the rutted gravel track he'd been driving on. 'You drive.'

'But your orders?'

'Just do it,' Tate said. He reached behind the seats and pulled out his FN and a map. He had the doctor show him the approximate site of the crash. 'Tell them I've gone in on foot.'

'You're mad,' the doctor said.

Tate didn't disagree.

Braedan steered his parachute into the negligible breeze and pulled down on the rear risers to flare the leading edge of his canopy. He brought his knees and ankles together and tucked in his arms. He tried to concentrate on his imminent landing, rather than the scene of carnage he'd witnessed from the air.

His boots hit the churned earth and he rolled onto his right side. The police had already arrived at the crash site, so there was no risk of an opposed landing.

Braedan and the rest of the men from the Fire Force and SAS sticks rolled their parachutes and strode across to the wreckage of the Viscount. He'd seen plenty of dead people in the past year, but his heart was pounding as he braced himself for what he might encounter.

Braedan slowed as he approached a group of police dressed in a mix of blue uniforms and camouflage fatigues. He could see the line of bodies at their feet, surrounded by opened suitcases and rucksacks. Clothing and personal possessions were strewn all around. A man knelt at the end of the line of dead passengers. He had his head in his hands, but even from this distance Braedan recognised the lanky frame of his own brother.

'Jesus Christ.'

Braedan ignored the lieutenant's words and the sergeant's barked orders for the rest of the stick of troopers to stop gawping. He walked straight past the police to Tate and stopped a couple of metres from him.

Hope was lying on her back in front of him. Braedan saw the blood on her belly and her chest, and he knew immediately that she had not died in the aircraft crash. His right fist clenched around his FN. As God was his witness he would kill the cunts that did this.

Tate lifted his head from his hands and turned to look at him. His face was painted with tears and dust and a string of drool hung from the left side of his mouth. His hair was wild and he looked like what he was – a man who had had everything taken from him.

Braedan lowered his rifle, butt to the ground, and held the flash suppressor loose in his right hand. He looked down at Hope. Her eyes were wide with a look Braedan had seen before – the knowledge that what was happening to her was real, not a nightmare.

He said nothing. What could he say?

Tate's speed and strength surprised him. One second he was an incoherent dribbling mess and the next he was leaping like a lion, hammering both fists into Braedan's chest, punching the air from him and toppling him backwards. Braedan's FN clattered to the dirt. Someone shouted behind him.

Tate slammed a fist into Braedan's face and he yelled as blinding pain and the snap of cartilage told him his nose had been broken. Braedan grabbed a handful of his brother's uniform and tried to push him off. Tate lashed out with another wild blow, but Braedan half-rolled under him, avoiding the punch. Tate tried again, but as Braedan started to sit up he brought his knee up at the same time and drove it into Tate's groin. His brother gasped and rolled off him. He lay in the dirt, doubled with pain.

Braedan got to his feet and gingerly touched his smashed nose. He spat blood, then reached his hand out to his brother. 'Come, sit up. Keep your head down, though.' To Braedan's surprise, Tate clasped his hand. He pulled his brother up into a sitting position.

'Quilter-Phipps!'

Braedan turned at the sergeant's bark this time.

'What the fuck's going on. Who is that man?' The sergeant was striding towards him, his face brick red with anger.

'My brother, Sarge. He's –'

Braedan turned to gesture down at Tate and was too late to sidestep the swinging rifle. Tate was on his knees and was wielding his FN by the barrel, like a club. The pistol grip smashed into Braedan's shin and he howled with pain and dropped to one knee.

Tate was on his feet in a flash, spinning the rifle as he rose. When Braedan looked up he saw Tate was pointing the weapon at him. He spat more blood. 'Put it down.'

'No.'

Braedan got to his feet, but didn't close the distance between himself and his brother. He stood there.

'What the bloody hell,' the sergeant said. He raised his own weapon. 'Put that rifle down, man. Now!'

Tate ignored the military man and aimed at Braedan's heart. He blinked away the last of his tears. 'You killed her.'

Braedan shook his head. 'Look, I'm sorry about what happened. I told her not to tell you, but she obviously did.' Tate risked a glance back at Hope's body. Braedan didn't seize his chance. He just stood there, hands by his side. 'She told me she loved you.'

'Shut up,' Tate said, barely audibly.

'She sounded miserable when she called me. She said she wanted me to pick her up from Salisbury Airport.' Braedan wiped more blood off his top lip.

'I should kill you now,' Tate said.

'Put the gun down, son,' the sergeant said, softer this time.

Braedan didn't turn, but sensed the experienced soldier was slowly circling closer. Tate paid the other man no mind.

Braedan thought, but didn't say, that his brother didn't have the balls to pull the trigger. Braedan didn't care. He'd faced stronger, tougher men in battle and lived. If he was going to die today, like this, then that was that. 'She told you . . . and she asked your forgiveness, didn't she, Tate?'

His brother licked his lips and blinked a few times. The tears started rolling again. Braedan couldn't remember the last time he had cried. Fuck. It was embarrassing. 'You cold, heartless bastard,' he said to Tate. 'She confessed to you and you rejected her, so she got on this bloody plane. She was coming to me not because of a one-night stand, but because you dumped her.' Braedan turned, walked three paces and picked up his own rifle.

'Stop!' Tate screamed. 'Why did you do it . . . why did you do that to her . . . to me?' Braedan could hear Tate was sobbing, but he didn't turn around to look at him. He just walked away, back to the war.

PART TWO

Zimbabwe

CHAPTER 15

Tanzania, 2009

Tate Quilter-Phipps raised the Dan-inject dart rifle to his shoulder and leaned out of the helicopter's hatch. The slipstream blasted him cool for a blessed few moments.

Victoria Regan, the South African pilot, brought the chopper down lower, until they were no more than ten metres from the rhino, above and to the left of the galloping cow. Victoria was an expert pilot – a former military flying instructor who now specialised in game capture. She bled off a little speed until Tate was positioned just aft of the animal as she charged along the short-grass plains within sight of the granite Moru Kopjes at the western edge of Tanzania's Serengeti National Park. Victoria reported that their speed was twenty knots, matching the rhino's.

'Steady,' Tate said into the microphone of his headset. Tate aimed the red dot of the sight mounted atop the dart gun on the muscle of the cow's upper left leg. He curled his finger around the trigger and got ready to pull it. He knew from experience that if he started to squeeze the trigger gradually, as one did with a rifle, air would begin escaping from the gun, lessening the power of the shot.

The rhino veered suddenly to the right, to escape a termite

mound, and Victoria made a smooth correction to keep Tate in the same position. Tate pulled the trigger in a single rapid motion, but just as he did so the young girl beside him suddenly lurched into his left side. The dart flew wide, missing the rhino by a good metre.

'Zoe!' he yelled. 'What the hell?' He leaned back into the helicopter and saw the American girl was on her knees, trying to retrieve her expensive Nikon camera from the floor.

'OK back there?' Victoria asked via the intercom.

'No. Take her up.' Tate swore and shifted his right leg in out of the slipstream. He made no move to help the girl. 'Get in your seat and put your seatbelt on,' he snapped.

'Sorry,' she said, sitting up again 'I just wanted to get a picture and –'

Tate held up a hand to silence her. 'I told you to keep your seatbelt on at all times. We're causing this animal enough stress as it is. Now I have to prepare another dart. Stay seated next time, all right?'

'I'm so sorry.' The twenty-two-year-old undergraduate from California buckled her seatbelt, her lip trembling.

Tate busied himself sliding the plastic fishing tackle box from under his seat so he wouldn't have to deal with her juvenile behaviour any more. He took out a sixty-millimetre needle and slipped a circular red plastic sleeve over the closed point, so that it covered the two small side ports located near the tip. He worked with practised ease, despite a frantic grab for the next dart's components as the helicopter hit an updraft of hot air. Once Victoria had her flying straight and level again Tate opened another compartment in the box and extracted a dart and a pre-loaded syringe fitted with a spinal needle. He injected the four milligrams of Etorphine into the dart's chamber.

'That's the M99, right?'

Tate ignored the girl's question. He knew Zoe was smarting from his rebuke and was now trying to impress him with her meagre knowledge in the hope that he might forgive her and start to like her. She was doomed on both counts.

'It looks like you're using the same dose as this morning, for the white rhino,' she said, leaning closer to him again. 'Isn't that a lot of Etorphine for an animal half the weight of the white?'

Tate frowned. It was a good question and she was right to notice the heavy dose of M99, the common name for Etorphine. 'Despite the difference in their sizes,' he said into the intercom, 'the black rhino has a justifiable reputation for being far more aggressive than the white, and the rule is never skimp on the M99. You want to put a black down fast, not only for your own safety, but also the animal's.'

'I see,' Zoe said.

Tate added the sixty milligrams of the tranquilliser Azaperone to the dart. 'The M99 will knock the rhino down, and the Azaperone will keep it drowsy.' The final ingredient in the cocktail was an enzyme, Hyalase, which would help the other two drugs be absorbed more rapidly. Next he fitted the needle to the end of the dart.

From the tackle box Tate took a large empty syringe and used it to pressurise the dart by pumping air into it until the red rubber stopper was seated firmly behind the chamber containing the immobilising agents. Finally, he fixed a bright pink 'fluffy' to the end of the dart and slid the whole thing into the butt of the airgun. Tate screwed the cover into place. 'Ready,' he said to Victoria. 'Stay in your seat,' he cautioned the girl. Zoe nodded.

'There she is. One o'clock,' Victoria called.

Tate looked out and put his right foot on the skid again as

Victoria brought the chopper down. As he'd been preparing the dart Victoria had been herding the rhino, keeping her in the short grass away from the kopjes and some stands of trees and bush, and moving in the direction of the ground party, with whom he'd been liaising. Tate glanced at Zoe to make sure she was behaving herself, then took aim again, laying the sight's red dot on the rhino cow's gluteal muscles, at the top of the left leg, over her pelvis. He pulled the trigger.

'Good hit,' the pilot said.

'Oh my God, Tate, that was awesome.' Zoe laid a hand on his forearm.

Tate shrugged her hand off as Victoria kept pace with the rhino. He'd sensed she'd find an excuse to touch him again. He hated people invading his personal space and if she kept it up he would need to have words with her.

'Wow, you're such a good shot,' she persisted in his headphones. 'I can shoot, too. My dad taught me. Do you think maybe I could dart the next rhino?'

'No.'

Tate could see the pink fluffy bobbing on the rhino's hide and the black rubber at the end of the plunger was now forward inside the dart's clear plastic chamber, telling him the drugs inside had been injected. It looked like a good hit. He hit the timer button on the digital stopwatch hanging from a lanyard around his neck.

'How long will it take for the rhino to drop?' Zoe asked.

'Three to eight minutes.' Tate didn't take his eyes off the animal. The rhino's charge had eased to a loping gate. Instead of avoiding a small bush in front of her, one of the few on the plain, she ran right over the top of it – a sure sign she was affected by the drugs. Two minutes later she slowed right down and was moving her legs in an exaggerated high-stepping motion. The rhino sank to her knees. 'Take us down, Victoria.'

Victoria made a tight turn and put them on the ground no more than fifty metres away from the rhino. She had done a good job keeping the rhino in open ground, as the cow had been heading for the safety of some thick thorn bush amid a couple of granite boulders and had fallen just short of the cover.

Tate, Zoe and a Tanzanian national parks scout named Teacher climbed out of the helicopter and Victoria lifted off again as they turned their backs to the swirling cloud of dirt, grit and twigs.

Tate had been in Tanzania for a month, supervising the darting of black rhinos in the Ngorongoro Crater and the Serengeti National Park. There had been about a thousand rhinos naturally occurring in the area until the 1980s, but the number of home-grown animals had been reduced to two by poaching. Numbers had been slowly built up in recent years, though, with rhinos translocated from Kenya and South Africa. Tate had been on a team that had brought in new stock from South Africa ten years earlier.

Rhino poaching, a perennial problem in Africa, had experienced a spike in recent times, ever since a Vietnamese government minister had claimed powdered rhino horn had cured his cancer. As if it wasn't bad enough that rhino were still being killed for a supposed cure for impotence and fever, this latest ludicrous claim had sent the market into overdrive. There was new pressure to conserve and protect the remaining populations, including Tanzania's small number of wild animals.

The project he was involved in was part of an ongoing monitoring program, checking the health and numbers of rhinos and fitting VHF radio transmitters. Once an animal was located and immobilised the team of researchers Tate was supervising would get to work installing a transmitter in each rhino's horn. A cavity would be drilled, the transmitter inserted and then the whole thing sealed up with resin.

'Keep watch in that *shateen*, Teacher,' Tate said, pointing to the curtain of thick bush nearby. 'Come,' he said to Zoe.

Tate untied the long strip of white cloth he was wearing like a sash around his waist and handed it to Zoe. 'You put on the blindfold, like we discussed. She's down, but she's not unconscious. She can still respond to visual stimuli and sound, so we want to cover her eyes and keep the noise down. And watch out for her horn, OK?'

Zoe nodded. Tate hoped she would at least get this simple task right.

'Hello, my girl,' Tate said as he approached the rhino. 'Get the blindfold on her, now.' Tate could see Zoe was mesmerised by the mere fact of being so close to the wild creature. That was understandable, but her repeated inability to respond to orders was not. 'Now!'

'OK, OK.'

Tate gripped the rhino's horn and held her sagging head up while Zoe tied the cloth around her eyes. When she was done he lowered the head and began assessing the animal. Tate called to Teacher to come and help them. The cow had come to rest on her chest, with one of her legs tucked up under her body. 'We need to roll her onto her side,' he said to Zoe. 'She's been running flat out for some time and her muscles are producing lactic acid. We need to straighten the legs to allow the acid out and oxygen in, so that the muscles don't produce more. Lactic acid can cause tissue and muscle damage, which can lead to compartmental syndrome, which could cripple her.'

Teacher arrived and the three of them heaved and rolled the

rhino onto her side. 'Good,' Tate said. He unzipped his bumbag and pulled out his stethoscope. The first thing to check was her heart rate. 'Good,' he said to himself. Tate unclipped the hand-held radio from his stout buffalo leather belt. 'Nigel, Nigel, this is Tate, over.'

Tate paused and tried contacting Nigel and the ground party again. There was no answer. He wasn't surprised, as the radios were limited to line-of-sight range and there was a ridge studded with granite kopjes between them. He called Victoria and organised to use the orbiting helicopter as a radio relay.

Zoe was taking pictures of the rhino, but as she had a three-hundred-millimetre lens on her Nikon she had to back up about twenty metres to get her shot. Tate was about to tell her to come back closer to him, but then decided he was better off with her out of the way. Teacher had his back to them. His rifle was balanced on his shoulder and he was gripping it by the barrel. He wasn't a model of efficiency, by any means, but at least he was looking in the right direction.

The rhino had her head lowered and each long exhalation from her nostrils raised mini dust clouds. Her breathing was fine. Tate yanked the dart from her rump and took a tube of antibacterial ointment from his bumbag. He pushed the long nozzle of the tube deep into the puncture wound and squirted until the ointment overflowed. This would prevent a subcutaneous infection under the rhino's thick skin.

He picked up the radio again. 'Victoria, Victoria, Tate . . . ask Nigel how far away he is, over.' Tate stood there sweating, keeping a close watch on the rhino while he waited for the reply. The ground party should be close. Ideally, they didn't want to keep a rhino immobilised for more than thirty minutes. He checked his stopwatch. Ten had passed already.

'Tate, Tate, this is Victoria. Bad news. Nigel says they've just got a puncture. The guys are working to change it as fast as they can, over.'

'Affirmative.' Tate knew there was no point in cursing or telling them to hurry. This was Africa and shit had been happening since the continent was part of Gondwanaland. His number-one concern now was for the rhino. He knelt by its head and grabbed its large front horn in one hand and stroked its big face with the other. 'Hush, my girl. Not long now. Be patient.' He loved these big, prehistoric things more than anything else in the world – certainly more than any human being he'd met in the past thirty years. The rhino let out a long, dozy snort.

Tate crossed his legs and settled himself on his bum, next to the rhino. The girl was still a distance away taking photos. Despite his concern at the delay, he realised there was nowhere else in the world he would rather be. The sky was clear and the Serengeti Plains stretched away to the east for ever and ever. Tanzania was different to his native Zimbabwe and the rest of southern Africa. He'd been to places with a justifiably rich reputation for their densities of game, but nowhere else had matched the sheer spectacle of the natural bounty of the Serengeti during the wildebeest migration. The seasonal movement had passed them now, which made it easier to track and work with the rhino, but he'd been fortunate enough to stand in the middle of the Ndutu Plains and see nothing but wildebeest, zebra and their attendant marauding predators for as far as his eye could see. It was a humbling experience to gaze on nature as she was meant to be . . . well, almost. All that was missing from the landscape were more rhinos, and that was man's fault.

Life was laid bare for all to see on the plains. And death. It was amazing, Tate thought, to see the interactions between predator and prey in the Serengeti and the adjoining Masai

Mara, in Kenya. In his part of Africa predators hunted using an element of stealth. Lion used long grass to get close to their prey, and leopard ambushed impala and bushbuck from the deep cover of thick riverine bush. Here, however, prides of lion lived and moved within plain sight of the animals they fed on. It struck him that, unlike the human world, everyone knew their place. You could see who your enemies were on the short-grass plain, and it was up to you to take the right strategies to avoid them, or face the consequences. No one could sneak up from behind you and steal from you, or deliver a killing blow without you knowing. Unlike in the human world, Tate mused.

Some people, such as Zoe, paid good money to do what Tate did for a living, and he did count himself lucky sometimes. The sadness was always there, however, threatening to drag him down, but as he looked at the drugged rhino and felt her warm breath on the back of his hand he was as content as he could be in this life. He would give her some more Azaperone soon if the ground team didn't arrive just now. If they were delayed further he would call in Victoria, then give the rhino a shot of Naltrexone to reverse the drug, and they would leave her for another day. Tate looked across at Teacher and saw him stiffen. The scout slowly moved the rifle from his shoulder.

'Zoe,' Tate hissed.

'What is it?' Zoe yelled.

'Shush!' He beckoned for her to come to him as he rose to his knees. Teacher held his rifle with the butt into his shoulder, ready to fire. He glanced over his shoulder and mouthed the word 'Kifaru'. It was Swahili for black rhino.

'Shit.' Now was the time to swear.

Zoe turned. 'Oh, my G–'

'Shush!' Tate said, glaring at Zoe.

'Sorry, I –'

Tate held up his hand to her. The radio squawked and he turned down the volume knob and held it to his ear. Victoria was coming back out of a wide circuit. 'Tate, Victoria . . . you've got trouble, man. There's another *bladdy* rhino trotting towards you from the kopjes. Looks a bull.' The other rhino must have been sleeping in the bush between the rocks, Tate thought. He clicked the press-to-send switch once to tell Victoria that he understood and that he was not in a position to talk. He was answered with another click.

Teacher backed slowly towards them. Tate heard the rustle of trees and a loud snort.

'Oh my God!' Zoe said as she saw the black rhino bull emerge from the thorn bushes at a trot. The stupid girl had ignored everything Tate had told her about keeping quiet once they were on the ground, and staying behind him. She was pointing her camera at the newcomer.

The rhino lowered his head and charged.

'Trees!' Teacher raised his rifle to his shoulder and fired a shot into the ground just in front of the animal, but it didn't heed the warning.

Zoe ran towards Tate rather than the nearest tree. He grabbed her by a slender arm and propelled her ahead of him. 'Run! Find a tree and climb it.'

She turned and stumbled, tripping herself up in her panic. Tate dragged her to her feet and glanced back. Teacher's nerve or his faith in his own shooting abilities had failed him, because he was running as fast as he could for the nearest stand of trees.

Zoe screamed, but Tate shoved her forward, away from the oncoming rhino and its attendant dust cloud. He could feel the vibration of its charging feet running up his own legs and pounding in his chest. 'Climb!' he ordered as he thrust her into the trunk of a sapling that barely looked strong enough to carry her weight. She reached up and grabbed a spindly twig that snapped when she pulled down on it. Her red nails scratched at the trunk.

'For Christ's sake, climb!'

'I can't!'

Tate wrapped an arm around the back of her thighs and hefted her up into the stouter branches of the tree. She was tiny and he was able to hike her up onto his shoulder; when she finally managed to grab a bough, he gave her another boost up with a palm under her butt.

Tate didn't need to turn to know the rhino was almost on him. He'd be gored or smashed between that huge skull and the trunk before he could get himself up to the lowest branch. Tate dropped to the ground and wriggled so he was lying on the opposite side of the tree trunk to the rhino. He heard the snorted puffs of angry breathing.

Leaves and small twigs rained down on Tate as he clung to the base of the trunk, trying desperately to become part of the bark that he pressed his face to. Above him, Zoe screamed in terror as the rhino rammed his head into the trunk a second time.

Tate risked a peek around the tree and saw the rhino standing there. More debris landed on him, and he looked up to see Zoe slipping from the perch on which she'd managed to sit. She screamed again and was suddenly hanging from the branch above her, her legs pedalling in midair above the rhino.

'Shit,' Tate said.

The rhino lowered its head again at the new sound and sniffed.

Tate heard the scream of the helicopter's jet engine and the chop of its rotors in the hot air. He looked up and saw that Victoria was banking around, heading towards them. The animal held its ground, but as Victoria flared the chopper again she sent a tornado of dust their way. Grit and sand shrouded everyone's view, including the rhino's. Blinded and frightened, the animal trotted around the tree. Tate heard a scream and thud as Zoe, her arms nearly pulled from their sockets, let slip her grip and fell.

Tate stumbled forward blindly until he found a part of Zoe, grabbed at it and dragged her away. 'Run!' She needed no urging this time and was able to find her feet. She sprinted away.

Tate looked over his shoulder and saw the rhino. It had heard them, and its ears guided it. It turned, seemingly spinning inside its own body length. It was homing in on the sound of Zoe's footsteps and the snapping of twigs in her path.

'Hah!' Tate yelled, waving his arms over his head. 'Hah! Over here!'

The rhino paused and registered Tate as its new target, then charged again. Tate ran for his life, hoping Victoria, who had climbed and begun circling again, could see what he was doing.

Thankfully, it looked as though she had, as Tate turned and saw out of the corner of his eye the helicopter wheel around and set down in front of Zoe. Victoria beckoned to her and pointed to the rear hatch. Zoe jumped onto the skid and dragged herself inside as Victoria started to lift off again.

Tate's arms and legs were pumping, but the rhinoceros quickly gained on him and lowered its head for the kill. Tate saw the shadow of the helicopter sweep over him and suddenly it was in front of him, filling his eyes and ears and mouth with choking grit and dust.

Guessing where the aircraft was and praying he was nowhere near the tail rotor, Tate held his arms out in front of him until his chest slammed into the hovering helicopter's skid. He blinked and yelled '*UP!*' to Victoria, and as soon as she knew he was hanging on she lifted into the air.

Tate registered the rhino passing below him, and if he hadn't bent his knees his feet would have been hooked on its horn. It had been a gutsy move by Victoria to land in the path of a charging rhino, but if she hadn't Tate would have been dead. Victoria flew slowly sideways and then sat the chopper down. Tate scrambled into the back of the helicopter and loaded another dart faster than he'd ever done in his life.

'Let's go get it,' he yelled.

By the time the road party had arrived, Tate was kneeling beside the male rhino, bare-chested and covered in sweat-streaked dirt and dust. He'd used his bush shirt as a makeshift blindfold. Tate issued his orders rapidly, splitting the ground crew into two teams, one for each rhino.

Teacher arrived on the scene, looking shamefaced. Zoe, meanwhile, had stayed in the helicopter after Victoria landed, sitting in the back with her head in her hands. Eventually, she summoned the courage to climb down from her seat and walk tentatively to Tate's side. Tate looked up when he realised she was there.

'Oh my God, Tate . . .'

He saw Zoe's faced was smeared with dirt and streaked with tears. Her chest was rising and falling as she sobbed. 'Oh my God, Tate, you saved my life.' She wiped the back of her hand across her eyes. 'I thought I was going to die and –'

'Get some water.'

'I can clean up when we get back to camp.'

'Not for you.' He glared at her. 'Get some water and wet the rhino's back. We have to keep it cool. These animals are in danger until the drug is reversed and they're back on their feet. Come on, get to work. You're wasting time.'

Zoe started to cry.

*

That evening, on his way back to his tent from the bush shower enclosure, Tate paused in the shadows cast by the flames of the campfire and hissing gas lantern. 'He's probably gay,' Tate heard Zoe whisper from the fireside. A male laughed. Nigel, the British graduate student.

Tate walked into the ring of light and the laughter and conversation stopped.

'Tate, hi,' Nigel said. Zoe raised an enamel mug to her lips and took a deep drink. Tate saw the red in her cheeks and knew it was more than sunburn or the firelight. She had a nasty scratch down one cheek. Perhaps he should have shown her more sympathy.

She coughed as her drink went down the wrong way. 'We were just talking about a professor I knew back at Stanford,' she said.

Perhaps not, he thought. He didn't care what the girl thought of him. It had been clear, since she'd arrived a week earlier, that Nigel had the hots for her. Nigel had been taciturn all week, which was annoying because, unlike Zoe, Nigel was actually a good worker and took the time to learn how to act in the bush. Unlike the girl, he listened.

There were two other people around the fire, Angela, a volunteer from Australia who had paid a substantial amount of money to a rhino charity to come along on the capture operation, and François, a French vet. François and Angela stood and excused themselves, saying it was past their bedtime. Tate didn't know if they were sleeping together, but it wouldn't have surprised him. François had a habit of doing that sort of thing with the volunteers.

Zoe stood. 'Yep, me too. I want to be bright eyed and bushy tailed for tomorrow. I'm sorry about today, Tate, if I was a little slow climbing the tree. Thank you, again, for saving me.'

A little slow? Tate would have laughed if it hadn't been so serious. He could take care of himself in the bush, although he'd used another of his lives today, but if one of the graduate students or eco-tourism volunteers had been seriously injured or killed, the project would have been suspended indefinitely.

'We won't be needing you tomorrow, Zoe,' Tate said.

She set down her mug, next to the near-empty bottle of Captain Morgan Spiced Gold rum, and squared up to him, hands on hips. 'I don't need a rest, Tate. I'm good to go.'

'No, you're not, and I'm not talking about a rest, either. You're off the project, effective immediately.'

'Tate . . .' Nigel said.

Tate held up a hand to the boy. 'I think you should go to bed, Nigel, and give us a moment.'

Nigel shook his head.

'Very well – Nigel, you can be a witness. Zoe, you endangered yourself and other people today by not following the instructions you were given in the briefing. If it was your first day in the bush I could understand it, but the other day you were more interested in getting pictures of the rhino than monitoring its vital signs. On Monday you started giggling while we were stalking the black rhino on foot. You've had your week's probation, but now I'm afraid you're going to have to pack tomorrow.'

'No fucking way!'

Tate was taken aback by her language.

'My father is a major, and I mean *major*, donor to the charity that sponsored this operation, and I have a thesis to research, so you can*not* simply dismiss me out of hand, Tate. I'm not going.'

'Yes, you are, Zoe.' Tate wondered if he was the first person in Zoe's life who had ever said no to her. 'I'll arrange for Teacher to take you to Arusha in the afternoon.'

'You can't do this.'

'I can, and I am.'

'Dr Quilter-Phipps . . .' Nigel began, but the look from Tate silenced him.

'Goodnight to you both,' Tate said.

Zoe started sobbing, as if that might make him reconsider. Tate looked back and saw that Nigel already had his arm wrapped around the girl's shoulders.

Tate left them and walked back to his safari tent. The semi-permanent research camp on the banks of the Mbalangeti River was luxurious compared to some of the places he'd lived and worked at in the past thirty years. Too much of the money raised or donated by people such as Zoe's father went on creature comforts as far as Tate was concerned.

He unzipped the mosquito-mesh door and kicked off his rafter sandals. He winced as he unbuttoned and took off his dirt-and sweat-stained bush shirt. They'd been lucky to escape with their lives today, and while he felt for Zoe, he knew there was no way she could stay on the rhino capture team. She was a spoilt child, which was not her fault, but she also refused to follow the rules.

Tate lay down on his camping stretcher with one arm under his head. A lion started its low, asthmatic calling nearby. He knew there would be repercussions – Zoe had probably already emailed her father – but he didn't care. He closed his eyes and nodded off.

The noise of the zip woke him and he sat bolt upright. 'Who's there?' His rifle was out of reach.

He caught her scent. Shampoo, soap, woman. She zipped the mesh door closed, but there was enough moonlight coming in through the weave for him to recognise her slender silhouette. Tate turned his head slowly to one side. 'Zoe, I –'

'Shush, Dr Quilter-Phipps. I understand why you said what you said before and I, like, totally understand,' she said softly.

'No.'

'Yes. I do, and I'm grateful to you for saving me today, and for teaching me so much, and I want to apologise for being such a brat. I want to make it up to you.' She lifted her green tank top over her head and stepped out of her flipflops. She had no bra on and her young breasts stood firm and high.

Tate swung his legs over the side of the stretcher and ran a hand through his unruly mane of greying hair. 'Go back to your tent, Zoe,' he sighed.

She started unbuttoning her khaki shorts. 'It's all right. I want this.'

'Yes, well I don't. Red light, or whatever you Americans say, OK?'

'Uh-uh. Not OK.'

She let her shorts drop and pulled down her g-string and kicked the flimsy piece of lace across the tent floor. Despite himself he couldn't help but stare for a moment at her smooth bare skin. 'Put your pants on.'

She stood there, naked, with her hands on her slender hips. 'I'll do whatever you want, you know. Just, like, tell me.'

'All right. Get dressed and get out of here.'

'You're serious?' The surprise was clear in her tone.

'Yes.'

She scoffed. 'Oh my God, you *are* gay, aren't you?'

'No, just discerning.' He regretted the words even as he said them.

Zoe stared at him for a few long, silent seconds, then opened her mouth wide and screamed.

By the time Nigel and Teacher arrived, Zoe had put her shorts and sandals back on, and half-replaced her tank top. She'd pulled one shoulder strap until it stretched, but she couldn't tear it; however, when the young men arrived they found her under a tree outside Tate's tent with one breast all but exposed.

'He tried to . . . he tried to attack me,' she sobbed, her hands covering her eyes.

Nigel squared up to Tate in the dark. 'What do you want?' Tate said to Nigel.

'An explanation would be a good start, Doctor.'

'Go back to bed, all of you.'

'I don't think so,' Nigel persisted.

A jackal mocked them from the darkness beyond the camp, its high-pitched keening adding to Tate's growing irritation. He ignored the English boy and turned to the girl instead. 'Blackmail's a dangerous game, Zoe, and it won't work with me.'

Zoe looked at Nigel and her breast rose and fell with a sob. 'He . . . tried to have sex with me.'

'Nonsense,' Tate said.

'I think Zoe deserves to be heard, Dr Quilter—'

Tate rounded on Nigel. 'This is ridiculous. She came into my tent and offered to have sex with me if I'd let her stay on the project. Isn't that right, Zoe?'

She sobbed again. 'How could you say such a thing?'

'Pack your bags, Zoe, you're leaving first thing tomorrow. I'm going to bed.'

Victoria had taken the helicopter back to Arusha to refuel, and when she returned she brought with her Farina Khan, the Tanzanian country manager for the World Nature Fund, which was sponsoring the rhino-monitoring project and paying Tate's consultancy fees.

Tate was in his tent, typing a detailed account of the previous day and night's shenanigans, as it appeared an unrepentant Zoe was still sticking to her lies this morning. Nigel and the other students and volunteers were huddled around her at breakfast, and Tate gave them a wide berth. He knew Farina was coming, and looked forward to a speedy resolution of this nonsense.

He heard the helicopter landing and hit print. The portable printer whined and scratched away, and Tate pulled the three sheets free and quickly scanned them. He had rhinos to dart – the helicopter's time was precious. When Victoria returned to Arusha in the evening she could take Zoe with her. Tate walked out into the morning glare. It was hot already and the dust that stirred up the rotor blades was hanging in the now dead still air.

'Tate, we need to talk,' Farina said loudly as she strode towards him. Khan was all business, as always. Tate had lived and worked with Africans all his life – he'd been one of the last white game wardens in the Zimbabwean Parks and Wildlife Service – and he'd long ago embraced the African custom of preceding any conversation with a short but polite greeting. Khan was good at her job, but her directness still rankled him. Behind Farina was a white woman Tate was sure he didn't know, but who somehow still looked very familiar.

'Hello,' Tate said, extending a hand to the woman striding to keep up with Farina, and momentarily ignoring the woman who paid his wage. 'I'm Tate Quilter-Phipps.'

She smiled at him and took his hand, but said nothing for a few seconds. Even before she spoke, though, the wheels of his mind were spinning fast and he began to feel an odd constriction in his chest, almost as though someone had turned the valve on an adrenaline drip plugged straight into his heart.

'You don't recognise me, but I'm not surprised. It's been thirty years,' the woman said.

Farina said something, but Tate didn't hear it. He looked into the woman's blue eyes and saw the light dusting of freckles on the tanned face. When she smiled, awkwardly under his gaze, he knew who she was, and it brought back all the pain that had never really gone away, just lain like a cancer somewhere deep inside his body, slowly eating him away.

'You used to go out with my aunt, Hope,' the woman said, but he was beyond the need to be reminded. Now he just wanted to forget all over again. Her smile fell away, but she tried to resurrect it.

'You're little Natalie,' he said, finally letting go of her hand.

'Not so little any more,' she said. 'I'm dangerously close to forty.'

'Natalie is a journalist,' Farina interrupted, 'from *Outdoor Adventure* magazine's Australian edition. She's come to do a story on the rhino-monitoring program and the success of the translocations from Kruger to Serengeti. You remember I mentioned someone from the magazine would be visiting in my email last week?'

Not really, he thought, but he nodded dumbly. If Farina had mentioned Natalie Bryant's name in an email he certainly would have remembered. He would have told Farina to offer the story to someone else, or to find another project for Natalie to cover. God, he thought to himself, she was just as beautiful as Hope.

'Natalie, Tate will find someone to show you to your tent where you'll be sleeping the next two nights. In the meantime he and I have some business to discuss.'

Tate stood there a moment, uncomprehending, then said, 'Right. Right. Nigel?' He called the young researcher over, introduced him to Natalie and told him to take her to the accommodation they kept for the seemingly never-ending stream of visitors, donors and hangers-on who dropped in and out of the project camp on a regular basis.

'What do you think you're playing at, Tate?' Farina hissed once Natalie was out of earshot.

'Did her daddy email you already?' Tate asked.

Farina shook her head. 'Zoe contacted her father last night and I had him on the *phone* from America this morning threatening to call the Tanzanian police to open a rape docket on you.'

'I didn't touch the girl, Farina. She came on to me.'

Farina waved her hand, as though swatting away a fly. 'I'm sure you didn't, Tate. We all know you're not . . . well, we know you wouldn't take advantage of a young girl like that. And if you did, I'd personally cut your balls off with a panga since you rejected me that night in New York. What I can't understand, however, is why you would be so stupid as to send the daughter of one of our biggest donors home!'

'She's a disaster waiting to happen. She nearly got herself – and me – killed yesterday.' Tate quickly outlined his version of events while Farina stood there, hands on hips in the heat, impatiently waiting for him to end.

'You took her in the helicopter and then on foot with you while you approached an animal without the ground crew in place.'

He bridled at her tone. The truth of the matter was that he thought that if he kept Zoe under his wing for a day or two she might finally start paying attention to all she'd been told in her briefings, and wouldn't get in anyone else's way. Reluctantly, though, he now conceded Farina had a point. It could look as though he'd been giving her favourable attention as a prelude to making a move on her.

'What does it matter?' he asked Farina. 'Even if I let her stay on here – against my better judgement – her father wants me tried for attempted rape.'

Farina led him into his own tent and took a seat in a canvas director's chair at Tate's fold-out aluminium camping table. Tate sat on his stretcher. 'I don't think he's serious,' she said.

'How can he not be serious – it's his daughter and he's swallowed her lies.'

Farina shook her head. 'He actually said to me that he thought his daughter was infatuated with you and that she . . . what did he say? *Could come on a little strong around men sometimes.*'

'She's a spoiled brat who'll do anything to get her way.'

Farina agreed. 'And I think her father knows that, too. He intimated that if you let her stay on he would let this matter pass and would ensure she maintained a strictly professional relationship between the two of you.'

'And what did you say?'

Farina looked away, unable to hold his gaze. 'I told him I agreed this would be the best course of action.'

'This *matter*,' Tate said, rising from the cot, 'never happened, Farina!'

'Tate, calm down,' Farina said.

'No. I quit.'

CHAPTER 16

'Knock, knock,' a female voice said.

Tate looked up from stuffing clothes into his kitbag.

Natalie Bryant tried not to show it but she was pissed off that she'd taken four days out of her African schedule to make her way to this place and would now miss out on seeing a rhino capture. She'd been interested as much in the process as the work the charity was doing in the Serengeti. She was writing a book, as well as a series of articles for *Outdoor Adventure*, and wanted to see for herself what her father and grandfather and other pioneers in rhino capture and translocation had been up to. As well as being the main talent for her magazine article, Tate Quilter-Phipps was also someone she needed to interview for her book. She hadn't told Farina about her hidden agenda, or emailed Tate in case he tried to fob her off before she could meet him in person. She knew from her own father's reluctance to be interviewed that some people just did not want to talk about the war years in Rhodesia.

'Farina said you had urgent personal business to attend to, back in Zimbabwe, is that right?'

Tate zipped his pack. 'Why wouldn't it be?'

'It's probably none of my business anyway.'

'You're right there.'

'Are you always so abrupt?'

'Yes.'

She laughed, but then saw he was serious. She remembered him, vaguely, as being the quiet, shy one, and had heard her parents and grandparents remark on it occasionally in the years since Aunty Hope's death. In that respect he was so very different to what she remembered about Hope. 'But you are going back to Zimbabwe?'

Tate packed a hairbrush, toothpaste and toothbrush into a toiletries bag and zipped it closed. 'Yes.'

'Me too.'

He looked at her and raised his eyebrows. 'When was the last time you went back?'

'I've never been back. My parents left in 1979. People used to call it the chicken run, so I've been told.'

'George and Susannah,' Tate said, nodding, as if fragments of her story were being plucked from the files of his scientist's mind and slotted into place. 'Yes, we used to call it that, but by the following year, as independence approached, people started calling it the owl run . . . the option the wise chose.'

'But you stayed.'

He shrugged. 'My work . . . it was all I ever knew, all that mattered to me after . . .'

'After my aunt?'

'Yes.'

They were both silent for a while, remembering their own versions of that year.

'You stayed in the national parks service, I read, until recently.'

He nodded.

Natalie was starting to feel glad he was leaving. He would have been a nightmare to interview anyway. He was not far off monosyllabic. She couldn't blame him, she supposed, for being rude. All she'd done was drag up some bad memories for him at a time when he probably had a lot more than 'urgent personal business' on his mind. Her journalist's instinct told her Tate Quilter-Phipps was leaving for a different reason. It didn't matter, though, as the World Nature Fund had been little more than her free ticket to the Serengeti. She was about to say goodbye to him when he straightened again, his packing finished.

'Why are you going back to Zimbabwe? Does it have anything to do with what happened to you during the war?'

As a journalist she liked asking probing questions, not answering them. 'I could give you my counsellor's answer – that I'm going back because what happened has always been a part of me, and possibly the root cause of some issues I've had, and the only way to exorcise these demons is to go back to where it all began and confront them head on.'

'But . . .'

'But the truth is, I got a junket to Africa courtesy of the NGO that employs you, and a tour company called Maasai Wanderings. I've tacked on a flight to Zimbabwe as well to see my gran and grandfather. Also, I'm writing a book about growing up in Rhodesia, during the war, and my grandparents' work in rhino conservation. That's another reason why I wanted to talk to you.'

Tate snorted. He didn't look impressed.

She could see, behind the eyes, more files being shuffled in this odd man's mind. With his bushy, uncombed greying hair and cheap glasses he could have passed for an absent-minded professor, but his bare arms and legs were tanned and muscled and his body was as lean and hard as a strip of old biltong. Tate had lived his life in the bush, and the African sun and wind and dust had shaped his body into something that could survive in the extremes of the veldt. He was actually more handsome now than she remembered him and Natalie couldn't help but wonder how his twin brother, who had saved her life, looked these days.

'Your grandparents are good people,' he said at last. 'I see them occasionally.'

'Then you'll have heard they're probably going to lose the farm?'

His eyebrows arched above his glasses. 'No, I hadn't. The whole ranch? Even the rhinos?'

Natalie nodded. It was going to be part of her book. From all she'd read online, and from her grandfather's emails, it seemed that the numbers of Zimbabwe's last wild rhinos were fast dwindling and that government-sanctioned land invaders were making a renewed assault on the private game conservancies.

Tate shook his head and looked at the floor of the tent. 'This is terrible. I have to see them. Paul and Pip are out on their own – all the other farms around them have gone. There's no security other than what they have on the property. If their farm changes hands their rhinos will be dead in a week.'

Natalie felt the anger rise from her core. 'What about my grandparents? All you can think about is their rhinos. Can't you imagine what it's like to lose your home? My grandfather's ninety-two and my gran's not far behind him. They've got nowhere else to go.'

He looked at her blankly. Perhaps he couldn't imagine. From what she knew of him he'd never married, never had children. He'd probably lived in national parks houses and research camps all his life. She doubted Tate really was absent-minded, but nor did it seem he was particularly connected to the reality of most people's lives.

Tate pursed his lips and nodded. 'I see your point, but to be perfectly honest with you, yes I am more concerned about their rhinos. Paul and Pip have people who will care for them – you among them, presumably. Those animals will soon have no one.'

'So what can you do for the *rhinos*?'

'I can try and convince your grandfather to let me relocate them to a conservancy in the Lowveld. The war vets have got their eyes on that area as well, but there are a number of foreign-owned properties there and it's been harder for the invaders to make inroads.'

Natalie didn't know if this was a good thing or not. Her grandfather had told her that one of the reasons they had been allowed to keep their farm up until now was because he had been involved in lengthy negotiations with the parks and wildlife service about the eventual reintroduction of some of the Bryant family's rhinos into the Zambezi Valley. Natalie put this to Tate, who shook his head vigorously.

'Can't be done and shouldn't be done. There isn't the money in Zimbabwe to relocate rhinos back to the valley yet, and even if there was, parks and wildlife would be incapable of monitoring and protecting them around the clock. They'd be killed almost as quickly as if Paul's farm was handed over to a poacher.'

'My grandfather reckons there's still a black rhino living up there, somewhere near Kariba.'

'Makuti?' Tate shook his head and laughed. 'Look, your grandfather's a great man, but he's *mupengo* – crazy – when it comes to that old piece of folklore. More than anyone else I'd love to believe there was a black rhino that was still roaming wild around Makuti, but there's no scientific basis to his claim. He's collected so-called eyewitness accounts but most of those were drunks driving to or from Kariba at night.'

'Well, I'm going to write a story about it,' Natalie said defiantly.

'Good for you. Like most journalistic pieces about conservation issues I'm sure your story will be based on falsehoods, totally lacking in scientific rigour, and needlessly sensational and sentimental.'

Natalie ignored his taunts. 'Instead of criticising, you could help me with some facts and figures. I googled you – you're something of a legend in rhino circles.'

Tate scoffed. 'A legend who's broke and out of work. Your grandfather can tell you all you need to know about rhinos, I'm sure.'

'Out of work? So you're not leaving to attend to personal business?'

He realised he'd been caught out. 'My mother is widowed and living back in Bulawayo. She's finding it hard to make ends meet. I don't think she can afford to buy enough food to live on. That's my business and it's why I'm going home.'

'Oh. So I might see you around town when I'm there?'

'I'll be busy, so I doubt it.'

'I've been in touch with your brother. He knows about my book and he said he'd be happy to talk to me. Perhaps the three of us can get together.'

Tate stuffed a couple of dirty shirts into his backpack and zipped it closed. 'I don't think so.'

'Right, well maybe I could drop you an email to see if we can catch up in Bulawayo,' she tried.

He looked at his watch. Victoria would be wanting to take off. 'I'm sorry, Natalie, but if I'm going to get a lift out on the helicopter, I have to leave now. Good luck with your book project. I hope you find what you're looking for.'

Tate hefted his pack onto one shoulder, picked up his laptop bag and walked out of the tent.

*

Natalie spent the afternoon interviewing members of the rhino research and monitoring team – it was, after all, the main reason she was here. Several of them had digital photos of the captures from the last couple of days, which they offered her for use in her article, but most of them were either blurry, taken too far away from the subject, or overexposed.

Natalie had cross-trained as both a photographer and journalist and she knew that without good quality pics her editor wouldn't be interested. Hopefully she could bulk out the story with some pics of her own while she was on safari in the next few days.

Nigel Wilson, a British postgraduate student with wavy blond hair and too many copper and elephant-hair bangles on his sun-burned arms, was clicking through some of his photos. Ironically, the best of the bunch was a tight vertical shot of Tate Quilter-Phipps kneeling and cradling the blindfolded head of a black rhino. The look in Tate's eye was something she barely thought him capable of – love. How odd, she thought, that if things had turned out differently this rude, unsociable man could have been her uncle. She shuddered.

'What's he like to work with?' Natalie asked.

Nigel looked at her, then back at his screen. He was obviously trying to work out the right thing to say. 'I don't know if I'm the right person to ask.'

'How long did you work with Dr Quilter-Phipps?'

'Six months,' he said.

'Six months, day in, day out; you sound like the right person.' She smiled at the young man.

'He's one of the best in his field – perhaps the best. He's totally devoted to conserving rhinos and he knows more about them than anyone I've ever met. He's got experience in South Africa, Zimbabwe, Botswana, Kenya and here, of course. The rhinos we've been implanting with tracking devices were all either brought here by Tate, or they're descended from the stock he brought up here from South Africa.'

'But . . .'

Nigel gritted his teeth and grimaced. 'But he doesn't have any people skills at all. He expects you to know what to do and how to act from the moment you arrive.'

'He doesn't give you any training or instruction?' Natalie interrupted.

Nigel reconsidered. 'No, he does give everyone a briefing, but you only get told something once. We're all human – except Tate. No one's allowed to forget something, or get scared, or make a mistake. He's a perfectionist.'

'Sounds like a bit of an arsehole,' Natalie said.

Nigel shook his head. 'No, I don't mean that. Um . . .' He ran a hand through his unkempt hair. 'I want to be like him, but I don't, if you know what I mean.'

'Not really.' Natalie looked up from her notebook.

'I want to have his single-minded devotion to conservation. I want to be out here, in the bush, every day, not worrying about the heat, the dust, the ticks, the danger, the lack of company – I want to be as professional and dedicated and motivated as him, but . . .'

'You also want a life.'

Nigel nodded. 'That's right. Tate doesn't have one.'

As a journalist Natalie was a trained observer and listener. In the few short hours since she'd arrived she'd moved about the camp gathering information. She'd seen other students consoling an American girl called Zoe and she'd heard muttered complaints about Tate Quilter-Phipps. The rhino expert was leaving in an unexpected rush. Natalie put two and two together and kept coming up with scandal.

'Has Tate ever been romantically involved with one of the research students?'

Nigel shook his head. 'No, which makes . . .' He looked back down at his computer and clicked on the next picture. It was Tate Quilter-Phipps in a helicopter, leaning out and aiming a dart gun at a rhino, which was close enough to be easily caught in the same frame as the conservationist.

'Which makes the issue with Zoe seem so out of character?' Natalie ventured.

Nigel stared at the screen for a few seconds, then looked up at her. 'We've had quite a few students – the majority of them girls – come through the research camp since I've been here. I know of at least two of them who made a move on Tate, even though he was old enough to be their father. At least one of them was pissed that he rejected her. And before you ask the question, no, he's never been interested in the guys, either. The dude's like a monk, you know?'

Natalie nodded, but said nothing. She knew that silence was often the best way to keep an interview flowing.

Nigel spread his hands wide. 'I mean, if I was fifty or whatever and I had these twenty-year-old babes throwing themselves at me, I'd be like, bring it on, you know? Maybe he succumbed to pressure with Zoe, but even so, I can't see him trying to force himself on her, or hurt her. I don't know . . . The guy's such a cold fish. What makes someone like that?'

Natalie shrugged her shoulders, although she was pretty sure she knew what made someone like that. She'd been rejected, too, and while she wasn't as uptight and grumpy as Tate, she knew what loneliness could do to a person.

Tate and Farina Khan sat in the green canvas mess tent in the centre of the research camp. They were alone, except for the

African cook who set a cup of tea down in front of each of them, then moved away. Like the research students, the man knew there was big trouble.

'Stay, Tate. Please. We'll work this out.'

Tate looked at his watch. 'Victoria wants to leave in fifteen minutes.'

Farina reached across the wooden trestle table and laid her hand on his. He looked down at it. 'Tate . . .'

He looked up at her and said nothing until she removed her hand. 'I didn't touch the girl, Farina.'

'I know. I've just been with her. She now says that she doesn't want to press charges. She says she'd been drinking and that it's possible she might have done something to lead you on.'

He snorted. 'She came into my tent and stripped naked, Farina. And I didn't touch her. She told me she thought I was gay.'

Farina gave a sympathetic smile. 'I wondered the same thing after that night in New York.'

He looked into her dark eyes and allowed himself his first grin of the day. People wrongly assumed that because Farina Khan was a Muslim from Pakistan she wouldn't drink, smoke or swear. She did all of the above with an impressive level of diligence and in the hotel bar at the WNF NY conference one night she'd put her hand on his thigh and whispered into his ear that she wanted him to come back to her room with her. He'd been tempted, but he'd politely declined. Nothing would come of it, he'd told himself, and she wasn't his type. Not that he even knew what his type was any more.

'There's more important work for me back in Zimbabwe,' he said, and it was the truth.

'Tate, we've raised a huge amount of money from all around the world for this project. Zoe's father is just one of our major donors. It's important work.'

Slowly he shook his head. 'No, it isn't. It's window dressing and it's convenient. There are a hundred more important, more deserving projects that you could have funded with this money. You picked the Serengeti because it's a nice safe place for rich American and English kids to come for a holiday.'

Farina slapped the table with an open palm and the cook retreated back into the kitchen tent. 'That's *not* true, Tate. This work is vital to the future of the East African population of the black rhino and your role is as important now as it was when your team moved these animals up here.'

'My role here is to be a babysitter for spoiled children. Zimbabwe's population of black rhino is just about extinct, but your organisation's too scared to put money into the country.'

'We don't want to be seen to be endorsing a corrupt regime,' she retorted.

'Rubbish. You're not in Zimbabwe because there are no foreign media allowed in, so you'll get no PR out of it, and because Zoe's father wouldn't want his little princess travelling there.'

Farina glared at him, her palm still flat on the table. 'You're infuriating, Tate. You don't care about anything other than yourself, do you?'

He'd never thought about it that way, but she was wrong. He didn't care anything about himself.

CHAPTER 17

Natalie Bryant pulled her hair back into a ponytail and tied it with an elastic band. She gripped the padded sides of the viewing hatch of the Land Cruiser and rode the rocking of the springs as the vehicle raced across the Ndutu Plains in the Serengeti National Park.

For this part of her trip, she was spending three days on safari, in the company of a small group of well-heeled tourists, and would write a glowing article on the wonders of the Serengeti for the magazine, to repay her free airfare and accommodation. However, what she really wanted to do was to make some headway with her book. Her meeting with Tate had been a disaster on that front, so she was hoping she'd get more out of his brother. For the time being, though, she was enjoying the ride as a tourist.

Natalie hadn't seen an African elephant, or a lion or a rhino in the wild since she was ten years old, and that was too long a time. Her arms were brick red and she could feel her face was similarly burned by the unforgiving sun and the buffeting hot wind that blew in her face.

She smelled elephant. Their mouldy, musty smell preceded them and she liked that she'd been back on the continent long enough to learn again how to identify an animal by its odour.

There was something primal about that, and you couldn't get it from a television remote and a cable TV wildlife channel.

Like an addict in recovery offered the needle once more, she'd weakened and succumbed to Africa's grasp. She'd been glad to leave the continent when she had, and had sworn off the place for years. She'd felt no vindication in the way Zimbabwe had crumbled into ruin over the past decade – her grandparents still lived there so she couldn't adopt the told-you-so smugness of the when-we crowd – but she'd been more than happy to live her life in exile in Australia.

But life changed. She had changed.

Natalie would be forty in a month's time, and she didn't want to be back in Australia when that happened. It wasn't some primal urge, however, that had sent her back to Africa – it was a man.

'You know, Natalie,' said Susie, a single woman from New York who was on the same package safari, 'the only thing I miss is having someone to share all this with. Know what I mean?'

Natalie nodded. She'd lived with Stephen for seven years, had known him for eight. He was a merchant banker, South African, originally from Durban. She found it easy to hate him now, and her therapist had told her that was OK, but at times like this she felt exactly the same as Susie. She'd catch herself wondering what Stephen would have thought of the safari guide's jokes, or the blood-red sunset over the plains.

They'd both lived in Africa until roughly the same age, but Stephen had been learning to surf while Natalie's family had struggled to keep farming while her father spent most of his time away, flying helicopters into battle. And the war had come right into her home.

Stephen was a couple of years older than her and had entered into an early midlife crisis, leaving her for a twenty-four-year-old secretary at his firm.

'You never really opened up to me, Nat,' he said to her, on the day he moved out. It was a low remark. She didn't think she had anything to do with Stephen following his cock to a bimbo young enough to be his daughter. Not that their sex life had been bad – at least Natalie had thought it was all right.

You never really opened up to me. What the hell did that mean? Sure, she had the occasional nightmare, but she didn't feel the need to tell him about it. Her therapist disagreed, but Natalie had a policy of only taking the right advice from her. Natalie had *suffered* according to her therapist, but in Natalie's mind it was nothing compared to what had happened to other people during the war.

She drank, probably to excess at times, but she kept herself fit thanks to three mornings a week in the gym back in Sydney and a sadistic female personal trainer. Stephen liked a drink, too, but he could be sanctimonious when he thought she'd had too much, particularly when it was his turn to drive.

They had decided against kids, which was probably a good thing, Natalie thought. Unlike most of her friends, she had never been clucky, nor felt the presence of some hidden clock. In fact, when her workmates and friends started having babies she found herself repulsed, at times, by their clinical descriptions of pain and damage.

Maybe she never opened up to herself. That was the sort of thing her therapist should have been asking, considering the amount of money Natalie paid her. Fuck her, she thought. And fuck Stephen too.

Meeting Tate Quilter-Phipps had been the start of something, though.

Nothing romantic – the scientist was far too prickly and, despite his lean good looks, too nerdy for her. Tate cared more about animals than he did about people. She wondered what his brother was like these days.

It hadn't been a coincidence that she'd ended up travelling to the Serengeti to do a story on a rhino-monitoring project being coordinated by Tate. She'd seen the name – there couldn't be two of those in the world, let alone Africa – and googled like crazy. It had seemed to her, as it sometimes did when the pieces of a story started falling into place, that there was some other force at work, guiding her. She'd even gotten the same chill down her spine and the tingling in her fingertips that she did when she was writing something good.

She knew from his bio, which she'd found online appended to a paper he'd written, that he was the same Tate Quilter-Phipps her aunt had been dating. There was nothing much from his early career, other than an old feature story about him being one of the last white men in the Zimbabwean Parks and Wildlife Service. The story, predictably, was about rhino conservation.

But there was nothing online about the twin brother, Braedan. No Facebook, no Myspace, no LinkedIn. If Braedan had a presence on the Net, he kept it well hidden. Her grandmother had contacted the twins' mother and got hold of an email address for Braedan, which was how she'd found him and established that he was in Zimbabwe and would be happy to chat to her when she arrived. She wondered what the man who had saved her life looked like now. She wondered what he was like, if he was a still a hero.

CHAPTER 18

Zimbabwe

Braedan threw up.

He steadied himself with a palm against the toilet wall and shuddered. Shuffling backwards – at least he'd stay aimed towards the bowl – he groped outside in the darkened hall behind him for the light switch. He flicked it, but nothing happened.

'Fucking ZESA.' Just muttering the curse made him gag again, and he pitched himself forward and sank to his knees as the vile concoction of curry, Captain Morgan, cheap Mukuyu cabernet sauvignon and Castle lager spewed forth.

'Braedan? Are you all right in there?'

He ran a hand down his face, shuddered again and coughed. What the hell was her name? Mary? Margaret? He'd met her the night before in the Keg and Sable in Borrowdale, a relatively up-market Harare suburb. No, he corrected himself, make that this morning sometime. He was in her house and there was no electricity. Maybe that was a good thing.

'Ja, fine.' He padded barefoot down the hallway, coughing, feeling the dust cling to the soles of his sweaty feet. She needed to get the cleaner in more often, he reckoned, but everyone had to be paid in forex now, so people were cutting back on their staff. Braedan swayed in the dark and lurched into a door, which creaked open.

'Come back to bed.' At least she sounded as *babelaas* as he was. Good.

The curtains weren't closed as tight in this room as the others and a chink let in some weak light. It was cold and rainy outside. He'd almost forgotten how cool it could get in Harare. It was a child's room – a son's. There was a signed cricket bat propped in a corner, an ancient computer gathering dust on a cheap chipboard desk, and the centre-spread from an edition of the *Zimbabwe Hunter* magazine – a cutaway view of a lion showing its vital organs and the best places to shoot it. On the facing wall was a two-year-old calendar showing a fading blonde babe in a bikini.

'Babe? Please won't you fetch me some water out the fridge,' the woman called from her bedroom.

Braedan pulled the door softly closed. He wondered at what point in the small hours of the morning he'd become *babe* and a domestic, but he held his tongue in the hope that there might be breakfast in this. '*Ja*.'

He navigated by instinct to the kitchen and swallowed hard when he saw the empty bottle of Spiced Gold on the bench. They'd kicked on a bit after she'd driven him home. Braedan opened the museum-piece Frigidaire and found the water jug. He took a glass from the sink, swilled the rum out of it and filled it with room-temperature water. The electricity must have been off most of the night. 'Fucking ZESA.'

Braedan drank some water, gargled and spat in the sink. When he closed the fridge door he saw a picture of her kids. The boy, he of the guns and girls, looked about twenty, the daughter maybe a couple of years younger. Christ, he thought, he hoped she wasn't asleep somewhere in the house.

He took the water back to the bedroom. She was lying on the bed, on her back, one arm over her eyes. The pose presented her breasts in their most flattering light. She was blonde, though the dye job wasn't as good as the girl's on her son's wall, and she'd be in her early forties. But she was in good shape – he'd clocked the treadmill in the garage when she parked her Fortuner – and her belly was flat and her arms toned. She looked over, reached for the glass and coughed.

'Your kids aren't living at home, are they?'

She grimaced. 'Gawd. Did I tell you I was married? No, they're not at home. Shane's in the UK and Jenny's at varsity in Cape Town.' She coughed again.

Braedan nodded. '*Ja*. You told me your husband's doing contract work in Afghanistan. Same as me. That's how we got talking. You also told me you wanted to divorce him.'

'I did?'

He nodded and sat back down on the bed. He bent to reach his jeans, which were lying on the floor. Saying it reminded him that he had had second thoughts about going home with her. It was almost like sleeping with an army friend's girl, and he wouldn't have done that when he was a troopie. Well, not often.

She reached out and put a hand on his forearm. 'Stay. It gets bloody lonely here, you know?' He left the jeans where they were.

He did know, but he couldn't be bothered telling her his sob story. His wife had left him for a doctor, while she and Braedan had been living in Australia. Lara had got them residency because of her qualification as a nurse. She'd qualified during the last year of the war, although she'd never actually worked in a hospital in the new Zimbabwe. She'd become Braedan's wife in 1980 and they'd got some land from her folks, had an OK life for nineteen years.

Then the farm invasions had begun. Braedan and Lara had been farming tobacco, and they had been one of the first to be targeted by the politics of greed and envy. If it hadn't been for their two daughters, who were home at the time from school, Braedan would have gone out to the yard, behind the chickens, and dug up the FN wrapped in oiled blankets that he'd buried there in 1980. It was a fantasy of his, one he still liked to indulge in every now and then when he was feeling depressed, that he'd gone down fighting for the farm with a gun in each hand. It might have been better for all of them if he had.

He'd been a failure in Sydney, pure and simple. All he knew was soldiering and farming, and he'd been too old to join the Australian Army, and no outsider could afford to buy into a farm in Australia and run it. There hadn't even been a farm manager's job and, besides, Lara had been recruited by a hospital in the city.

He knew a lot about cars, but he wasn't a skilled mechanic. He'd drawn up plans for tobacco sheds on his own farm and supervised their construction, but he wasn't an architect or a builder. He was a jack of all flipping trades and master of none.

Braedan paused, reached for his cigarettes and matches on the side table, and lit one. 'Please,' said the woman on the bed. What the hell was her name?

'Sorry,' he mumbled through his first drag. He shook out another Newbury and lit it for her, off the end of his. He passed it to her and she coughed as she took her first hit of nicotine for the day.

'You didn't tell me,' the woman said, shifting herself up into a seating position, her back against the padded bedhead. 'Are you married?'

'*Ja*.'

'Oh.'

'Bit late for second thoughts, hey?' he said.

She smiled and nodded, her cheeks colouring slightly. 'Don't worry,' he added, then exhaled towards the ceiling. 'I'm just waiting for the divorce papers to come through.'

'I'm going to divorce mine . . . as soon as he's paid off the house.'

Braedan laughed, but not at her joke. He wondered if that's what Lara had been waiting for too. It was the way it had happened. Of course, she'd paid more off the house than he had, although in the last five years he'd worked in that dust-blown shithole and been shot at plenty of times in order to make his belated share of the mortgage repayments.

After they'd arrived in Australia he'd found himself a job, a string of them in fact. He'd hated every one of them. He'd worked nights in a service station, behind the till. In Australia, he learned on his first day in the country, customers filled their own cars with petrol. One night a South African woman had come up to the counter and started berating him about the state of the toilets. She told him he should send someone in, immediately, to clean up the mess in the ladies room.

It was late, and he'd had two people that night already who'd driven off without paying. He knew the Indian owner of the service station would blame him and make a big deal out of it. What the hell, he thought. He didn't have a gun, so he couldn't shoot the thieves. Besides, people didn't shoot each other in Australia. 'There's no one to clean the toilets,' he told the ex-Kugel, who sounded as though she'd just stepped off the SAA jumbo, 'we're fresh out of *kaffirs*.'

She stormed out, but the problem was that the bloody basket-weaving hippie woman queuing behind the South African had heard what he said and called the manager to complain about him. The Indian gave him a 'verbal warning' and told him racism wasn't tolerated in Australia.

He'd walked out on the Indian, without a word. Lara had been furious at him and had begged him to go back and apologise. Apologise, be damned. He'd lived around black people all his life and he wasn't a racist – despite what the fucking *munts* had done to him. He hadn't, in fact, used the K word since he was a young troopie in the army. He'd only said it to take the piss out of the South African. To hell with the bloody curry-muncher if he couldn't take a joke.

'I'm thinking I might go to Australia when we split up,' the woman on the bed said to him. 'I've had enough of this place. You said last night you lived there for a while. What's it like?'

He wondered if he should just leave. He looked down at his jeans and trainers on the floor, again contemplating making a run for it, but when he turned back to her she'd raised one leg, bent at the knee, and he got a glimpse of her neatly trimmed bush. She put a hand out and patted the sheet. One of her blood-red nails was chipped. He remembered the sting on his back as she'd scratched him.

'You wouldn't like it,' he said.

She raised an eyebrow and drew on her cigarette.

'You'd be arrested and fined for smoking inside, with double demerit points for doing it in bed, and if you'd driven in Australia after drinking like you did last night you'd be publicly executed.'

'Serious?'

'*Ja*. Seriously, I lost my licence for driving at forty-three kilometres an hour.'

'Now you really are joking.'

He shook his head. 'True as nuts. I was working as a courier and it cost me my job.'

She shook her head. He'd had other speeding offences as well, and the camera trap had exhausted the last of the points he had left on his Australian licence. He didn't tell her about the drink-driving conviction, because he was still embarrassed at having been dragged through the courts like a criminal.

'I've heard they have a lot of rules there,' she said.

Braedan nodded. '*Ja*, too many politicians and not enough problems. They make up new laws all the time.'

'My daughter wants to work there, once she graduates. She's going to be a radiographer.'

Braedan was about to say he hoped she'd find a nice doctor, like his wife had, but he didn't want her sympathy. 'I should go,' he said, standing.

'Wait . . .' She exhaled a stream of smoke from the side of her mouth and gestured to his penis with the glowing tip of her cigarette. 'You have unfinished business, China.'

He looked down. 'What do you mean?'

'Only once last night. I think the drink got the better of you, hey?'

Braedan had never been able to walk away from a challenge. He stubbed out his cigarette, reached out and grabbed one of her ankles. As he dragged her down the bed she giggled and quickly reached over to drop her smoke in the ashtray on the side table. By the time her arse was on the edge of the bed, he was hard. He spread both her legs and kept his feet on the floor as he leaned over and drove into her.

'That's better,' she said.

He locked eyes with her. There was the hardness there of the survivor. All his tribe had lost something; some in the war, some in the peace. They lived as they played – there was no tomorrow for most of them.

'Fuck me.' She gritted her teeth, bared them. 'Harder.'

He took out his frustrations on her, in her. The wife who'd left him, the life he'd lost, the farm, the kids. Later, when he pulled on his jeans and buttoned the shirt that smelled of stale sweat and smoke, she kissed him and let him go. And he felt she'd used him the same way, for the same reasons.

As he walked out of her house he looked up at the sky. There was a glimpse of sun through the clouds, but it was a metaphor of hope, only.

There had been no water, as well as no electricity, in the house so she hadn't even been able to offer him a shower before he left. It was probably just as well, he thought, as he was sure the woman – what was her damn name? – would have wanted to climb in with him, and he doubted he could have risen to the occasion one more time.

The power and water shortages had been worse over the past couple of years, but the country's basic infrastructure was so degraded that both would continue to be a fact of life. Harare was the only place in the world he knew where people could make dinnertime conversation about their bathing habits, and where the flicker of an electric light coming on could provoke applause. It hadn't been uncommon, during the worst of it, for people to draw the water from their swimming pools to drink and wash in.

Braedan opened the door of his battered, rusted Nissan 1400 *bakkie*. The starter whirred for a while before it finally caught. He checked the top pocket of his bush shirt and found a few crumpled, grubby US dollar bills. The fuel gauge was broken, but he was sure he at least had enough to get to the airport. Tate would have money – he hoped. He caught a whiff of himself – sweat and woman. Normally he might have smiled to himself, but the encounter had left him feeling uneasy, even angry. Maybe it wasn't her. Maybe it just was the prospect of seeing his sanctimonious, pain-in-the-arse brother again.

His mother had called him, just the day before, and told him Tate was coming in from Kenya, and ordered him to pick up his twin. Any other time Braedan would have found an excuse not to, but he was driving his mother's old *bakkie* and he did have to get back to Bulawayo at some stage. The downside was that he'd have to sit next to Tate all the way home for five hundred or so kilometres.

Braedan lit another cigarette and indicated right to turn onto Harare Drive. The little pickup's puny springs squeaked as he lurched over the uneven surface and in and out of a pothole that nearly swallowed the Nissan whole.

He stopped at a robot and ignored the Africans who tried to sell him a newspaper or some cell phone airtime. He had money for neither. His phone would still receive messages and there was no one he needed to call. The news was the same as always – bad.

Morgan Tsvangirai, the leader of the main faction of the Movement for Democratic Change, was threatening to pull out of the GNU. It was a fitting acronym, Braedan thought. The Government of National Unity had been as crazy and direction-less as a wildebeest, or a gnu as they called them in East Africa, since its inception. Like the wild-eyed, shaggy beast, it had pranced around and around in circles, waiting to be taken down by the king of the beasts. Mugabe had done that, through inaction and attrition of the opposition's will.

Braedan accelerated away as the one functioning traffic light at the intersection turned green. At least there was some power in this part of town. At the second intersection his luck ran true to form again. All the lights were out and he who had the strongest will, or a company vehicle, had right of way. Braedan nosed out into the chaos and spun the back wheels as he dropped the clutch and floored the pedal to escape an oncoming blue ZUPCO bus. The smoke-belching giant crabbed and missed his tailgate by centimetres.

He punched some buttons on the ancient car radio, but all he could pick up was the Dead BC; the ZBC, or Zimbabwe Broadcasting Commission, radio service was a hundred per cent propaganda and its television channel was even more dire. The TV played tits and drums, endless poorly shot videos of happy Africans dancing and singing, in between news broadcasts about how evil Britain and America were and, by association, how evil and inept its lackeys in the MDC were.

According to the radio news His Excellency the Comrade President claimed Tsvangirai had turned his back on the people of Zimbabwe by announcing his withdrawal from the GNU. Braedan saw the move for what it was: a quick, desperate shot at some international publicity. The MDC had been unable to influence any government decisions of any consequence while it had been part of the GNU, so pulling out really had no effect on the people of the country either way. At least the rest of the world, which in truth knew or cared very little about Africa, would now hear that things were not OK – again – in Zimbabwe. The fact was, nothing would change in Zim until the big man died.

A glossy black Hummer H3 roared past Braedan, eliciting a toot from the oncoming Land Rover it nearly collected as it swung out over the solid centre line. The colour and dark tinted windows told Braedan it wasn't a white man driving the expensive vehicle. There was money around in Harare – always had been. It was just the owners of it who had changed.

Emmerson Ngwenya, the Zimbabwean government's Assistant Minister for Land Redistribution, told his driver to keep the Hummer's engine running and the aircon on as he stepped out of the gleaming black vehicle and walked into Harare Airport's arrivals hall. His protection officer, a CIO agent by the name of Ncube, preceded him through the door and looked around.

The pair walked upstairs to a VIP lounge that overlooked the baggage carousel through frosted windows. A pretty girl with long, straightened hair and a nicely rounded bottom brought him a vodka on the rocks and Emmerson smiled back at her as he accepted his drink with a polite thank you.

'My pleasure, Minister,' she said, holding the tray across her front demurely as she pirouetted away.

'Find out her cell number for me while I'm downstairs,' Ngwenya said to Ncube.

The other man nodded and grinned. He was more than just a bodyguard. Tobias Ncube was Emmerson Ngwenya's right-hand man in a number of non-governmental pursuits the minister carried out in his spare time.

'What time are we meeting the Vietnamese?' Ngwenya asked when he was sure the girl was out of earshot.

'Three-thirty, at the Monomotapa.'

Ngwenya sipped his vodka and savoured the fiery spirit as it warmed him all the way down. How such heat could come from somewhere so cold . . . The drink reminded him of his time in Russia: the women he'd bedded and the racist communist instructor he'd killed. 'Good,' he replied.

'What will we tell them about Hwange?' Ncube asked.

Ngwenya rolled an ice cube around his mouth while he thought about it. The stick of ex commandos he had hired to find a black rhino in Hwange National Park had failed to kill their quarry the night before. They'd blamed the full moon and cloudless skies that side of the country was experiencing. Apparently the wily old bull had kept picking up the sound of its pursuers and was continuing to evade them. The military men were inept, and Emmerson had decided he would not be using them again, even if they managed to kill the animal they were tracking. Everyone knew rhinos had poor eyesight, so it was a mistake by the panicked leader of the gang to blame the good light for their failure. It was just another excuse. The hunters had probably made more noise than a tank ploughing through the bush of the national park.

'We tell them nothing, except the truth – that there are fewer and fewer rhinos that are easily accessible and those that are left are harder to track. We leave out the bit about our men's incompetence.'

Ncube nodded.

'I can stall them,' Emmerson continued. 'I do not dance to their tune. In time, we will have all the horn we need. I don't mind keeping these men hanging on – it makes them more anxious and this may push the price even higher.' The lounge attendant returned and asked him if he would like another vodka.

Emmerson checked his gold Rolex. 'No thank you, sister.' She smiled at him again. Beautiful, he thought.

The first passengers off the Kenya Airways flight from Nairobi were presenting themselves to the immigration officers at the booths at the far end of the arrivals hall below them.

He spotted his nineteen-year-old daughter striding haughtily across the hall, the first person to clear immigration. It was as it should be. Emmerson rose and brushed an imaginary speck of dust off his Ralph Lauren chinos. He nodded to the girl again, and walked downstairs to be ready to greet his daughter as she emerged.

Natalie was the second last person to clear immigration, as she and the other people travelling on foreign passports had to wait to purchase visas. The process seemed to take an age, as forms were filled out, ornate stickers affixed to blank pages, money counted – slowly – and receipts laboriously completed.

She could see Tate Quilter-Phipps standing by the carousel, a mix of impatience and equivocation flitting across his face. He looked over at her every now and then, not smiling.

It had been sheer coincidence that they'd been on the same direct flight from Nairobi, and by an even weirder twist of fate they'd been seated nearly next to each other, on either side of a vacant centre seat.

'I'm not stalking you, honest,' she'd said to him as she placed her bag in the overhead locker and sat down.

He smiled, looked down at the book already open in his lap, then back over at her. 'I'm . . . sorry if I sounded abrupt with you when you arrived in the Serengeti. Things weren't going to plan, that was all.'

'It's fine, I understand,' she assured him.

He nodded and went back to his book, brushing a long strand of grey hair out of his eyes. After their inflight meal had been served Natalie summoned the courage to interrupt him again. 'I've got to get from Harare to Bulawayo. Can you recommend a good bus service?'

Tate looked at her over the top of his reading glasses. He said nothing, but closed the book on game management he'd been reading, and folded his glasses and stowed them carefully in their case. 'How long are you staying in Harare?'

Natalie had given up on getting anything more useful out of him for her article or book. The words tumbled out of her. 'Um . . . I don't know. Maybe only a night . . . I've got family friends I can contact . . . or . . . I don't know. I'd like to get moving to Bulawayo as soon as possible to see my grandparents. I'm on my own funds now, so I've got to watch the pennies, but I've heard there's a pretty good bus from Harare, and –'

'I've got a car in Harare. I left it with a former colleague. I'd very much like to see your grandfather again, so perhaps I could . . . perhaps you'd like . . .'

'A lift? That'd be fantastic, thank you so much,' she gushed. She could see he was regretting the offer already, but she didn't care. She needed to get to her grandparents' farm as quickly as possible, and she did want to have another try at prising some more information from this strange, shy, prickly man. 'And your brother?'

'I'm sure my mother will know where he is – if he isn't sponging off her. She also stays in Bulawayo.'

Natalie had got the tingling feeling in her fingertips again. The story . . . it was all coming together. She'd have time to prepare herself for coming face to face with her past on the drive to Bulawayo with Tate. She had a lot to discuss with Braedan Quilter-Phipps and she'd need to get herself in the right frame of mind. A long drive across Zimbabwe would help.

She fetched a trolley of her own – Tate wasn't rushing to help her – and hefted her wheelie bag off the carousel as it passed her. 'OK. Ready,' she said.

He led off wordlessly. A dozen Zimbabwe Revenue Authority customs officers sat or leaned against walls near a row of inspection cubicles. None of them bothered to stop Tate or her, or to ask them what they were carrying. Natalie had heard horror stories of people being shaken down at border posts and the airport and forced to pay a range of real and bogus duties. These men and women simply looked at them with bored eyes. It seemed as if even the government officials were tired of doing the president's dirty work.

They walked down the corridor and exited to the left. Natalie stopped and gripped the push rail of her trolley. She wasn't ready to see Tate's twin brother just yet, but there he was, smiling.

CHAPTER 19

Braedan wasn't ready for her to be so beautiful, or for her to look so much like Hope.

The last time he'd seen her she'd been nine years old. He'd thought about the little girl many times over the years, and seen her in his nightmares time and again, but there was never any extrapolation of the woman she might have grown into. In his mind she was always the trembling, dishevelled, terrified little girl in his arms.

But this chick was hot.

And there, next to her, was his brother, still affecting the absent-minded professor bunny-hugger look that he pulled off so well. He saw Tate's look of annoyance. 'Howzit?'

Tate frowned. 'What are you doing here?'

'*Ja*, I'm *lekker*, and you?' He ignored Tate now and stared at the girl. The woman. She had to be forty now, he supposed, but she didn't look it.

She wore what people who didn't live in Africa thought people should wear in Africa. But the khaki skirt was stylishly cut just above her knees, and the green bush shirt was tailored to show she'd keep on beating gravity for a few years more at least. She was blonde, like Hope, though she wore her hair in a bob. The family resemblance was there, most especially in the eyes. Even the old granny, Pip, still had those striking eyes in among all the wrinkles.

'I'm –'

'Natalie.' He smiled and took her hand. Her palm was a little clammy, but he didn't let go, and she didn't try to pull away. She just looked at him, as though she was remembering what he was remembering. 'It's been some time, hey?'

She nodded.

'Have you got a car, or did you come in an ET?' Tate interrupted. Most whites Tate knew wouldn't be seen dead in an emergency taxi – the minibuses that were the main form of public transport for African people.

'Very funny,' Braedan said. '*Ja*, I've got a car, but guess what . . . you don't.'

Tate looked annoyed, like he always did, thought Braedan. Bastard thought he was smarter than everyone, but now he was stranded. He could see he was looking for his African friend, Lookout. 'Your buddy called Mom, but she couldn't get through to you in Tanzania or wherever the hell you were. He says he was taking it to get fuel and he got sideswiped by an ET. Your car it is, *ah*-broken.'

'When's the car going to be fixed?' Tate asked.

'You seriously think your out-of-work MDC China is going to pay to have your car fixed? Man, you still don't get it, do you? How can you keep trusting these people when they never fail to disappoint you?'

'So what must I do?'

'You must, *boet*, catch a glide to Bulawayo with me. Mom's orders.'

'A glide?' Natalie asked.

Tate scratched his bush of grey hair. 'He means a lift, with him. I need to go to Bulawayo to see Natalie's grandfather anyway.'

'Yes,' she chimed in. 'And you must come too, Braedan. I know he'd like to see you after all these years.'

Braedan led them into the car park and Tate followed, pushing the trolley he'd taken from Natalie which was piled high with their baggage.

Natalie fell into step beside Braedan. 'So,' he said, 'I knew from your email you were coming to Zim around now, but I didn't expect to see you walk off the aircraft with Chuckles here.' He thumbed back at his brother. Braedan didn't have to turn around to know Tate was scowling.

Natalie tried not to smile. 'It was a bit of a surprise for me too.'

'So tell me more about this book you're writing.'

She quickened her step to keep up with him. 'I'm writing about my experiences during the war, growing up and . . . well you played a pretty critical role. You did save my life, after all. I'm going to tie the story in with what's happening in Zimbabwe today and the problems my grandparents are having keeping their ranch and the rhino-breeding program going.'

Braedan nodded. 'This is us.' He stopped beside the tiny *bakkie* and felt a moment of embarrassment. 'It's a loaner.'

'Nice wheels,' Tate said. 'Mercenary business a little slow?'

'Very funny. You can ride in the back, like one of your *shamwaris*.'

'All the way to Bulawayo?'

'I'll drop you at the Rainbow Towers if you prefer. They have a bus service.'

Braedan saw that Tate was half-considering the idea of being dropped off at the highrise hotel that had once been the Sheraton, but then Tate glanced at Natalie and said, 'All right, I'll come with you.'

'We can swap around,' Natalie said. 'You know it's illegal to ride around in the back of a ute – a *bakkie* – in Australia, but it's something I remember fondly from my childhood.'

Braedan shrugged. 'From what I remember, everything's illegal in Australia. Suit yourself.' Braedan and Tate loaded the packs and bags into the tiny tray of the Nissan. The vehicle creaked and sagged as Tate climbed it. There was hardly enough room for him to stretch out, but he rearranged the luggage to make himself as comfortable as possible.

Braedan shifted two empty brown Castle Lager bottles off the seat as Natalie climbed in. She fished for the seatbelt sash, but then couldn't find the connector to click it in. 'Don't bother,' Braedan said. 'It's missing. Just hold the belt across you if we come to a roadblock. Those bastards will look for any excuse to fine you.' He glanced back and saw Tate look away. He wondered if his brother had the hots for Natalie. He didn't care.

'So this book,' he said, 'is it like some kind of therapy for you?'

She gave a small laugh. 'I'd forgotten how forward people can be in this part of the world. But yes, I suppose you could call it that. I haven't thought a lot about what happened during the war for quite some time, but lately I've been coming back to it . . . or it's been coming back to me.'

He nodded and fished his cigarettes from his shirt pocket. He offered her one.

'No thanks,' she said.

He shrugged and lit a Newbury as he drove. He scanned left and right as they came to the T-junction. There was a black man with a Scania, a heavy steel pushcart running on an old car axle and tyres, on the left. The intersection looked clear, so Braedan started to accelerate. He checked the rear-view mirror quickly and saw that Tate was asleep already, nestled in among the bags. He shifted his eyes back to the road, but thumped on the window behind him to try to wake his brother.

Natalie had started to say something about how marvellous her trip to the Serengeti had been, but Braedan was only half-listening. He saw the man with the Scania start to move. The next second the man was running, pushing the cart ahead of him. Braedan started to swerve, to miss him, but a Mercedes rounded the corner in the other direction. He slammed on the brakes.

Natalie was pitched forward and she yelped as her forearm connected with the dash. 'Hey, I don't have a seatbelt, remember?'

He ignored her. The cart filled his view through the wind-screen. Braedan rammed the gear lever into reverse and dropped the clutch, but there was only a grinding noise. He jiggled the stick, but it still refused to engage. 'Tate!' he yelled.

Braedan looked back over his shoulder. The cart man had run around back and was heaving on the handle of Natalie's black carry-on bag. 'Shit.' The smart bastard would know that this was the one that had the passport, the money and the stuff that was too valuable to put in a big check-in bag. His useless brother was looking around, as though he was still half-asleep.

'What is it?' Natalie's voice was edged with concern.

'Stop!' Tate yelled. He stood in the back of the *bakkie* with his fists clenched by his side. The man dragged the bag all the way out and started running.

'Lock yourself in,' Braedan said to Natalie. 'There might be others.' He opened the door and grabbed the tyre lever he kept by the side of his seat. He slammed the door closed and ran after the fast-disappearing man. 'Look after the rest of the stuff,' he yelled back to Tate. His woolly-headed brother was standing in the tray of the *bakkie*, watching him. Bloody useless, Braedan thought.

The black guy was probably thirty years younger than

Braedan, but his arms and legs were like skinny sticks. Braedan hadn't been working out since he'd come home from Afghanistan, but over there he had pumped iron and run on the treadmill every day. He was in a business where his workmates came from some of the best military units in the world – British SAS, South African Recces, American SEALs – so he had to stay in shape to keep up with them. Plus, if Natalie was like most experienced travellers she'd probably pushed the limit on the weight of her carry-on bag, so the thief had to be lugging close to ten kilograms as he ran.

'Stop, you thieving bastard!' Braedan yelled.

The man made the mistake of looking back and he tripped. Braedan was on him a second later, raising and swinging the tyre lever. The younger man was wheezing underneath him and he yelped like a dog as Braedan brought the edge of the steel bar down on the back of his legs. He hit him again. A horn honked behind him and Braedan turned to see the Nissan *bakkie*, with Natalie at the wheel. Tate was standing in the back, with his palms flat on the roof of the cab.

'Leave him alone, Braedan,' Tate called. 'You'll kill him if you're not careful. He looks done in.'

Braedan stood. He was furious. The rage had overtaken him, as it had often done in combat. He looked down at the moaning form below him. He kicked the man in the ribs, then hoisted Natalie's bag and strode to the *bakkie*. Braedan pointed the tyre iron at Tate. 'You stupid prick, this wouldn't have happened if you hadn't fallen asleep.'

'You drove into his bloody cart,' Tate retorted.

'Enough, guys,' Natalie said. 'Let's just get out of here. And thank you for getting my bag back.'

Tate looked down at the injured man. 'I think we should wait and see if he's OK. He might need help.'

'Help? That fucking *munt* just tried to rob us. Jesus Christ, Tate, what is it with you and these people?'

Through his peripheral vision Braedan could see people moving closer, the way they always did when there was an accident or a fight or anything out of the ordinary. Africans seemed to come out of the woodwork at times like this. He knew he should get in the car and drive, but Tate was doing everything he could to piss him off.

'You just never know when to stop, Braedan, when to back off.'

Braedan reached up and grabbed a handful of his twin brother's shirt and jerked him off the back of the truck. Tate landed in a heap at his feet. 'Get up!'

Tate reached for his glasses, which had fallen off and were lying in the dirt. 'I'm not going to fight you, Braedan.'

Braedan was breathing hard, the tyre iron still hanging loose in his hand. He wanted to kick the shit out of his brother for being such a waste of oxygen. *You should fight me,* he thought. *You should fight me and you should kick the living shit out of me and get all the shit in our lives out into the open and be done with it for good.*

Natalie was out of the car, standing with her hands on her hips. 'Hang on, what's going on here? You two are acting like twelve year olds. What's all this about? Tate fell asleep, that's all. It's not a crime, Braedan.'

Braedan shook his head. 'It's not about him falling asleep.'

Tate straightened himself up and slowly climbed back up into the *bakkie*. 'No,' he agreed. 'It's about Hope. It always is.'

CHAPTER 20

'So that's why my dad hates you?' Natalie asked as Braedan drove through Kadoma, another once-prosperous town whose local economy had been gutted by years of government excess and mismanagement.

Braedan had explained, matter-of-factly Natalie thought, that Tate's anger was still due to Braedan sleeping with Hope when she had been Tate's girlfriend. Natalie had known there was something about Hope's death that her family had always shied away from talking about.

Her mother, Susannah, often seemed reserved when talking about Hope. When Natalie was growing up she'd thought her mother was trying to blot out the tragic details of Hope's death, but as she'd grown older she'd begun to wonder whether there was a side to Hope that didn't fit with the family's innocent golden girl. When she'd asked her mother, in the context of the book she was writing, what she remembered of Hope, Susannah had told Natalie that Hope was a bright girl who liked to party.

Braedan stubbed his cigarette out in the Nissan's overflowing ashtray and shook his head. 'No, your old man never liked me. I don't know why. Me sleeping with your aunty is why Tate hates me.' Braedan jabbed his thumb back over his shoulder, at Tate's back, which was pressed against the rear window of the *bakkie*'s cab.

'Do you blame him?' Natalie asked.

Braedan shrugged. 'Hope's been dead thirty years and he still can't get over it. Took me a long time, too. I still don't really know how it happened between us. I mean, I always fancied her, from the first time I saw her, and no one forced her to come out with me the night before she died. Tate blames himself – and me – for her being on that flight home. Whether he's right or not, it was just bad luck that General Walls was on the other flight and that the terrs got the wrong plane and all those civvies were murdered.'

Natalie nodded, although she knew he was oversimplifying what had happened, and his role in it, and he was not acknowledging the horrible way Hope, and the other passengers, had died. Perhaps that was his way of coping.

She could see what her aunt might have seen in both the Quilter-Phipps men. Tate was the brooding, sensitive environmentalist and intellectual, while Braedan was the muscular, hard-living man of action. Also, as Natalie was learning, Tate was aloof to the point of rudeness and Braedan was forward to the point of arrogance. He'd seduced his brother's girlfriend then claimed no responsibility for the tragic chain of events that followed.

'You say murdered,' Natalie said, 'but Joshua Nkomo claimed the Air Rhodesia Viscount flights regularly transported military personnel and that it was a mistake of war that an aircraft full of civilians rather than Walls's plane was shot down.'

Braedan scoffed. 'Who are you, the devil's advocate, or just a bleeding heart commie?'

'I'm a journalist and I'm trying to get my facts straight.'

'That's a laugh. There was a woman reporter from South Africa who wrote that the female survivors on board the Viscount – including your aunt – had been raped before they were killed. It was a lie, and as bad as the whole mess was, I heard that your grandmother found that the worst thing about Hope's death. The *facts*, Natalie, are that your aunt and the other people who survived the crash were bayoneted by the same terrs who shot down the Viscount. That's murder.'

She nodded. 'I agree. I read the reports, the inquests.'

Braedan changed gears and slowed as a policeman waved them to a halt as they approached a roadblock. '*Ja*, well I saw the bodies. Her body.'

Natalie had been haunted by the image, confirmed in the archived reports of the inquests, of Hope rolling on top of the eight-year-old girl in her charge to protect her, and being stabbed to death. The child had been dragged from under her and killed in the same manner. 'How . . .'

Braedan shrugged, as if he knew there was no point in trying to find an explanation or reason for the atrocity. They pulled up at the roadblock.

'Good afternoon, how are you?' the policeman asked through the driver's window.

Braedan had his hands on the steering wheel. He stared fixedly through the windscreen. Natalie remembered there was no quicker way to insult an African person than by not replying to a greeting or asking a question before taking the time to say hello. The policeman sneered, but then turned his head as a voice came from the rear of the *bakkie*.

'*Kanjani*,' Tate said from the back, and then launched into fluent and rapid Shona that Natalie had no chance of deciphering. In a few seconds the scowl was gone from the young policeman's face and he was laughing. Tate leaned his head around to the driver's window. 'Show the man your licence . . . if you have one.'

'I *have* one.' Braedan fished in his jeans pocket for his wallet.

'What were you talking about?' Natalie asked Tate through the open window while the officer took his time studying Braedan's licence.

'He told me that you should be riding in the back of the *bakkie* and I should be in the front,' Tate said.

'Very funny,' Natalie said.

'He was serious.'

The policeman grinned. 'Good afternoon, madam.'

'Afternoon.'

'Ah, you may proceed.' The policeman returned Braedan's licence and touched the peak of his cap in a salute to Natalie.

Braedan put the Nissan in gear and drove off without even making eye contact with the officer.

'He was only doing his job,' Natalie observed.

'Hah! These bastards have been cowed, crooked and conned for so long they've forgotten what their bloody job is,' Braedan said. 'They stood by while white farms were invaded and innocent men beaten and murdered. They don't get involved in criminal investigations any more because there's usually a *political* angle, and when the pricing controls came in a couple of years ago they were at the head of the queues looting all the shops.'

Natalie had read about President Mugabe's ludicrous policy of fixing prices at below cost, when inflation was running out of control. He had forced supermarkets and other retailers to lower their prices to such an extent that they went out of business. Police and military personnel were given first preference for shopping when the new prices were introduced, and corrupt officers bought up entire stocks of stores then sold them at a huge profit on the black market in Zimbabwe or transported their goods across the border to Botswana where they sold them to similar retailers and made tidy profits in foreign currency.

'Things have improved, haven't they, since he did away with the Zimbabwean dollar?' Natalie asked, playing devil's advocate again.

Braedan shrugged. 'You can get just about anything you want these days as long as you have US dollars or rand to pay for it, but you're paying well over the odds. That's OK if you've got a job that pays you in forex, but if you don't . . .'

'What are you doing these days? My grandfather said he'd heard you'd been in Iraq.'

'*Ja.*' Braedan lit another cigarette. Natalie was a reformed smoker who occasionally bummed one from girlfriends when she'd had too much to drink. She wanted one now, but said nothing. 'And Afghanistan as well. Those places are *kak*.'

'Why did you come home to Zimbabwe?'

'It wasn't nostalgia, I'll tell you that. The money was good, hey, but the outfit I was working for, Corporate Solutions, got a bad reputation in Iraq and lost its contracts.'

'What happened?'

'On or off the record?'

She smiled. 'I could say off the record, but you know there's really no such thing.'

'Well, it's no skin off my nose anyway. I was part of a crew headed by a South African nutter called Van Zyl. He killed a senior Iraqi army officer. The camel jockey was in civvies and Van Zyl said he ran a roadblock, but I was there. He was executed. We were all arrested by the local police, but no charges were laid, not even against Van Zyl. The rumour was our boss was being paid by the CIA and they wanted the Iraqi dead. I hope the boss got a lot of money, because the rest of us were kicked out. There was a bit of work in Afghanistan after that, guarding convoys, but that dried up when the smaller firms like CS were muscled out by the American players.'

'Couldn't you have got a job with one of them?' Natalie asked.

Braedan shook his head. 'Who wants a geriatric Rhodie when there are twenty-two year olds leaving the army every day for the big bucks? My wife left me and I didn't want to go back to Australia, so I came back here.'

They rolled into the town of Kwe Kwe, which Natalie recalled as being spelled Que Que in her youth, and drove around the clock tower, which she also remembered. Like many things in Zimbabwe, the clock was broken. Braedan pulled up outside a liquor shop.

'Back in a minute.' He got out and said, over his shoulder, to Tate, 'Want anything?'

'No.'

Braedan shrugged and disappeared into the store. Natalie started in her seat when someone rapped on her window. She turned to see a small boy holding a tin cup made out of an old fruit tin, with a handle riveted to it. An elderly man with dark glasses and frizzy grey hair stood behind the boy, with his hand on his shoulder. Natalie had been surprised she hadn't seen more beggars in Zimbabwe, given the widespread poverty and unemployment. She reached into her shirt for the travel wallet that hung around her neck and pulled out a dollar note.

'Thank you, madam.'

She looked back through the rear window of the *bakkie* in time to see Tate pulling a sandwich from his daypack. It looked like it had come from the flight they'd both been on. Tate handed the boy the food, and the youngster beamed with gratitude. He was breaking it in two as he and the old man shuffled off.

Braedan returned with half-a-dozen loose bottles of Castle Lager in his hands. Natalie leaned across and opened the door for him. Braedan upended one of the bottles and hooked the edge of its cap under the lid of a second bottle and levered it off with a loud *pop*. 'Call of the wild, hey?' He offered the open bottle to Natalie.

She hesitated. 'Is this legal, drinking in a car?'

Braedan smiled. 'You're not in Australia now.'

She took the bottle, but nuzzled it between her legs as they drove off through town. Braedan kept his bottle out of sight, too, as he weaved around a ZUPCO bus belching black smoke and crabbing up the main street.

The shops looked tired and in need of a lick of paint and a lot more business. Some stores were closed completely: newspaper behind broken windows or rusting wire mesh security screens pulled down and locked. A queue of people snaked around the corner from a Zimbank branch. *Diesel, yes, petrol, no*, the chalkboard in front of a fuel station read. Shortages might have eased since Zimbabwe's transition to foreign currency, but the country's problems were still a long way from being solved. It all seemed so terribly sad.

And yet . . . there was something about the place. Natalie had suffered nightmares for years after what had happened to her. After her kidnapping and Hope's murder, Natalie's father, a decorated helicopter pilot, had resigned his commission and taken the family to Australia. Natalie had learned to love the peaceful order of Australia, but being back was stirring a mix of dormant emotions in her.

'You know,' said Braedan, pausing to take a long swig of beer once they cleared the small town's limits, 'I always thought it was a shame your family left Rhodesia.'

'Why's that?' she asked.

'It was like somehow the terrorists had won, even before the end. I kind of thought there was no hope, once you'd left. I don't know why your dad never liked me, but he was a legend in the air force. He was one of their most experienced chopper pilots and a hell of a brave *oke*. Him leaving must have hurt his squadron's morale. But, like, the whole country got a shot in the arm when . . .'

She looked at him, waiting for him to finish. 'What?'

'Nothing.'

He turned to glance out the window, but she saw the colour in his cheeks. She wondered if he had been going to say that the country's morale had jumped when he rescued her from the terrorist gang. He'd stopped himself, perhaps not wanting to sound boastful. Perhaps he wasn't as arrogant as he at first appeared. She changed the subject. 'I remember Aunty Hope's funeral. You weren't there.' She didn't tell him how much she'd wished he was. She had been devastated by Hope's death – they all had been – but Natalie remembered seeing Braedan just before Hope left for Kariba. She knew now, piecing it all together, that was the night he must have slept with her. Or had they been seeing each other more often?

'My unit was sent on a raid into Mozambique a couple of days after the Viscount crashed. Just as well probably, as Tate might have killed me if I'd shown up.'

Natalie couldn't share his smile. She knew she would soon have to write about her memories, and that many, like those of Hope's funeral, would hurt her. 'I remember the coverage on TV. The government made such a big thing about it. Ian Smith came to our house. My father won't talk about it – any of it. Not about me being taken, or Hope being killed. I tried to get him to, for the book, but he's put up a wall.'

Braedan nodded. 'Maybe a good thing.'

'What are you going to do here, for a job?' Natalie asked, changing the subject completely. She didn't want Braedan to go all strong-silent-type on her now that she'd found him and got him talking.

'I don't know,' he said. 'There's not much an ex-troopie and ex-farmer can do in this country. I'd like to get work as a safari guide, but the tourism business is still dead. If I can't find anything I might join the other three million Zimbabweans living in South Africa and Botswana and try and find work there. Trouble is, though, that I'm a middle-aged white man, which hardly puts me at the head of the hiring line in any African country.'

It was dark when they came to Gweru, the main city of Midlands Province. The power was out, so it was a gloomy, slightly eerie crawl through the town she'd known as Gwelo. Natalie and her family had lived just out of town for a while, on the Mvuma Road, near the sprawling Thornhill Air Base where her father had been posted for a couple of years as an instructor.

'In the old days, before we had candles, we used to have electricity,' Braedan said as he braked to avoid running into a truck that was driving without lights.

Natalie gripped the dashboard to avoid being thrown through the windscreen. It struck her as crazy that she would be driving in the black night with no seatbelt, while drinking a beer. It was unsafe and foolish, but at the same time it was oddly exciting; liberating, even.

'Another beer?' she asked Braedan, and leaned forward to pick two rolling bottles off the floor of the cab.

'*Ja*.'

Natalie unzipped her daypack and took out a Swiss Army knife. She used the bottle opener to open the beers and passed one to Braedan.

He raised the bottle to her. 'Welcome home to Africa, fucked-up place that it is.'

After eleven attempts, and being constantly told that the cellular phone network was busy, Natalie finally got through to her grandfather on his cell phone and told him she was nearing Bulawayo.

Grandpa Paul sounded delighted, as always, to hear from her, and when she told him she was getting a lift with the Quilter-Phipps boys he ordered her to make sure they stayed for supper.

'I'm sure their mom will want to see them,' she told him.

'Can they hear me?' Grandpa Paul asked her quietly. Natalie looked at Braedan, who was intent on drinking and driving and didn't appear to be paying attention to what she was saying.

'No.'

'Then make sure they both come to dinner, Natalie. Their mother's on a government pension that barely pays enough for her to buy a loaf of bread or a few potatoes a month. She'll want to see both the boys, but we'll be doing her a favour if we send them home fed.'

'OK Grandpa, I understand.'

The lights were on in Bulawayo, but the town still seemed dead. They passed a couple of restaurants that were open, but business was slow judging by the small number of cars and *bakkies* parked outside. Young men loitered in the shadows of shop awnings. She'd loved coming here, before the incident on her grandparents' farm. She loved the big wide streets, and the carpet of purple blossoms shed by the jacaranda trees, and Lyon's Maid ice cream from the little place near the Haddon and Sly department store. Nineteen seventy-nine changed all that.

Once out of town the road towards Plumtree and the Botswana border took them through open, undulating grass-lands studded with granite kopjes. It was beautiful, empty and wild. She'd loved this drive as a child, but now she was heading back to the land of her nightmares.

'Remembering?'

She looked across at Braedan. 'Oh, yes, sorry. Lost in my thoughts.'

'It happens. This country's got too many ghosts and not enough soul any more.'

'Yet you've come back.'

He drained his third beer and slipped it under his seat. 'I'm like a lot of people here – I've got nowhere else to go. The ones with money and relatives overseas have gone; the ones with small kids have gone to find them a better education; the ones with professional qualifications have gone to places that appreciate them, and that leaves the ones like me.'

'My grandparents have stayed.'

'*Ja* . . . and then there are the idealists. The ones who believe that if they hope and pray and have faith in the goodness of man and the strength of the human spirit then things will come right.'

'You sound like you don't believe it.'

'I don't. But don't get me wrong – I like your grandparents, always did.'

And it was true, he did. And they seemed genuinely pleased to see him and even sour old Tate, Braedan thought.

They'd passed through two security gates manned by smartly dressed Africans who'd made them sign in and radioed ahead for permission for them to proceed. The parallel fences looked in good condition and Braedan had heard the *tick, tick, tick* that told him the fences were electrified and the power was on.

The Bryants met them on the gravelled drive outside the same farmhouse they'd lived in when Braedan had parachuted into the field at the back. Braedan took in the place while Natalie's grandparents hugged and kissed and fussed over her. The fire damage had long since been repaired and the place looked a little larger than he remembered – some extensions over the years, he thought – but like everywhere else in this country it was another reminder of the life they'd all once lived, good and bad. A Land Cruiser *bakkie* was parked under a carport next to the house, and Braedan could see it was packed with camping gear.

Old Paul Bryant must be at least ninety, but his eyes were clear and his handshake was strong. 'Good to see you, again,' he said, and Braedan could still hear the slight twang of the Australian accent in the old man's voice. He wore a two-tone farmer's bush shirt of green and khaki and shorts that looked as though they were handmade, with a simple elastic waist.

'Howzit, Mrs Bryant,' Braedan said to Natalie's grandmother. Pip was tiny – he'd remembered her as being short, but she'd shrunk with age. She'd made her face up a little and he could see where Natalie and Hope had got their looks.

'Braedan, how lovely to see you.' Pip gave him a hug and she felt as though she might snap in his arms if he put the slightest amount of pressure on her. She turned from him and beamed up into Tate's face. 'Tate, Tate, Tate . . . it's been too long, how are you, my boy?'

Paul clapped a bony hand on Braedan's shoulder and winked at him. 'Come, let's get a beer in before dinner.' Braedan let Paul lead him inside as Pip bustled along between Tate and Natalie.

Braedan smelled roast chicken as they entered the house, and a rotund African woman came out from the kitchen and said good evening to him and Tate. Braedan returned her greeting in fluent Ndebele and noted, with a touch of self-satisfaction, Natalie's surprise at that.

'Dinner will be ready in about twenty minutes,' Pip Bryant said. 'Portia,' she said to the maid, 'please won't you set another two places for dinner.'

'Really, Mrs Bryant, we're fine,' said Tate.

Braedan felt like smacking him. He was starving and the smell of the chicken was making his stomach do parachute landing rolls.

'Nonsense, Tate, you will stay for dinner. Portia's doing two chickens in any case, so it's fine.'

Pip wasn't unfriendly or unwelcoming towards Braedan, but she seemed much more interested in Tate. It figured, Braedan thought, as they were both rhino people. It seemed they'd had a bit to do with each other over the years.

And there, on the mantelpiece, over an already stacked fire of mopane wood interspersed with old mealie cobs, was Hope. If Paul Bryant noticed Braedan staring at the black and white studio print, he gave no indication of it. 'And what have you been up to lately, Braedan? I heard from your mother you'd been in Iraq and Afghanistan. Tricky places to fight a war, eh?'

Braedan gave the answers he usually did to such questions, about how hard it was to tell friend from foe, and how both countries were locked in internal conflicts that foreign troops could hardly begin to understand, let alone solve. But his eyes were drawn back to Hope's face. It must have been taken not long before her death, and it sent a shiver down his spine.

Paul suggested they go outside, on the pretext of showing Braedan the garden.

'Paul, dinner's nearly ready,' Pip said.

'Won't be a mo,' he replied.

Braedan wondered how much the Bryants knew about what had gone on between him, Hope and Tate. They would have quizzed Tate after Hope's death about why she'd got on a plane back to Salisbury so soon after arriving in Kariba. Tate probably told them there'd been an argument, but he would have been too embarrassed to tell them what the argument had been about. Still, Braedan mused, George and Susannah would have raised their eyebrows at the time Hope got home the night before she left; they would have put two and two together, but maybe they would have protected Hope's parents from the truth. He suddenly regretted being so candid with their grand-daughter. Would she put all that in her book? It was all so sad, but it was also ancient history.

'How does it feel being back here, on the farm?' Paul asked him, and Braedan took a sip of cold Lion Lager from his glass while he thought about that one. The old man was sharp, for sure.

'It's funny, hey,' he said at last. 'It was thirty years ago, but coming back here makes it all feel like it was just yesterday.' Braedan reached for his cigarettes and saw the grandfather's eyes brighten.

He looked furtively back at the farmhouse. 'Can you score me a loose one, Braedan?' he whispered. Braedan smiled and shook a cigarette free of the pack and lit it for Paul. He breathed deep, his eyes closed. 'She'd kill me if she knew. I expect you know all about Natalie's book by now. How do you feel about going over all that again?'

Braedan shrugged as he lit his own cigarette. 'It was different for me. I was just doing a job. Natalie wants to find answers, and to tie what happened back then into what's happening in the country now. Me, I'd prefer to forget it.'

'That's impossible,' Paul said, exhaling.

Braedan nodded. 'I know what you mean. It was different for you, in your day . . . during the Second World War, I mean. You won. You were a hero.'

Paul held up his hand. 'Enough of the bullshit, mate. I don't like that word. Fact is, for a good part of the war I was a coward, and it wasn't until I met Pip that I straightened myself out. But what you did, Braedan, was truly inspirational, at a time when people needed inspiring. The sensible thing for you and your men to do that day, the right thing, was to wait for reinforcements to arrive. But you didn't. You went out alone and you saved my granddaughter's life. That's a story that needs to be told.'

'Enough of the bullshit, *mate*,' said Braedan, imitating the Australian accent.

Paul laughed, then clapped Braedan on the shoulder again. 'We should get inside. The women will be clucking like those two chooks were a few hours ago. But first, I've got one more thing to ask you.'

'Sure.'

Paul preceded his question by telling Braedan that he had lost a rhino to poachers three days earlier – the second animal killed in the past twelve months. 'Things are so desperate here, one of my security guards was turned, by a bribe. I reported it to the police and he was arrested, but I just heard today he's been released on bail. He'll probably get out of the country before he can be prosecuted.'

'The rest of your guards?' Braedan asked.

'Good men, as good as you'll find, but they're human, Braedan. My senior guard, a former national parks warden, died of the Big A a month ago. I'd like to promote someone from within, but the truth is none of them has the leadership potential, or the will to take the fight to the poachers. They're not saying anything to me, and outwardly they're behaving as professionally as ever, but the fire's gone out of their bellies, Braedan. I think someone's getting to them.'

Braedan finished his cigarette and thought about what Paul Bryant was saying. He had nowhere near the interest or passion for wildlife and its conservation as his brother did, but this might be interesting work, with the prospect of a little action.

'I've got a grant from an Australian-based rhino conservation charity,' Paul went on. 'It's not much, but I can pay you in US dollars and you'll have a vehicle and a house on the farm, and I'll get your weapons permits sorted for you.'

Braedan had a mounting pile of debts both in Zimbabwe and Australia, and he was months behind on his child support payments. He wanted to see his daughters, Ashley and Jess, but couldn't afford an airfare to Australia, let alone the tickets to fly them both to Zimbabwe. He was, he knew, a burden on his mother as well. His life was a mess and he had few prospects. Anything Bryant could pay him would be more than he had now. He had one final question, though, before he accepted the offer.

'Why didn't you offer this to Tate? He's ex parks and wildlife and knows all there is to know about rhinos and anti-poaching operations . . . He could help you in so many more ways than I could.'

Bryant stubbed out his cigarette and threw the butt into a flowerbed. He took a sip of beer and swilled it around his mouth, before wiping his lips and looking Braedan in the eye. 'Tate's not a soldier, Braedan. You are. You have what it takes.'

CHAPTER 21

Tate didn't like sit-down meals, where one felt obliged to engage in meaningless small talk. Even in the field, where there were often a dozen or more researchers and students working on a project, Tate preferred to eat alone.

He found himself seated between Philippa and Natalie. Pip seemed to want to coddle him all the time, and Natalie kept leaning on her elbows so she could engage Braedan, seated opposite her, with more talk of his travels to various war zones.

Old Paul Bryant had come up with the terrible idea that the brothers and Natalie should travel with him and Pip to Hwange National Park the next day, to join them on the annual game census.

Natalie was obviously excited about the idea of going on the count, but Tate was a lot less enthusiastic. 'I was hoping we might have a word about the future of your rhinos, Paul,' Tate said, in between mouthfuls of chicken. He had no desire to camp out in the park and sit in the bush for twenty-four hours counting animals in the company of a bunch of farmers, for-eigners and amateur environmentalists.

Paul rested his knife and fork on the table. 'Come to Hwange with us if you want to talk, Tate.'

Tate had twice raised the issue of Paul relocating his rhinos to a larger conservancy, preferably in the Save Valley, in the southeast of Zimbabwe, where they might be less vulnerable than sitting on a farm out in the middle of Matabeleland, surrounded by properties that had already been overrun by war veterans. Tate himself was considering an emailed offer of a job as warden of the Save Valley conservancy and he would dearly love to have Paul's fourteen animals under his care.

'In any case,' Paul said, resting a hand on Braedan's shoulder, 'my rhinos are going to enjoy a much safer future thanks to this young fellow agreeing to be my new head of security.'

Tate stared across the table at his brother. 'What?'

'*Ja*, I'm going to be overseeing security and anti-poaching patrols.'

Tate was incensed. 'He knows nothing about rhinos!'

They all looked at him. Tate reddened. He realised he'd sounded churlish, but it was the truth.

'Braedan doesn't need to know about rhinos, he needs to know about catching poachers,' Paul said gruffly.

The war hero, Tate thought. He said nothing more about the appointment during dinner, but he was annoyed that instead of talking about much more sensible options for securing the long-term future of his rhinos, Paul Bryant had latched on to his wastrel brother as a solution. What Tate really wanted to ask Paul was what was going to happen to his precious animals after he died. The old man seemed in good health for his age, but he wouldn't be around forever.

Paul offered Tate and Braedan the use of a Toyota Hilux *bakkie* to travel to the game count. Tate weighed up the pros and cons of accepting the offer and coming along, or of getting a lift back to Bulawayo, then catching a bus to Harare.

In the end, he agreed. Braedan said something, which Tate didn't catch because he wasn't paying attention, and Natalie laughed uproariously. Tate looked to Braedan and saw him wink at the woman. Tate felt nauseous.

At Pip's insistence the brothers agreed to stay the night at the farm. Tate had decided he would go see his mother the next day, before leaving for Hwange. Pip showed Braedan and Natalie to their rooms, then laid a bony hand on Tate's forearm and whispered, 'Come with me.'

The guest rooms were in a wing of the house that had been added after the guerilla attack on the farm. Pip led Tate back into the old part of the house. She stopped by a door and Tate suddenly realised where he was.

Pip opened the door. 'I've kept it just as it was, well, apart from some of the fire damage that we had to repair.'

Tate saw the bed and the posters on the wall of rock stars he'd never known so couldn't remember. One, of a young man with long straight black hair, was singed at the edges. But mostly it was all exactly as it had been the last time he'd been in this room. They'd sat on the bed – he remembered it squeaking and his flush of panic, in case her parents heard. But all he'd done was kiss her. He was so shy, he didn't even know if, or how, he should touch her, but that kiss had left his head spinning.

It was his imagination he was sure, but he almost thought he could still smell Hope's perfume.

'I couldn't show Natalie,' Pip said in a hushed voice, 'as she'd probably *freak out* or whatever it is young people say. But you . . . I thought you'd . . .'

Tate, himself, was feeling a bit freaked out, but he knew people had to deal with grief in their own way. He had thrown himself into his work, Pip had maintained a shrine to her daughter; both of them thought of Hope every day of their lives. He didn't know what to do, or say. He felt Pip's spindly arm encircle him and hold him as tight as she could. Awkwardly, he put his own arm around her.

'I miss her so,' Pip said, her voice catching.

Tate felt the tears well behind his eyes. He wanted to blurt out that it was his fault Hope had been killed, that he didn't deserve to still be alive.

'Goodnight, Mrs Bryant,' Tate said, extracting himself from her embrace and walking out the bedroom door.

With the extra company and her grandparents' easy manner over dinner Natalie had not dwelled on what had happened to her in this house when she was a child. It was different, though, when she said goodnight and went to the room Grandma Pip had prepared for her. It wasn't Hope's room, thank goodness.

A scops owl called in the night, in a tree outside her window. Its soft, high-pitched *brrr brrr* might have sounded benign to anyone else, but it jarred her nerves. It was hot, which was normal for this time of year, but it was also very humid. She lay on her bed, a ceiling fan rotating slowly above her, and when she ran a hand under her T-shirt and down her tummy, she felt a sheen of perspiration. The owl called again, and she shuddered, despite the heat.

When she closed her eyes she saw the flash of light again, heard the boom and smelled the smoke. The men were banging on the door. She thought it was someone coming to rescue her from the fire. When the door crashed open she saw the face of nightmares long faded, leering at her, reaching for her.

She screamed.

Natalie sat up in the bed and clutched the sheet to her. She'd been more tired than she'd thought after the flight from Kenya and the long drive from Harare to Bulawayo, and she had drifted off to sleep, but the nightmare had woken her. She pulled her knees up to her chest and wrapped her arms around her legs.

It was irrational, she tried to tell herself. She felt suddenly embarrassed and hoped no one had heard.

It was still, and even hotter than before. Overhead, the ceiling fan had stopped turning. The power was out, which she knew was common in Zimbabwe. The president and his lackeys were more interested in making money for themselves than investing it in infrastructure. She'd read that water shortages were also common, although fortunately her grandparents had a bore on the farm.

Natalie crooked an arm behind her head and stared at the ceiling. She was thirsty. The wine had helped her relax back into the house, and kid herself she would be fine, but it had also dehydrated her. She swung her feet over the side of the bed. The polished concrete floor was fractionally cooler than the thick air that blanketed her. Natalie stood and padded, in her pyjama shorts and T-shirt, to the door. It creaked as it opened.

Without the starlight that illuminated her room, the hallway was pitch-black. She almost turned and went back into the bedroom. Don't be silly, she told herself. She hadn't been afraid of the dark as a child, until the attack on the farm in 1979. Since then she'd not so much been scared of the dark but of what it might conceal.

Natalie reached out and felt for a wall. She felt the hall runner, threadbare as it was, under her feet and started moving along the hallway. With each step she found her eyes adjusted a little more to the darkness. Her right hand, which had been running along the plaster, came to a void. Ahead of her was the door at the end of the corridor that led to the lounge room and kitchen.

Natalie realised where she was. This was the last room of the original building. Hope's room. Her room when she stayed over. She felt for the door handle and started breathing faster, suddenly afraid she couldn't get enough air into her lungs. She licked her lips . . .

It's all right, it's all right, she tried convincing herself. She failed. God, what was behind the door? She wanted to know, but couldn't bring herself to turn the knob. There was the light, the boom, the smoke, the smell of the man's sweat as he put a hand over her mouth and dragged her away. There was Aunty Hope's things, her pictures, her records, her perfume . . . There were the flowers on her coffin and Grandma and Grandpa crying as they lowered her down . . . There was . . .

Natalie gasped and spun around as a hand touched her arm.

'Sorry,' Braedan said, his wonky smile showing through the dark.

Her heart was pounding. 'God, you nearly gave me a heart attack.'

'Are you all right?'

'I was thirsty.'

'Kitchen's straight ahead, as far as I remember,' he said.

She nodded, trying to compose herself. 'This room . . . it's where I was sleeping that night.' Her hand was still on the door-knob.

He reached out and wrapped his hand around hers. 'You don't have to go through there.'

She looked at him, searching for his eyes to try to read them, but it was too dark. Was he just a muscle-bound grunt who'd saved her because it was his job, and slept with her aunt because he could . . . or was there more to him?

'Myself, I'm all for a little compartmentalisation of the soul, but don't ask me to spell that,' Braedan said.

'Compartmentalisation?'

'Some fears aren't worth facing.'

She laughed, and he put his finger to his lips as he lifted his hand from hers. 'I'm going to get that drink of water.'

'I'm thirsty too.'

He followed her through the next door and she felt safe with him behind her, watching her. She remembered burrowing her face in his uniform as he'd picked her up. She'd cried and cried as he'd carried her through the bush. 'You're safe now, you're safe now, my girl,' he'd said to her. She was just a child. And he had saved her.

In the kitchen Natalie opened the door of the fridge. 'Water?' she asked.

'I see a beer in there. Do you think your grandpa would mind?'

'He only has one a night, so I think you're safe.'

'Right. I saw him have at least three. I think he was sneaking them on the sly while your gran wasn't looking.'

'Shush,' she said. She took out an old plastic Coke bottle filled with water and passed him a bottle of Lion, then closed the door. 'We'll wake the house if we're not careful.'

'Outside?'

She nodded, and followed him out onto the front stoop. Braedan sat down on the step. He had on the same shirt he'd worn in the car, but unbuttoned as though he'd just thrown it on, and she suddenly noticed he was only wearing boxer shorts. He pulled his cigarettes from his pocket.

'Um . . . do you mind if I bum one of those?' She sat down next to him, the concrete cool on the bare skin at the back of her thighs.

'If any more of the Bryant family come out of the smoking closet I'll be forced to quit myself!'

'What do you mean?' She slid a cigarette from the offered packet.

'Nothing.' He leaned in closer to light her cigarette.

She coughed. 'Rough.'

'Zimbabwean – the finest sweepings from the floors of the finest empty tobacco sheds in the world. We can't even kill ourselves with decent cigarettes any more.'

She didn't laugh.

'Sorry.'

'It's OK.' She took another puff and exhaled. 'What does it feel like for you, being back here?'

He shrugged. 'Place was just about in ruins last time I was here. I went to plenty of farms that had been revved. It was the same old story. You got used to the destruction, to the heartbreak of the families involved.'

She didn't buy the tough guy act. 'Yes, but you didn't save a little girl at every farmhouse.'

He looked up at the stars and blew out a long stream of smoke. 'No. At a couple of places we got there too late, and little kids died.'

Natalie felt her whole body sag. 'I'm sorry, Braedan . . . I haven't really thought about what else you might have been through.'

'*Ag,* forget it. Like I said, there's some things I like to keep locked away, in a compartment, in here . . .' He tapped his heart. 'But, yes, I could tell you some stories of the fun we used to have, hey. We used to *jol* like there was no tomorrow in those days.'

For many of them, she thought, that was probably still the case. Natalie looked up and the sky was studded with stars. 'It's hard to imagine people having fun during a war, but I can remember my mom and dad having some big parties.'

His eyes caught some starlight and she could imagine how handsome he must have been in his youth – he was still a very good-looking man. There was something of that heroic youngster still in him, though dulled by too many years of hard living. She could see how Aunty Hope had been momentarily weakened by his mix of charm and bad-boy cockiness.

Braedan stubbed out his cigarette. 'I haven't felt so alive since those days. Funny, because a few of my mates didn't make it. It was all for nothing.'

He looked at her, and she couldn't read the expression in his face. He reached out a hand, towards her, and she felt her heart stop. Was he going to touch her? Could he somehow tell that she'd just been thinking he was attractive? Had she given him some kind of sign? She didn't think so.

'It's all right.' His fingers brushed her shoulder. 'Spider,' he smiled, flicking the tiny bug away.

She exhaled. 'Phew. For a moment, I thought . . .'

'Thought what?' His face was a picture of contrived innocence as he got to his feet. 'Early start tomorrow. Night Natalie.'

'Night Braedan.' *You cheeky bastard.*

The next morning Tate awoke and went to the dining room to find Pip waiting for him.

'Paul's taken Natalie and Braedan for a quick tour of the farm. He thought you wouldn't want to go, as you've seen it all before. You've probably seen more rhinos than any man in Zimbabwe.' She gave a little laugh, but Tate knew she was embarrassed by the deliberate snub. The tour must have been arranged the night before, without his knowledge.

'That's fine,' he said, sitting at the table. Portia came in and asked him what he wanted for breakfast. 'Some mealie-meal porridge, please, if you have it.'

'Is that all?' Pip asked. 'We can do bacon, eggs, sausage . . . whatever you want.'

'I learned to eat pretty sparingly during all the years I spent with parks and wildlife.'

Pip nodded, and when Portia had left the room she said, 'My husband means well, Tate.'

'I know he does, Mrs Bryant.'

'Please, I've asked you a million times, call me Pip.'

He nodded.

'He *is* worried about what will happen to the farm, to the rhinos, after we're dead, but he's right to believe they're currently safer here than anywhere else.'

Tate poured himself tea from a pot covered with a crocheted cosy. 'What makes him so sure? Because he's appointed my brother head of security?'

Pip shook her head. 'You two really don't get on, do you?'

He let the question hang as he took his cup of black sugarless tea and sipped it.

'Well,' she continued, 'Paul has a good friend, an African friend, by the name of Kenneth Ngwenya. Kenneth and his children are very well connected with ZANU Popular Front. One of his sons is a government minister.'

Tate was surprised by the connection. 'Not Emmerson Ngwenya?'

'Yes.'

'My God, Mrs Bryant . . . Pip . . . he's . . .'

Pip took a sip of her tea. 'A little shit.'

Tate spluttered as his tea went down the wrong way. The profanity seemed so much stronger coming from this dainty old lady in her freshly pressed flowered pantsuit. He smiled. 'A good summation. You know he's responsible for a good deal of rhino poaching.'

She nodded, then paused as Portia brought in Tate's porridge and a fried egg on toast for Pip. 'Thank you, Portia.' Once the maid left, Pip leaned forward, elbows either side of her plate.

'That's the worst kept secret in Zimbabwe, but, yes, Emmerson is bad news all right.'

Tate shook his head. 'I don't understand it. How can Paul think his rhinos are safe if he's friends with one of the most corrupt families in the country?'

Pip sat back in her chair. 'No, no, no. Kenneth is a wonderful man, very highly principled. He was a schoolteacher when we knew him in the old days, and because of his service during the liberation war he was eventually made director general of the education department. He did some very good things in the early days, after independence. Also, his daughter, Thandi, is a lovely girl. She's an MDC minister. Brother and sister both in cabinet on opposite sides. The foreign media love that. Emmerson is the black sheep, so to speak, but Kenneth keeps him in check.'

'Yes,' said Tate, 'I've heard of her, but this Kenneth . . . he must be, what . . .'

Pip nodded, knowing where his question was headed. 'Yes, pushing ninety, like me. That's what worries me, Tate. There's this new round of land invasions going on, and if Kenneth were to pass away, Paul and I would lose our protection and Emmerson would be in here like a shot. He is, after all, Assistant Minister for Land Redistribution.'

'The fox in charge of the henhouse.'

'Exactly,' Pip said. 'What I'm trying to say, Tate, and I hate going behind Paul's back, is that I think you're right and that my husband is wrong. I think we need to move the rhinos to the conservancy before it's too late. But he's terribly stubborn, Tate, and he is absolutely devoted to those animals, as am I.'

Tate blew on a spoonful of porridge and thought about how terrible it would be if all the rhinos in Zimbabwe were killed by the likes of Emmerson Ngwenya and his cronies. He looked across the table into the elderly woman's piercing blue eyes. 'We'll make a plan, Pip. I won't let your rhinos be taken and killed.'

The morning was cool enough for Natalie to put on a light-weight cardigan, but the sky was clear and blue, promising another warm day. Natalie sat next to Braedan in the first of three tiers of canvas-covered bench seats in the back of an open-topped Land Rover Defender. Grandpa Paul sat in the front passenger seat, next to an African man in a green uniform.

Natalie had her camera with her and when the Land Rover stopped she snapped a picture of a yellow-billed hornbill, which had landed on a tree next to them. The morning sun shone through the bird's semi-translucent beak. It was a beautiful time to be out.

The African guide, whose name was Elias Masian, stood on the driver's seat and held up a T-shaped aluminium antenna, attached to a black box about the size of a handheld radio, which hung from a strap around his neck.

'We've got radio transmitters implanted in the horns of six of our rhinos,' Paul explained as Elias donned a set of headphones and slowly turned around, searching for a signal.

'We can't afford GPS transmitters, but with a property our size it's not too much of a drama as the rhinos can't wander far.'

Their drive took them from the farmhouse past the circle of six two-bed thatch-roofed chalets, where paying guests stayed, and a kitchen and dining room. The guest accommodation was empty, though, as usual. Tourists had been driven away from Zimbabwe long ago by stories of its ruined economy and the vio-lence associated with the early rounds of farm invasions, not to mention a succession of elections in which the government maintained its hold on power through torture, beatings and murder.

Paul waved to a maid who was opening one of the chalets. 'We still try and keep the place in good order, for when the tourists start coming back. It's a shame, you know, that people think Zim's a dangerous country. In fact, for travellers it's one of the safest places in Africa, but still governments around the world warn their citizens not to come here.'

Natalie nodded. She believed her grandfather, but she also knew it would be a long time before the tourists who had taken to holidaying in neighbouring Botswana and Zambia decided to give Zimbabwe another chance.

Natalie spotted a family of warthog nuzzling in the grass, and a herd of zebra that trotted away from the game-viewing vehicle once they realised they'd been spotted. Grandpa Paul told Elias to stop when they came across his herd of sable antelope.

'Beautiful, aren't they? I never get tired of looking at them,' he said to her, and she had to agree. The males were black with white blazes and impressive curved horns arching towards their backs. The females were a rich red-brown and the herd boasted half-a-dozen youngsters. The sable had been introduced to the ranch by her grandparents, but there were still naturally occurring populations of kudu and impala, some of which they spotted as they cruised slowly along a rutted dirt road. 'Enjoy your African massage,' her grandfather said when he turned and saw Natalie gripping the bar in front of her seat.

Braedan snapped his fingers. Paul swivelled in his seat and turned to look off to the left rear, where Braedan was pointing. 'There's one,' Braedan said softly.

'Ah! Chete! Come, my girl!' Paul called, then whistled loudly.

The rhino cow emerged from a thorn thicket and trotted towards the vehicle. Elias glanced at the animal, and then ignored her, returning his attention to rotating his antenna and listening into his headphones.

'Do you have that apple I asked you to bring from the kitchen, Nat?' her grandfather asked.

Natalie reached into her camera bag and pulled out the apple as the rhino came closer. She handed the apple to her grandfather, then snatched up her camera. She peered through the viewfinder then leaned back involuntarily as the rhino's head filled the screen. When she lowered the camera she saw the huge animal was right next to the truck. Chete snorted and Natalie could feel her hot breath as Chete raised her big head. Grandpa Paul held up the apple and Chete reached for it with her hooked lip. Paul held onto the fruit as Chete leaned in close and bit off half of it. Her grandfather scratched the rhino behind one of her long ears.

'What happened to her horn?' Natalie asked. Her heart was beating fast, being so close to this huge prehistoric-looking animal.

'We cut it off,' Grandpa Paul said.

'I have found Chengetai,' Elias said, removing his headphones and settling back down into the driver's seat.

'Good,' Paul said. 'We'll go find the cranky old cow just now. Now, what was I saying, Natalie?'

'You were talking about cutting off the rhino's horn, Grandpa. I've read about that being done, but some experts have said it doesn't stop poaching.'

Her grandfather crooked an arm under the rhino's head and lifted it away. To encourage her to turn away from the Land Rover a little he held out the remainder of the apple with his other hand. When he had a gap he opened the door. 'Come give me a hand, please, Elias.'

Paul got out of the Land Rover and for a second Natalie

thought he might be crushed between the bulk of the rhino and the vehicle. Elias walked around the front of the truck. 'Climb down, I want to show you something.'

Natalie climbed down, her heart beating a little faster at the prospect of being on foot next to the rhino, and Braedan got off the other side and walked around the rear of the Land Rover to join them. Once they were all present, Paul reached down and grabbed Chete's right front leg. Elias made soothing, cooing noises in the animal's ear and leaned against her, steadying her.

'Look here, on her foot – see the notch?'

Natalie moved closer and bent down until she could see the narrow arrowhead groove in the animal's foot. 'Is that naturally occurring?'

'No,' her grandfather said. 'The problem with dehorning in other parts of Africa was that it didn't stop poachers tracking rhino. It's hard work dehorning every animal on a farm, let alone in a big national park, so you've always got some who have been dehorned and some who haven't.'

Natalie nodded, then stepped back a couple of metres so she could get some pictures of her grandfather while he talked.

'Morning, sir,' said a voice behind them. Natalie turned and saw a jowly African man walk out of the trees. He was dressed in the ranch's green uniform and carrying an AK-47.

'Morning, Doctor,' Grandpa Paul said. 'You're out early. You should be at home in bed, still with your wives.'

'I was just checking on the patrols, sir.' The man smiled and Paul introduced him as Doctor Nkomo, the acting head of security on the ranch. Braedan and Natalie shook hands with him. 'I am not a real Doctor,' he explained, 'but my mother had high hopes.'

'I was just talking about our dehorning program,' Paul said. 'We've got, what, Doctor, seven rhinos dehorned now?'

'Six, sir,' Doctor said.

'Ah, my bloody memory,' Paul said. 'I just can't seem to remember numbers any more . . . Anyway, what the poachers would do, in the early days of dehorning, was track a rhino and when they caught up with it they would kill it, regardless of whether it had a horn or not.'

Natalie stopped taking pictures. 'But why would they kill it if it had no horn – out of spite?'

Paul shook his head and he and Elias lowered Chete's foot to the ground. She snuffled and nuzzled his belly, almost pushing the elderly man over. Elias scratched Chete under the chin and tried, in vain, to keep her from the man she clearly adored. 'There, there, my girl,' Paul said, feeding the rhino the rest of the apple. 'The poachers would kill a dehorned rhino simply to save themselves the effort of tracking the same animal again in the future. Also, if even a tiny stump of horn had begun to grow back, they would take that. So, we now carve the notch in the foot to –'

Natalie's eyes widened as she understood. 'To send a message to the poachers. It's like a code.'

'Precisely,' Paul said.

'How do you get the word out? I mean, it's no good making marks in the hooves if the poachers don't understand what the new tracks mean?'

'Doctor?' Paul said, looking to the security man.

'Mr Bryant, he tells us to go out to the shebeens when we are on leave, and that when we drink we must tell everyone in the bar what we have been doing here. We talk about carving the marks in the *bejanes'* feet, and we lie about the numbers of guards.'

'I like it,' Braedan said. 'But what's to stop poachers going after your good rhinos, the ones without the marks in their feet.'

Paul spread his open palms wide and looked soulfully at Chete who, having received her treat, had ambled away to snack at an inviting bush. 'Nothing at all. It's a war of attrition, Braedan, as you'll soon learn. If a poacher spends an extra few hours or a day on my property looking for a horned rhino, if he knows it's not worth following the tracks of a dehorned one, then that might give us the time we need to catch him. If he decides to let the dehorned one go, then that's a minor win for us . . .'

'Why don't you dehorn all of them, Grandpa?'

'I hope to soon, while I'm still here and while all my rhinos are still here. But it takes time and money, and Zimbabwe's running out of both of those commodities.'

'Aren't you worried about leaving the rhinos alone, while you go off to the game count?' Braedan asked.

Paul shrugged. 'What can I do? I can't be here all the time. I have to trust my security people and that's where you come in. Part of your job, Braedan, will be to train Doctor here to take over from you eventually. He was second-in-command to the guy I've just fired.'

Natalie noted the flash of resentment on Doctor's face. She wondered if he felt insulted at having a white stranger put in over his head.

'When do you want me to start?'

'As soon as we get back from the count, if that suits you,' Paul said.

'Fine.'

CHAPTER 22

They left the farm just before eleven and it was already scorching hot. Paul and Pip led the mini convoy out of the gates to the house and down the long access road through the bush to the main gate. Tate followed in the Hilux, apparently very happy to be on his own, while Braedan and Natalie brought up the rear in Braedan's Nissan.

'You're taking this game count thing very seriously, I see,' said Natalie, nodding at the green bush shirt and matching shorts Braedan was now wearing. The shirt bore the machine-stitched logo of Kiabejane, the name of the Bryants' ranch, on the left breast. The name meant 'home of the black rhino'.

Braedan smiled. 'I'm not interested in counting animals in a national park.'

'What do you mean?' Natalie asked.

He winked at her. 'You'll see.'

Doctor was standing at the entry gates, next to the security guard on duty. He smiled and waved at the Bryants, and at Tate, but his face was cold as Braedan and Natalie passed under the boom. Natalie waved and Doctor pointedly ignored her farewell.

You'll keep, Braedan thought.

Once they were off the farm there was another two kilometres of dirt track before they reached the main road back to

Bulawayo. This had been the feeder road for three other cattle farms in the district, all of which had been taken over by so-called war veterans.

'Check the fences,' Braedan said, pointing out the window.

Natalie nodded as she wrote something in the notebook balanced on her leg and Braedan tried hard not to let his eyes linger on her smooth thigh.

'Are you taking notes for the book?'

She nodded.

'They let the fences fall into disrepair,' he continued, 'and then the cattle roam wherever they bloody well want. When there's an outbreak of disease, like foot-and-mouth, it spreads to hell and gone before anyone can do anything about it.'

'Who's *they* exactly?'

'Farm invaders, war veterans, *wavets*, new farmers: call them what you like. They say this land is theirs and that we whites didn't deserve it, but as soon as they get it they strip the farms bare of anything of value then let the land go to ruin. Farms didn't only go to veterans of the liberation war, they went to politicians, party faithful, serving soldiers, public servants. Plenty of them have jobs in town and hardly ever get out to their farms. Sometimes you see them in their brand-new Hiluxes that they get cheap through government grants, coming out to their property for a *braai* on the weekend, and that's as close as they ever get to working the land.'

Natalie looked out the window. There was a clutch of roughly built mud huts with thatched roofs.

'A couple of families, living like they did two hundred years ago,' Braedan said, following her eyeline. 'That's all there is on this farm.'

'If they want to live that way, then who are we to say they shouldn't?'

Braedan shook his head. 'Don't give me that politically correct crap, Natalie. That farm probably supported a hundred, maybe two hundred Africans when it was white owned. These places were like mini communities – mine was, too. We had a little school for the kids and a chapel, and my wife used to run a small dairy herd just to provide milk to the compound where the Africans lived. All those people – dozens of families – were kicked off when we were. Overnight, the men had no jobs and the women had no homes or food for their kids.'

He checked his rear-view mirror as he passed the huts. He saw a couple of kids in baggy hand-me-downs crossing the road, along with a mangy dog. Paul's theory was that the men from this small settlement were prime suspects in the poaching of the last rhino to be killed on his property. The people living there were ZANU–PF supporters who had been bussed in, at the government's expense, four years earlier and told to take over the then white-owned farm. The thugs, none of whom were old enough to have fought in the bush war, had threatened and beaten the workers on the farm so that when they were ready to make their move on the owner's house the staff fled in fear of their lives rather than rallying to support their employer. Once the whites had been hounded out, the invaders had raided the house, looting furniture, carpets, light fittings, copper wiring and plumbing, and the pipes and pumps that watered the lands. It had all been sold and the money spent long ago. Those 'war veterans' who hadn't drifted away eked out a meagre living by growing a few straggly lines of mealies and running some thin, tick-covered cattle on what had once been a thriving ranch. The old herd of fat cattle had been slaughtered years ago.

'Those people back there,' Braedan said, glancing again in the mirror, 'have taken to poaching on your grandfather's farm to survive. Their party and their government have no need of them any more. They set snares to catch buck, to eat and sell, and he thinks they're responsible for killing at least one rhino.'

Natalie turned her head to look back through the dust thrown up by the *bakkie*, but the houses were out of sight now. 'So what are you going to do, now that you're going to be working on the ranch?'

'This.' Braedan stopped the *bakkie* and opened the door.

'What are you up to?'

He liked the sound of her accent, predominantly Australian but with traces of the old Rhodesian still there. Her clothes, unlike his, had become less safari. She wore short denim shorts and a lemon-yellow T-shirt, and slops. He would have liked to spend the next five hours in the car with her, on the drive to Hwange, even if she did insist on psychoanalysing him for her book. But he had a job to do.

Natalie got out as well and her eyes widened as he reached into the back of the Nissan and drew out a rifle from under his pack and a stack of extra camping gear her grandfather had loaded into the little vehicle.

'I need you to drive the Nissan into town for me, to my mom's place, OK? You can go to the count with Tate.'

'What's going on?'

Braedan took a daypack from the rear and slipped it on. He worked the bolt of the rifle, walked off the road and started into the long grass on the verge. He waved without looking back at her. 'Bye, honey, I've got to go to work.'

Natalie fumed all the way to Bulawayo. She followed Tate to the house in Hillside where his mother lived. It was, she thought, the poorest looking house in the best neighbourhood of the once prim and proper colonial town.

Sharon Quilter-Phipps opened the sliding security gate by herself. Either the electricity was off or she couldn't afford an electric motor for her gate.

She was a bony woman wearing a faded cotton sundress. Natalie followed Tate through the gate. Weeds sprouted through the gravel on the driveway and the brittle yellow grass looked as though it hadn't been cut for months. The paint was peeling from the wooden eaves of the sagging shingle roof. A skinny dog barked at Natalie and jumped up so that its paws scratched at the driver's door of Braedan's little truck.

'Down, Roxy!' Sharon said.

Tate's mother wrapped her near skeletal arms around her son as soon as he got out of Grandpa Paul's truck. Tate dwarfed her, and while he reached an arm around her shoulders, Natalie could see his body was rigid in her embrace.

'How are you, my boy?'

'Fine, Mom,' he said, extricating himself from her hug.

'Roxy, DOWN!'

For a small woman, she could yell, Natalie thought. Perhaps it was a necessary quality for bringing up twin boys. Tentatively, Natalie got out of the Nissan, now that the dog was fussing around Tate's legs. It looked like an African dog, one of the whippet-like animals that had been called KDs, or kaffir dogs, when she was a child, in a less politically correct era.

Tate mumbled introductions and Natalie took Sharon's dry, papery-skinned hand. She could see what her grandfather had meant, without even looking inside the house. Sharon was like thousands of other pensioners in the country who had seen their pensions whittled away by rampant inflation and a government that cared nothing for them. It wasn't only whites who had been hard hit by the government's ruinous economic policies, Natalie knew, but at least elderly African people could usually count on the support of their extended families. The children of many retired whites, like Sharon's, had left Zimbabwe to start their lives anew. Tate and Braedan were back, temporarily at least, but up until yesterday Braedan had been unemployed, and, from what Natalie had learned, Tate seemed to drift from one conservation assignment to another.

'You won't stay for lunch?' Sharon asked Natalie.

'We have to get going, Mom,' Tate said. 'We're going to Hwange.'

'Haven't all the animals been killed up there?'

'No, Mom,' Tate said, using the tone a condescending adult might use with a child. 'We've got to go. Bye.'

Natalie would have liked to have stayed and chatted with Sharon. It would have been interesting to get her views on the current situation; Natalie intended to touch on the plight of the poor whites in Zimbabwe in her book. Tate said nothing as he pulled out of the gate and followed the Bryants, who had been waiting out on the road, into central Bulawayo.

In the silence Natalie wondered what on earth she was doing here. Things were moving too fast for her liking, although she guessed that was part of life in this mixed-up country. She'd planned to spend a few days at least on her grandparents' farm, and maybe to line up some sit-down interviews with Braedan. Instead, she and Braedan had been thrown together on the long journey from Harare and she'd barely had five minutes with her grandfather. It seemed pointless trying to make plans in this place. Now she was on another long road trip, this time with a man for whom talking was as comfortable as a trip to the dentist.

Tate stared straight ahead, through the windscreen, as he slowed at a busy intersection where the traffic lights were out. There was probably no power at all in this part of town. It could have been a recipe for disaster in other parts of Africa, but somehow, through some unseen signals, Tate was able to coast across the intersection without any horns blaring or tyres screeching. Even in the face of chaos, there was a kind of natural order in Zimbabwe.

She had a few childhood memories of Zimbabwe's second largest city, but what struck her as they drove through the town was the absence of white people. Blocks of flats which had once housed single whites and urban professionals were now run-down, unpainted, with torn curtains or sheets tacked in the windows. The whole country seemed down on its luck. In many ways, other parts of Bulawayo reminded her of an Australian country town, with its wide streets, parking down the centre of the road and shady covered verandahs in front of the shops and pubs. Zimbabwe was like a parallel universe, where growth and prosperity had not only stopped but had done a U-turn. It was like so many other places, only sadder.

Once out of town they headed north on the Victoria Falls Road, which would take them to Hwange National Park. The grass on either side looked parched, like straw, and the trees were a dull khaki. Tate was driving with the windows open.

'Perhaps we could have a little aircon?' Natalie asked.

Tate sighed and worked the electric window switch. He stabbed the airconditioning's 'on' button.

'Sorry. If you don't like it . . .'

He shook his head. 'No, it's fine. One gets used to economising in a country like this. Airconditioning is terrible for fuel consumption, but fuel's not the problem it once was.'

Natalie felt like reminding him that it wasn't his vehicle and his fuel they were using, it was her grandfather's, and that she didn't think he would mind. She sensed, though, that if she tried to argue something with Tate he might not utter another word for the rest of the long journey. That might be OK, but she did also have a story to cobble together about the rhino program in Tanzania, to pay off the contra deal she'd received from Maasai Wanderings.

Her editor wanted a break-out box biography of Tate Quilter-Phipps so she had to persist with him. 'You were the last white warden of Hwange, weren't you?'

'No.'

'Oh.' This was going to be even harder than she'd thought. She now wished her grandparents had more than two seats in their Land Cruiser pickup.

After a long minute Tate said, 'I was *one* of the last white wardens in the parks and wildlife service. There were a few of us who hung on until not long ago. I was never warden of the whole of Hwange, just of a couple of the camps, Robins and Sinamatella, at different times.'

'I read a quote from an overseas wildlife fundraising organiser who said that without you there would be no black rhino left alive in Zimbabwe today.'

'Rubbish.'

Natalie laid her pen down on her notebook. She thought of herself as a capable journalist and normally she could get blood from a stone. A usable quote of more than one syllable from Tate, however, might be the greatest challenge of her career. She stared out the window, trying to think of a way to get him talking. Flattery clearly wasn't the answer. She saw more mud-walled huts and waved back at a little girl in a hand-me-down T-shirt. She wondered if these were more farm invaders, or just desperately poor people.

When she glanced at him she saw Tate staring through the windscreen, his hands gripping the wheel, his shoulders slightly hunched. She hoped he was just socially inept and not a psychopath. She closed her notebook.

'Write this down.'

She looked at him, but he didn't acknowledge her. She opened her notebook again.

'Charles Moyo.' He paused until he heard her pen on the paper. He didn't so much as glance at her. 'Matthew Sibanda. Patrick Mangwana. Augustine Nkomo. Sylvester Gono. John Little.'

Natalie wrote in shorthand, and Tate spoke the names slowly and deliberately. She would check spelling and write them in full later. For now, she wanted him to keep talking. She waited.

'There are still rhino in this country today because of those men,' Tate said at last.

The dry countryside flashed by. Tate drove in silence. She grew tired of waiting.

'OK. Who are they? Wardens? Are they conservationists? Parks' employees?'

'They're all dead.' Tate blinked a couple of times. 'If you want a story,' he said, 'then write the story of those men, who all gave their lives in the fight against poaching in this country. It's a war, you see, and it never ends. Men like those don't receive medals – they hardly even get paid these days – but they go out every day, on foot, with rags on their back and hardly any food in their packs, and they hunt poachers. They kill them, and sometimes they are killed.'

'John Little?'

For the first time he looked her way, and raised an eyebrow. 'You *would* single out the only white man, wouldn't you?'

She said nothing to that. Natalie searched her memory to see if she had ever interviewed anyone as rude as Tate Quilter-Phipps. No, he was the rudest.

'John was a helicopter pilot. A New Zealander. He was a bush pilot in the Okavango Delta for a number of years – had a bad crash there taking a media crew out and almost died. He used the compensation payout to buy his own helicopter, a little Robinson R22.'

Natalie scribbled away, but felt a chill because Tate was talking about a dead man.

'We couldn't afford to pay him, although a charity in Australia provided just enough money for John's fuel and maintenance of his helicopter. He was probably the most valuable resource we had in the fight against poaching in Hwange.'

Natalie paused. She didn't need to ask the next question.

'John had spotted two gangs of poachers in three weeks. Rhino killings were at a ten-year low. He would spot them, then hover overhead until we could get an anti-poaching call sign to his location. Twice, he was fired on by poachers armed with AK-47s. He was fearless. Then one day he crashed and was killed in the fire that engulfed his helicopter. I paid for an independent air-crash investigator to come up from South Africa. There was little doubt in the man's mind that John's R22 had been sabotaged.'

'My God. I never realised . . .'

'Never realised it's a war or that people would murder a civilian? The other men whose names I mentioned were all rangers killed in the line of duty.'

'That's terrible.'

Tate nodded. 'Yes, but many more poachers than rangers have been killed. Properly equipped, properly trained and properly motivated, we can hold the line. At least we could in the days before the government became involved.'

Natalie was confused. 'Aren't you talking about government-employed parks and wildlife rangers fighting the poachers?'

'Yes. What I meant was,' Tate looked at her again, 'senior members of the government are now organising the poaching.

Rhinos are being shot to order by a man at the top of the tree. He's the same man who I believe ordered the sabotaging of John's helicopter. I can't prove it, but I will, one day.'

'Who is it?'

'Emmerson Ngwenya.'

CHAPTER 23

'Happy Birthday, Grandfather!'

Kenneth Ngwenya kissed his beautiful grand-daughter, Naomi, on the cheek and opened the small parcel wrapped with shimmering paper and a red bow. His fingers were stiff with arthritis and Naomi used her long, pink-painted glossy nails to undo the knot in the ribbon. Kenneth opened the gift box and there was a small device made of white plastic, with a grey screen on it. 'Thank you, my dear. May I ask, what is it?'

Naomi laughed, as did her two sisters, Patricia and Tumi, and her cousins, Emmerson's children Kenneth and Sally, who were all gathered around her. 'Oh my God, Grandfather, it's an iPod!'

'An iPod?'

Thandi shook her head. 'Don't tease the girls, Dad. You know what an iPod is. Don't you?'

Kenneth winked at his daughter. She was as lovely as her children. Thandi was a successful businesswoman, a holder of two university degrees and an MBA, a heroine of the struggle and a wonderful mother. She had also been elected as a member of parliament at the last elections and was the MDC's Minister for Women's Affairs in the fragile government of national unity. Her three girls were all university educated – Naomi was a lawyer, engaged to a doctor; Patricia was an engineer; and little Tumi, who was now twenty-three, was a chartered accountant.

Thandi had encouraged them all to pursue good careers, which Kenneth fully supported, but he thought it might be nice to see one great-grandchild before he died.

Kenneth's son, Emmerson, stood in the corner of the room, his arms folded. He had barely spoken to his sister. Kenneth's pride in having two children who had risen to the exalted positions of government ministers was tempered by the fact that Emmerson and Thandi were on opposite sides of the political divide, and hated each other.

'It is lovely, child,' Kenneth said to Naomi. 'Thank you, and thank you all for such wonderful presents. I shall listen to Duke Ellington on this little machine as soon as you put his music on it for me, Naomi.'

'Duke who?' Naomi rolled her eyes and Kenneth laughed. He was so fortunate. He just wished Patricia was still here with him. And Winston. He looked across at Emmerson.

'Maybe I should have bought you an iPod instead of a new house, Father. That gadget seems to have been your favourite present today.'

The mood quietened. Kenneth knew Emmerson's own children respected him to the point of fear, and Thandi's children were also intimidated by their famous uncle.

Thandi turned on her brother. 'Don't be so churlish, Emmerson. The girls bought these presents from their own wages.'

Emmerson unfolded his arms and took a step out of his corner. 'What are you saying?'

'Nothing.'

'Liar,' Emmerson, said, jabbing a finger at Thandi. 'You think you are so clever.'

'Not in front of the children,' Thandi hissed. 'Girls, go outside and see to the *braai*.'

Naomi glared at her uncle but backed down after just a few seconds of his cold, hard stare. Young Kenneth and Sally knew better than to get in their father's way, and were already gone. Thandi's three girls filed out quietly after them. It saddened Kenneth that on the rare occasions they all came together as a family, Emmerson and Thandi usually ended up yelling at each other. Today would be no exception. He sighed.

'I'll go see to the *sadza*,' said Emmerson's wife, Grace.

She was as quiet as a mouse, that Grace, Kenneth thought, as he watched her disappear into the kitchen. She was very well dressed and had a pleasingly rounded bottom and nice full breasts, not that sex was much on Kenneth's mind these days. He had always been faithful to Patricia, and he assumed she had been to him through the long years he'd spent in prison. He wished he could believe that Emmerson was true to his wife, but he very much doubted it. His son had a reputation as a ladies' man which he seemed to do little to deny. Indeed, Kenneth thought Emmerson was probably proud of the way he carried on with women half his age. There had been the pretty Kwaito pop star at the last ZANU–PF conference Kenneth had attended – what, twelve years ago? How time flew as one got older. The way Emmerson had writhed on the dance floor with her, and the way he had kissed her, openly, with his wife still somewhere in the banquet hall of the Kingdom casino at Victoria Falls had shamed his father, as it no doubt had shamed his wife. Kenneth had had words with him the next morning, but Emmerson, possibly still drunk, had told his father to go to hell. It had taken two years for them to speak to each other again. Emmerson had begged forgiveness, and Kenneth had accepted his apology. What else could he do – he was Emmerson's father.

But Kenneth had wondered about the timing of the apology. It had been a tumultuous time for Zimbabwe, back in 1999, when Emmerson had come to him, offering a heartfelt apology and promising he had also apologised to his wife for his philandering, and that it had come to an end. The Third *Chimurenga*, as the propagandists had dubbed it, was in full swing. As someone who had lived through the Second *Chimurenga*, the liberation war against the white colonial regime, Kenneth had been mildly offended to see the reclamation and doling-out of white-owned land to party supporters – some of whom had not even been born during the struggle, let alone been old enough to take part in it – painted in such terms.

Kenneth was not against land redistribution. In fact, he had championed the notion throughout the struggle, and after independence. He did not want a farm for himself – he was a schoolteacher, and despite his time as head of the Zimbabwean education system, that was how he still thought of himself – but he recognised every Zimbabwean's right to a piece of land to call his own. Land redistribution had gotten off to a good start, after the people's victory in 1980. When white-owned farms came up for sale, the government had first right of refusal to buy them and give them to people who were more needy. Britain had promised funding for compensation to white landowners, but this fell by the wayside as successive British governments paid less and less attention to the newly independent Zimbabwe and increasingly distanced themselves from promises made by their predecessors.

Kenneth felt the government could have done more than it did, even without the British funding, to compensate whites, or perhaps to encourage or even force them into joint ventures with African farmers. He'd spoken to several dispossessed whites in recent years who said that if they'd been told they had to take on a black partner, years ago, then they would have agreed to do so. They might not have liked the arrangement, but it would have been better, in hindsight, than being forced off their land by the mobs that ran riot during the past ten years.

'What I was saying,' Thandi said to her brother, hands on hips, 'is that I'm proud that my children all have professions – proper jobs with good wages, with which they can afford to pay for their grandfather's birthday presents.'

Emmerson spread his hands wide. 'What you are *inferring*, my educated sister, is that I did not pay for our father's home – this beautiful new home in which we are standing – out of my own pocket.'

Thandi shrugged. 'I said no such thing. I'm sure the money was yours, but where did it come from, Emmerson? Are ministers paid so well that they can afford a second home that costs nearly half a million US dollars?'

'How dare you!'

'Emmerson, Thandi, please.' Kenneth coughed. His chest was bothering him more and more as he grew older.

Thandi rounded on him, her eyes ablaze with the same fire he'd seen in them when he'd met her in Mozambique in 1975, on his release from prison. He'd crossed the border the day after Robert Mugabe. Kenneth, Mugabe and other senior figures in the struggle had been released by the whites on the understanding that they would beseech their underlings – ZANU in Mozambique, and ZAPU in Zambia – to enter into a fresh round of peace negotiations with the Smith government. Instead, they had joined the struggle and injected fresh resolve into the ranks of the comrades being trained outside Rhodesia's borders.

Kenneth had been swayed by the unassuming, highly educated Mugabe during the long hours they'd spent studying and discussing politics together in jail. On release, Kenneth had turned his back on the Ndebele-dominated ZAPU and ZIPRA, lead by Joshua Nkomo, and joined the ranks of the mostly Shona

ZANU. Kenneth had seen himself as being above tribal allegiances. He had also been able to see what others in his tribe and his former party had not – that Robert Mugabe would gain the upper hand in any power contest. There was enough of the pragmatist in Kenneth to want to serve the winning party.

'Thank you,' Kenneth said, but the silence between the siblings barely lasted a few seconds.

Thandi had reluctantly deferred to her father, but Emmerson saw an opportunity and jumped in. 'Are you saying I stole money, Thandi? Go on, I dare you to make such an allegation in front of our father. You people . . . you poison this country with your lies and unfounded accusations.'

This time Thandi ignored her father's raised hand. 'Thieving, parallel market currency exchange, call it what you will. You made millions by using your privilege to change US dollars on the parallel market and then buy back more forex while people were starving in the streets and dying of cholera in the country. You grew fat on our people's misery and your leader orchestrated the whole mess.'

Emmerson took a step towards her, puffing his chest out. 'How dare you? Be careful what you say in public, *sister*.'

'Is that a threat, little brother?'

Emmerson's nostrils flared and he half-raised a fist. For a terrible moment Kenneth feared his hot-headed son might strike his older sister. They had been like that as children. Thandi had sometimes goaded Emmerson to the point where he would lash out at her, even though she was a foot taller than he. Kenneth had missed too much of their childhood after that point. He knew he was partly to blame for the way Emmerson had turned out. The boys had missed a paternal presence during their formative years and Patricia, for all her goodness, was a hothead who wore her hatred of white rule like a badge of honour.

'It is a word to the wise, though I don't know if you fall into that category any more. You run with a bunch of dogs that are fed scraps by the British and Americans. You are a traitor to your party and your people, Thandi.'

'In case you haven't read the papers,' she retorted, 'even your own partisan rag, the *Herald*, we are all one big happy family now, Emmerson.' She put on a smile of mock sweetness. 'And the MDC is committed to searching out corruption and putting an end to it.'

Kenneth slumped back in the deep leather-upholstered arm-chair that had come with the house that Emmerson had built him. It was a big house. A beautiful house. But it was too big and too showy for a man of Kenneth's modest tastes. He'd lived well enough when he was director of the education department, and he and Patricia had saved enough to buy a nice house of their own, in Burnside. It was big enough for their grandchildren to stay when they visited, and nice enough that he did not feel embarrassed when friends, such as Paul and Philippa, called on him. Patricia had never warmed to the Bryants, and as such the Bryants did not call on them while she was still alive, but Paul and Pip came often to see him now his wife had passed away. In return, Kenneth enjoyed his regular trips to the Bryants' ranch, and he was fascinated by the good work they were doing conserving the endangered black rhino.

In his wisdom Emmerson had decided that his widowed father needed to live in a six-bedroom mansion. He appreciated his son caring for him, as was the way it should be, but, really, he thought, *six* bedrooms for one old man? Kenneth sighed.

His children bickered back and forth. It seemed this time that Thandi was pushing harder and Emmerson's threats were not nearly as veiled as they usually were. It had been embarrassing enough for Emmerson when the independent press, muzzled as they were by the government, broke the story that the sister of ZANU–PF heavyweight Emmerson Ngwenya had turned her back on the ruling party and joined Morgan Tsvangirai's rebel Movement for Democratic Change. Things must have become even more uncomfortable for Emmerson when Thandi went on to win a seat in parliament in the 2008 election, and then became the party's spokesperson on women's affairs.

'The Government of National Unity is a joke, Thandi,' Emmerson spat.

Kenneth was as surprised as his daughter to hear Emmerson speak so bluntly.

Thandi had no comeback. It was true. After months of stalling over accepting the election results, which the MDC claimed to have won outright and ZANU, even after massive electoral fraud, still maintained it had won by a small majority, Robert Mugabe had finally conceded to the formation of a government of national unity.

'Is it true,' Kenneth asked his daughter, 'that Tsvangirai is considering pulling out of the Government of National Unity?' He couldn't bear to use the ungainly acronym, GNU, which was also the East African name for a wildebeest. The wildebeest was described by some as an ugly animal, with the long face of a horse, the curved horns of a buffalo, and a billy goat's beard. It looked like it had been put together by a committee, and it had a penchant for running around in circles and shaking its head. Commentators had predictably drawn parallels with the shaky new government.

Thandi looked at the floor. 'It's not for me to say, or to speculate, Father.'

'Ah! There you have it,' Emmerson said. 'You people and your colonial masters don't get what you want – unconditional surrender from Africa's greatest leader – so you turn and run away. Typical!'

Africa's greatest leader? Kenneth wondered if his son really believed that. There was a time, not even that long ago, when Kenneth would have agreed. Mugabe had promised so much, and the early days, despite what had happened in Matabeleland, were peaceful and prosperous.

Kenneth turned away from his children and watched the images from Afghanistan, playing on CNN on the widescreen television his son had insisted he needed. The volume was down, but the tragedy of war was evident in the eyes of the victims. It didn't matter which side was doing the killing. Kenneth asked himself if he really believed what he had just thought. *Despite what happened in Matabeleland?*

If he was honest with himself – and it pained him to realise that he had not been thus, all his life – Kenneth knew he had begun to lose faith in Robert Mugabe in the early to mid 1980s when the *Gukurahundi* had begun.

The word was Shona for the early rain which washed away the chaff before the spring rains; it referred to operations by the Zimbabwean Army's North Korean-trained 5th Brigade against ZIPRA and ZAPU rebels, following independence.

'Father?'

Kenneth looked up, away from the television and away from his terrible thoughts of his own guilt. *All that is needed*, Edmund Burke had written . . . and he, Kenneth Ngwenya, the principled schoolteacher, so-called hero of the Second *Chimurenga*, a good man, had done nothing. Evil had prevailed in Zimbabwe because too many of them had allowed it to happen. The recent elections had also been marred by terrible violence; Mugabe's ZANU–PF thugs had tortured and killed opposition activists and forcibly extracted the votes of illiterate people in rural areas through beatings and threats. 'Sorry, Thandi, my mind was elsewhere.'

She had her hands on her hips again. 'Did you hear what Emmerson just said? I cannot believe it!'

Kenneth shook his head.

'He said, Dad,' she drew a breath, 'that Mugabe will never stand trial for the deaths of thousands of people – thousands of our people in Matabeleland in the 1980s.'

Kenneth brought his palms together in front of his face, as though he was about to pray. Perhaps he should, perhaps they all should. 'He is too scared to go peacefully.'

'That man is scared of nothing, he is the hero –'

'Shush, Emmerson, at least let our father speak.' For a moment the younger brother deferred to the older sister.

But Kenneth had no more to say. The fact was that many people – no one still knew exactly how many, but best estimates put the figure between two and ten thousand – had been slaughtered by the 5th Brigade in Matabeleland during the early years after independence. Ex-ZIPRA cadres, dismayed at their party coming in as runner-up in the race for power against Mugabe's Shona-dominated ZANU, and angry that their erstwhile leader, Joshua Nkomo, had entered into a political alliance with Mugabe, had staged a show of force in Matabeleland and denounced the newly formed ZANU Popular Front party. The response by the army to this localised rebellion was disproportionate in the extreme. As well as killing former Ndebele freedom fighters, civilians were executed en masse, some in the most horrible ways imaginable. Pregnant mothers had been bayoneted, their unborn children torn from their wombs; people had been buried alive or burned to death in their homes; and ordinary people were tortured before being executed, for no other reason than they came from the Ndebele tribe.

His tribe.

'I tried to turn my back on tribalism,' Kenneth whispered. 'We all did. You, Thandi, went to Mozambique and became a senior member of ZANU. You, Emmerson, also turned away from your people, as I did. We all bear the blame for what happened.'

'Well,' Thandi huffed, 'at least I've seen the light.' She got down on one knee beside her father and laid a hand on the arm-rest of his chair. She leaned in close to him. 'Please, Father, come meet Morgan, he is a good man. At this time, more than ever, we need the voice of experience in our party.'

Kenneth only stared straight ahead. It had been the same with Emmerson. He'd come back, asking for forgiveness right at the time Mugabe was having one of his regular cabinet reshuffles. The President had needed another Ndebele in his government to try to counter the impression that his was a one-tribe government. Kenneth wasn't a regular visitor to Zimbabwe House, but he was still on the list for significant state receptions, and the annual Hero's Day reception. His old friend Robert invariably acknowledged him at these functions and on one occasion they also exchanged a few words.

'Your son shows promise, Kenneth,' the President had said to him at a reception for a visiting Chinese delegation.

'He throws himself into everything he does with great vigour,' Kenneth had said. He and his son had made their peace just the week before, but Kenneth had been scared by the inflammatory language Emmerson had used on television a few days before when describing how the people would rise up and kill any white who decided to use force to defend his farm in the face of eviction. He'd shaken his head at the hate he'd seen burning in his son's eyes.

After independence Emmerson had transferred into the new Zimbabwean Army, a force that was a blend of ZIPRA and

ZANLA guerillas, black soldiers who had served in the Rhodesian African Rifles, and even a few whites who stayed on in technical roles, such as pilots and armoured-car crews.

'I turned my back on nothing,' Emmerson said, interrupting Kenneth's thoughts. 'We united under a strong man, the President, and he is as strong now as he was when we put down those armed rebels in Matabeleland. Father is right, we cannot live by tribalism. There can be no mercy for people who would destabilise the peace of this country.'

'You twist my words, Emmerson.' Kenneth lowered his forehead to the tips of his clasped hands. *Perhaps I should just go to church and pray,* he thought. *There is nothing else that will mend this family, let alone this country.*

Enough of their words, Emmerson thought as he walked out of the lounge room and into the kitchen. It was no wonder his sister had become a politician.

Despite his own high office, Emmerson Ngwenya still thought of himself first and foremost as a soldier. He was a man of action, not words. If he had his way he would take the traitor Tsvangirai, and his white puppet masters, Bennet, Colthart and the others who told him how to dance, line them up against a wall and shoot each of them in the back of the head with his Makarov.

He opened one of the double doors of the new stainless-steel fridge he had bought for his father – something else the old man had neglected to thank him for – and took out a bottle of Coke. He fixed himself a double Scotch, then added the soft drink and held the tall glass under the ice dispenser while the cubes plopped out. He downed it in three gulps, then poured himself another.

The cell phone clipped to his belt vibrated.

'Hello.'

'It is Nguyen here, how are you?'

'Fine, and you?'

There was a pause. 'I am fine, thank you. Ah . . . we had discussed a time for the delivery, and that time has passed. I know this is Africa, but . . .'

Emmerson snarled. How dare the oriental insult him with the veiled reference to 'Africa time'. Nguyen van Tran was a political officer – a spy by any other name – with the Vietnamese embassy in Harare. Emmerson had made a deal to deliver another rhino horn to him. Nguyen had a diplomatic bag leaving for Hanoi tomorrow, and the horn should have been delivered to him yesterday. Emmerson had known the call would come, but he was still annoyed at the man's supercilious tone.

'It will be here, soon. There have been problems. When is your next shipment?'

'You are lucky. This one has been delayed by three days. Yours is not the only . . . ah, commodity, that has failed to arrive on time.'

Again, the insult, the implication of failure. Emmerson would like to beat the smile off the dapper, oily little man. But the deal was too lucrative, so he bowed and scraped, just as the Vietnamese wanted. 'No problem. It will be there, trust me.'

'I do trust you, but I can always look for alternative supplies. The market grows stronger by the day.'

It was true. The demand in Asia for rhino horn was increasing faster than it had for years, right at the time Zimbabwe was running out of the animals. Emmerson saw the pros and the cons of this situation and knew that he could make himself rich. He'd needed an alternative source of funds since the President had formally done away with the Zimbabwean dollar and the economy had switched to foreign currency.

The President was clever, Emmerson knew, but his decisions didn't always benefit the rank and file of the party. Mugabe had, eventually, made a concession to world opinion by forming the Government of National Unity with the hated MDC. Emmerson had been appalled at the time, and privately thought his leader was showing the first sign of weakness, but he'd been impressed these last few months with just how little power had been ceded to the opposition, and very pleased at the talk of Tsvangirai pulling out of the GNU. It was like a game of chess, he thought. Chess was a game Emmerson had never had the time or patience to learn. He remembered his father trying to teach him once, when he was six; Emmerson had swept the pieces from the board with his hand. That was how to win a game. By force.

It had been the same with the switch to a foreign currency economy. The wily old President had been smart, politically, to do away with his country's own valueless currency. Inflation had ended and virtually overnight traders were legally able to buy and sell goods that had been missing from shop shelves for years. There was fuel in the service stations and food in the supermarkets. By adopting foreign currency and bowing to pressure to form a government of national unity with the MDC, the president had also released the pressure valve of international media interest in Zimbabwe. As far as many people overseas were concerned, peace had returned to the country. Prices were still high, as nearly everything had to come from South Africa, but wealthy families like the Ngwenyas wanted for little.

Except cash.

Until recently Emmerson had made his money, as his sister pointed out, by continually changing hard currency for Zimbabwe dollars then back again. If you could get hold of US dollars from the reserve bank at the ludicrously low official rate – and as a government minister Emmerson could – then sell them on the street again at a stupendously inflated black-market rate and repeat the transaction, there was no limit to how much money a man could make. But that had ended with the switch to a hard currency economy, and Emmerson had seen the end to his cashflow problems in the skyrocketing demand for rhino horn in China and South-East Asia.

Emmerson had retired from the army as the commanding officer of the 1st Zimbabwe Commando Regiment. He had access to a network of serving and ex Special Forces soldiers that he called on from time to time to help him in his work as Assistant Minister for Land Redistribution. At his order, and with payment from a slush fund he'd personally set up, these men had beaten opposition politicians, intimidated farm workers who had dared to stick up for their white masters, and, lately, located and shot rhino to order.

He had a team of six men deployed at this very moment, looking for an animal to fill Nguyen's latest order. 'The men blame the moon – it is nearly full,' Emmerson said into the phone.

'The moon? Is this one of your African superstitions?'

Emmerson gritted his teeth. These people, he thought, were more racist than whites. Who was Nguyen to call him superstitious when he was paying tens of thousands of dollars for a pointed lump of matted hair? 'They are hard to track, especially at night when the moon is high. They see the men coming.'

'Ah . . . I understand, but unfortunately my, ah, backers at home are not so understanding. I don't need to remind you that a good deal of money has already changed hands.'

Emmerson gulped down half of his second Scotch and Coke. 'Yes, yes, yes. I know. My men are on the job. I expect a call at any time.'

There was another pause on the end of the line. 'I do hope

you are not leaving this business to your underlings. I am going to Victoria Falls the day after tomorrow. Your men, I gather, are in the area?'

Emmerson knew they had probably said too much over the phone, but who would be listening? The only threat he faced from the police or CIO was that they were probably also involved in poaching rings of their own and might see him as a competitor. Parks and wildlife were the only ones Emmerson had to worry about, and they were a toothless bunch of bunny-huggers. 'Not far from there, yes.'

'Normally, I would not wish to get ah . . . personally involved, but time is of the essence and I would feel, ah . . . more confident in our relationship if you were to take a stronger interest in this transaction.'

'You want me there, to do the handover?'

'Ah . . . yes.'

Emmerson licked his lips. He had kept himself at arm's length from the killing of the animals and the transport of their horns. It had all been done by his foot-soldiers and Nguyen's minion, a security guard at the embassy. The Vietnamese was putting him on the spot. He weighed the risks quickly. He did not want to appear weak, and there was nothing to stop Nguyen shopping elsewhere for his *commodity*. Emmerson needed this relationship more than Nguyen did. The President was an old man and Emmerson, despite his very public support for his leader and party, feared that ZANU–PF would crumble once Mugabe was gone. Emmerson needed to make as much money for the future as he could, while he was still in a position to do so.

'I will be there,' Emmerson said at last.

'Good. I am pleased. I will be staying at the Kingdom.'

'I will see you there.' Emmerson ended the call. Perfect, he thought. It would give him an opportunity to call on the twenty-three-year-old croupier he'd met the last time cabinet had sat at Victoria Falls. He loved the way she screamed his name when she rode him.

CHAPTER 24

Braedan knelt and traced a finger around the spoor. It was a black rhino, and there was no notch carved in any of the tracks he'd seen. That meant it still had its horn.

He'd found the place where the poachers from the nearby community had been coming and going from the ranch. It was a dry creek bed, sandy and studded with smooth granite boulders. The electric fences followed the contours of the land, but the soft bed was easily dug away to make tunnels so a man could crawl under the wire. Someone had used a cut-off branch to smooth away their tracks, but the brushing marks stood out as clear as footprints to Braedan's eye.

Braedan was disappointed. It was an obvious point to enter and exit the farm and he'd found it in less than two hours of walking outside the ranch's fence line. He used the same method of entry as a poacher would, sweeping his tracks up to the fence, digging away a gap with his hands, then sliding the sand back into place. Between the fences was the dirt access road. Braedan saw that one of the ranch's vehicles had not only passed recently but had stopped at this point, in the dry bed. Doctor – or perhaps the former head of security – clearly knew this was a spot worth checking.

Braedan had decided he would put a man in a hidden observation post, to watch this entry point. Doctor gave a good show of efficiency, but it had been laughably easy to enter the ranch.

Braedan paused by the tracks and listened to the bush. It was good to be back. A Cape dove cooed nearby and a woodpecker tapped out a Morse code welcome on a mopane. Braedan wiped the sweat from his eyes with a green handkerchief. It was humid for this time of year. There was a line of cloud building on the horizon. He set his rifle between his knees and tied the cloth around his forehead and knotted it. He'd worn a sweatband like this when he'd been a troopie. He picked up his weapon and moved forward.

A zebra gave its high-pitched braying call ahead of him. There were also wildebeest, impala, kudu and leopard occurring naturally on the ranch. Braedan spotted a length of wire in the grass. He stopped and knelt again. His fingers traced it to a loop that had been fashioned in the free end. The other was fixed to a sapling. A snare.

'Bastards,' Braedan whispered.

The so-called new farmers, who had squandered the wealth of the farm they had stolen, were now sneaking onto Paul's property and snaring game. It could have been to feed themselves, or to sell illegally in town, but either way it was still theft. Braedan pulled the Leatherman from the pouch on his belt and snipped off the wire near the trunk. He wound it into a loop and hooked it on his belt. He'd bring back the evidence to show Paul.

Braedan scooped up a handful of powdery dust and let it trickle through his hand. He watched its fall and saw the wind was building. However, he was still downwind of the rhino, so it wouldn't smell him as he approached it. He wanted to see how close he could get to one of the animals – how easy it would be to shoot one. The rhino he'd seen on the drive with Natalie and

Paul had been as tame as a pet. He wondered if they were all as easy to approach. He guessed it would depend on how many had been hand-reared and how many had been allowed to grow up 'wild' within the confines of the ranch.

He thought about Natalie. She was beautiful and smart, and at the same time there was something vulnerable about her. She reminded him so much of Hope it almost hurt. He wondered what sort of effect her presence was having on his cold, intro-verted brother. Braedan felt a prick of jealousy, knowing that Natalie was at this moment in a car with Tate, but he forced the thought from his mind.

He returned his attention to the job at hand. Black rhino were unpredictable and prone to aggressiveness. Tame or not, they might not take kindly to the presence of a stranger on foot in their domain. He followed the spoor along a well-trodden game path.

A pile of dark brown droppings littered the track. Unlike the white rhino, black rhino did not defecate in specific middens to mark their territory. They let it go wherever they felt like it. Braedan reached into the pile. It was still warm. He crumbled a cricket-ball sized piece in his hand. Black rhino browsed from trees and bushes rather than grazing grass. This one had been feeding on a russet bushwillow and each little twig in the drop-ping had been sheared off and chewed with teeth set at an angle of precisely forty-five degrees. This one was close.

He felt a charge of hunter's adrenaline. It was like being back in the war, hunting gooks. The rhino couldn't shoot back, but in time he might find himself stalking armed poachers around the farm.

Braedan had confirmed his terms of employment before Paul Bryant had left for the game count. The wage was only $15,000 a year. He'd earned nearly that much in a month, contracting in Iraq and Afghanistan, but those days were gone and he had no other prospects in Zimbabwe. The deal included food and board, in the security manager's cottage on the ranch, and a vehicle; yet even though the wage was reasonable compared to the pittance most people in this country earned, there would be little left over to put towards his debts. He was already a year behind on his child support payments and Lara was threatening to sue him. Also, he would have to set aside part of his pay for his mother. She'd supported him for the past year and he knew it had drained her meagre savings. She was living on the charity of her neighbours and an organisation called SOAP – Save our Old Age Pensioners. He felt disgusted that she had been feeding him for a while from her care parcels.

Braedan didn't want to think about his life and where it was heading. His new job would allow him to exist, but not get ahead. He might never be able to afford an airfare to Australia to see his kids, or to fly them over for a visit, and if he couldn't contribute to their education, then his wife might make sure he never saw them again. He knelt in the dust to check the spoor again, sighed, and shook the depression away. This was where he belonged, on the ground, in Africa. Right or wrong, he was at home here.

He had a rifle in his hands and he was back in the Rhodesian bush of his youth. The sun was tanning his bare arms and legs, which were now crisscrossed with scratches from thorns. Everything about this environment was hostile, from the cruel sun overhead to the snakes and scorpions that lurked in the grass and rocks at his feet. Even now a leopard might be watching him from a tree and today might be the day it chose to feast on a human instead of an impala. And the rhino, which he'd been enlisted to protect, might charge and gore him just for the hell of it. But he loved it here.

He heard a snort.

Braedan melted into the shadow of a stout leadwood tree. As a precaution he raised the butt of the .303 into his shoulder. He peered through the curtain of crisp, golden-brown leaves and saw movement. It was an ear, rotating like an antenna, searching out the snap of a twig or the swish of fabric against grass that would give away a stalking hunter.

Braedan could hear his own pulse. He licked his lips as he watched the rhino. It was no more than fifty metres from him. He glanced up, looking for branches within reach. He'd have to climb the tree if the rhino saw him and charged. Tiny mopane flies buzzed around his face, seeking the moisture from his eyes and mouth.

The rhino shifted its body so that it was facing him head-on. It lifted its head and sniffed the air. Braedan took a pace backwards and almost jumped as something hard and pointed pressed into his back. Slowly he turned and saw Doctor Nkomo's unsmiling face at the far end of a Brno .458 hunting rifle.

Doctor let go of the stock of the rifle, but held the heavy weapon up with his right hand alone, his finger curled around the trigger. He motioned for Braedan to continue moving backwards.

Braedan was furious. He was angry with himself for not hearing Nkomo sneak up on him, and indignant that the man had the hide and the stupidity to stick the barrel of a loaded rifle in his back. He was ready to give the man a piece of his mind, followed by a *klap* in the face.

When they had backed up sufficiently for the rhino to lose interest and trot off in the opposite direction, Doctor spoke first. 'What are you doing here?'

'I could ask you the same question,' Braedan said. 'What the fuck do you think you're doing sticking a loaded weapon in my back?' There was another man, a younger African with his hair in tight dreadlocks, carrying a .303 who stood a pace behind Doctor, his weapon held at the high port, across his chest, ready for action.

Doctor's face remained impassive, despite Braedan's growing anger. 'You were stalking a rhino, with your rifle up at your shoulder. Why?'

Braedan stuck his jaw forward and narrowed his eyes. 'What I was doing was checking the security here. Mr Bryant knows all about it.'

'Then why didn't he tell me?'

'Because, like me, he probably wanted to test the security here. It was ridiculously easy for me to get onto the ranch.'

Doctor had his rifle lowered now, but still had his finger through the trigger guard. 'You came in via the dry riverbed. We know that is where the poachers have entered in the past. We are not stupid.'

'Then why don't you do something about it?'

'You think we did not?'

Braedan didn't know what Doctor was talking about. Had they, he wondered, been following him all along?

Doctor gestured to the young man behind him. 'This is Edward. He is one of our new men. His job, and that of another man, is to stay hidden and watch the riverbed from a place in the rocks on the edge of the cutting. He radioed in to tell me an unfamiliar white man had snuck in under the fence. I told him to follow you – although I was fairly certain it was you. But I had to make sure.'

Braedan exhaled. He set his rifle down, butt first in the ground, and reached into his shirt pocket for his cigarettes. He took one out and lit it, and as an afterthought offered the pack to the others. Doctor declined, but Edward smiled, for the first time, and took two. He put one between his lips and filed the other behind his ear. Braedan lit the smoke for him. His heart had slowed to its normal rate, and the tension was draining from the encounter, but Doctor was still not happy.

'You did well,' Braedan conceded. 'But I found this.' He unhooked the snare wire from his belt and held it up.

Doctor shrugged. 'I am sure the former head of security was taking money from the war veterans and turning a blind eye to their snaring. Mr Bryant thinks the man became greedy and began working with them to kill rhino. Since he left, my men and I have collected many snares. We must have missed that one.'

'I saw boot prints on the game trail, near where I found the snare.' Braedan pointedly looked down at Doctor's *veldskoen* ankle boots.

'We patrol on foot here. You will find the footprints of myself and my men everywhere on the ranch.'

Braedan rubbed his jaw. Doctor was surly and arrogant, and clearly still annoyed that Braedan had been installed over his head. Braedan wondered whether Doctor might have taken up where his predecessor had left off, or whether young Edward might be doing a little snaring of his own to fill in the long hours of guard duty. On the other hand, everything Doctor had told him could be the truth and, apart from missing a single snare, he'd been running an efficient security operation since his former boss had been fired.

'You don't trust us, do you?' Doctor said.

'I didn't say that.'

'So what do we do now?'

Braedan checked his watch. 'Well, since there don't seem to be any poachers about today and we've just been tracking each other through the bush, I suggest we go back to the house and have a beer.'

For a moment Braedan thought he saw Doctor almost smile.

The drive from Bulawayo to Hwange brought back many memories for Tate, most of them good, a few of them heart-wrenching.

The afternoon sun was slanting in through the Hilux's sloping windscreen, so they'd kept the windows wound up and the airconditioner on. Tate preferred using Land Rovers in the bush. Their boxy shape and small straight-up-and-down windows meant the driver was in shade most of the time.

He was thinking about vehicle comparisons partly to keep his mind off Natalie. She was beautiful – even he could see that – but if he looked at her too much or talked to her too much he was worried the dam of emotion inside him might burst. He'd seen the way Braedan leered at her, and as far as Tate was concerned they could have each other. She was writing a book about herself – a self-absorbed, self-indulgent quest if ever there was one – so it would make sense that she spend more time with her saviour, Braedan. He'd given her what he thought she needed for the magazine article she was supposedly writing about the plight of the black rhino. He'd almost felt ashamed of talking of the deaths of the men – good men – killed in the war on poaching. It was almost as though he was sullying their memory by condensing each of their deaths into just a headline for the benefit of her pampered first-world audience.

Charles Moyo – killed in a contact with poachers, 1984, shot in the head by an AK-47 round. Tate had thrown up the first time he'd seen a man's brains spilled in the dust. *Matthew Sibanda – stabbed to death, 1989, in a supposed shebeen brawl.* Tate later found out that Matthew had overheard two men talking about a rhino horn buy. He'd followed them when they left the village bar, but they had picked up the tail, recognised him as an off-duty ranger and murdered him. *Patrick Mangwana – died 2003, screaming in the bush as he bled to death because there was no helicopter to take him to hospital, and no diesel fuel for the one serviceable Land Rover left at Robins Camp.* Tate had gripped the slippery, torn end of Patrick's femoral artery in a bid to slow the blood flow, but it had been of no use. He'd been drenched in a good man's blood and had held Patrick's hand as he'd died.

Tate had felt a perverse satisfaction seeing Natalie's face whiten with the telling of these stories. She'd had her own brush with death in the bush war, and her aunt had been murdered, but she needed to know that the fighting had never really ended.

He followed the Bryants off the tar road, near the town of Hwange, home to the once thriving Wankie Colliery and associated power station. Both ventures were in near ruins now. Unemployment meant hunger, and hunger meant more poaching. The road to Sinamatella Camp had seen better days. The Hilux's hard suspension juddered on the corrugated dirt surface. Tate eased off on the accelerator to avoid the Cruiser's dust cloud.

'It's beautiful countryside,' Natalie said, breaking the silence.

Tate nodded. She was right. He could tell the rains had been good here as there was a decent amount of water in the Lukosi River when they crossed it. Tate pointed out a couple of female kudu drinking from a pool of water. They took flight as the four-by-fours passed, curling their short white tails over their rumps as they bounded away in a series of high leaps.

'They're scared,' Natalie observed. 'The poaching must be bad here.'

Tate said nothing. He had neither the time nor the

inclination to educate her about the situation in the park. Unlike many whites, Tate wasn't prepared to write off Hwange or any of Zimbabwe's other national parks. Rumours abounded about the extent of poaching, and these half-truths were recorded as gospel in countless email messages of doom and gloom. Conventional wisdom had it that there were no animals left in Hwange, that game had been massacred en masse by government soldiers and that poaching was rife.

The truth was that poaching occurred in Hwange, as it did in every single national park in Africa. During his time as a camp warden Tate had lost men to poachers, and his men had killed poachers. People living near the park – many of them farm invaders who had been unable to maintain the land and keep it productive – took to snaring. The target of these indiscriminate traps was buck, such as impala or kudu, but all too often inquisitive predators – lion, leopard, painted dog and hyena – ended up getting snared. A poacher returning to check his wire nooses would not be game to go near a snarling, writhing leopard and unless parks and wildlife rangers stumbled across the trapped animal it would usually die in extreme pain.

In response, anti-poaching patrols and researchers working in the park devoted countless hours to walking the bush and collecting wire snares. A marvellous interpretive centre devoted to the endangered African painted dog had been built near Main Camp, Hwange's headquarters. The substantial building had been constructed with mud bricks reinforced with snare wire collected by the centre's anti-poaching team.

Snaring was concentrated on the fringes of the park, but Hwange was massive and Tate knew that deep in the park, far from the reach of poachers and all but the hardiest of self-sufficient travellers, there were marvels to be seen. On patrol Tate had encountered herds of thirty or forty sable and roan, antelope considered endangered in other parts of Africa; herds of a thousand or more Cape buffalo; painted dogs, and elephants by the hundreds.

'I'm looking forward to the count,' Natalie said, obviously too stubborn to take his hint. 'I'd like to show the world that there are still some animals up here. It'll be important to lure tourists back to Zimbabwe once things change, don't you think?'

Such sweeping generalisations infuriated him. 'You're not going to see many animals.'

'Oh. Is the poaching problem really that bad? I thought –'

He pointed out the window, to where they occasionally had glimpses of the river. 'Look at the water. That river should be dry at this time of year. They had very good rains here last summer, and that means the game will be spread out all over the park, instead of congregating at the last remaining sources of water. There are animals here for sure, but we won't be seeing many of them.'

'Oh.'

At last, she was quiet.

Natalie wished she had stayed with Braedan. She disliked the fact that he had not told her what he was doing. He was like a commando on some secret mission, sneaking off into the bush with his rifle.

He'd looked good, though, from behind. The shorts were too short to be worn anywhere else in the world except by gay men, but Braedan filled them out to perfection. The muscles in his back and shoulders had rippled like a lion's. She glanced at Tate, who was concentrating on a washed-out stretch of the appalling road they were travelling. She'd be glad when they got to wherever they were going, so she could at least get out and have a conversation with her grandparents.

The road started to climb towards a mesa and when they rounded a bend Natalie saw a green and yellow striped boom gate. Thank God, she thought. Sinamatella rest camp was something approaching civilisation.

A national parks employee in khaki trousers and a shirt bleached to a pale tan stepped out of the shadows of a guard's booth, said something to her grandfather and then raised the boom and waved the Land Cruiser through. The man had a green beret on his head. His eyes, initially bored and listless, brightened as he noticed the driver of the second vehicle.

Tate hit the electric window button and Natalie marvelled at his transformation. 'Oscar!'

The guard stepped back, beaming, as Tate opened the door. Tate shook the man's hand, first in the normal western manner, and then in the African way. Natalie noticed that both men rested their left hands on their right forearms as they shook. By showing their other hand was empty they were according each other great respect.

'I am so happy to see you, *sah*,' the ranger said.

Tate opened his arms and folded the African man in a hug. 'You are looking well, my friend,' he said.

'And you too, *sah*.'

Tate bellowed a laugh, and it was so out of character that Natalie stared open-mouthed. 'You lie, Oscar, but it is a good lie. Your wife and children?'

Oscar nodded vigorously. 'We have three now, one daughter and two sons.'

'Good for you.'

'Ah *sah*?'

'Yes?'

Oscar looked down for a moment, as if embarrassed. When he looked up into the taller man's eyes again, Natalie heard him say, in a quiet voice, 'I have named my youngest son Tate, *sah*. I hope you do not mind.'

Natalie saw Tate's shoulders shake before he hugged Oscar to him again.

Natalie joined her grandparents under a high-pitched thatch roof that shaded an open-air restaurant and bar overlooking a huge expanse of wilderness. Tate was still busy wandering around the camp, chatting with the staff, all of whom seemed pleased to see him again.

'We brought you here when you were a little, little girl,' Grandma Pip said. Below them was an endless plain of flat-topped acacias and thorn trees, bisected in the foreground by the serpentine meanderings of a river.

Grandma Pip had a battered pair of black binoculars out and had spotted a herd of zebra in the distance. She was giving Natalie directions where to look, but Natalie couldn't see them. The zebra were the size of ants from this distance.

'It's your city eyes,' her grandmother said. 'It's the same whenever we get visitors. Your vision's limited, living in a city. Your eyes can only see a certain distance because of all the buildings and whatnot. It takes time for you to adjust to Africa, where you can see forever.'

Never a truer word spoken, Natalie thought. Out of the corner of her eyes she watched Tate laughing with a waiter in a brightly patterned shirt. They had ordered Cokes, which were taking a long time coming while the waiter and Tate reminisced about old times, but there was no food on offer in the restaurant and a curio shop next door was shut, its shelves empty. They were the only tourists here to take in the magnificent view, but Oscar had pointed out other vehicles in the row of bungalows lining the edge of the drop-off, and some four-by-fours in the campground further along the mesa. These, Oscar explained, were people who had also arrived to take part in the game census.

Natalie lowered the old binoculars and looked across at Tate again. When he smiled he looked more like his brother. Braedan might be down on his luck, but he seemed totally at ease with himself and his world. Tate, however, carried some unseen burden. Seeing him square-shouldered, smiling and laughing, made him look attractive. Very, in fact, though still in an unkempt, scholarly sort of way.

'Dear?' Natalie looked around at her grandmother, who had a small smile of her own on her lined but lovely face. 'See the elephant down there?'

'Where?'

Natalie looked through the binoculars again and her grandmother laid a hand on her forearm to steer her in the right direction. 'Oh, I see it now.'

'They're both very attractive, the twins, don't you think?'

Natalie half-lowered the binoculars. 'Grandma . . .'

'Remarkably good shape, I'd say, for their age,' her grandmother continued. 'Tate's a good man, don't you think?'

This was too weird for words, Natalie thought. She looked down into her grandmother's blue eyes and saw the girlish sparkle. 'Actually, I think he's a bit of a cold fish,' Natalie said softly. An understatement if ever there was one.

Grandma Pip kept her hand on Natalie's arm and gave it a squeeze. 'He's hurting, that's all. He just needs someone to tell him it's all right.'

'What's all right?'

'You know.'

Natalie didn't, but she nodded anyway.

Tate was full of admiration for the staff, who had remained motivated and committed to the fight against poaching, but at the same time he was depressed by the obvious lack of resources. Many of the national parks vehicles were dead or barely running, and the field rangers' gear was tatty and worn.

They left Sinamatella Camp for the last leg of their journey, to Robins Camp, in the far northwest of the park, towards the Botswana border. On the way they stopped for a break at Masuma Dam. Tate pulled up beside Paul in the dirt car park on the top of the hill and they got out and walked down some flag-stone steps into the welcoming shade of a thatched hide set into the brow of the slope.

The attendant, like the staff at Sinamatella, greeted Tate like a long-lost friend. Tate had lived in the park for years, but he hadn't expected to be so moved by the reaction of the people who had worked under him.

Before they'd left Sinamatella, while the Bryants were still watching game from the restaurant patio, Oscar had taken him aside, looking around him as though he might be overheard. 'Things are bad for the rhino here,' he'd told Tate.

'Yes, I know, Oscar. But the new warden, he's maintaining patrols in the IPZ, yes?'

Oscar had looked over his shoulder. The intensive protection zone, or IPZ, was an area demarcated around Sinamatella Camp where many of Hwange's rhino had been concentrated so that they could be better monitored and guarded. 'Yes . . . and there are many good people here, but in other parts of the park things are not so well organised.'

'Is it a matter of resources? I can speak again to the charities in the UK and Australia.'

Oscar nodded. 'But it's not just money. Some of the patrols find that when they are sent to a particular area, a rhino is then shot far away. We have not had contact with poachers for many months.'

Tate could see Oscar was wary of making an outright accusation, and was obviously nervous about having this discussion. 'You think someone inside Parks is tipping off the poachers, letting them know where the patrols are?'

Oscar pursed his lips. 'I think people are working against us. Important people.'

'Who? Emmerson Ngwenya? It's said he's behind the latest spate of poaching.'

'I did not say that,' Oscar said. 'I cannot say that.'

Tate clapped him on the arm. There was little he could say or do, other than promise to raise the matter with Parks authorities.

At Masuma the late-afternoon sun glanced off the waters of the dam. A hippo let out a honking laugh. A Nile crocodile motored silently from one side of the dam to the other in search of prey. A trio of old male buffaloes – called *dagga* boys because of the coating of dried mud or *dagga* that stuck to their black coats – ambled down to the water's edge through a stand of mopane reduced to toothpick-like sticks by grazing elephants.

Mrs Bryant sidled up to him, interrupting his reverie. 'Natalie's grown into a nice girl, hasn't she?'

Tate looked down at the small woman. He wanted to say something rude but couldn't bring himself to. He nodded.

'Did she tell you her boyfriend left her for a younger woman?'

'No, she didn't, Mrs Bryant.'

'Pip.' She laid her hand on his arm. 'Tate, one of the good things about getting old is that you can say what you like, because most of the time people don't pay attention to you.'

'OK,' he sighed.

'Then be nice to my granddaughter or I won't let you near Paul's rhinos ever again. Understood?'

'Yes, Mrs Bryant.'

She patted his arm. 'Good boy.'

CHAPTER 25

Fat drops of rain smacked the Toyota's windscreen. Tate peered into the blackness beyond and shook his head. There would be no more counting animals tonight.

It was what he'd feared when he'd seen the clouds looming the night before, during the briefing and *braai*. He'd smelled the rain on the stiffening breeze and he, like some of the farmers who'd come to the park for the census, had correctly predicted the rain.

During the day they'd sat in the small stone hide overlooking Crocodile Pools. The pools had, in fact, been connected into one long body of water that stretched around the bends to their left and right. Tate had been able to keep Natalie's questions to a hushed few, saying that their voices would travel and scare the animals. Now, however, with the rain beating louder on the roof of the cab, there was no need for them to keep their voices down. Nothing could hear them, and they couldn't see a thing through the rain. Lightning struck somewhere nearby, with an explosion that made Natalie jump in her seat.

'Was that close?'

'No.' He smiled, but was glad she couldn't see. She projected an image of toughness, but like most journalists she was a city person, secretly terrified by nature. Tate had some sympathy, though. He was under no illusions about his own weaknesses.

He'd been flown to Australia, years ago, to talk about saving the rhinos. He didn't imagine Sydney was a particularly big city by world standards, but he'd felt a curious sense of fear and disorientation wandering its streets. He hated cities.

'If I wasn't here I imagine you'd be out in the rain, sitting under a tree with a poncho on or something, scanning for rhinos.'

This time he laughed out loud. 'Good lord, no. I'd be sitting right here, inside the vehicle. There's no point being uncomfortable for the sake of it, and it's bloody hard to track a rhino at night in the rain.'

'You were fitting GPS transmitters in Tanzania, weren't you?'

He looked at her, wondering if she had put away her notebook as a pretence. Was that just a way to get him to open up? He resigned himself to getting this over with. Rhinos could always use publicity and he would give her his standard spiel. 'Yes, on some of them, but the authorities here don't have the money for that sort of thing. Some of the rhinos here in Hwange are fitted with radio telemetry transmitters.'

'Why do you do what you do?'

He was taken aback by the sudden change of tack. 'What do you mean?'

'There's no money in it, is there?'

'Not that it's any of your business, but, no, I don't get paid very much. Why do I do what I do?' He thought about Hope's body, lying in the dust by the wreckage of the Viscount. He thought of the rhino that had sniffed the air and trotted by his Land Rover, just as he was about to blow his brains out. He couldn't tell her any of that. He could use the stock phrases about the need to save the rhino so that they would be there for the next generation to see. But that was bullshit.

'Is it because of Hope?'

'I . . .'

He swallowed. He didn't know how she could be reading his mind.

'I'm writing a book, Tate, as well as a magazine story. What happened to me – to all of us – in 1979 is part of it. It's not ancient history – it affected us all, and probably still has a bearing on our lives. Braedan was a hero who's now . . . well, who's now down on his luck. You've dedicated your life to what a lot of people are saying is a hopeless cause. Braedan and I are linked by what happened at the farm, but you're part of the story too. You were Aunty Hope's boyfriend, and as far as I know you've never married or lived with a woman.'

'It's not a story,' he said, almost to himself.

'Sorry?'

He snapped his head around and sought her eyes in the dark. 'I said it's not a bloody story. It's not something you can make up and put in your book.'

'I'm not making it up.'

'No, but you'll sensationalise it, and you'll write it so that people cry, and you'll use it and what happened at the farm as a way to explain your own failings . . . and it'll be another nostalgic, post-colonial African tragedy.'

She opened the door, got out and slammed it shut.

Tate slumped back in his seat and wound down the window. The rain had slowed to a misting drizzle. He folded his arms. He knew he should call her back. If she came across an elephant or a lion she'd scream and run and that would be the end of her.

After a couple of minutes he reluctantly opened his door. He saw the flaring orange glow of a cigarette, smelled the smoke. He got out, stretching away the cramps of sitting too long. He was damned if he was going to apologise to her. 'You can't stay out here all night.'

She turned at the sound of his voice, inhaled deeply, then blew the smoke skywards. 'Hope flew to Kariba from Salisbury and turned around and flew back the same day. Why does someone do that, Tate?'

He put a hand on the door.

'Are you getting back inside the car? Are you hiding from me, Tate?'

'Stop it.'

'Stop what?'

He sighed, and felt the little strength that remained in him seeping away. 'Stop trying to understand things you were never meant to know.'

'Like what? Like how Hope died . . . *why* she died?'

He stared at her, and even in the dark she looked so much like Hope, even sounded enough like her, that it hurt.

He'd bottled it all up for so long. The poison was eating him from the inside out, a little more each year. Time didn't heal a wound like this, it made it worse. The older he got, the more bitter he became and the less likely it was that he would ever find happiness, either by himself or with another woman. He should have killed himself that day. He'd tried, unsuccessfully, to justify his meagre excuse for a life by devoting it to saving something innocent. But there were fewer than nine hundred rhinos left in Zimbabwe and at the rate they were being killed they'd all be gone in a year or two, and then there would be no reason left for Tate Quilter-Phipps to stay alive.

Tate took a deep breath and stared at her. 'I killed your aunt.'

She said nothing for a moment. A hyena mocked his confession from the blackness, whooping with derision.

'You didn't know the aircraft was going to be attacked.'

'I rejected her. She came to me to apologise for something she'd done and I wasn't man enough to accept her apology and forgive her. I was a petty, vindictive bastard and she got on that Viscount because of me. If I'd been a better man, a bigger man, she'd be alive today. I killed her, Natalie. Put that in your bloody book.'

Natalie opened her mouth to reply, but a half-dozen loud popping bangs made both of them turn and look out over the river.

Tate held up his hand before she could ask what the noise was. 'Gunfire. AK-47.'

'Oh my God.'

A branch whipped Natalie's face as she stumbled through the bush in Tate's wake.

He'd ordered her to stay in the vehicle and her immediate reaction had been to refuse. She was a reporter and she'd come to Africa – at least as far as her magazine was concerned – to do a story on rhinos. If what Tate had said was true and those shots were rhino poachers, then this would propel her story from colour piece to hard news. Now, however, with her bare legs beneath her green safari skirt soaked from the wet grass and her arms and cheek scored with scratches from thorn bushes, she wondered if she shouldn't have done as he'd told her. Her heart was beating from fear and the sudden exertion. Tate was tall and it was hard keeping up with his long stride. He seemed to place his feet like a sure-footed animal, whereas it seemed every step Natalie took landed her in another hole, or stubbed her toe into another fallen log.

The hyena whooped again in the distance and the sound sent a shiver of primal fear down her spine.

The full moon was glowing white gold through a break in the scudding rain clouds. Natalie looked up and suddenly felt terribly exposed in the light. She hurried to catch up with Tate, and almost bumped into him. He stopped and raised a hand, then moved slowly into the shadow of a tree, Natalie close behind him. When she peeked around his shoulder she saw a dark mound on the ground. On the brisk, cool wind she caught the harsh smell of blood.

'No,' she whispered.

He turned and glared at her. She said nothing, but stayed close as he moved forward cautiously.

The rhino lay on its side and Natalie clapped her hand over her mouth at the sight of the horrible wound where its horn had been. Rather than sawing the horn off, the poachers had hacked the skin away from the skull, scalping it. Tate knelt beside the animal and put a hand on its grey flank.

'A female,' he said. 'Breeding age. Bastards.'

Natalie saw the ragged stitch of bullet wounds in the creature's flank, each oozing a trail of coagulating dark blood. 'How could anyone do this?'

Tate moved his hand to the rhino's head and fingered a v-shaped notch on the outside edge of the right ear. He leaned across the carcass and lifted the left ear, which had two similar notches on the bottom. The cuts were clean and had obviously been made by humans rather than a predator.

'What do those mean?'

'The ear notches assign a number. The Vs in the outer edges of the ears and a hole punched through the ear all represent a number. There are two notches assigned for the number one, and one each for the numbers three, five, thirty and fifty. A hole in the centre of the right ear is worth a hundred and hole in the left ear is two hundred. By using a combination of these markings you can number a rhino population well into the three hundreds,' he said without looking up at her. 'This one has a thirty notch and a ten on her right ear, and these plus the two number one notches on her left ear mean she's rhino number forty-two in the local population.'

'Amazing. But what do we do now?' Natalie asked.

Following the poachers on foot, unarmed, was out of the question, although as she jogged after Tate back through the soaking, barbed trees Natalie couldn't help wonder if Braedan might have handled the situation differently. As it was, she was quite happy to go with Tate's plan of heading back to Robins Camp.

They drove through the night, and although the illuminated dial of the speedometer rarely climbed over fifty kilometres an hour, it felt as though they were doing twice that on the rutted, mud-slicked roads. Several times she reached out to brace her palms on the dashboard as the Toyota's tail slid out on corners and Tate wrestled with the wheel to get the vehicle back under control. A lightning bolt struck a tree not a hundred metres off to their right and Natalie felt her heart lurch as she remembered the crackle of the poachers' rifle fire. To calm herself she forced herself to observe and remember as much detail as she could for the article she'd write about this night, and the chapter she'd devote to it in her book.

Tate honked the horn as they rolled under the thatched entrance gate at Robins Camp and stopped beside the warden's house, set just outside the perimeter fence. All the lights were out and no one stirred. None of the national parks staff were in the reception office at this late hour. Tate leaned on the horn again and a bleary-eyed man in parks green trousers and a ratty blue anorak stumbled down the last few rickety stairs of the fire-observation tower that rose like a medieval redoubt above the camp restaurant, which had been closed for several years.

'Where is the warden?' Tate yelled over the noise of the engine. The man pointed in the direction of the staff village, behind the tower. Tate quickly briefed the duty ranger on what had happened then sent mud spinning as he floored the accelerator and bounced down the track towards the cluster of asbestos-roofed cottages where the rangers and domestic staff lived. The rain had stopped and Natalie heard African music coming from one house. Two men stood outside, dressed in shorts and T-shirts and holding brown bottles of beer. A battered green national parks Land Rover Defender was parked next to the mostly barren, rock-rimmed garden in front of the dwelling.

'Where's the warden?' Tate barked.

One of the men nodded towards the interior of the building.

Natalie followed Tate out of the vehicle and caught up with him as the warden, a surprisingly young man in a still-starched khaki shirt, emerged. He looked less the worse for wear than the two rangers who leaned against the outside wall of the house. Tate told him, rapid fire, what had happened. 'We must go, now!'

The warden nodded. He spoke to the other two men in Ndebele and they set their beer bottles down and strode off. One of the men began calling at the top of his voice and lights went on in two other houses.

Tate paced up and down while he waited for the national parks men to get themselves organised. Natalie turned at the sound of another vehicle's engine and a white Land Rover, pre-ceded by the sweep of its headlights, pulled up beside them. Two men got out and Natalie recognised, but couldn't remember the name of, the coordinator who was overseeing the game census. There was another man, with his right arm in a plaster cast, who was introduced to her as Nicholas Duncan, a researcher from New Zealand doing his PhD on black rhinos.

Tate filled them in on the rhino's death and Nicholas asked if there were notches on its ears.

'Yes. Its number was forty-two.'

Nicholas shook his head. 'Bastards. That's Chizzi. I thought she might be pregnant – she's been seen with a male on and off lately.'

'I was on the team that relocated rhino from Chizarira National Park to here years ago. Your Chizzi was probably one of them or a descendant,' Tate said, his words heavy with the remembrance. 'One step forward, two steps back.'

Natalie wondered what it must be like to live in a place as remote as Hwange, spending your days in the bush following rhinos. 'What did you do to your arm, Nicholas?'

He smiled. 'Stupid, really. I was up in the microlight, doing a test flight. It's brand new and we're going to fit a radio tracking antenna to it. A couple of days ago I landed – safely I might add – and had started to walk back to camp from the airstrip when I was charged by a *dagga* boy. The buffalo was in the trees on the edge of the runway. He knocked me down and tossed me with his horns. I was lucky that my arm was the only thing he broke before one of the rangers came running and shot him. I feel terrible that people back home and in Australia have paid for the aircraft and I can't use it for another month.'

The warden rounded up his four rangers, who were all now dressed in green field uniforms and carrying a mix of AK-47s and FN self-loading rifles. Tate spread a map of the park on the bonnet of his vehicle and pointed out where the poaching attack had occurred. 'You can follow me, if you like.'

The warden nodded, ordered his men to climb into the back of his Land Rover and got in. There was a painful groaning noise from the starter motor when he turned the key.

'*Sheesh*,' Tate fumed. Natalie saw his knuckles were white on the steering wheel. The Land Rover continued to refuse to start. Tate got out and slammed the door of his vehicle. 'Give him a push start,' he yelled at the rangers. They climbed out and, with Tate helping, pushed the Land Rover. The warden let out the clutch and the vehicle lurched, belched a cloud of diesel smoke and the engine started. Tate was getting into the Toyota when the Land Rover's engine died.

Three times more they tried starting it, but the Land Rover refused to be coaxed into life. Tate went to the driver's door and stood with his hands on his hips. 'Get into my vehicle. I'll drive.'

The warden shook his head. 'Ah, that is not possible. It is against regulations. What if we have to drive off-road to chase the poachers? You cannot be involved in the pursuit. You no longer work for parks and wildlife.'

Tate stood there glaring at the man. 'Bloody hell, they're getting away while we speak.'

One of the rangers spoke in Ndebele to the warden, but the senior man silenced his interjection with a short, angry rebuke. The ranger looked away in shame.

'I will call the police in Hwange town. They will come, when it gets light,' the warden said.

Tate ran a hand through his thick hair. He looked to Natalie like he was about to explode, but then he took a deep breath. Nicholas, too, looked like he wanted to enter the debate, but Natalie guessed that as a researcher he was beholden to the warden. She couldn't work out why the man wouldn't take up Tate's offer.

Natalie sensed the rangers were on Tate's side and seemed to resent their boss, though none of them dared to speak up against him again. Nicholas spoke, breaking the deadlock. 'Too bad I can't fly.'

'Why?' Tate said, turning on him. 'You'd have little or no chance of seeing the poachers on the ground. If they had a vehicle hidden nearby they could be halfway to the Zambian border by now. If I thought it would do any good I'd fly it.'

'You can fly a microlight?' Nicholas asked.

Tate nodded. 'I used one in Namibia for a year, monitoring desert rhinos.'

Nicholas beamed. 'Choice!'

'Why?' Tate's eyes suddenly widened. 'Was Chizzi . . .'

'Yep, you guessed it. I put a transmitter in her horn. If they haven't found the transmitter and killed it, you can track the poachers through the signal from her horn.'

Tate could hardly believe that Natalie had talked him into letting her fly with him.

Tate had asked Chris, the coordinator of the volunteer counters, if he would fly with him and operate the radio direction finder. Chris had been keen to help, but his first duty was to the people scattered around the northwest sector of Hwange National Park. Although the poachers were probably well on their way, Chris wanted to drive around to all of the teams of counters and check on them.

Nicholas had been equally frustrated. There was no way he could monitor the frequencies on the tracker and hold the antenna aloft with only one good hand. 'We can try fixing the antenna to the wing now.'

Natalie had stepped in at that point. 'How long will that take?'

'An hour and a half, an hour if we work quickly.'

'Tate, like you said, if the poachers have a car they could be a hundred kilometres away in an hour if they've already reached the tarred road. I'll come. You can show me how to work your radio thingy, right, Nicholas?'

Nicholas had nodded.

It had infuriated Tate that Natalie had been right. It was easy to use the direction finder once someone learned the basics, but Tate hated the thought of being responsible for her. 'It might not be safe, if we find them.'

She'd scoffed. 'Rubbish. You're not taking a gun, are you?'

'I wasn't planning on it,' Tate had said. 'The warden seems less than keen on catching up with the poachers, so I doubt he'll lend me an FN. If we track the poachers down my plan is to shadow them and then radio back here and have Nicholas pass on the location to the police.'

'See,' Natalie had said defiantly, 'nothing unsafe at all. Are we going to get started or are all you men going to stand around talking for another hour?'

The moon was setting and the sun was entering the narrow band of clear washed-out sky between the horizon and the lower edge of the clouds which, while breaking up, still covered most of the sky. The unseasonal conditions were by no means ideal flying weather for the tiny craft.

Natalie and Tate got into their seats and Nicholas showed Natalie how to use the intercom. She put on a headset and Nicholas adjusted the microphone closer to her lips. 'Can you hear me, Tate?' she said.

'I can,' he replied. He checked the gauges and started the small engine.

'*Brrr*, it's cold now, and I bet it'll be colder once we get airborne,' she said.

Tate knew she was nervous, and so she should be – he knew what cornered poachers were capable of. 'It's always coldest just before dawn. We'll be fine soon.'

He looked back at her, forced a smiled and gave her a thumbs-up. She replied and then lowered her head to concentrate on the receiver. 'OK,' Natalie said, her voice clear in his headphones as he started to taxi, 'I've punched in Chizzi's frequency on the receiver. It's scanning now.'

'OK. Here we go.' Tate opened the throttle and the microlight raced along the airstrip.

'Wow,' Natalie said once they were airborne, 'What a rush! I've never experienced a takeoff like that, not even in a small aircraft.'

'It's being so close to the ground, racing along, that makes it so much more noticeable once you're airborne,' Tate said. He kept his voice calm, but he never tired of the 'rush' either. Tate turned the microlight to the north, following the dirt road towards Victoria Falls. Ten kilometres later they crossed from the national park to the Matetsi Safari Area, the government-controlled hunting area to the north of the park. 'Keep sweeping the antenna. The gain at the front is higher than behind, so that'll give us a direction.'

Tate climbed and slowly increased the speed to a hundred and forty kilometres an hour. He'd flown a microlight at speeds of up to two hundred and twenty in the past, but he wanted to conserve fuel in case they picked up a strong signal. He looked back and saw Natalie's face was grim as she held her arm out into the slipstream, moving the antenna array from side to side. The device looked like an old-fashioned TV antenna, attached to a pistol grip, and was joined to the receiver with a length of coaxial cable that snapped in the breeze. Natalie looked up at him and grinned.

She was brave, he conceded. She had no need to be up here with him, but she had insisted on coming. He wondered if it was just a journalist's pursuit of a story.

'Tate! Hear that? There,' Natalie said. Tate held up his left hand to silence her.

'Come right, to about one o'clock,' she said, ignoring him.

Tate made the turn and increased the throttle. As the air-speed rose he heard the faint bleep in the headphones. 'Well done. You've found it.'

They both concentrated on the sound now and Natalie issued

minor direction corrections. Tate glanced back and saw she was pointing the antenna straight ahead now. The signal seemed to pulse louder and clearer with every beep. 'Sixty beats per minute,' he said into the boom microphone connected to his headset. 'That means they're on the move.'

A herd of buffalo, startled by the drone of the little aircraft, took flight and Tate briefly watched the scattering of black dots coalesce and wind their way across an open *vlei* like smoke caught on the wind. He pointed ahead when he saw the ribbon of black tar. He looked back and Natalie nodded to confirm that she had seen the main Bulawayo to Victoria Falls road.

From Robins Camp to Victoria Falls was only about a hundred kilometres, though the first fifty was on rough gravel roads through the Matetsi area. They had seen no vehicles and the signal was still coming from straight ahead, somewhere up the main road. The poachers, Tate realised, must have had a vehicle waiting outside the northern entrance gate. They had moved fast on foot to the park boundary, then probably rendezvoused with their lift and sped north. Natalie had been right; if they had waited even an hour to attach the antenna to the microlight they would have lost them.

Tate lowered the nose but the needle moved frustratingly slowly on the airspeed indicator. Zimbabwe's roads were still in relatively good condition, with a maximum speed limit of a hundred and twenty kilometres per hour, but a decent vehicle could easily cruise at a hundred and forty.

'Look. Vehicle ahead,' Tate said. Natalie leaned out around Tate's body and put her thumb up to show she had seen the black Toyota double-cab *bakkie* ahead of them. 'He's not travelling as fast as us.' If this was the vehicle, Tate wondered, was the driver taking it easy so as not to be stopped by traffic police?

'Is that them?' Natalie asked into her microphone.

'One way to find out.' Tate banked to the right and told Natalie to keep the antenna pointed straight ahead, in the direction they were flying.

'I'm losing the signal. It's getting fainter,' she said.

'That could be them. I'll try and confirm.' Tate turned lazily to the left, then increased speed and headed north again, but on a track parallel to the main road. The signal returned, stronger, but not as loud as before. They pulled ahead of the pickup and carried on.

'It's getting weaker again, now that they're behind us,' Natalie said, the excitement of the chase plain in her voice.

Tate said nothing but carried on to the north, coaxing as much as he could from the small droning engine. He looked back over his shoulder then pulled around in a tight one-eighty turn that made Natalie groan into his headphones.

'Tate, it's very strong again!' she said as she pointed her antenna back at the *bakkie*, which passed underneath them. As soon as they overflew the vehicle, the signal dropped off. 'Gotcha!'

CHAPTER 26

Emmerson Ngwenya had left the pretty young croupier lying on her back in his hotel room, gently snoring off the effects of the Johnny Walker Blue Label she had shared with him as they partied and fornicated late into the night at the Kingdom hotel and casino in Victoria Falls.

He stepped out of the lift and walked across the polished floor to the reception desk. 'Send up a bottle of French champagne and some strawberries and orange juice to my suite.'

'Of course, Comrade Minister,' said the girl at the desk, smiling and batting her eyelids. Emmerson winked at her. He wondered . . . No, he told himself, it was time to think about business. And if all went well with the Vietnamese then he could continue to have as many women as he wanted.

His protection officer and driver, Ncube, was waiting for him at the entrance and got out and opened the rear door for him. Emmerson glanced up at the grey skies and saw the water beaded on the polished black metal of the new Mercedes. He hadn't heard the rain last night – not surprising given the volume of the girl's screaming. He smiled to himself.

The girl had pouted when his cell phone had rung just after one am and he insisted, despite her protests, that he must answer it. She'd paused, sitting astride him, as he took the call.

The soldiers had told him they had the goods, at last, and had offered to bring them to his hotel.

'No, you'll look out of place. I'll meet you on the road at six.'

'Yes sir,' the commander of the hunting party had replied. While they had settled on a location for the meeting the croupier had placed her palms on his chest and started moving again, squeezing him between her thighs and raising and lowering herself slowly on him. He'd waggled a finger at her as he continued the conversation, but his protest had been half-hearted. Rather than being distracted by the details of arranging the pickup of the rhino horn he'd been further inflamed by a jolt of adrenaline at the thought of what he was about to do, and the money he would make on the deal. As soon as he'd ended the call he'd grabbed the cheeky maiden by the hips and rammed up into her with his considerable force and exploded inside her. She'd told him she was HIV negative and he'd told her he was negative as well. In fact he'd never been tested, but he hadn't been able to be bothered walking to the hotel bathroom to search for a complimentary condom. He didn't know whether rhino horn worked as an aphrodisiac or not, but the thought of making $50,000 for a few hours' work certainly did.

Ncube had placed a copy of the morning's *Herald* on the back seat for him and Emmerson unfolded it as the car sped out of Victoria Falls, past a stream of people walking into town to work. The newspaper failed to hold his interest, however, and his mind turned to ways he could maximise his returns from his latest business venture.

The problem with rhinos, Emmerson knew, was supply and demand. Demand was threatening to outstrip supply at a great rate. The solution, he knew, was not to send armed gangs out into the bush to track down wild rhinos. That was too difficult and, as recent experience had showed him, too unreliable. He needed a guaranteed, possibly ongoing supply of rhino horn, and he knew just where to find it. But that would have to wait.

'You asked me to tell you when we were twenty kilometres out of town, Comrade Minister,' Ncube said, glancing back from the road. 'Coming up now.'

'Very good, Tobias,' Emmerson said, peering through the windscreen. 'Up ahead . . . see the deserted woodcarvers' stalls? Pull over here.'

Once, hundreds of carvers had lined the roads from Bulawayo to the Falls selling all manner of artefacts. However, since tourists had abandoned Zimbabwe the curio business had collapsed and the line of rusting tin-roofed lean-tos, which had once been packed with a wooden menagerie of giraffe, rhino and elephant, were now abandoned.

Emmerson wore a Ralph Lauren linen bomber jacket against the morning cool. He slid his hand inside and brushed the envelope containing $10,000 in US greenbacks. He shifted in his seat as the Makarov pistol in the waistband of his chinos was digging into his back. One had to take precautions when the stakes were high.

'Comrade Minister?'

'I see them,' Emmerson said. Two men emerged from behind the abandoned stalls. One wore an old green army greatcoat. The air was still crisp, Emmerson noted as he opened the door, but not that cold. He guessed the coat was to cover a slung AK. He was expecting three men, and assumed the third was waiting with a vehicle somewhere behind the shacks. While the soldiers had come highly recommended, Emmerson didn't know them personally.

The other man wore a khaki bush shirt and jeans crusted

with dried mud. He carried a bulky parcel wrapped in hessian. Emmerson felt his pulse quicken. They exchanged greetings. Emmerson wondered if these men realised just how many times more than ten grand the horn was worth.

'Nine hundred and ninety-eight grams,' said the man in the bush hat.

Emmerson had told them that he would still pay them the price they had agreed per kilo, the full ten thousand. The Vietnamese diplomat, Nguyen, had initially offered him $40,000 per kilo, but Emmerson had bargained that price up to $50,000. He knew that once ground into powder the horn would fetch nearly $300,000 in Asia.

Emmerson reached for the envelope and the other man passed him the package. Emmerson slid away part of the hessian and marvelled that people would pay so much for something so worthless and unattractive. He started to smile, but when he ran his finger along the length of the horn his smile turned to a scowl. He unwrapped the package and held it up to the morning light. A piece of wire protruding from the horn. 'Idiots!'

Emmerson heard the whine of an approaching engine.

Ncube strode away from the shelters and out to the road. 'Boss! Police coming up the road!'

Natalie watched the operation in fascination, mentally recording all the details. Tate had banked away from the road when they saw the *bakkie* pull over and park behind what looked like a row of empty market stalls. He wanted to stay well out of range in case the poachers became suspicious.

As they orbited high above the bush the clouds began to clear and brilliant sunshine warmed their faces. Tate had radioed Nicholas Duncan at Robins Camp and he had acted as a relay man, passing information about the vehicle's location to the national parks rangers, who then passed it on to the police at Hwange.

When the Mercedes limousine had showed up and then pulled off the road, Tate had radioed news of its arrival to Nicholas. 'This could be a pick-up, over.'

'Affirmative, Tate,' Nicholas had replied. 'I'll get the rangers to tell the cops to put foot.'

'It'll be a miracle if they can get their act together,' Tate said to Natalie, while they had orbited.

But the plan had worked and Natalie had spotted a white Land Rover crammed with armed officers hurtling up the road from the south. 'It's the cavalry!'

'Don't speak too soon,' Tate said, as he turned back towards the road and lowered the nose of the microlight. 'There's no sign of any police from Victoria Falls, so these guys could still get away. If they take off now there's no way the cops will be able to keep up with them.'

'Look,' Natalie said into her microphone, leaning around Tate and pointing, 'there are two men getting into the Mercedes. They're leaving!'

The car's rear wheels sent up a spray of mud and painted twin lines of rubber as it slid out on to the tar road. The pickup truck was not far behind. Tate could see the light on top of the police Land Rover flashing and a cloud of black smoke blooming from the exhaust as the officer driving geared down and floored the accelerator. But the Defender was heavily laden and had clearly seen better days.

Tate brought the nose of the microlight around until he was over the road then turned and dived. 'Hang on,' he said to Natalie.

The airspeed indicator climbed through one-fifty, to one-sixty and finally one-eighty. Slowly they gained on the two vehicles below. 'Come on, come on,' Natalie urged the aircraft.

Eventually they passed over the *bakkie,* and then the Mercedes.

'Fuel's getting low,' Tate said. He radioed Nicholas and asked for an update on what was happening with the police at Victoria Falls.

'No good, Tate,' Nicholas replied. 'Hwange station can't get in touch with the Falls. Seems their phone and radio links are out of order.'

'Dammit.' Tate looked back at Natalie and she saw the indecision on his face.

'We can't let them get away, Tate.' The police Land Rover was fading to a speck in the distance behind them. Tate nodded, then pushed the controls forward. The microlight started to drop.

The men in the *bakkie* must have seen the little aircraft coming down out of the sky before the driver of the Mercedes, because the pickup driver started flashing his lights and honking on his horn, but the Mercedes continued to speed on.

Natalie felt her stomach leap as Tate dropped lower still, until he was flying no more than ten metres above the road. Natalie looked back over her shoulder. 'The Merc's slowing, Tate.'

'Good,' Tate replied, his concentration fixed on the road ahead and his instruments. Natalie saw he was throttling back to one hundred and twenty kilometres an hour. Trees flashed past on either side at a terrifying pace. 'If I can keep him at this speed or slower the police might be able to catch up.'

Natalie looked over her shoulder and checked the car again. 'He's speeding up, Tate! He's going to try and get under us.'

Natalie gripped the edges of her seat as she felt the aircraft sink even more. 'Tate!' The bonnet of the black car was right below them. The driver blew his horn, but still Tate kept coming down. The roadway looked close enough to reach out and touch. Natalie screamed as the microlight's wheels touched the road. The machine bounced back up into the air and lurched sickeningly as Tate fought to regain control.

'On the right!' she yelled into her microphone. The pickup driver had veered out to the right and accelerated hard. The truck was overtaking the Mercedes – and the microlight. 'Oh my God! He's got a gun!'

Tate jinked to the left as they heard the *pop-pop-pop* of bullets leaving the barrel of an AK-47. The driver of the Mercedes also swerved instinctively.

Natalie felt sure Tate would give up now and climb to a safe altitude. It was what she would have done. She screwed her eyes up tight at the sight of the winking rifle barrel. The noise shot her back to her childhood and she clenched her fists around the seat supports as the dreadful images of the night at her grandparents' farm flashed across her mind.

'. . . something,' Tate said, his words intruding on her nightmare.

'What?' she yelled into the microphone.

'Throw something!'

The two vehicles were side by side now, the pickup driver struggling to overtake the Mercedes. The gunfire had stopped and when Natalie dared look at the *bakkie* she saw the rifleman had pulled his weapon inside. He was fiddling with something on the rifle, yanking it back and forth as though there was a problem. Natalie looked around her then realised she was still holding the radio tracking scanner. It was the size and weight of a large hand-held radio. It was all that she could see that was loose.

Tate eased the microlight over to the right until he was between the two speeding vehicles below. 'Up ahead! Tractor!'

Natalie peered around Tate and saw the tractor slowly trundling along the left-hand side of the road, its two nearside wheels straddling the yellow line that ran along the edge of the highway. Tate edged a little more to the right. The windscreen of the pickup was below her, no more than two metres away. She saw the wide-eyed face of the driver staring up at her. The gunman seemed to have fixed his rifle and she saw its barrel poke out of the open window again. She was suddenly filled with hate for these men who had tried to kill her – and for the man who had abducted her all those years ago. She had been scared all her life, since that moment, and it was time to fight back. Natalie gave an animal-like growl as she pulled the coaxial cord from the tracking device, raised her arm and then hurled the grey box downwards with the strength born of thirty years of pent-up rage.

The radio tracker hit the windscreen in front of the driver's face and the safety glass shattered into a silvery mosaic. The driver of the *bakkie* swerved violently to the right onto the verge of the road, then swung hard back to the left.

At the same time the driver of the Mercedes instinctively slowed and dropped back when he saw something fall out of the microlight.

Tate dropped the microlight and bounced off the roadway again. The driver of the *bakkie* braked hard while still trying to overcorrect back to the left. The Mercedes driver hit the brakes but was too close to avoid slamming into the side of the truck as it flashed across his path. Both vehicles skidded off the road.

Emmerson Ngwenya wasn't wearing a seatbelt and he was thrown violently against the driver's seat in front of him. His left shoulder ached and his arm felt weakened as he opened the rear door with his right hand and stumbled out. The car was a write-off and steam hissed from the burst radiator under the crumpled bonnet.

Ncube, who had disabled the airbag on the limousine two weeks earlier and sold it to a second-hand auto-parts dealer, was slumped over the steering wheel, which had crushed his chest. His broken ribs had skewered his heart and lungs. The windscreen was cracked and bloody where his forehead had connected with it.

The *bakkie* had been pushed down the road sideways by the force of the impact of the Mercedes and all four of the truck's tyres had blown. The idiot of a driver, however, was still trying to get away, his buckled rims screeching on the tar. The man who had been in the front passenger seat, with the AK, was slumped over the dashboard. A third man, the one who had handed over the horn to Emmerson, opened the rear door of the double cab and got out. He, too, looked unsteady on his feet.

Emmerson and the man both turned to look southwards as they heard the increasing volume of a police siren. Ahead of them, in the sky, the lunatic pilot of the microlight had climbed and was now turning back towards them.

The driver of the Toyota gave up on his futile attempt to get his vehicle working. He was probably in shock, Emmerson thought. The man got out and looked to his comrade. 'What about Enock?' he asked, gesturing to the slumped man. Enock groaned.

'Forget him.'

They looked at Emmerson. 'We must run,' the driver said.

Emmerson shook his head. 'I am a minister of the government. I cannot run, but I cannot order you to stay. I will have to stay and face the music.'

The man who had handed over the horn just shrugged and the driver said, 'Let's go.'

'Here,' Emmerson said, stepping back to the open rear door of his car and reaching in. 'Take the horn.'

The men looked at each other and the driver grabbed the hessian-wrapped trophy. As they turned, Emmerson reached behind him, drew out his pistol,and shot both of the poachers. One man died instantly, the bullet slamming into the back of his head and exploding out of his mouth; while the other, still clutching the rhino horn, writhed and screamed on his belly and futilely reached around with his other hand for the wound in his back. Emmerson took a step closer and fired into the man's head. Next, he walked over to where the third poacher was groggily trying to sit upright, one hand braced on the dashboard of the wrecked Toyota. Emmerson took aim and fired again, the round entering the man's forehead just above the bridge of his nose.

Emmerson looked up the road, towards Victoria Falls, and saw the microlight touch down on the road and roll towards the wrecked cars. Glancing back over his shoulder he could clearly see the police Land Rover. He looked down at the hessian-wrapped package that could have paid off his latest debts and bought him endless nights' pleasure with the girl who waited in his hotel suite. The warrior in him wanted to shoot the white man who was now striding towards him. The man was being followed by a woman with blonde hair. He stood with the pistol hanging from his right hand. Emmerson's eyes widened as he recognised the pilot.

'Drop your weapon!' the man called. He appeared to be unarmed himself.

'Who are you to tell me what to do? I am a government minister.'

The man slowed, recognition dawning on his face. 'You're Emmerson Ngwenya.'

'What business is it of yours?'

'You're behind it . . . all of it . . .'

'I don't know what you're talking about, and what business do you have, causing an accident that killed my driver?'

The man and woman stopped about ten metres in front of him, no doubt wary of the pistol he held.

'Oh my God,' the woman said, looking at the bodies lying on the grass beside the road. 'You killed these men?'

Emmerson nodded. 'They were poachers. My driver and I stopped for a rest at the abandoned carvers' market back there and these men tried to sell me something. I told them I was a member of the Zimbabwean government and they threatened to kill me. When the accident happened I was trying to get away, but you put an end to that. These men turned on me again and I acted in self-defence.'

'Drop the gun!' a senior police officer called from further down the road, where the Land Rover had stopped. The squad of armed policemen was dismounting and fanning out, rifles raised and ready for action.

Emmerson let the pistol slip from his fingers and clatter to the roadway.

'You were here to collect the horn, weren't you?' Tate said. 'You killed these men so they couldn't tell the truth to the police. You're going to gaol.'

Emmerson looked to the police, raised his hands above his head, then turned back to the white couple. He noticed the woman's face for the first time. There was something about her that he recognised immediately, but it took him a moment to realise just what it was. Her hair, her eyes, her build were all eerily familiar.

He stared at the woman and saw that her mind was turning in the same direction. He smiled at her as the police came up behind him.

CHAPTER 27

The police left a guard with the microlight, which was now low on fuel, and drove Tate and Natalie to Victoria Falls, where they were required to sit for three hours in an interview room and wait until it was their turn to give their statements. They didn't see Emmerson Ngwenya again all that day.

Tate tried to find a policeman who would give them a lift back to the aircraft with some spare fuel, but none of the constables seemed particularly keen to assist them or to drive back to relieve the man who had been left on guard duty.

'I've got some friends who work at the Vic Falls Safari Lodge, and they can probably do us a good deal,' Tate told Natalie as they stood outside the police camp deciding their next move. 'Perhaps we should just stay here for the night and go back to the park tomorrow.'

'I'm all for a bed at the moment,' Natalie said. 'And I never leave home without my plastic.' She held up her gold card and he smiled at her.

The police were able to radio Robins Camp and let Nicholas know that Natalie and Tate were alive and well and that the missing rhino horn had been recovered – although no charges had been laid. Natalie felt better that her grandparents knew where she was, and she passed on a message via Nicholas that she and Tate would be back at the national park the next day, around lunchtime.

Tate had the police constable at the charge desk call them a cab and they were soon on their way out of town. The safari lodge was four kilometres from Victoria Falls, set in the bush near the border of the Zambezi National Park. A minibus pulled up ahead of them and they had to wait while a party of Chinese tourists was checked in first.

Natalie felt tired and dirty and did her best to be polite and friendly to Tate's friend, Neil, who was fortunately working as the duty manager. He looked a little surprised when they told him that neither of them had any luggage, but Tate promised to fill Neil in on the whole story later. Natalie walked in a daze behind the African porter who showed her to her room. Tate walked behind her.

'This is the honeymoon suite!' the porter said, pushing open double wooden doors.

'Wow . . .' Natalie's spirits perked up immediately, although she suddenly felt guilty. She turned to Tate. 'I can't take this, really. They can't give me this room, Tate.'

'I'm afraid they can,' he said, folding his arms and leaning against the wall just inside the doors as Natalie explored, taking in the lounge, upstairs bedroom and the view out over the deck towards a waterhole where a huge bull elephant sucked up brown water from a waterhole with his trunk and poured it down his throat. 'It's the only room Neil's got left.'

'The only one?'

Tate nodded. 'I'm afraid I have to stay here with you, assuming that's all right. If not, Neil says he can put me in the staff camp somewhere.'

Natalie opened a door. 'No, it's fine, Tate. There are two rooms here.'

'Fine.'

Natalie excused herself, saying she needed a shower and a sleep. She shut the door to the master bedroom and let herself into the ensuite bathroom. She peeled off her dirty clothes and half-skipped into the huge double-headed shower. She washed her hair and soaped herself and, unable to bear the thought of being filthy all over again, opened the door, reached out and got her knickers. She washed them with soap, hung them up, then got out and wrapped herself in a fluffy white bathrobe. She dried her hair with the built-in dryer and made a mental note to call room service after she woke to see if they could get her some toothpaste and a toothbrush.

When she had finished in the bathroom Natalie drew the curtains shut and sat on the bed. She started to shake.

In the cool, semi-dark of the room she wrapped her arms around herself, hugged herself tight and drew her knees up towards her chest into a foetal position. She lay like that for half an hour, fighting off the images that hovered at the edge of her consciousness.

The face was older, fleshier, aged by too much booze and too much good food in a country where so many had too little to eat. The eyes, though, were exactly the same. The pupils red-rimmed, the whites turning to yellow. She remembered, suddenly, the strong smell of native beer on his breath all those years ago. At the scene of the car crash she'd smelled stale Scotch in the air. The drink might have changed, but the man had not.

The sound of the mortars took her back to her grandparents' farm, back to 1979. The face was waiting for her there, in her nightmare.

Tate was too wired to sleep. He showered and changed back into his bush clothes and padded barefoot out to the deck. He found an old copy of *Getaway* magazine on a coffee table and was idly flicking through it as he sat and watched the old elephant ambling off from the waterhole back into the bush.

It had been a tragedy, losing another of the country's precious rhinos, yet they had recovered the horn and come close to busting the man who was quite possibly the mastermind behind the biggest poaching syndicate in the country. There had been rumours for some time that Emmerson Ngwenya was a kingpin in the rhino-horn trade, and now Tate knew those rumours were true.

Whether or not the police actually believed the politician's cock-and-bull story about stumbling on to the poaching gang didn't matter. Tate had all the evidence he needed. The question now was what to do with it. The government-run media would never publish the true version of the story, and while the independent newspapers would have a field day with it, the police would never open a docket on a minister who was so openly favoured by the President.

Tate wondered why a government minister, even one who enjoyed such extraordinary protection, would travel out in an official vehicle for a rendezvous with a bunch of poachers in person. Desperation perhaps? Was he in a hurry to collect the horn? Or was the wild-eyed, firebrand champion of the government's disastrous land reform program simply addicted to risk? Whatever the reason, it made Ngwenya a dangerous man.

Tate stretched out in the deckchair and contemplated a nap, but a piercing scream from inside the suite made him leap to his feet and rush back in. He hesitated by the closed door to Natalie's room, but the wail of terror continued. Tate opened the door and saw her sitting up in bed with the palms of her hands pushed hard up against her closed eyes. He reached out and grabbed her forearms, but she shook violently against him.

'Natalie . . . Natalie! Wake up.'

'No, no, no!'

'It's a dream, Natalie . . . You're OK.'

She blinked and stared at him, her eyes adjusting to the gloom of the room, then jerked her body again to try to free herself. 'Don't touch me!'

'Natalie, it's me . . . Tate.'

'Tate?'

He could see the recognition softening her contorted features, but tears began to drip down her cheeks. He sat down on the bed next to her and wrapped an arm around her. She smelled warm and clean in the cocoon of her thick fluffy robe, but her whole body shuddered under his embrace.

'Oh God . . .' she cried, and buried her face in his shirt. 'I feel like such a stupid child.'

Unsure what to do, he tentatively reached out a hand and stroked her hair. 'It's all right, Nat . . . You're safe now.'

'Christ, I hate being so weak,' she said, her voice still muffled against him. 'But it's him, Tate. I know it is.'

He was confused. Gently he pushed her away from him and looked into her reddened eyes. 'Who, Nat? What are you talking about?'

'Promise me you won't think I'm crazy?'

He shrugged. 'Sure.'

'Emmerson Ngwenya . . . I'm sure he's the man who kidnapped me from my grandparents' house.'

Tate sat back and looked into her face. He wanted to hold her again. There was something about the way it had felt. It was the closest he'd been to a woman in many years. It wasn't a sexual feeling, more a pleasant feeling of connection. He'd felt strong

– stronger than he had in years – when she'd leaned against him and he'd let his dusty shirt soak up her tears. She'd made him feel needed. He reached out a hand, again not sure if he was doing the right thing, and placed it over hers, on the bedspread. She made no move to shift it, so he left it there. 'But Braedan killed all the men who raided the farm, didn't he?'

She shook her head. 'I've been researching it, as best as I can. The records are patchy and the three historical books that mention it all have discrepancies. One of the accounts says the men on the follow-up sweep reported finding a blood trail, from a wounded man, though this was glossed over in the other books.'

'But at the awards ceremony, in all the newspaper reports at the time, they said Braedan shot the man who had hold of you,' Tate said.

'Oh, Tate . . .'

She started sobbing again and he leaned in closer to her again. Her body melted into his and he sat there once more with his arms around her, rocking her gently as she cried and cried. He had no idea what any of this meant, but her encounter with Ngwenya had clearly triggered something deep inside her. It was possible, he thought as he breathed in the sweet scent of her shampoo, that Ngwenya had been involved in the raid on the farm. He was from Matabeleland and had served as a ZIPRA guerilla before throwing his support behind Mugabe's Shona-led ZANU–PF when Nkomo's ZAPU disintegrated in the 1980s. He was the right age to have fought in the war. And now that he thought back on it, Tate, too, had noticed the predatory intensity of Ngwenya's gaze as he'd stared into Natalie's eyes. Tate squirmed, then relaxed, as he felt Natalie snake one of her arms around his body. She clung to him and he held her while she sobbed.

After a while she got up to go to the bathroom and he heard

the shower running again. Tate wondered what to do and, unable to decide, went back out into the lounge and put the kettle on. When she emerged from her room she had dressed again, in her green shirt and skirt and sandals. Her hair was damp and, although her eyes were still red, she had stopped crying. 'I'm sorry about all that.'

He waved a hand in the air. 'No problem. I've made tea. Would you like some?'

'Um . . . that's sweet, but I think I might need something a little stronger.'

Bugger it, thought Tate, once more feeling out of his depth. He opened the minibar. 'No, not stocked. Wait a minute, I'll just pop downstairs.' And he disappeared quickly out of the room.

Natalie was left standing there, hands on hips, wondering what had got into the man. She felt embarrassed at the way she had broken down in front of him. But God, she thought, it was good to be able to let some of this out.

She was grateful that there had been another human being in the room when she'd needed one, and that Tate had dropped his usual automaton impersonation. He'd even called her 'Nat', which made her smile now. She looked down at the tea and took a tentative sip. It was too hot and he had used powdered coffee whitener. What she needed was a gin and tonic, but if there was nothing in the minibar, why hadn't he thought to simply call room service?

Natalie walked out onto the balcony and looked out across the lengthening shadows. The dull greens and browns of the Zimbabwean bush were slowly being softened to golden coppery tones as the sun entered the hazy zone of dust and smoke above the horizon. There was still an hour or so of light left and it seemed the rains that had washed out the game census last night had not made it as far as Victoria Falls. The countryside was achingly beautiful and Natalie wished with all her heart that this was her first visit to Africa, that she could simply appreciate the place for its natural wonders. But she couldn't. She was African. She was born of the blood-red dirt that baked below her and she was destined to carry the continent's sorrows in her for all her days.

The doors opened behind her and Tate stood there, grinning like a slightly confused puppy. 'I've organised you a drink. But you've got to come downstairs.'

She sighed. She felt self-conscious now about her tears and clinginess, and all she really wanted to do was hole up in her room with a drink and watch TV. But she didn't have the heart to turn Tate down. 'All right, maybe just for one.'

'OK. Come on.'

Natalie followed him down the stairs back through reception. Outside, two open-topped Land Rovers were filling with the Chinese tourists who had arrived just before them, and an assorted group of Europeans – Germans, she thought, judging by the accents – tricked out in a menagerie of animal-print scarves and designer safari outfits. Natalie groaned inwardly. If he told her they were climbing aboard one of these vehicles she was going to turn on her heel and march straight to the nearest bar.

'Hang on a minute,' Tate said.

After the vehicles filled and drove off Tate told Natalie to wait just a little longer. She turned at the sound of the squealing brakes and saw a much older cut-down Land Rover creak around a corner and pull up into the driveway. An African man in oil-spattered overalls got out and slammed the slightly wonky door to close it. 'I am leaving the engine running in case it stops, *sah*,' he said.

'This is Edson,' Tate said, introducing the hotel mechanic, who wiped his hand on his grimy clothes before shaking Natalie's. 'Neil said we could take this old Landy for a spin. Our sundowners are in the cooler box in the back.'

Natalie waved a hand in front of her face to ward off the diesel fumes, then nodded her thanks to Tate who had opened the passenger door for her. Once she was in he slammed it closed after two attempts. They waved goodbye to Edson and Tate headed out into the slanting gold of the afternoon sun.

Natalie closed her eyes for a second and relished the feel of the warmth on her face and the breeze stirred by the movement of the roofless vehicle. The windscreen was folded forward, flat on the bonnet, so she felt as though she was almost floating through the bush. She had no idea if Tate knew where he was going, but she said nothing as he turned down a rutted dirt road flanked by copper-coloured mopane trees.

'I love this time of day,' Tate said over the noise of grinding gears. 'The photographers call it the golden hour, but I expect you know that.'

She nodded. The breeze was ruffling her skirt and she smoothed it down with her palm. She'd left her knickers drying in the bathroom, and while she hadn't thought twice about walking about the suite naked under her skirt, she now felt quite self-conscious about it. She looked at Tate and he smiled at her. She felt herself blush a little, although he couldn't know why.

Tate changed gears and pumped the squeaky brakes. He pointed out over the open bonnet, then raised a finger to his lips. Natalie swivelled in her seat and saw the sable antelope. It was a magnificent creature, nearly as tall as a horse, jet-black with a white blaze and pale underparts. He raised his snout to sniff the negligible afternoon breeze and tossed his massive curved horns a little.

'Beautiful,' she whispered.

'Rare across much of Africa, yet we still have good popula-tions of them here in Zimbabwe,' Tate said quietly. 'It's the way of this crazy, screwed-up place. Some people will tell you there's nothing of value here, but there's always something hiding, sur-viving somewhere, hoping things will get better eventually.'

The sable bounded away and Natalie felt good just knowing it was out there, alive and well in its natural environment. Tate carried on down the road and took a fork to the right that led them to a small waterhole. He drove around it and parked at the base of a fat old baobab tree. Its spindly branches held an array of nests, and the fleshy bark of its bulbous trunk glowed and shone a pinky-brown in the afternoon light as though it had been polished.

Tate switched off the engine.

'Are you sure you'll be able to start her again?'

He laughed. 'We're parked on a bit of a slope. I can roll-start her. I drove one of these things for years when I was younger.'

He looked away into the distance. For now, though, Natalie wanted to keep both of them in the present, away from their terrible past. 'What about that drink?'

He nodded, returning to the present, and got out and hefted the plastic cooler block out of its purpose-built cradle at the rear of the old Land Rover. He also slid out a folding table, which he set up. Inside the cooler was a plastic bag with a white linen tablecloth, which he snapped out with a flourish and laid on the table. Natalie laughed at his the-atrics, and he set out miniatures of gin, a couple of cans of tonic, and a shiny metal tumbler. Tate fixed her drink, com-plete with ice and pre-sliced lemon, and selected a Lion Lager for himself. He rarely drank alcohol because he couldn't afford it and he didn't like the feeling of losing control, but the sundowners were on the hotel, and he felt he'd earned a beer after what had happened.

'What shall we drink to?' she asked, raising her glass.

Tate looked down at the waterhole, about a hundred metres away, where a pair of warthog were staring at them, getting their measure before deciding whether or not to come down to drink. One of the hogs lowered itself into a muddy depression and started wallowing enthusiastically, grinding his belly and genitals into the black ooze at the edge of the waterhole. 'How about him? He looks as happy as a pig in shit.'

Natalie laughed. It was the first time she'd heard him crack a joke. 'To pigs in shit.' They clinked cup and bottle and the stringent, ice-cold drink sliced through the dust and the foul aftertaste of her afternoon nightmare and sent a jolt of pure pleasure down to her core. 'It's so peaceful here.'

He nodded. 'I wish life could be like this. Simple. As it was meant to be. But we humans have screwed up the environment so much that even moments like this are only an illusion.'

She agreed with him, but she wanted there to be more to Africa, more to this moment. 'But is it completely hopeless, Tate? If it is, then why do you bother?'

He shrugged, took a sip of beer and appeared to ponder her question. She feared for a moment he might retreat back into his shell, or snap at her with a barb designed to show her how naïve or shallow she was. 'No, it's not completely hopeless.'

Natalie took another sip of her drink. 'I'm pleased to hear it.'

'We white people nearly wiped the rhino off the face of Africa early last century. It wasn't ignorant black poachers or greedy Chinese herbalists who were responsible for almost killing all the rhinos. It was us. We white men killed rhinos because they carried the Rinderpest disease where we wanted to run cattle, and because we wanted the head of a big horny beast to put up on the wall. Stupid, really, when you think about it. Of all the uses for dead animals, trophies seem to make the least sense. But they stopped the slaughter, just in time, down in Natal where there were only about fifty Southern White Rhino left. From those few survivors a species was saved, and today the southern white's numbers are around seventeen thousand. That's a success story.'

'But can it be done again, with the black rhino?'

Tate shrugged. 'It's ironic, but war and apartheid saved the black rhino from total annihilation this time around. South Africa was too busy looking inwards, sealing off its borders and being shunned by the rest of the world, to allow wholesale poaching to carry on. At the same time up here in Rhodesia we were far more preoccupied with killing each other than killing our wildlife, so that bought the rhino some breathing space while it was being wiped out in the countries to our north. Greed's the only factor here, and it's hard to find an antidote to that.'

'So *nothing* more can be done?'

Tate took another sip of beer and climbed up onto one of the squared-off front fenders of the old Land Rover. Natalie hoisted herself up on the opposite one. The sun-warmed aluminium felt pleasant on her bum, through the thin material of her skirt. 'We can keep fighting a rearguard action against the poachers, but it's only a matter of time and numbers and the poachers have both on their side. It'll be years before a new, truly democratic Zimbabwean government could get back to the business of properly resourcing the parks and wildlife service, and seriously protecting the country's wildlife. Whoever eventually takes over from Mugabe is going to have to fix the water, the electricity, the economy, the roads . . . animals are going to have to wait in line, and by that time the rhinos may all be gone. No, I think it's time for some more radical solutions. Farming, for example . . . If we can't stop people in Vietnam and China buying rhino horn and believing in its powers, then who's to say we aren't better off just accepting the market will always be there and doing something to try and regulate it?'

She was shocked. She'd heard the argument before, but it surprised her coming from someone like Tate, who'd fought the war on poaching all his life. 'What, if you can't beat 'em, join 'em? Are you saying rhinos should be farmed for their horns?'

He shrugged. 'All I'm saying is that at the rate they're disappearing – around fifteen a month – they'll all be dead in a few years. But in the same period we could have supplied the same number of horns into Asia without the loss of a single animal if the horns were removed and sold. It would bring foreign currency into the country and, if it was managed properly, it's a renewable resource that simply keeps growing.'

'But surely that would be seen as an admission of defeat?' Natalie said.

'Yes and no.' Tate set his beer bottle down on the bonnet of the truck and turned to face her. 'There's a plant in South Africa called the pepper bark tree. Have you heard of it?'

She shook her head.

'Well, the pepper bark is seriously endangered. There are just a handful of trees left, in only a couple of locations. For years the bark was harvested – poached – by traditional healers who took what they needed to make a tea that was used to treat coughs and colds. It seemed to work. In fact, it worked so well that some smart *sangomas* started marketing it as a cure for HIV-AIDS. Tuberculosis and respiratory-tract infections are common illnesses for people with AIDS, so some patients may have experienced some relief from using pepper bark.'

'I understand . . . but what has this got to do with rhinos?'

He took a sip of beer and set the bottle down again. 'There was a boom in sales and the poachers started ring-barking trees – stripping the bark off where they once might have taken just a sliver at a time. The trees were in serious threat of dying out altogether, but then some South African national parks people decided to enter the pepper bark market. They started taking cuttings and growing their own trees and selling the plants and the bark direct to the traditional healers. They made money for the national parks, kept the *sangomas* happy and, for now, saved the trees.'

'Yes, but you don't believe pepper bark cures AIDS?'

'Of course not,' Tate said, 'no more than I believe rhino horn relieves fever or acts as an aphrodisiac or cures cancer. But if we can hold the line, until those traditional beliefs die out naturally or people are finally convinced they're not true, we might buy ourselves enough time to save a species.'

It was a radical solution to a desperate problem, but she wondered if legalised farming of rhino horn could ever function properly in a state where the government seemed hell-bent on stealing all the natural resources and ruining commercial agriculture. Four female kudu, one with a small fawn, tiptoed nervously past the warthog to the edge of the waterhole. The lead animal looked at Natalie and blinked its big doe eyes and rotated its antenna-like ears, alert for the slightest sign of danger.

Tate slid down off the fender, took Natalie's cup and fixed her another drink from the cooler box. She was tired, despite her troubled nap, and the drink was going to her head. She asked him some more about the places he'd been and he told her of his travels around Africa and some near-death scrapes while capturing and monitoring rhinos.

He leaned against her side of the truck while they talked, the distance between them closing all the time. She could sense him relax as he finished a second then a third beer as the evening shadows edged across the waterhole. It was funny, she thought, how it had taken the danger of the aerial pursuit and his near suicidal flying to bring about this change in Tate. She found him a curious mix of inconsistencies. He'd proved he could be fearless in defence of rhinos, but he was also willing to discuss the possibility of decriminalising the rhino-horn trade.

'We should be getting back,' Tate said as the sun disappeared behind the mopane trees and the bare red earth fringing the water turned a dark purple. She wished they could have lingered a little longer. Tate held out a hand. She didn't need any assistance getting off her fender seat, but let him take her hand anyway, and help her down. He held it just a fraction longer than he needed to, and she smiled at him. He blushed, which was cute, then opened and closed her door for her and walked around to his side of the Land Rover.

'Tate!' she hissed. He followed her outstretched finger and saw the elephant emerge from the trees off to the left, not thirty metres from them. The old bull shook his head, sending out a halo of dark crimson dust against the sunset. He looked at them through a long-lashed eye. 'Hurry,' she said.

Tate held a finger to his lips and eased his way into the driver's seat then quietly closed his door. The elephant had been heading to the waterhole, but his interest was clearly aroused now that he had spotted the Land Rover. His massive skull seemed to rock with each step he took towards them. Natalie slid closer to Tate across the middle seat of the Land Rover and reached a hand out onto his thigh to steady herself. She felt him wince slightly as she gripped him, but she kept her eyes on the elephant.

'It's fine,' Tate whispered. 'Stay very still.'

The elephant seemed to fill her entire field of vision as he raised his trunk against the pink and gold sky. Natalie flinched as she heard a low rumbling growl from the animal's throat. The elephant reached out its trunk until it was protruding over the row of seats behind her. She didn't dare move as it snaked around behind her neck. The elephant shifted a little to the left and sniffed her.

The tip of its trunk looked like a couple of fingers and she heard a gurgling noise as the two nostrils drew in her scent. Natalie nearly screamed when the wet end of the trunk brushed her shoulder. She had never in all her life been this close to one of these huge creatures. She was terrified, but awed at the same time.

Tate held up a palm and the elephant dutifully sniffed him as well. Then, seemingly satisfied that all was right and that the humans and their vehicle posed no threat to him, the bull sauntered off to the waterhole.

'*Sheesh*, you could have washed it before you brought it back, *bru*,' Neil said when Tate pulled up outside the entrance to the Victoria Falls Safari Lodge.

'You might want to do something about the brakes,' Tate said, climbing down, 'And the tyres . . . and the starter motor . . . and the clutch . . . and . . .'

'All right, all right!' Neil held up his hands and laughed. 'I get the picture.' He leaned close to Tate as he reached in to retrieve the now empty cooler box. 'It's all sorted, my China. I've organised a candlelit dinner on your balcony with the lady.'

Tate watched Natalie walk into the hotel and hoped she hadn't heard. 'It's not like that, Neil. Can't we just have dinner with all the other guests?'

Neil shook his head. 'Well if it's not like *that*, man, it *should* be. She's hot. Besides, the table's already set and there's a waitress up there waiting to take your orders. If I was sharing a suite with a babe like that I'd be ordering room service for a week.'

Tate set off after Natalie, wondering how he'd explain his friend's misplaced generosity. The doors to the suite were ajar and she stood there in the middle of the lounge, arms folded, looking out at the table set with glittering candles in a silver candelabra.

'I . . .' He didn't know what else to say.

'It's beautiful, Tate. Thank you. You don't need to say anything.'

His head was swimming from the beers on the drive and the glass of champagne he gulped down as soon as the smiling African waitress poured it and placed it in his hand. He really wasn't used to drinking this much. He stood there, swaying slightly, hypnotised by the sight of the candlelight reflecting off the golden skin of her face and arms, and her smile.

He wanted to say something. He wanted to tell her how beautiful she looked and how much she reminded him of Hope, but in a good way. He knew the words would come out all wrong and that he would either sound like a maudlin old fool or some sort of sad loser.

'Come, sit down,' she said. 'I'm thirsty.' She picked up a big glass of iced water and downed half of it while he laid a hand on the back of his chair and lowered himself into it. 'Relax, Tate. We've already established I'm not going to bite.'

He felt his face flush, but sat and picked up the menu. He ordered soup and the beef. Natalie ordered the same.

'It's been a hell of a day,' she said.

He took the champagne from the ice bucket and refilled both their glasses. 'It has indeed.'

'Scary . . . terrifying, in fact. Tragic, frustrating, and beautiful this evening. How is it that this place can conjure up so many conflicting emotions in such a short time?'

He shrugged. 'I suppose it's what keeps me here. The unpredictability of it. I don't think I could ever live anywhere safe and normal. It'd drive me crazy.'

She laughed. 'Funny, I would have said the opposite of you, that you craved order and normality.'

He frowned. 'You know, until just now, I probably would have said you were right, yet here we are.'

'Yet here we are.' She leaned across the table and her eyes sparkled in the candlelight. She clinked her glass against his. 'Thanks for a wonderful day.'

Tate drank some more of the champagne and thought that he could have sat there all night looking into those eyes. As the first course came and went – they were both ravenous – she asked him about his research work, and about rhinos he had translocated from one part of Africa to another. He was passionate about his work and enjoyed talking to her about it. He felt relaxed in her company, in the sense that he no longer regarded her as a prying journalist who might feign interest in him to get him to say something controversial, but he was also acutely aware of his growing attraction to her. It scared him.

She twirled a finger in her hair as she told him of some of her own adventures as a journalist. While she worked for a travel magazine now, she had started on local newspapers, covering police and court stories as a young cadet, then moved on to a major daily newspaper where she covered federal politics for a while. She tried to talk it down, to make it sound like just another job, but he could see that she, too, cared about what she did. 'I got sick of politics – I learned pretty quickly there wasn't much difference between politicians, whatever their party, but it did have its moments.'

'Really?' Tate said.

'The crowning glory of my political reporting career was when a cleaner from Parliament House told me he'd busted a senior politician having sex with a member of a rival party.' She leaned across the table, adopting a conspiratorial tone.

'And,' she said, placing her elbows on the table, 'guess what?'

'What?' He didn't recognise the names of the people she was talking about, but they were obviously well known in Australia. Natalie reached out and laid her fingers on his, which were resting on the table on the base of his wineglass. He felt tingling jolts of electricity racing from his extremities to his heart. 'They *did* it in the chamber, in Parliament House . . . in the speaker's chair! What do you think of that?'

He didn't care about these strangers and it was all he could do to smile and laugh a little instead of stare down at her hand on his. His heart was pounding so much he was sure it must be visible to her.

'The story went national, but afterwards I felt bad about it. I mean, they were just two people, having fun, and I'd helped shame them. I didn't like that side of journalism and I was much happier when I got a gig as deputy travel editor. I loved it, and from there moved to the magazine. But it's funny, now, thinking about those two in the parliamentary chamber. I'd never have the courage to do something like that . . . I'd be too scared of getting caught, wouldn't you?' she said.

'Um . . .' He was trying to follow her conversation, but her smile and her eyes were entrancing. He felt himself flush once more, at her question. How was he supposed to answer that?'

'Have you ever . . . you know . . . in a public place?' She hadn't moved her hand.

'Well . . . um . . . there was a train trip, coming home from boarding school, when I was seventeen. There was a girl . . .'

'Tate!' Natalie squealed. 'You sly *dog*! I *am* impressed. God, that's a fantasy of mine – on a train.'

He felt his cheeks burning and suddenly regretted saying anything, though at the same time he was pleased by the reaction he'd provoked in her. The waitress knocked and opened the door. She looked inside, hesitantly, then smiled when she realised everything was OK and Natalie wasn't screaming because a black mamba had slid into the suite. She wheeled in a trolley bearing their main course and a bottle of red wine. 'Courtesy of Mr Neil,' she said when Tate pointed out he hadn't ordered more wine.

'Oh dear,' Natalie said as the waitress left them again, 'I'm afraid I'm going to be pissed tonight and unwell tomorrow.'

Tate shrugged and poured some red for both of them.

'So, about this train . . .' Natalie grinned at him. She'd had to remove her hand from his when the food had arrived, but Tate could still feel her touch on his skin.

'Not much to tell, I'm afraid.' He chewed some steak and took a sip of wine. 'There was a girl . . . she and I used to see each other on our way to and from boarding school at the beginning and end of each term. I didn't really know her that well. But someone had smuggled some beer and cigarettes onto the train and everyone was drinking. And later, as we chugged through the night, we found ourselves alone . . .'

'Don't stop.' She took a big sip of wine.

'There's not much more to tell.'

She narrowed her eyes a little. 'Don't tease.' Her voice seemed deeper, huskier. 'I want details.'

He thought about what she had said, that this was her fantasy. He swallowed. He could feel his penis shifting in his pants, chafing against the fabric as it started to swell. 'We were both young . . . inexperienced. We talked, for a long time, into the night. I'm sure she made the first move, but we ended up kissing.'

He didn't know whether to go on. He could see her breasts moving up and down with her breathing, though she said nothing. There was a crooked smile playing across her face.

'It was my first proper kiss with a girl. It was . . . God, it was so long ago, and I haven't thought about it for ages, but now that I do I can still taste her.'

Natalie shifted in her seat, but her eyes didn't leave him. He felt a pressure on his leg and realised it was her foot. Instinctively he moved his leg, but her foot followed him and pressed against his, her calf resting against the inside of his leg.

It felt hot in the room, and he was breathing quicker. He took a gulp of wine. The corners of her mouth lifted slightly as his eyes widened and she increased the pressure of her leg against his. Instead of moving he tensed the muscles in his own leg, meeting her rubbing with resistance.

'Don't stop . . .' she whispered.

He was confused. There was not a lot more to tell. They had kissed and he had eventually plucked up the courage to brush a hand against her breast, through the fabric of her school shirt. He'd figured that if he had gone too far she would pull away and tell him so, and he could claim it was an accident. But she hadn't. Instead, she'd issued a soft moan through their passionate kiss and that sound came back clearly to him now as he watched Natalie chase a stray drop of wine from her lips with the point of her tongue. Emboldened, he'd fumbled with two buttons and slipped a hand beneath the layers and into the heavily engineered bra. Did Natalie want to hear all that?

'Did you actually . . . you know?' Natalie's finger was near her throat now, tracing a line down the edge of her shirt, along the skin. Tate watched its path and didn't care that her eyes dropped to see what he was looking at. Her finger slid slowly lower until it came to a rest at the V formed by her top button.

He looked back up into her eyes. 'No . . . not that . . . but it was a night of several firsts for me.'

A knock at the door made both of them look away. 'Are you finished your main courses yet?'

Natalie exhaled. 'I'm finished. I'm full. That was lovely, thank you.' She dabbed her mouth with the serviette as Tate gratefully shovelled the last of his food into his mouth. Natalie had moved her leg and he felt a slight sense of relief now that the moment of tension seemed to have been broken.

'Dessert?'

'Not for me,' Natalie said.

'Nor me,' said Tate.

The girl smiled broadly as she collected their plates. 'Then I will leave you in peace. Goodnight, sir. Goodnight, madam.'

Tate walked the waitress to the door and handed her a tip. When he closed it he saw Natalie was standing as well. He didn't know which part of the room to move to. If he suggested the lounge suite she might take it the wrong way. They were both borderline drunk. If he said he was going to bed, what would she make of that? She lowered her eyes and to his shame Tate felt the bulge in his shorts. He turned back to the door, making a show of attaching the security chain. 'It's not unsafe here, but you never can tell, particularly with what we've been through today and . . .'

When he turned to look back over his shoulder he saw that she had advanced on him, closing the distance between them. There was no reason for her to be walking towards the door. The reminiscing about the girl on the train, the feel of her provocative touch on his leg, the finger at her neck, the look in her eyes and the slight parting of her lips all coalesced in his scientist's brain and told him, with undeniable certainty, that there was no way he would ever, in a million years, be able to explain what was going on right now, and what he was feeling. A heat rose in him and pounded in his chest. She was within reach of him, but she had stopped, and now she stared at him.

She was beautiful, she was single and she had touched him in a way that told him he should take her in his arms right now. Natalie smiled and though he had seen her do that so many times since they'd met, he knew now why it transfixed and pleased him so. The eyes, the mouth, even the hair . . . they were all Hope's.

Tate closed his eyes as the desire consumed him, fed by the despair that welled up from inside him. He had to tell her. He opened his eyes again and spread his arms, palms outwards. He was about to confess to her when Natalie surged forward and fell against him. 'Oh, God, Tate . . .' She raised herself up on her toes and sought his mouth with hers. Tate was overcome with surprise by the force of her and nearly fell backwards. Instead, he locked his arms around her and wheeled her, in a kind of dance, until she was leaning with her back against the hotel room door. He couldn't resist the hot, wet allure of her mouth and he kissed her hard. It had been so long since he'd held a woman or kissed like that. Natalie clawed at his back and he dropped a hand to her bottom and pulled her closer.

Natalie ground against him and he felt his erection quickly return to full bloom. She moved her lips from his and he felt her hot breath on his ear. 'Touch me.'

He needed no further urging. Tate moved his free hand

between them. Natalie's skirt had already ridden up partially as she hooked a leg around him. He felt the warm, smooth skin of her thighs and to his shock encountered no barrier as his fingers brushed her soft, damp curls. He'd recalled the moan that had come from the girl on the train and now he felt himself making the same involuntary groan. Natalie murmured her assent as he parted her and she kissed him again on the mouth, hard enough for him to feel her teeth graze his lower lip. She was touching him now, searching for his zip. He craved her touch, but he was even more aroused by the way she was moving against him. He had found the hard little nub between her soft lips and Natalie's breath was coming in short, sharp bursts as he teased and rubbed her.

She closed her eyes and threw back her head and the sight of her neck, and her blonde hair hanging down, and the feel of the way she craved more of his touch aroused him more than anything he'd experienced since he'd lost Hope. Natalie reached for him and managed to undo the top button of his shorts. He could feel her orgasm building as her breathing intensified in response to his touch. She nodded her head up and down in short, sharp movements, urging him, telling him he was doing it right. She bit down on her lower lip and drew in a deep breath.

Just as it looked like she might climax on his fingers, Natalie pulled down his zipper and wrapped her hand around the girth of his cock. She pumped her hand once, twice, three times as he increased the movements of his own fingers.

In that moment of almost overpowering desire he half-closed his eyes and she appeared before him, unbidden, although she was never very far away. He saw her long blonde hair and there were tears streaming down her cheeks. He heard again, as he did in his nightmares, the last words Hope had said to him. *'It was nothing, Tate. I'm so sorry. Please forgive me.'*

Tate broke away from Natalie and, hurriedly zipping his pants, opened the hotel room door and ran out onto the landing.

CHAPTER 28

Braedan and Natalie sat in the beer garden of the Brass Monkey pub, next to the TM Supermarket in the Bulawayo suburb of Hillside. A glossy starling pecked at a chip that had fallen from Natalie's plate, and Braedan waved it away.

The three weeks since she and Tate had chased the poachers had gone by too quickly, and she hadn't achieved half of what she'd needed to in order to make a start on her book. She and Tate had been summoned to see the police again the morning after their intimate dinner. Tate had mumbled an apology to her and had said something about wanting to keep their relationship purely professional. She'd felt hurt and had wanted to discuss it with him, but Nicholas Duncan had driven to Victoria Falls to collect them and they could hardly discuss what had gone on in his company, on the trip back to Hwange National Park. Once back in the reserve Tate had said he would stay at Robins Camp for a couple more days of meetings with senior national parks staff who had come to investigate the rhino's slaying. Natalie had taken the Toyota back to her grandparents' place by herself, leaving Tate to hitchhike back once his business was concluded.

On the ranch, her grandparents had smothered her with attention after her ordeal with the poachers. Braedan had been working nights, out patrolling the ranch with his men, and sleeping days, so she'd barely had a chance to talk to him. Just when she'd arranged to spend a free day with him, the national parks and police officers had arrived. This trip was turning into a nightmare, but she'd finally managed some time alone with Braedan again so she could interview him.

Natalie picked at her roast chicken, but she wasn't particularly hungry. Her eye was drawn once more to the front page of the *Bulawayo Chronicle*, despite her fervent wish that the words would somehow disappear.

'RHINO RANCHER UNDER SUSPICION OF POACHING AS MINISTER'S NAME IS CLEARED' read the headline of the lead story.

'Everyone knows that paper's full of shit. It's just another government mouthpiece, like the *Herald*,' Braedan said, stirring sugar into his coffee.

'I *know*, but it all seems so hopeless.' She folded her arms and slumped back in her seat. 'My grandfather's an old man, Braedan, and I'm worried what this will do to him. I didn't know it, but Grandma Pip told me he had a heart attack a few years ago.'

'He's a tough old bugger, hey,' Braedan said.

But she wasn't reassured. 'Aren't you worried about the loss of the rhino horn from the ranch?'

Braedan nodded. 'Of course. Especially as it happened on my watch, but at least the rhino wasn't killed, thank God. Ngwenya's getting desperate, but the real risk is not that he'll kill another rhino, but rather that he'll take over the whole ranch.'

Natalie felt sick at the lies splashed across the front page.

Bulawayo: Police are investigating the loss of a rhino horn with a value of hundreds of thousands of dollars from a ranch near Plumtree owned by once-lauded conservationists Paul and Philippa Bryant.

The *Chronicle* can reveal that a snap audit by parks and wildlife officers found last week that the Bryants were unable to account for a horn believed to have been removed from a healthy black rhinoceros.

Police spokesman Inspector Wayne Chisango said rhinos at the Bryant property were regularly dehorned as a deterrent to poachers and the horns surrendered to the Zimbabwean Parks and Wildlife Service for safekeeping.

'Acting on an anonymous tip-off, rangers made an unannounced inspection of the ranch on Thursday and found that eight of the ranch's fourteen black rhinos had been dehorned, but parks and wildlife had records of only seven horns in their custody,' Inspector Chisango said.

When questioned by police Mr Bryant was unable to account for the missing horn. Inspector Chisango said Bryant was continuing to assist police with their investigations as the *Chronicle* went to press.

In other news, a government spokesman announced today that embattled Assistant Minister for Land Redistribution Cde Emmerson Ngwenya has been cleared of all allegations of involvement in the poaching earlier this month of a black rhino from Hwange National Park.

Mr Ngwenya was involved in an altercation with poachers when he and his ministerial driver stopped to render assistance to the drivers of a vehicle that appeared to be broken down, near Victoria Falls. When the occupants of the vehicle, who turned out to be rhino poachers, pulled a gun on Cde Ngwenya, the Minister and his driver fled the scene. Hwange police had been alerted to the presence of criminals in the area and were in pursuit of the poachers. In a shootout following a traffic accident between his government vehicle and the poachers' bakkie,

Mr Ngwenya shot the three poachers when they again tried to kill him.

The MDC-T faction tried to get parliament to reopen the police investigation that cleared the innocent Mr Ngwenya of any wrongdoing, but government members of parliament, voting with other opposition parties, successfully defeated the move in parliament yesterday.

'This man is a hero and deserves a medal for bravery, not the baseless and spurious muck-raking that is the hallmark of the MDC,' the President said following yesterday's vote.

Natalie tossed the paper back on the table in disgust. 'You think Ngwenya's behind the missing rhino horn?'

Braedan set his empty coffee cup down on its saucer and leaned forward, his elbows on the table and his hands clasped. 'I'm certain of it. Think about it – it all fits. He's obviously the head man in the poaching syndicate, right?'

Natalie nodded. 'I doubt even the most ardent of government voters believes that rubbish about him just stumbling upon the poachers. Tate and I saw his limousine parked near the poachers' vehicle. They were talking and no one was threatening anyone. He was there to collect the rhino horn, for sure.'

'Of course he was, but he couldn't take it with him. He couldn't be caught with the evidence when the police arrived, so he killed all the witnesses who could have linked him to the crime. So what does he do, given that he couldn't get away with the rhino horn?'

'Steals a horn from one of Grandpa Paul's rhinos without killing it?'

'Exactly.'

'But why didn't he just get someone to kill the rhino, and how did he take the horn?'

'Aha!' Braedan raised a finger over his head as if it was a light bulb being switched on. 'Because he's not stupid. Ngwenya sent someone onto the property armed with a dart gun, loaded with M99 probably – it's the same stuff Tate uses when he wants to immobilise a rhino. Ngwenya's man drugs the rhino and chops off the horn. When the job's done the poacher gives the rhino the antidote and slips away.'

'Sounds like a lot of trouble to go to,' Natalie said.

'It is. You're supposed to be a qualified vet to immobilise a rhino, although it is possible to do a course and be registered to hold M99 for use in relocating game. Either way, you have to know exactly what you're doing.'

'Then why bother going to the trouble to find and pay someone who can do this?'

'Two reasons.' Braedan held up his index finger again. 'One, it's quiet. No one heard gunfire and no one was alarmed, at first. Two, the rhino lives, so it can sire more offspring and, in time, regrow its horn. It's not the first time this has happened. In South Africa there have been rhino killed on private game reserves by people using darts to give the animal a silent over-dose. I've also heard of a case of a noble-minded poacher darting a rhino and then bringing it around once the horn had been cut off. There's even a term for it down south – "Eco Poaching".'

Natalie shook her head. 'And Ngwenya wants the rhino alive on Grandpa's ranch because he wants to take over the place . . .' Braedan nodded, but Natalie knew it wasn't as simple as Ngwenya walking onto the property and staking his claim, as thousands of so-called veterans of the liberation war had done with farms across the country. 'But the ranch has survived all the farm invasions so far, with the exception of some crop-growing land that Grandpa Paul ceded to the local community.'

Braedan leaned over and stabbed the newspaper on the table.

'But now we have this. Ngwenya probably called someone in parks and wildlife as soon as he'd taken the horn from the drugged rhino and set them onto your grandfather. The inference is that he's selling the horns from his own rhinos, animals entrusted into his care by the state for captive breeding.'

'That's preposterous,' Natalie snorted.

'I know that, and you know that, but it gives Ngwenya a green light to make his next move,' Braedan said.

Something else struck Natalie as odd about the theft of the horn. 'How come no one noticed the rhino's horn was missing? I mean, it's a pretty big animal.'

'You're right,' Braedan conceded, spreading his hands. 'But to be fair, your grandfather sometimes gets a bit mixed up with the names of the rhinos and numbers of horned and dehorned animals. I don't know them all by sight yet, so I'm partly to blame for not being on top of it. Doctor Nkomo should have known, because the men he supervises, to track the wild rhinos, should have reported it to him. There seems to have been a forty-eight hour period where the rhino involved wasn't spotted by anyone, and when he finally was, the news was already out about the missing horn. We had two scouts away on leave – mysteriously they both claimed to be sick and had to go to the clinic the morning before the horn was taken – and that left Doctor short of two trackers. Also I was in town getting supplies that day. It was a catalogue of errors that we're trying to ensure doesn't happen again, and as the man in charge I'm as much to blame as anyone.'

There was something else that was troubling Natalie. She'd seen photos of Emmerson Ngwenya on the web when she was researching Zimbabwe's troubled state of affairs, but it had been a very different experience when she'd seen him first-hand, standing wild-eyed in the middle of the road holding a gun, dead bodies around him. He had smiled at her and she had felt the physical, lung-crushing grip of pure terror.

'Natalie?'

'What?' She looked up at Braedan. 'Sorry, I was somewhere else.'

He smiled, but it didn't cheer her. 'A million miles away by the look of it.'

'No, thirty years away,' she said.

'Do you want to talk about it?'

She folded the newspaper so that the headline was face down. 'No, not right now, but I want you to.' Natalie reached into her daypack and pulled out a digital voice recorder, little bigger than the cigarette lighter Braedan took from his pocket and used to light up. 'I've been waiting weeks to talk to you.'

'I've been dreading this, but yes, I suppose now's as good a time as ever,' Braedan said, smiling through the exhaled smoke.

She liked being in his company. He was self-assured, easygoing, and when he smiled his eyes glowed. She was sure he was suppressing some terrible memories, but unlike Tate, Braedan seemed to have the ability to get on with life and to find the humorous or the irreverent in even the bleakest of situations. 'I suppose the rhinos are safe without me for another hour, even if half of them are stoned on drugs at the moment.'

Natalie placed the recorder on the table and waited for the waiter to clear their plates away. She'd barely finished half her chicken and felt guilty about leaving it, in a country where the poverty line was an impossible aspiration for so many. 'I'll have a Castle,' Braedan said to the man. 'I have a feeling I'm going to need a beer.'

She took out a pen and notebook and flipped it open. Natalie always took notes, just in case the recorder wasn't working properly or it ran out of batteries without her noticing. God, she thought, why was she even putting herself through all this? Writing a book was a much bigger endeavour than putting together a feature story for a magazine or newspaper – the difference between taking out a kayak for a quick paddle on one of Sydney's rivers and crossing the Atlantic in a rowboat. It was daunting enough given the number of words she would have to write, but as she flicked the toggle on the recorder she realised that she was also about to embark on the most difficult interview of her life.

'Tell me about what happened, the day you parachuted into Grandpa Paul's farm. The day you saved me . . .'

He flicked an imaginary flake of tobacco off his lip then closed his eyes for a moment as he drew another deep lungful of smoke. Halfway through exhaling he opened his eyes and pierced her with his stare. 'What, specifically, do you want to know?'

'All of it.'

He shook his head. 'Most of it's in three or four books about the Bush War and the RLI. You can read about how we jumped in, how the boys and me were pretty much on our own – no air support, no command and control for most of the time.'

'I've read the books.'

'Then what do you really want to know, Natalie?'

'I want to know what really happened.'

He swallowed and looked away from her. 'It's all in the history books.'

'No, it's not. Look at me, Braedan.'

He beckoned to the waiter for another beer. The first one had disappeared quickly and he set the empty bottle down on the table.

'The man you shot, the man who had hold of me . . . he wasn't the one who kidnapped me from the farmhouse. He was part of a different group of terrs.'

Braedan shrugged, accepted his next Castle with a nod of thanks, and raised the bottle to his lips. 'So what? There were two groups operating in the area and they linked up. The guy I shot must have taken you off the other one.'

She closed her eyes, forcing herself to recall the images she had spent thirty years trying to forget. 'There was so much shooting.' When she opened her eyes again she saw he was looking at her, but he glanced away once more.

'*Ja*. The lead was flying.'

'I think they might have been shooting at each other before you arrived.'

He picked at the sodden label of the bottle, peeling it. 'That's possible – not even unusual. What you have to remember is that in 1979, when things were coming to a head in Rhodesia, the blacks were also fighting among themselves. Mugabe's ZANLA and Nkomo's ZIPRA hated each other, on tribal and political grounds. It was a three-way contest sometimes. The Special Branch and army intelligence guys used to keep scoreboards of terrs killed by each other and terrs killed by us. We used to joke about it, saying our aim was to kill more of them than they killed of each other.'

Natalie nodded rapidly. 'Yes, yes, I've heard all that before, but there was something else going on there in the bush. You know the real story, don't you?'

He reached for his cigarettes and lighter and finished his beer. She wondered if he was going to walk out on her and leave her stranded in the pub. Braedan's cell phone chirped the high-pitched call of a woodland kingfisher from his pocket. '*Ja?*'

Natalie could tell immediately that something was wrong.

'We're on our way.' He ended the call.

'What was that all about?'

Braedan stood and pulled a few grimy dollar bills from his

wallet and left them crumpled on the table. 'Your grandfather's farm. The gooks are trying to invade it again.'

They flew back to the Bryant ranch, the little Nissan *bakkie* squeaking noisily on its wornout springs as they bucked along the uneven surface of the main road and swerved to miss the occasional pothole or goat.

'What should I do?' Natalie asked as Braedan slowed down.

There was a crowd of about fifty Africans gathered around the ranch's entrance gate, which was locked. Braedan took the phone from his pocket, driving one-handed, and scrolled down his contact list until he came to the number for the member in charge at the Plumtree police camp. He handed her the phone. 'Call this number if things go bad.'

'Bad?' She was wide-eyed with fear.

'OK, if things go worse.' He smiled for her, though he felt out of his depth. He stopped the car a hundred metres from the crowd and leaned across her to open the glove compartment. She smelled clean and fresh, despite the heat of the day. A woman in the crowd turned to them, pointed, and started ulu-lating. Other heads swivelled and took up the chant. Some of them started dancing. Braedan saw the glint of light on a panga, the wicked blade bobbing above the black heads.

He remembered the day he and Lara were kicked off their own farm, and the crippling sense of helplessness he'd felt. He'd thought, at the time, that if he'd been a single man he might have made a fight of it – barricaded himself in the farmhouse with his FN and his .458 hunting rifle and taken as many of the bastards with him as he could. But that was just a fantasy, an oft-replayed daydream in which his life ended in a blaze of glory instead of in a series of dead-end jobs and a mounting pile of debts.

Braedan clenched his fists as he approached the mob. These were ordinary people; pass them on the street in Bulawayo or Harare and they would most likely return a polite nod and ask, 'How are you?' Individually they were the peaceful, smiling heart and soul of Africa; as an angry mob, they were its secret nightmare.

'Kill the Boer!' the woman broke her ululating to chant.

'Kill the Boer, kill the Boer!' the mob responded, taking up the chant and turning to face him.

At another time he might have laughed at the words. He was not a farmer any more and he'd certainly never been an Afrikaner farmer – a Boer – but this new generation of so-called war veterans had delved back into the old Cold War era language of the *Chimurenga*, when 'Boer' had been the term for any evil whitey, whether they were residents of Rhodesia, South Africa or the old South-West Africa.

Braedan could see Doctor on the other side of the locked gates, about a hundred metres up the access road, leaning against the bonnet of one of the game viewers. He had Elias, the senior game scout, with him. Doctor lifted a hand in a laconic wave and Braedan nodded to him.

Braedan scanned the group of protesters and located the eldest man. He had a tight cap of grey curls and he stood, immobile, while the younger demonstrators danced and chanted around him. He alone was actually old enough to remember the war as an adult. Braedan turned side-on to ease his way into the press of bodies, and while he felt a couple of brushes and shoves, the crowd reluctantly cleared a path for him.

'*Mangwanani, baba,*' Braedan said to the man, using the correct form of greeting for an older man, and one who clearly held sway with the mob. Braedan guessed from his heavy-set features that he was Mashona, a stranger to the land of the Ndebele.

'*Mangwanani.*' The man was unsmiling.

'How are you, *baba*?' Braedan said.

'I am fine, and you?' The reply was instinctive.

'Fine, thank you, all things considered. May I ask what you and your friends are doing here?'

The younger men in the group were growing tired of chanting for the sake of this one white man, who was showing no signs of being intimidated, and some had stopped in order to listen to the conversation between him and the older man, who introduced himself to Braedan by his old *Chimurenga* name, which was Comrade Styx.

'The people are here to claim the land that was stolen from them over a hundred years ago. This land is ours and our ancestors died here fighting to defend it,' Styx said.

'The owner, Mr Bryant, has given away twenty per cent of his land. I recognise some of the people here who live as his neighbours,' Braedan said, looking around the quietening crowd.

The old man shook his head. 'This land was never his to give, and besides, it was poisoned land, nothing grew on it. He gave up his barren land and kept only the good.'

Braedan gritted his teeth. It was the same across the country. Where land had been ceded it had been left idle and become overgrown or, at best, planted with straggly, undernourished subsistence crops. There was nothing wrong with the land Paul Bryant had given up, voluntarily, just the ability and commitment of the 'new farmers' to prepare and work it.

'Mr Bryant is breeding rhinos here, on behalf of the Government of Zimbabwe. This ranch is an intensive breeding zone, monitored and approved by the parks and wildlife department. You have no claim on this place. It is protected by law.'

'*We* are the law in this country now, white man,' the so-called comrade said, aiming a crooked finger at Braedan's chest. 'The people are taking back what is rightfully theirs, and if rhino are to be bred then it will be by the rightful inhabitants of Zimbabwe, not some Boer.'

The woman who had whipped the mob into a frenzy on Braedan's arrival had positioned herself behind the old veteran; at the sign of his defiance she threw back her head and started whooping her war cry again. The others in the crowd joined her and Paul felt the bodies press closer around him.

'*We are the law, we are the law, we are the law . . .*' they chanted.

They may as well be, Braedan thought, as it seemed no one was actually running the country at the moment.

Eyes turned then at the sound of a vehicle's engine. A black double-cab Toyota roared up the access road, past Braedan's Nissan, and pulled up a few metres from the crush of people surrounding the lone white man. Braedan caught a glimpse of Natalie standing outside his truck, nervously bobbing her head from side to side to try to keep him in sight, the phone clasped in her right hand.

If she was thinking of calling the police she needn't bother, because four uniformed officers dismounted from the cargo area at the rear of the Toyota and brushed the dust from their uniforms. The doors of the double cab opened and out stepped Emmerson Ngwenya, dressed in pressed khaki bush clothes, along with another man in a black T-shirt and jeans, and two men in cheap suits and dark glasses.

'Shit,' Braedan said. The crowd parted and he walked across to Ngwenya.

'I might have known you were behind this,' Braedan said.

Ngwenya used a meaty index finger to slide his Ray Ban sunglasses up the bridge of his nose. 'You talk to me like I know you . . . as though we have something to discuss.'

'What are you doing here?'

Ngwenya smiled and spread his arms to show off the men he had brought with him. 'I am doing my civic duty, assisting the local police and these two gentlemen from the Central Intelligence Organisation in their investigation of wrongdoings at this ranch. You read, no doubt, of the unaccounted rhino horn that went missing from here?'

'Yes, I read about it,' Braedan said.

Ngwenya looked past him, to where Natalie was standing, and Braedan saw the flare of panic in her eyes.

'A striking woman, and the second time I've seen her in recent weeks. She's the Bryants' granddaughter, isn't she?'

'What's that got to do with you?' Braedan hissed. He shivered at the way Ngwenya lowered his sunglasses to take a better look at Natalie.

'Anything that happens on this ranch is my business.'

Braedan licked his lips. 'I know what you want, but you won't get it while I'm head of security here.'

Ngwenya laughed. 'Head of security? You couldn't protect a kitten, let alone a pair of old white farmers and some rhinos.' Ngwenya spun on his feet and raised his arms. 'You cannot *protect* something that is not yours!' he said loudly. 'This land, this farm belongs to the people of Zimbabwe and I am here to liberate it for them!'

The ululating, cheering and dancing began again and a cloud of dust generated by stamping feet began to rise around Braedan. He locked eyes with the politician just before Ngwenya pushed the glasses back up his nose.

'What do you want?' Braedan said again.

Ngwenya looked to his sidekick and snapped his fingers. The man walked back to the Toyota, reached in and pulled out an orange plastic folder. He delivered it to the minister, who passed it to Braedan. 'You can hand this to Paul Bryant after you organise for his trained monkeys to open the gates and escort the police and CIO to the farmhouse.'

The crowd broke into a song, '*Pamberi ne Chimurenga*' – 'Forward with the Struggle' – the words of which Braedan recalled from the war days. Braedan opened the folder and read the first page of a document that was addressed to the government department responsible for redistribution of land. It was headed: 'PROPOSAL FOR TRANSFERENCE OF OWNERSHIP OF KIABEJANE RANCH TO THE LOCAL COMMUNITY AND REDESIGNATION OF SAID PROPERTY AS COMMUNITY TOURISM AND WILDLIFE CONSERVATION CENTRE.'

He scanned the summary of the proposal and realised he had underestimated Emmerson Ngwenya's intelligence and cunning. Paul had had enough friends at the highest levels of the parks and wildlife service to hang on to the ranch during the earlier farm invasions, but the news of the missing horn would not help his case once it came time for the government to consider Ngwenya's proposal to redesignate the ranch as a community project. Brigadier Emmerson Ngwenya, Braedan read in the document, would be chairman of a 'governing council' which would oversee the new grassroots conservation and tourism operation, with all profits being returned to the local people.

'We have a warrant to enter this property, by force if necessary,' one of the suits said.

Braedan looked up from the folder. He was surrounded and outgunned.

'Come,' Braedan said to the politician, as if he was talking to a dog.

CHAPTER 29

Tate lowered the binoculars and rubbed his eyes. They were so sore from scanning the far-off bush and staring through the rippling heat haze that his dirt-encrusted fingers were muddy with tears when he inspected them.

He'd been in the hills above Lake Kariba in the virtually abandoned Charara hunting concession for three weeks, with not the slightest sign of the probably mythical animal he was looking for. A different man might have given up, might have been overwhelmed by the heat and the dust and the flies and the danger, but Tate knew this was where he was meant to be.

It reminded him of the old days, before everything went wrong. He had been at his happiest as a young field ranger, patrolling these very same hills. He'd been at home here, alone and content to live in splendid isolation. And although he was happy here now, he was fast coming to the conclusion that he was on a fool's errand, looking for a ghost. The legendary last black rhino of Makuti was most surely long dead and gone.

Tate pulled out his notebook, opened it to today's date and recorded his observations. *12 pm – nil sighting, nil spoor*. He checked his handheld GPS and recorded his current location. He closed the notebook and fastened it with a rubber band. The information was recorded on the GPS as well, but Tate had an inbuilt distrust of gadgets.

He'd quartered the area slowly and methodically, starting from the corner near where he'd left the main Harare to Chirundu road, not far from the old Clouds' End Hotel. He'd had little expectation of finding any sign of a rhino close to the road, but he'd used those first few days to get himself accustomed to being back in the bush on foot again. For too many years he'd been tracking rhinos from helicopters and Land Rovers, using an array of high-tech monitoring gear. Now he was travelling on his own two feet, with only his knowledge of the land, and a plastic-wrapped file of letters, notes and maps collected by an old man with senile dementia, to guide his way.

But if Paul Bryant wanted to pay him to go off into the wild for a while, then that was fine with Tate. It gave him time to think, and time to be by himself. Annoyingly, he also had plenty of time to replay in his mind, over and over again, the evening he'd spent with Natalie at Victoria Falls. Sometimes he wished he'd taken her to bed, but then memories of Hope would come back to haunt him and he'd feel guilty all over again.

As well as looking for the probably nonexistent rhino, Tate had busied himself looking for signs of other game as he'd walked within earshot of the main road. He'd found the spoor of some small buck – common duiker mostly – plus the occasional small cat. He'd also uncovered snare wire aplenty. As much as it pained him, he left every snare exactly as he found it, and took time to clear his own tracks. He didn't want any of the poachers to know there was a white man on their patch.

Paul's instructions had been succinct.

'Go out there for me, Tate, and find Makuti, the last black rhino, if he's still alive. I'm too old to go traipsing those hills, but I have to know, before I die, if the story's true.'

'It's not, Paul. I can tell you that now and save us both the time,' Tate had replied.

Paul had held up a sun-spotted hand. 'Always the cantankerous bastard, aren't you? I'm a firm believer that where there's smoke there's fire. I saw stranger things come true in the war, my boy. Here's the file.' And he had passed over the stained, dog-eared folder.

Not receptive, but curious nonetheless, Tate had opened the folder and skimmed its contents. Despite his convictions he'd felt the frisson of excitement when he'd started reading.

Lomagundi Lakeside
 Kariba
 September 1997
 Dear Paul,
 Howzit. You won't believe it, but I spotted your old friend again, during a hunting trip into the hills with a South African client. The hunter had bad eyes and didn't see him, but I did, and he looked in fine form. Makuti sniffed the air a moment, turned his rump to me and trotted off. I wished I'd had a camera, but it was good enough that I was able to get a clear view of him. I've attached a copy of a map showing the location. Look forward to seeing you here again next year.
 Cheers,
 G.O.F.

Paul had explained that he'd been in regular contact with the old hunter, Gerry O'Flynn, over the years and it was he who was responsible for most of the correspondence and entries in the dossier. Tate knew of O'Flynn, or Flynn as he had been called when he was still alive, and he wished he could put as much credence in the reports as Paul had.

Flynn had given up hunting for much of the seventies,

joining the Rhodesian SAS, and he even had some supposedly confirmed sightings of rhino in the Makuti area from the war days. These, Tate conceded, could very well have been true, as there had been a healthy population of black rhino around Lake Kariba in the Zambezi Valley and, by extension, into the mountains on the Zimbabwean side of the Zambezi River after independence and well into the 1980s before they were all either killed or relocated.

But Paul had clearly been paying Flynn to mount occasional searches like the one Tate was undertaking now, and it seemed that for many years Paul had joined Flynn on safari in search of the mythical Makuti, the supposed last black rhino.

Tate unstrapped the blanket from the bottom of his rucksack and laid it in the shade under the tree. He sat down, took off his sweat-dampened broad-brimmed felt hat and scratched his scalp. It had been five or six years since he'd last seen Flynn, propping up the bar at the old Kariba Yacht Club. Flynn had been an expert on rhinos, and on tracking them, and had still been leading tourists on walking safaris into Matusadona National Park, taking clients to see the virtually tame rhinos that had lived around the main camp at Tashinga. These were the orphan offspring of adults killed by poachers, and as tight as the security had been around these precious survivors, poachers had still managed to get close to them and kill one that had grown to maturity. Word had it that Flynn, who was as addicted by then to the bottle as he was to the money he made off rhino tracking, had inadvertently led the poachers to the adult male on one of his escorted walks. Flynn had been found a short time later at his hovel in Kariba, stabbed to death.

The reports since 2004 were in Paul Bryant's hand. They were notes of discussions he'd had with an assortment of people he'd met in and around Kariba and Makuti. There were the two glitter-stone quarry men who still eked out a living digging up the unusual rocks that people who still had money for such things used to tile the edges of their swimming pools. The diggers claimed to have seen a rhino trotting along a distant ridge line as they returned to Kariba from a trip to Chirundu. Paul had recorded that he had paid the men $20,000 Zim dollars – only a few US dollars' worth at times, but no doubt a tantalising reward for the miners. Were they canny men who had heard an old man asking about rhinos and seen a way to make some money, or could their story have been genuine?

Away from the road the poachers' tracks and snares had become fewer and further between, until they had petered out altogether. Tate had returned to his car at the end of each week and, reconnecting the battery, had coaxed it back into life and driven into Kariba for more supplies. On his last trip, three days' earlier, he had carried with him enough kapenta, biltong, noodles and other dried foods to last him a further two weeks on foot in the bush. Water he would find in the streams and pools in the hills. He would be moving deep into the safari area and he wanted to carry on until he was sure, once and for all, that Paul had been wasting their time. But there was no bitterness in his quest. In a way, he wished he could stay out here forever.

Tate opened his pack and pulled out the portable camping stove. He had enough of the small gas canisters to last him three weeks if he was careful with their use and limited himself to boiling water twice a day. He set a tin pannier on the stovetop, filled it with water he'd drawn from a rockpool that morning, and lit the gas. While he waited for the water to boil he heaved himself slowly back to his feet. His right knee protested. As much as he loved this simple, rough life in the bush, he knew full well it was a younger man's calling.

Tate hobbled the first couple of steps until his knee loosened a bit, and stopped at the squat bushwillow tree. He unzipped his shorts and started urinating. He looked at the foliage of the tree and absently noted that some of the branches had been recently grazed. He caressed the snipped-off twigs with his free hand.

As he'd moved further into the bush he'd been pleased to find a little more spoor of more and differing kinds of mammals. There had been the scat and teardrop hoof prints of majestic sable antelope – though he'd yet to see any on his wanderings so far – and the middens of impala rams who had staked out their territories. He'd also seen the big bovine pats of buffalo dung, and patted the oiled stock of his old .358 Brno hunting rifle instinctively as he reminded himself to keep an eye out for any *dagga* boys who might be snoozing nearby. Elephant had crossed the area often, and though he saw no fresh spoor, it was always nice to know they were still around, moving as silently as grey ghosts. As with the buffalo, he would be content to limit his encounters with the huge mammals to discoveries of their dried dung. He had no wish to get into a dangerous confrontation with any animal, not even a phantom rhino.

'What's been eating you?' he asked the bushwillow shrub aloud. It wasn't the first time he'd caught himself talking to no one.

Tate had been checking the trees and bushes he passed on his transepts for signs of browsing and inevitably the stripped and broken branches had been fed on by kudu, which only browsed, or impala, which were both browsers of trees and grazers of grass, depending on the season. He rubbed his thumb against a cleanly cut twig.

His hands were shaking as he zipped his fly and fumbled in his pocket for his reading glasses.

He put on his glasses and leaned in closer to the bush. The stem he'd just touched, and several others around it, had not been stripped of leaves or snapped off, but rather looked as though it had been snipped by a pair of garden secateurs at an angle of precisely forty-five degrees. 'My God.' There was only one animal in the African bush that left this telltale sign when browsing.

'Black rhino.'

'Ladies and gentlemen, the Qantas Club welcomes members and guests travelling to Johannesburg on flight QF 64. Your flight is now ready for boarding.'

George Bryant folded his copy of *The Australian* and tucked it under his arm. He picked up his blue blazer and snapped out the extendable handle of his wheelie bag. He prided himself on only ever travelling with carry-on luggage, his bags conforming to the gram and the millimetre to cabin-stowage requirements.

He nodded a polite thank you to the woman at reception and walked out and down the escalators to join the throng of people clustered at the boarding gate. His fellow passengers were a mix of Australian backpackers and honeymooners, and South Africans either going home after visiting relatives in Australia, or going back to visit family members unlucky enough, in George's view, to still be stuck there.

George took out his iPhone. He thought briefly about sending Susannah an SMS, but there was no point. He switched his phone off instead. She'd been polite, when saying goodbye, but he knew she was looking forward to having the house to herself while he was away.

Any pretence of tenderness or affection had disappeared from their communications, verbal and typed, years ago. These days, George and Susannah, while still married on paper, were no more than flatmates. They didn't have a bad life, he supposed. They had a lovely house in Pymble, on Sydney's upper north shore, which was big enough for them to lead their separate lives without annoying each other unnecessarily. Two cars, separate bedrooms, separate home offices. It was all very civilised.

To split up would be too much of a hassle. They would have to sell the house, and then they'd both have to buy new places. With the property market stagnant at best, it wasn't a good time to sell.

He didn't want to think about that. George had joined a blue chip insurance company soon after they'd migrated to Australia in 1980. Susannah had urged him to try to join the Royal Australian Air Force. He'd been reluctant, but Susannah was a domineering woman who usually got her way, so he'd gone for an interview with defence recruiting and duly suffered the humiliation of rejection. He'd been a squadron leader in the Rhodesian Air Force and had flown in wartime operations for ten years, yet he'd been told by a flight sergeant that he would have to join the Australian Defence Force as an officer candidate or a recruit and complete his basic training and flight training all over again. 'You'll have to go through a selection board and, to be honest, mate,' the flight sergeant had said with a patronising familiarity that had irked George, 'you blokes are a bit on the nose after the way you've stuffed up your own country.'

George had stormed out and told Susannah that he'd be happy if he never flew or even saw a helicopter again as long as he lived. What George hated most was that his years of war service had all been for nothing. All the fighting, all the dying, all the bloodshed had counted for nought when Robert Mugabe, the Commonwealth's great black hope, had been sworn in as the President of the new Zimbabwe.

'Heading home?' a man in the queue asked him in a South African accent, as they waited for the flight attendants to sort out an issue with a bent boarding card.

'No, to Zimbabwe,' George said.

'You're not from there?'

'A long time ago, but Australia's my home now.' George's reply was automatic, as it had been for decades, but as he'd packed for this trip he'd wondered what it might be like to make a clean break, to leave Susannah and Australia for good. His life wasn't bad, but it was like living in an emotional coma. Zimbabwe was a mess, but perhaps it could bounce back, once Mugabe died. He'd taken his family away from Rhodesia to escape the killings, but ever since then he'd been slowly dying inside.

'*Ja*,' the stranger nodded, 'those people ruined your bloody country, now they're doing their best to screw up mine. There's no bloody hope at all. Me, I'm going back to Jo'burg to try and get my daughter to come back to Australia with me. She thinks everything's going to work itself out in South Africa, but I keep telling her she's crazy, man.'

George just nodded. He didn't want to continue the conversation.

'She called me a *when-we* in an email the other day,' the man continued. 'Isn't that what they called you Rhodesians who left? Now they're using it on us South Africans, hey? Well, I don't mind being called that because *when we* ruled our country it was bloody paradise, hey?'

George simply nodded again. He had been one, as well – a *when-we*. The fact was that life expectancy, education standards and every other indicator of civilised society – roads, water, healthcare, electricity, economic performance – had all plummeted under black rule in Zimbabwe, just as they had in South Africa. From what George had read, the new Government of National Unity had achieved nothing of note, so even the beatings and torture that members of the opposition Movement for Democratic Change had suffered had all been for nothing.

George got most of his information about Zimbabwe from the internet. He regularly read online newsletters and newspapers that painted a grim picture of life there. More than once he'd come across the name Thandi Ngwenya. Although he sometimes felt slightly guilty doing it, he'd googled Thandi several times and had kept up to date with her rise through the political ranks.

The man ahead of George said goodbye as he entered the aircraft and turned right towards economy. George was grateful. He'd feared the man might be flying business class and, worse, that he might end up sitting next to him. As much as he agreed with everything the South African had said during their brief exchange, he hated such conversations.

He read all the emails – the jokey ones and the tragic ones pointing out time and again how bad things were in Africa these days – and dutifully forwarded them on to his circle of ex-Rhodesian and South African friends. He bemoaned the state of Africa at dinner party after dinner party and, like all the other expatriate guests, silently patted himself on the back for being smart enough to move his family to Australia all those years ago.

It hadn't been easy. The air force had given George and Susannah a nice lifestyle that they'd never really had to pay for. They'd always lived in air force houses and George had eaten and drunk in the mess most days. His wages had been enough to cover Natalie's school fees and Susannah had never had to work for a living. When they'd made the decision to leave they'd done so with precious little savings.

George had started in the insurance business at entry level and had enrolled in an accountancy degree part-time. He'd slowly worked his way up to his current position as chief financial officer of the company. He'd learned about the markets over the years and had invested what spare money they'd been able to save.

The nightmares came, especially in the first year, but less and less often as time went on. He rarely saw the burnt-out hulk of the crashed Viscount any more, or the charred bodies. Last night, though, he'd seen and spoken to Winston in his sleep again – the first time in many years. He knew the conversation was directly linked to this trip, and had half-expected to see his mouth forming the word 'why' as his blood oozed out onto the floor of the helicopter. In real life, of course, Winston had been dead for hours by the time his body was loaded into George's helicopter. But in the dream, he always wanted answers from George about why he'd been killed by the security forces.

George stowed his wheelie bag in the overhead locker and handed his blazer to the flight attendant. The business class ticket had cost a small fortune and Susannah had raised her eyebrows and told him that an economy seat would have saved them a couple of thousand dollars.

Them? Susannah had worked the first eight years in Australia, but not since. She'd been employed in an upmarket dress shop and developed a taste for designer labels. They'd chosen the north shore because of the number of South Africans that lived there, but it was also a well-heeled part of Sydney, where women were expected to dress to a certain standard, no matter how little their husbands earned. George had suggested moving to Perth when a position in the insurance company was advertised internally, as there were more Rhodesians there than South Africans, but Susannah had objected, telling him that all her friends were in Sydney. She played tennis most days, which kept her figure looking almost as good as it did in her twenties, but did nothing to contribute to their finances.

George didn't really mind going to work every day; in fact, as the years wore on, he realised he actually preferred being at work to being at home. When he'd been a pilot, during the war, Susannah had seemed the perfect wife for a few years. She was pretty, fiercely patriotic, and she'd been a good mum to Natalie, especially after the trauma of Natalie's abduction. However, in Sydney she'd complained about having to do housework every day *and* work in the dress shop. She'd quit her job once Natalie finished school and they no longer had the fees to worry about. But even though she didn't work she still never seemed to have time to do the housework. Eventually they'd hired a cleaner, which had stopped Susannah from whining for a while.

The other passengers filed into business class and George glanced at them every now and then over the top of his newspaper. The flight attendant brought champagne and he thanked her and took a sip.

Susannah had had a healthy appetite for sex when they were younger, even though George knew he sometimes left her wanting. After the stress of missions, especially those in which either his own men or soldiers they'd been ferrying had been killed, he'd sought relief through beer and whisky and there had been plenty of occasions when he'd been too drunk to perform. He'd thought that moving to Australia would give them a chance to rekindle the spark they'd shared as newlyweds, but that hadn't happened.

He had more energy, working nine to five, but Susannah complained of being too tired after long days on her feet in the dress shop. After she became a lady of leisure it seemed the hours on the tennis court wore her out. Also, she lunched with her friends when they weren't on the court – and sometimes went for drinks after matches – and then it was she who was sometimes too drunk for sex.

Australia was different to Rhodesia. George had driven home

drunk from the officers' mess or a pub most nights of the week when they'd lived in Africa, but since the early eighties drink-driving had been taboo in Australia. Susannah had been stopped by the police one afternoon on Mona Vale Road, near the St Ives Village shopping centre where she'd been lunching, and ordered to undergo a random breath test. She'd been arrested and charged with drink-driving and had had to go to court, where she lost her licence for six months.

After the initial embarrassment she'd curbed her drinking for a while, but her abstinence didn't last. She took more back roads, or the occasional cab, and often George would come home to find her with a bottle of wine open in front of her as she dozed in front of the television.

George didn't think about sex much at all these days. He and Susannah had, as people said, drifted apart, and there was little chance of drifting back.

To his shame, it had been one of their mutual friends, a former South African, who had told George that he might like to keep an eye on his wife's tennis coach. George had dressed for work one day, in his suit, and left for the train, but then called his office from his cell phone – a real status symbol back then in the late eighties – to say he was ill. He'd killed a couple of hours reading the financial pages at a local café then picked up a rental car. He'd parked outside the tennis court and watched Susannah say goodbye to her friends after their match was over. Susannah had waited in her Ford Capri convertible until Ben, her tennis coach, had walked out of the clubhouse and got into his RX-7. Susannah had driven off and Ben had followed her, with George a discreet distance behind.

They'd spent the afternoon at a cheap motel on the Pacific Highway.

He'd flown hundreds of combat missions in the bush war and

put his life at risk more times than he could remember. He'd enjoyed it. Really, he had. He'd never felt as alive as he had in those years, despite the danger. He'd loved flying and he'd loved the time he spent on leave in his beautiful country with his beautiful, sexy wife and his perfect little daughter.

But all that had changed the day the terrs had raided his parents' farm and tried to steal his baby girl away. George's best friend in the world had been killed by friendly fire. His sister had been murdered shortly afterwards. He'd taken his young family away from Africa, to the safety of Australia, in the hope that they could live a normal life there. And that's when he'd started dying.

He'd grown scared. He was too much of a coward to confront Susannah over the tennis pro and he hated her, and himself, for his weakness. He was fairly sure she had cheated on him continuously over the years, but he'd thought it best, for Natalie's sake, to do nothing. He was also sure that Susannah knew that he knew, but she never said anything either. They just drifted apart. He'd talked about moving out, but in the end they'd decided it made more sense to keep living in different halves of the same house.

He was due to retire later in the year, and that scared him too. He didn't want to spend his days rattling around the big empty house with Susannah, each of them trying to avoid the other. She didn't like to travel at the best of times and had made a list of excuses as to why she couldn't accompany him to Africa to see his parents. Maybe, he decided on a whim, he'd check out some property while he was back. It wouldn't make financial sense to buy a place in Zimbabwe, even though he assumed he could buy a mansion with the proceeds of half his Sydney house, no matter how low the selling price. Maybe a beach house and a boat in Mozambique.

Mozambique. Thandi.

George looked out the window as the jumbo raced up the runway. They lifted off and the wheels retracted with a clunk. Sydney's orderly sprawl and sparkling blue waters disappeared as the pilot banked. George was, he knew, in limbo. There was nothing beyond a few possessions awaiting his return to Australia, and there was nothing but memories – most bad, but some good – where he was headed.

CHAPTER 30

Philippa wrapped an ornate hand-painted china serving dish in newspaper and handed it to Natalie, who laid it carefully in the packing crate with the rest of the antique service.

'Honestly, I don't know why I'm bothering with all this stuff. I should just give it away or smash it to pieces so those bloody coons don't get hold of it.'

Natalie didn't reply. Instead she took another sheet of paper and began wrapping a dinner plate. Her grandmother had oscillated between tears and anger all through the day as they'd worked to pack the contents of the farmhouse. She couldn't remember ever having heard Grandma Pip use a derogatory term for Africans before. In fact, it was the opposite – Philippa chiding other people for using one.

'Why do they hate us so, Natalie?'

'I don't know, Grandma.' Natalie could understand that some people felt genuine grievances over land. There were real veterans of the liberation war who had received nothing from Mugabe's government and had been justifiably angry as they'd watched the political fat cats get richer while they starved. But there was no doubt that the land redistribution had been an unmitigated disaster.

While the vast majority of white farming families had been evicted from their land in Zimbabwe, Grandma Pip and

Grandpa Paul's case seemed especially unfair. When the farm invasions began they had met with the local people – the real surrounding communities rather than the bus loads of outsiders who had been brought in by the ruling party to squat on white farms – and ceded several hundred hectares of arable farming land. The Bryants had used the land to grow crops, primarily to feed their dairy cows when dairy had been their main business. As her grandparents had grown older they had progressively downscaled the dairy and shifted their focus to breeding and conserving black rhinos. They were doing something for the nation, and living off the profits of their farming life rather than making money from their land.

Grandma Pip had confided to Natalie that while they still had money in the bank, it was fast disappearing. Kiabejane had once been a popular tourist destination, but tourists had all but abandoned Zimbabwe over the previous decade and the ranch's main revenue stream had dried up. They were supported by overseas charities in Australia and the UK, and the trickle of foreign volunteers who still made the pilgrimage to the ranch provided some extra hands and a small contribution.

'That Emmerson Ngwenya is hell bent on destroying us,' Pip said.

'But why, Gran? Why does *he* hate us so much?'

Her grandmother shrugged her bony shoulders and went back to her packing.

Natalie sensed there was much more to the story, but didn't have the heart to push the issue at the moment. Her grandmother was tired to the point of exhaustion and worried sick about Grandpa Paul, who was in hospital in Bulawayo, so it was no wonder she was repeating herself. Paul had suffered a mild heart attack at the police station, where he was being interviewed about the missing rhino horn, and the police member in charge had driven the elderly white man in his own car to the hospital.

Natalie wanted to tell her grandmother that it was a younger Emmerson Ngwenya who had abducted her from this very house all those years ago, but that would only add to her grandmother's anxiety. Natalie shivered. She could understand how heart-wrenching it was for her grandparents to leave the house they'd lived in for so long, but the place still held terrible memories for her and she would be happy to leave the farmhouse for good.

Philippa sniffled and wiped her eyes. Natalie wrapped an arm around her grandmother's thin bony shoulders. She felt so tiny, as though the life force was ebbing from her by the minute.

'I'm sorry, my girl. I'll be all right. We must go see to the rhinos.'

'All right, I'll go get Braedan,' Natalie said.

Braedan was outside in the dark with half-a-dozen farm workers, supervising the loading of a lounge suite from the formal sitting room onto the back of a flatbed lorry. '*Chova!*' he called, and the men pushed, but then he raised a hand and told them to stop. 'Hey, go easy with that, *mudhara*,' Braedan said to an old man with a cap of grey frizzy hair who had dropped his end of a couch with a loud thud.

Natalie's cell phone rang and she took it from the pocket of her jeans.

'Hello?'

'Natalie, it's Tate. I can't get hold of your grandparents. Their phone doesn't seem to be working. Is everything all right?'

'Hardly,' Natalie said. 'Emmerson Ngwenya's convinced the government to hand over the ranch to him. My grandfather's in hospital in town – he had a heart attack. It's a disaster here, Tate.'

'Oh.'

She wondered if that was all he had to say for himself. 'We're packing, Tate. My grandmother's been given two days to move out. My father's on his way from Australia, but it seems like there's nothing anyone can do.'

'I found the rhino,' Tate said down the static-plagued phone line. 'I've just got back into cell-phone range. Your grandfather was right, Natalie! It's not a myth – there's at least one black rhino still alive out here, in the wild.'

'That's wonderful, Tate,' she said, not bothering to mask her sarcasm. 'But it's all gone to shit here so it doesn't really matter how many rhinos you find out in the wild, because my grandparents' animals are probably going to wind up dead.'

George Bryant wheeled his bag down the air bridge at Harare International Airport and joined the queue at the immigration desk reserved for foreigners requiring a visa. It had been many years since he'd surrendered his Rhodesian passport for an Australian one.

'How long are you staying in our country?' the man behind the desk asked him.

George was tempted to say, 'I honestly don't know,' but instead answered, 'Two weeks.' It was all the time he'd been able to take off work. Even though he was retiring later in the year, the end of the financial year was looming. Wouldn't it be nice, he thought, if he could just call work and tell them he wasn't coming back?

George had booked the tickets as soon as Natalie had called him and told him the news of his father's heart attack, and the likelihood – now being realised – that the ranch was about to go.

In the arrivals hall George took a moment to recognise Jamie MacDonald, a pilot he'd served with in 7 Squadron.

'Have I changed that much?' Jamie asked him as he shook George's hand. 'Howzit, China?'

'Good, and you? And yes, like me you're older, fatter and greyer.'

They laughed. As Jamie led him out into the car park, he filled in the gaps since George had last seen him, on a visit a decade earlier. 'We lost the farm, of course, like everyone else, and Janet and I have been eking out a living in town. We grow some tomatoes and a few other bits and bobs in the backyard, and I fly charters when I can get the work. You made the right move getting out back when you did, George.'

George nodded, but he didn't want to appear as though he was gloating. 'And how is Janet?'

Jamie shrugged. 'Well enough, but she never really got over losing the farm. You see it in so many people's eyes. They soldier on, you know, but the light's gone out of their souls. Still, there's beer in the fridge – no electricity, though.' Jamie forced a laugh and wound down a window and paid a grimy dollar bill to the airport parking attendant.

It had been a long journey and George was tired, but he had much to do.

'So you're flying to Bulawayo tomorrow, is that right?' Jamie asked.

'Yes, but there's something I want to do, or rather someone I need to see, in Harare first tomorrow if possible.'

'And who's that – another of the old squadron boys?'

'No, it's a woman. A black woman.'

'Really? And who might that be?'

'Do you know anyone in government, Jamie? The thing is, I want to see the MDC's Minister for Women's Affairs.'

Jamie raised his eyebrows. 'I know a couple of the MDC guys

– I'm a supporter, or at least I was when I still had an income to speak of. So, you want to see Thandi Ngwenya?'

'Yes,' George nodded. 'Thandi Ngwenya.'

George woke at four in the morning, not sure whether he was hung-over or still drunk from the cheap Scotch Jamie had plied him with until midnight. He couldn't go back to sleep, and while it was no doubt partly to do with the jetlag, he knew it was also because he was thinking about Thandi.

Jamie and Janet had filled the bath tub in the ensuite with water two days before his arrival, when they'd had the unexpected good fortune of running water. George scooped some out with a jug and filled the hand basin. He washed his face and armpits and shaved with the cold water. It was more basic than his army days operating from forward airfields out in the bush.

He made himself coffee with water boiled on the gas bottle and hob sitting on the kitchen counter – there was still no electricity – and took his mug outside to watch the sun rise while he waited for Jamie and Janet to wake.

When they were up and ready Jamie started making calls on his cell phone. After four attempts he finally got the right number for Thandi Ngwenya's ministerial offices. His earlier calls had revealed that a young man Jamie had met at some MDC rallies was now working as a media adviser to the minister.

'I'm through . . . on hold,' Jamie said, giving George thumbs-up. 'Matthew, hi, it's Jamie MacDonald. Yes . . . Jamie MacDonald from the old days at Wedza. I was wondering if I might make an appointment to see Ms Ngwenya.'

George waited anxiously while Jamie whispered that his contact, Matthew, was checking with the diary secretary. 'Oh, I see. Booked solid all day, is she? It's just that I've got a very important visitor from Australia who's come all this way to meet her.'

Jamie shook his head, but George interrupted. 'Get him to tell her my name.'

'OK.' Jamie managed to stop Matthew from hanging up and urged him to pass on George Bryant's name. 'Do you really think she's going to know who you are or that your name's going to mean anything?' he asked George while he waited on hold again.

'We'll see,' George said, not knowing the answer himself.

Jamie held up his hand, signalling that Matthew was back on the line. 'She will? That's great news, Matthew. Thanks so much, hey. OK, we'll be there at eleven on the dot.' Jamie ended the call. 'Do you know how hard it is to see a government minister in this country? Who'd you sleep with to get so well known by a senior MDC politician?'

George felt his temperature rising, and smiled to himself. If only you knew, he thought.

Harare's traffic was chaotic, and the congestion was made worse by the fact that most of the traffic lights they passed through were out of order because of electricity shortages.

George wiped his hands on his chinos. He was nervous about seeing Thandi after all these years. He hoped that the fact she'd agreed to see him was a good sign. But there was no way of knowing if she would be able to help him at all, or if she would even bother trying. He'd found a picture of her online. The official portrait shot showed her smiling and well groomed, the consummate politician. He remembered the feel of her lithe young body under his in the beach hut in Mozambique, and the salty taste of her as he ran the tip of his tongue over the womanly swell of her hip.

The offices of the Ministry of Women's Affairs were on the twentieth floor of the Mukwati building in Fourth Street. Jamie dropped him outside the unattractive office block and went off in search of a parking space. Inside, George consulted a list of offices in the foyer and found the lifts. Electricity may have been a problem for Harare's residents, but not so for the politicians and bureaucrats who inhabited the Mukwati building.

On level twenty George presented himself to a well-fed African receptionist who took his name and motioned for him to take a seat on a grey imitation leather sofa whose surface was cracked and peeling. He sat forward so as not to let his head come into contact with the greasy marks on the headrest where other supplicants had perhaps fallen asleep waiting for an appointment.

A young man in a grey suit opened a side door and smiled at him. 'Mr Bryant? I am Matthew Mpofu. The Minister will see you now, if you'll please follow me.'

George stood and straightened his tie. His heart was pounding and he felt like a teenager again. Matthew opened a door and George saw her. She stood up behind an impressively large desk. The room was mostly lit by weak sunlight, diffused by years of uncleaned grime on a row of windows.

'Mr Bryant, Minister,' Matthew said.

'Thank you. Please leave us.' Matthew nodded and slipped out behind George, closing the door as he left.

George and Thandi looked at each other. George forced himself to take a breath. His chest felt tight and he could feel his face flush as the memories of her, and their time together, tumbled through his mind. She had aged well, he thought, her body curvy but still as perfectly proportioned as it had been when she was a teenager. Her hair was immaculately styled, straightened and coloured – far different to the afro he'd last seen her with – but when she smiled he was transported back to their time on the beach in Mozambique.

He remembered, suddenly, vividly, the taste of her mouth, the heat of her body, the dried sea salt on her skin that last time their bodies were locked together.

Thandi smiled. 'It's good to see you, George,' she said at last. 'After all these years.'

He felt embarrassed that he'd been unable to speak, to even say hello. 'Yes . . .' He took two steps towards her and held out his hand. She leaned across the expanse of her desk and took it. He held her hand, looking into her eyes at the same time and the emotion welled up inside him. He felt like a sentimental old fool. He had an immediate urge to tell her something . . . anything . . . but he was lost for words.

'Would you like tea?' she asked.

'Um . . . no thanks,' he stammered.

She eased her hand from his and sat down. He took one of the seats opposite her. The space made it a little easier for him to compose himself.

'You look well, George,' she said. 'You live in Australia, yes?'

He wanted to tell her that she looked as beautiful as ever, but the words wouldn't come. 'Yes . . . for, gosh, thirty years now.'

'So many people have left the country. It's one of the biggest challenges we'll face in the future, getting the good ones back. Black and white.'

He nodded. He looked around the office. In truth it was tired and spartan, but he didn't underestimate her achievement or the effort it must have taken for her to get here. 'You've done well for yourself, Thandi.'

She shrugged. 'It hasn't been easy. I served ZANU–PF for many years after independence, but as things deteriorated I couldn't stay with them and sleep at night. When I changed sides, I thought for a while I might die a pauper, leaving my children nothing.'

He'd been foolish, he realised. He'd been reliving stolen, selfish moments of passion from forty years ago, but Thandi had more important things on her mind. He could only imagine how much of a battle her life must be, as a politician in a country that was still to all intents and purposes ruled by a dictator. She'd compartmentalised him and their affair and was living in the here and now. All the same, he had to think hard to make small talk with her. 'Was it dangerous? We read stories about the violence and intimidation suffered by MDC politicians and activists.'

She tilted her head. 'There were moments when I was concerned, more for my children than myself, but that is all water under the bridge. At least we now have a voice in government, even if ZANU–PF continues to frustrate our attempts to bring real change to the country.'

There was so much he wanted to ask her, about what she'd done during the war years, about her family, but he didn't know where or how to start.

Thandi looked at her slim gold watch. 'George, I hate to sound abrupt, but what can I do for you?'

He felt silly again, thinking she might want to reminisce about old times. She was a busy woman and she'd made time for him. Quickly, he told her about the eviction notice that had been served on his parents, and his father's heart attack. 'I'm flying to Bulawayo this afternoon to see him. I don't know if there is anything you can do, Thandi, but I thought that since your brother was involved you might get him to see reason. If the community is going to take over the ranch, perhaps my parents could at least stay on as managers, to help ensure the safety of the government's rhinos.'

'Hmm,' she said. 'I've read about the problems at the ranch, but to tell you the truth I didn't know Emmerson was involved in this one. You say he's setting himself up as the chairman of the proposed community project that will run the rhino-breeding centre?'

'Yes. Look, Thandi, I don't live in Zimbabwe, and all I know is what I read online and in the newspapers. Your brother does not have a very good reputation internationally, especially when it comes to rhinos.'

She frowned, but nodded. 'Yes, I've read the same things. We barely speak these days. Corruption is rife in the government, and while there are some people who are dedicated to wildlife conservation, it would be naïve of anyone to suggest that there aren't senior politicians and bureaucrats who have been involved in poaching and the smuggling of wildlife products out of the country. There have been secret shipments of stock-piled ivory and rhino horn to Asia and the Middle East. I don't know if Emmerson is guilty of all the things people accuse him of, but as they say, where there's smoke . . .' She shrugged.

'My daughter, Natalie, was part of an operation that caught him in the middle of nowhere at a meeting with some rhino poachers. The government media said he killed two of the poachers, but Natalie thinks he was just covering his tracks.'

She nodded. 'Yes, I read the same story. I also read that your father has been accused of dealing in rhino horn as well.'

George slumped back in his seat. 'That's preposterous. My father's dedicated most of his life to saving these animals. He's hardly likely to start selling rhino horn on the black market at this stage of his life.'

'I know, George. There are so many allegations flying around it's hard to know who is doing what these days. The truth is, as much as I hate to admit it, there is a power vacuum since our new Government of National Unity was formed. The police don't know who to listen to – us or ZANU–PF. We control law and order on paper, but it's no secret that ZANU–PF enforces its will through intimidation and patronage. I'm sure the investigation into your father is based on trumped-up charges, but someone darted a rhino and stole its horn on your father's ranch out from under his nose. It does seem like the work of someone with at least some concern for the animal's welfare, don't you think?'

George ground his teeth. He couldn't believe that his father would deal with the people who he'd fought for decades. They weren't rich, but neither were they struggling. It had to have been an inside job. He would have to thrash this out with Natalie and the Quilter-Phipps boys as soon as he got to Bulawayo. 'I don't know what to think either, Thandi, but I do know that losing the ranch, and knowing their rhinos now have an uncertain future, will probably kill my parents.'

'I don't doubt what you're saying, George. And I'd be lying if I said I wasn't concerned at the prospect of my brother taking over a rhino-breeding ranch. It would be like putting the lion in charge of the goat herd. Let me see what I can do. I still have some friends in ZANU–PF. Perhaps there's something I can do to at least make sure the rhinos are protected. They are the property of the people, after all.'

George sensed the meeting was drawing to a close. He pushed back his chair and stood. 'Thank you, Thandi. My parents are heartbroken at losing the ranch, but if they had some assurance that their life's work wasn't for nothing, it might help them cope.'

Thandi stood as well and smiled. 'If what I plan comes off, then I think they might even be able to stay involved with the ranch. I can't make any promises, but leave it with me. When do you leave Zimbabwe?'

'Assuming my father's OK, I have to leave in two weeks' time.

I have to get back to my job in Australia.' Looking into her eyes he wanted to add, 'But I'd stay here in Zimbabwe, if it meant I could spend more time with you.'

'I understand. Perhaps we could have dinner here in Harare when you are finished in Bulawayo?'

George's heart lurched. Good lord, she wanted to see him again. Thandi extended her hand and he took it and looked into those big dark eyes that were still as sexy and enticing as they had been when he'd last seen her, forty years ago. 'I'd love to, Thandi.'

'So would I, George.' And she grinned back at him.

CHAPTER 31

Sharon Quilter-Phipps poured tea from a chipped china pot. Natalie added some milk to her cup and sat back on the wrought-iron chair in the shade of the jacaranda tree. It was a beautiful afternoon and despite the traumatic events of the last few days it was great to have her father and grandparents all together again.

'How are you feeling, Dad?' George asked as he stirred in some sugar and passed a cup to Paul.

'I'm fine. And stop asking me that,' Paul grumbled. Grandma Pip patted him on the knee and told him not to be so rude, and that George was just worried about him. 'I'm more worried about my rhinos,' he retorted.

'Your house and garden are looking lovely, Sharon,' Philippa said.

'Thanks, Pip,' Sharon said. 'I had a bit of a windfall recently from an old pension policy Fred had taken out in the UK years ago. I didn't know anything about it – Fred never let me have anything to do with the finances – then all of a sudden there were all these pounds sitting in my bank account.'

Natalie remembered the first time she'd been to Sharon's place, just a few weeks ago. The grass and garden had been overgrown and paint had been peeling from the house. Sharon, too, had undergone a transformation. She'd been wearing a threadbare house dress and her hair had been lank and greasy. Now she wore a new frock and her hair had been cut and permed. Sharon said she now had enough money to buy in water, and a large generator hummed away noisily behind the garage. The garden table was almost groaning under the weight of biscuits, scones and chocolates. Sharon was certainly doing nothing to hide her new-found wealth and it was nice to see at least one person in Zimbabwe for whom things seemed to be looking up.

Paul and Philippa were staying with Sharon for the time being until they could organise a house to rent in town. Philippa had been to see four real estate agents already, but had found out that rental properties were in high demand and rents were generally exorbitant. 'The problem is there are plenty of people in the same situation as us,' Philippa said after Sharon had asked how the house hunting had gone, 'farmers who've been kicked off their land in this latest round of invasions.'

Philippa set her cup down and reached for a handkerchief. She started to dab her eyes.

'Oh, Gran,' Natalie said, putting her arm around Philippa, 'you'll be OK. You'll find a lovely house.'

'Yes,' Pip sniffed, 'but it won't be *my* house, will it?'

George set his cup down. 'Natalie's right, Mom. You'll be fine, and who knows, Thandi might be able to do something. Now, Tate,' he said, deliberately steering the conversation away from the depressing subject of housing, 'tell me more about the rhino.'

Tate had arrived from Kariba late the previous evening and Paul himself had only been released from hospital early that morning. Natalie had collected him in one of the pickups they had moved off the farm. Sharon's backyard resembled a used-car lot at the moment, with the ranch's three *bakkies*, two Land Rover game-viewing vehicles, the Land Cruiser and the

Mercedes station wagon Paul and Philippa used as their personal car.

Tate reached under his chair for a manila envelope. 'I wanted to bring these to the hospital to show you, Paul, but Natalie ordered me to wait here for you.' He pulled out a sheaf of photos. 'She told me Philippa wouldn't let me into the hospital if I wanted to talk to you about rhinos.'

Pip had dried her eyes and she laughed.

Paul moved some teacups and spread the photos on the garden table so Natalie and the others could see. Braedan got up from his chair on the other side of the table and walked around behind Paul. He placed a hand on the old man's chair back and leaned in close between Paul and Natalie. Natalie noticed Braedan was wearing aftershave today. Tate's clothes were rumpled and, from the whiff she got every now and then, it seemed he hadn't even bothered to bathe or shower when he got in last night. Braedan, by contrast, was wearing a freshly ironed shirt and shorts. His muscled arms were one of his best features, Natalie thought, stealing a glance out of the corner of her eye. Natalie and Tate had only exchanged a few words since his return, and she expected he still felt as awkward about their fumblings in the hotel room as she did. There was a frailty about him that she guessed stirred some need in her to care for him. Maybe that's all that the chemistry between them had been – pity mixed with too much alcohol.

Braedan smiled at her and she felt her cheeks redden, wondering if he'd noticed her looking at him. Braedan didn't need anyone's pity.

'This one,' Tate said, pointing to a picture, 'was taken by a camera trap I set up near a waterhole.' The rhino's head had been raised at the moment the flash had gone off. 'He bolted soon after, but at least I got him. I knew the flash would scare him, but it was the best way for me to get a good image.'

Paul picked up the photo and stared at it, saying nothing.

Tate fanned out three more enlargements. 'You can see these others, taken at a different waterhole, aren't quite as good quality because I took them using a night-vision lens. It intensifies the ambient light, from the stars and moon, but I had a couple of cloudy nights so they're not as clear. It is the same animal, though, an old bull. You can see here how he's missing a chunk of his ear. Perhaps he was attacked by a lion or a hyena when he was a calf.'

Paul nodded slowly. 'So there's just the one.'

'That's all I've found evidence of. He's cautious, as you might expect of a forty or fifty-year-old animal that's evaded poachers for thirty years or more. I had to track him for two days after the first photo, to his next drinking place, but I photographed him twice there.'

'You've done an incredible job, my boy,' Paul said, picking up the other photos and studying them – again.

Philippa put her hand on Tate's arm. 'Yes, Tate, remarkable.'

'I don't see what this means, though, for your captive rhinos, Dad,' George said.

Natalie thought her father was being as curmudgeonly as ever. He'd never struck her as a happy person and she supposed his generally glum attitude had something to do with his experiences in the war. He'd lost his country and his old job as a pilot and she assumed that was enough to make any man bitter. She had desperately wanted to sit down and talk to him, as an adult, and get him to open up about his earlier life and the war, but he had refused to have anything to do with her book.

Paul looked up from the photos and fixed George with a stare. 'This means something, George. These pictures are a sign of hope – they tell us that nature can survive, even in the face of man's greed.'

George shook his head. 'Can I give you a hand to clear up, Sharon?'

'Oh, yes, of course. That's nice of you, George.'

'I'll help you, Dad,' Natalie said.

Natalie stacked the tray and her father picked up the side plates and they walked inside together. 'I'm worried about them,' her father said to her as they carried the used dishes to the kitchen.

'I don't know if it's fully sunk in yet – the enormity of losing the ranch,' she said.

George nodded. 'This whole business of searching for rogue rhinos in the bush can't be helping. From what I know of it, Dad's paying all Tate's expenses, but he's just lost his only source of income. He can't afford to play the eccentric naturalist any more. We've got to look at some nursing homes for them, too, while I'm here, Nat. They can't stay with Sharon forever and I'm worried they're too old to care for themselves.'

'They lived all right at the ranch,' she said, annoyed by his condescending tone.

'They had a small army of servants and workers there, Nat.'

He had a point.

'Sharon's little windfall mustn't have been too little,' her father said as they wandered slowly back down the hallway. 'Fresh paint, new furniture, good food on the table. Mom told me a while back that lots of pensioners were doing it tough here, and she mentioned Sharon in particular.'

Braedan's muscular bulk filled the door leading out onto the garden terrace.

'My mom was in financial trouble for a while,' he said.

'Oh,' George said, then lowered his voice. 'Braedan, I'm sorry for gossiping about your mother like that.'

Braedan waved a hand dismissively. 'Forget it. No harm done.

Have you two got a minute? I want to go out back for a cigarette. Mom doesn't like me smoking and Tate will have a hissy fit if I exhale in his general direction. Do you mind coming with me?'

George looked at Natalie and she shrugged. 'Very well,' her father said formally. She knew the two men didn't get on, and wondered what it was that Braedan wanted to say to them away from the others. They retraced their steps to the kitchen and walked out the back door.

Braedan pulled a pack from his khaki shirt and offered it to George.

'No thank you. Not for about thirty years, in fact.'

'Since the war?'

George nodded, but it was clear he wasn't prepared to indulge in small talk with Braedan.

'Natalie, Mr B, I'm worried about something that happened at the ranch.'

'Yes, well, the ranch is no more,' George said, folding his arms.

Braedan ignored the sarcasm. 'It's about the last rhino incident, the one that was darted and its horn removed. I –'

'Well,' George interrupted, 'I can assure you there's no way my father would have anything to do with trade in rhino horn, despite what these local keystone kops say.'

'I agree,' Braedan said. 'But someone tranquillised that rhino, dehorned it, gave the animal the antidote and then sold the horn. That's a sophisticated operation that wasn't carried out by your usual run-of-the-mill poacher.'

'Maybe it was Emmerson Ngwenya?' Natalie said. 'He knew security at the ranch was good, and that my grandfather had employed you to tighten it up. He would have known that gunfire would have alerted the security detail. Also, if he was pretty sure he was going to be taking over the ranch soon, maybe he didn't want to kill a rhino that would soon be his, and which he'd eventually be able to dehorn again.'

George nodded. 'You think Ngwenya wants to get into the business of sustainable rhino horn farming?'

'It's a possibility,' Natalie said.

Braedan exhaled cigarette smoke away from them. 'You're partly right, I think – someone wanted to get into sustainable harvesting of rhino horn, but I don't think it was Ngwenya.'

'Why not?' Natalie asked.

'You can't just send one of your foot soldiers in to dart a rhino with M99 and expect them to be able to revive the animal as well. M99's a controlled substance – you can't just go to a pharmacy or a veterinary surgery and buy or steal some. Even if you could, it's a very precise science, especially administering the antidote. It's pretty easy to kill a rhino with a dose of M99, but to care for it while it's down, and then revive it, is specialised work.'

'I don't understand,' George said. 'Are you saying there's a crooked vet involved with this? Surely the number of people in that category could be counted on one hand in Zimbabwe these days, and I wouldn't imagine any of them would do such a thing.'

Braedan took a pace to his left and looked through the kitchen, down the hallway. When he was sure no one was in earshot he ground out his cigarette. 'I really hate having to say what I'm about to say, but my mom, you know, she's not all there.'

'What do you mean, Braedan? She's lovely,' Natalie said.

'*Ja*, she is, but she's very old and I think she's suffering from dementia.' He looked over his shoulder again. 'I don't think there was any long-lost insurance policy from the UK. I don't think that's where she got the cash to fix up the house and start living like a human being again. And, I'm sorry to say, the money didn't come from me.'

'Braedan, no!' Natalie whispered, putting her hand over her mouth.

'Where do you think it came from then?' George asked.

Natalie's mind raced back to the night she'd spent with Tate at the Victoria Falls Safari Lodge. 'My God, Dad, sustainable farming of rhinos for their horns – I've heard someone else talking about that.'

'Who?'

Natalie looked at Braedan, who said nothing. 'Tate.'

'Tate? You're kidding. He's the biggest bunny-hugger I've ever met in my life,' George said. 'Always has been. Part of his problem, if you ask me. He couldn't relate to people so he immersed himself in wildlife.'

Natalie recognised the reference to Hope, and she wondered if Braedan had caught it as well. She felt dizzy as the pieces of the puzzle spun through her mind and fell neatly into place. 'Don't you see, Dad, it's *because* Tate cares so much about the plight of the rhinos that he's actually in favour of farming them. He's accepted that he won't be able to save them all from the poachers, so he's actually advocating farming and controlled dehorning. He wants to dehorn the remaining rhinos, sell the products to the Chinese or Vietnamese or whoever, and use that money to promote more conservation and captive breeding. He knows better than anyone in Zimbabwe how to use the drugs to put a rhino under and to wake it up again.'

'This makes me feel terrible,' Braedan said. 'I mean, on the one hand I really don't blame him if he's done something crazy like this to help our mom. There was no way either of us could have afforded care for her here, or to move her to a nursing home. I looked at the email that advised my mother about the money being transferred into her bank account. She barely knows how to operate the computer and it was Tate who was checking her email account and clearing it for her. She hadn't looked at her messages for weeks. At first I thought the message was one of those Nigerian internet scams, but it said all she had to do was check her bank account. Tate offered to check it for her, just before he left for Kariba, and when he came back with the statement it showed that the money really was there. I told Tate it didn't look kosher, but he just said she was lucky to have the money.'

Natalie sat down on the back doorstep. The news was like a body blow.

George's face started to colour. 'The stupid, thieving bastard.'

'Steady, Mr B,' Braedan said.

'Don't call me that.' Braedan just stood there. 'Your bloody brother's got my father in trouble with the police and he gave Emmerson Ngwenya the excuse he needed to take over the ranch. If he thought he was doing any good for anyone other than your mother, then he's more stupid than you are.'

Braedan squared up to the older man. 'What do you mean by that?'

Natalie looked at her father, and she was scared. He was clenching and unclenching his fists as he faced Braedan; neither man was backing down. George's face was an alarming shade of red and there was a vein pulsing in his neck. For a moment she thought that he was either about to have a heart attack or punch Braedan. The two men stared each other down, like a pair of old elephant bulls with locked tusks, each waiting for the other to move.

Her father exhaled noisily through his nostrils. 'Nothing. But your brother needs to be reported to the police, for all the good it will do.'

'Dad, please,' Natalie said, moving between her father and Braedan. 'We don't know for sure that Tate was involved. This is all just speculation, right, Braedan?'

Braedan relaxed his muscles a little and shrugged. He eyed George coldly. The tension between the two men was presumably related to Aunty Hope's death all those years ago. It was a long time, she thought, for her father to hold a grudge. Hope had been a grown woman who had made her own choices. It was tragic what had happened to her, but it was more than thirty years ago. People had to move on.

With a startling jolt of clarity Natalie realised that she was moving on. She'd come to revisit the ghosts of her past but she had been confronted by stark reality, and a living, breathing part of her nightmare in the form of Emmerson Ngwenya. She was still scared of him, and the power he wielded in this lawless country, but she also knew that her problems were not as serious as those facing her grandparents. Her demons were in her past and she doubted Emmerson Ngwenya was still out to harm her after all these years. His threat to her grandparents and their rhinos, however, was explicit and real.

In safe, orderly Australia Natalie had, she now realised, lived a carefree life. Ironically, that had given her time to dwell on her past. Now there was so much more to worry about than her experiences during that long-ago war.

Her father strode back into the kitchen and down the hallway, his shoes echoing on the timber floorboard. Natalie and Braedan followed him, and stopped just behind him at the front door. A black Mercedes had been buzzed through the security gate and was now parked on Sharon's gravel driveway. The front passenger door opened and a black man stooped with age, his curly hair grey and his face as creased and sagging as an old elephant's, grabbed the doorframe to ease himself out.

He stood there, wearing a charcoal business suit, white shirt and a maroon tie. He coughed into his hand, clearing his voice. 'I am sorry to intrude on your tea.'

Tate was gathering his photos, hurriedly stuffing them back into the envelope in case the newcomer saw them. Grandma Pip stayed seated, but was staring at the man. Her grandfather stood, as creakily as the man who had just got out of the car. 'Kenneth . . .'

'Paul. I would ask how you are, my old friend, but I know you are in pain.'

No one else spoke as the two old friends walked slowly towards each other.

'He's got a bloody hide,' Sharon Quilter-Phipps whispered loudly.

'Is that who I think it is?' George asked his mother.

Pip nodded. 'Yes. Kenneth Ngwenya. And Sharon's right. He has no right to be here after what his son did to us.'

In his nice suit and his fancy new Mercedes, Kenneth Ngwenya looked as though he came from a different world altogether from the whites sitting around their rusting garden table, clinging to the colonial traditions of an empire that no longer existed.

Paul and Kenneth clasped hands in the western and then the African manner.

'I am well, my friend,' Paul said, 'all things considered. And you?'

'Ah, I am fine. It has been too long, my friend.'

Paul nodded.

Pip turned away from the scene. 'He's no friend of ours.'

If Kenneth heard Philippa's response he chose to ignore it, but Paul was determined to show Kenneth what hospitality he could. He looked at Sharon, perhaps in the hope that she might offer to organise some more tea, but she just folded her arms.

'Pip,' Paul said, 'come say hello to Ken. It's been ages . . .'

Philippa turned her head and looked up at Kenneth, who was now within touching distance. He smiled at her.

'What did I ever do wrong to you or your wife or your children?'

Kenneth licked his chapped lips and looked first to Paul, then to Pip. 'You showed us nothing but kindness, Philippa.'

'We took Winston in as if he was our own son. He was like a brother to George.' George moved to his mother's side and put a hand on her shoulder. 'We brought food to your family while you were in prison . . . and then Emmerson goes and steals our *home*. How can you come into this house and call my husband your friend, Kenneth?'

Kenneth clasped his hands in front of him. 'I wish I could apologise for everything that has gone wrong in this country for the last thirty years, in the same way that I sometimes wish someone would have once taken the time to apologise to me and my family for what went wrong in the thirty years before that.'

Philippa glared at him, but it was George who interrupted. 'You mean those years when we had employment, a strong economy, first-world health and education systems and infrastructure that worked?'

Kenneth nodded. 'Yes, we had all those things, and a system where I could advance no further than the post of schoolteacher; where my wife was left to raise three children while I was locked in gaol for attending political demonstrations.'

'I sent her food, damn you,' Pip hissed.

'Pip,' Paul chided softly.

But Kenneth just stood there and nodded. 'Yes, and I thank you for it, even if my wife never did. What you didn't know was that she had been brutalised as a child. She was beaten by a white landowner who raped her mother. She and her mother were utterly powerless against that white man.'

'Yes, well,' said Pip, 'I'm sorry to hear that. But she didn't have a monopoly on tragedy. Sometimes I think this bloody country was only so fertile because of all the blood and bone that had been spilled onto it. And now you people have even stuffed that up – you've squandered the land and the wealth that people bled and died to create.'

'*Us people*,' Kenneth paused to cough again, then seemed to get his emotions in check, 'include my daughter, who is a minister in the new Government of National Unity. She is working to turn things around.'

'*Pah!* The MDC hasn't achieved a single thing,' Pip said.

'Perhaps, perhaps not,' Kenneth said, 'but they, too, have fought and bled and died for the right to try.'

Natalie watched her grandmother twitch her lips, then look down into her lap. This battle of wills was uncomfortable to watch, but no one seemed to want to interrupt it. It was as if these things, as cruel as they might be, had to be said.

'But it's all for nothing, Kenneth,' Philippa said, not looking up at him as she twisted a linen serviette in her fingers. 'Because the MDC couldn't stop the farm invasions and now we have nowhere to live.'

'It is true, Philippa,' Kenneth said. 'Your ranch is gone and I am afraid it is unlikely that you will get it back. It has been given to the local community to run as a conservation and tourism project.'

'Those bastards will kill our rhinos and strip our house before you know it, and your son, Emmerson, will be the first in the door.'

'I have some news.'

'I don't care,' Philippa said.

'Pip,' Paul said at last, 'let Kenneth have his say.'

'My son wanted to give me a farm for my last birthday,' Kenneth said, 'but I said, "No, I am a retired schoolteacher, what do I know of farming?" So I declined.'

'More fool you,' Pip snapped.

'Pip!'

She looked at her husband, and nodded.

Kenneth cleared his throat again. 'But my daughter called me yesterday. Until then I didn't know that my son had appointed himself as chairman of the community trust that was going to run your ranch and the rhino-breeding program. Thandi told me it was in the newspapers, but I don't read them because I never believe most of what's in them. But I'm rambling, I think . . . I don't pretend to understand the politics of the new government, but Thandi does. She told me that while Emmerson is the Assistant Minister for Land Redistribution – still a very powerful position – he has enemies within ZANU–PF. There is much jockeying at the moment amid the party faithful as they try and map out a future for themselves once the President dies or retires. There are many who are jealous of Emmerson's influence and wealth.'

'That's money he made from poaching rhinos,' Tate said.

'Yes, well, I know my son is alleged to have done many things in his life,' Kenneth continued. 'No doubt some rumours are true, but perhaps some are spread by his enemies.' When Tate started to speak again Kenneth held up a hand. 'Please, I am an old man and I don't find breathing as easy as I once did. Please let me finish. My daughter, Thandi, may be a senior member of the MDC but she still has contacts within ZANU–PF. She made approaches to a woman who approached a man who approached the President and suggested that perhaps

Emmerson would not be the best person to head up the rhino-breeding facility at your ranch, given the international speculation of his involvement in the rhino trade.'

'So the ranch will go to some other puppet,' Pip said.

'No, Philippa,' Kenneth said, finally letting some of his exasperation show in his words. 'I am to head the community trust that will now run Kiabejane.'

Philippa blinked and shook her head, as if to clear it. 'You?'

Kenneth smiled and spread his hands wide, palms up. 'I was as surprised as you are. The President apparently gave the order himself that I was to be given control of the ranch in thanks for my work during the struggle. Ironic, I know, given that I have not been a supporter of the man or his party for many, many years now. But life moves in a direction beyond our control.'

Philippa started to stand and George lent his arm for his mother to steady herself on. 'But Kenneth, what does this mean? Can you protect the rhinos from your son?'

Kenneth put his hands back down by his side. 'As I said before, Philippa, I know nothing about farming, or rhinos, or how to protect them. I fear that as an old man I would be no match for armed poachers or organised criminals . . . yet you two were able to hold them at bay for a long time, and to continue to breed rhinos.'

'We did our best.'

'Yes, Philippa, you and Paul did your best, and that is why I would like to invite you, on behalf of the community trust that I seem to have inherited, to come back to the ranch and stay on for an indefinite period as the managers of the ranch and the rhino-breeding program. I will see that you are paid a wage . . . it won't be a fortune, but you will have your house and your game animals and your prized vegetable garden. Perhaps in time you will be able to find another home, in town, but I would hope that in the intervening period you would work with me to train some bright young souls, unsullied by the politics of race and hate, who might one day take over the breeding program and run it the way you would wish to see it run when it is time for you to move on.'

'Oh, Kenneth.' The tears streamed down Philippa's cheeks as Paul wrapped an arm around her. Philippa reached out and took Kenneth's hand and when he clasped it she broke from her husband and encircled Kenneth in a hug.

CHAPTER 32

Kenneth Ngwenya was feeling lightheaded from the three beers he had drunk with his friends Paul and Philippa and their family and friends. Fortunately he didn't need to drive, as one good thing his son had done for him was to hire him a driver when his eyesight began to deteriorate.

Maxwell, the driver, took him out of Bulawayo into the lowering sun and the countryside out towards the Botswana border. Paul and Philippa had said that as much as they wanted to return to the ranch immediately, all of their possessions were at Sharon's and would have to be reloaded onto trucks the next day to move back.

Braedan Quilter-Phipps, Paul's head of security, said he would make his way out to the ranch later in the evening. Kenneth thought it looked like Braedan wanted to continue celebrating and he seemed to be quite fond of little Natalie Bryant, who had grown into a fine golden-haired woman. Natalie made him think of Paul and Philippa's daughter, who had been killed in the war. They had all lost someone. Kenneth wondered, as he often did, what sort of man Winston would have become if he had had the chance to grow old peacefully. The war; the terrible killings in Matabeleland in the eighties; the farm invasions – his poor country had known too much sorrow.

But now he had a farm to run, for a short while at least.

Maxwell stopped at the security gate and Kenneth introduced himself to Doctor Nkomo and told him the Bryants would be coming home the next day. 'Mr and Mrs Bryant will continue to manage the farm, so even though I am here as the new head of the community trust you are to take your day-to-day orders from them. Understood?'

'Yes, Mr Ngwenya,' Doctor said.

'Very good. There are going to be changes here. I will see to it that your staff numbers are increased. Every rhino here will have at least two armed guards with it or observing it twenty-four hours a day.'

'That is good, sir. We have had so little money for so long.' Doctor asked Kenneth to wait a minute while he ducked back into the small hut by the gate. When he emerged he handed Kenneth a walkie-talkie. 'If you need me or one of the other guards, sir, just press the button and call. The radio is set to our frequency.'

Kenneth nodded and ordered Maxwell to drive on.

Kenneth's bank account balance was healthy – too healthy for a man of his age. He had made some shrewd investments, and Emmerson, for all his faults, had regularly deposited large amounts of cash into his father's account, especially when he was trading the ruinous Zimbabwe dollar on the black market. Emmerson had asked for some of that money back recently – his fortunes had clearly changed – and Kenneth had of course given some of the money back to his son, but now his wealth was going to be invested in something truly worthwhile: getting this ranch back on its feet economically and beefing up its security. Kenneth had a feeling in his bones that the battle over the future of the rhinos that lived among the kopjes of Kiabejane was only just beginning.

Kenneth's cell phone played the rap song one of his cheeky

granddaughters had programmed as his ringtone. Maxwell laughed as he always did when he heard the phone and Kenneth mumbled about getting it changed. 'Hello?'

'Father, I need to see you.'

'Emmerson . . . where are you?'

'I am not far from Kiabejane,' Emmerson said into the phone.

'What a coincidence. I've just arrived.' Kenneth covered the mouthpiece and said to Maxwell, 'Take me to the farmhouse.' Maxwell nodded.

'I'll be there in ten minutes.'

Kenneth ended the call. They pulled up out the front of Paul and Philippa's house. Kenneth walked though Pip's beautiful garden and when he opened the unlocked front door Kenneth felt like a trespasser.

The house was empty. A few sheets of discarded newspaper lay on the carpet, and the walls were bare, patched with pale squares where pictures had hung for decades. It would be good once his friends were back in their home; the gesture made him feel that he, and Thandi, had taken one small step towards what Kenneth hoped would eventually be a nationwide movement of reconciliation between the races. Politics as well as colour had split the country and he hoped, too, that one day his son and daughter could again speak to each other as loving siblings rather than bitter enemies.

Kenneth's footsteps echoed on the bare timber of the hallway.

'Car coming, sir,' Maxwell said from behind him. Kenneth heard the engine and when he looked out a window he saw a black Hummer pulling up the driveway. His son got out, dressed in black jeans and a matching long-sleeved T-shirt. That had been a lot less than ten minutes. He wondered if perhaps his son had been waiting for him, or if he had followed him out of Bulawayo.

Emmerson walked through the open door. 'Leave us in private,' he said to Maxwell. The driver looked at Kenneth, and Emmerson glared at him. 'I pay your wage, fool. Leave us in private!'

Maxwell walked out, eyes downcast.

'Was that necessary?' Kenneth asked. He noted the chunky gold chain around his son's neck and the heavy rings on three of his fingers. Emmerson looked like an American gangster.

'That meddling bitch Thandi has robbed me, but I want what is due to me.'

'Don't use such language when you talk about your sister, Emmerson!'

'She is no relative of mine. This ranch belongs to me, Father. I don't care what she or anyone else has said to you, I am the one who has been selected by the community to run this place.'

Kenneth was affronted by his tone and suddenly tired of making excuses for him. His son was a thug, pure and simple. 'Your *community* is a bunch of unemployed criminals and party hacks too lazy to work for themselves. They have squandered the land already given to them and now they want to walk onto this place and strip it like a flock of vultures on a corpse. Well I am not going to let that happen. The Bryants are good people who have done a great service for this country and they are returning here tomorrow.'

'What?' Emmerson turned and slammed the front door shut. Kenneth shuddered. He never thought he would live to see the day when one of his children frightened him. Emmerson advanced on him, pointing a finger. 'Listen to me . . . tomorrow you are going to call the Ministry of Land Redistribution and you are going to tell them that you are too old and infirm to head the community trust. You are going to tell whoever will listen that I am taking over this place.'

Kenneth took a pace back and folded his arms. 'No, Emmerson, I will do no such thing.'

'Why? Don't you trust me to care for this rich white man's house and all his precious animals? What do you think, Father? Do you think I am a poacher? Do you think I am a killer?'

Kenneth shook his head. 'I don't know what to think about you, my son, but I am not going to sign this place over to you. The Bryants are going to return as managers and begin a program to train local people – *real* local people not out-of-town parasites from Harare – how to run this place in the future.'

Emmerson took another step closer until his face was just inches from his father's. His nostrils flared and Kenneth could smell alcohol on his breath. 'If those rich *boere* racists dare to set foot on this land they will be signing their own death warrants.'

'I will pretend I did not hear that.' Kenneth reached out. 'Emmerson, we have to do what is right in this world. It's not too late for you . . .'

Emmerson shrugged off his father's hand and pulled a cell phone from his jeans, opened it and dialled a number. 'He said no. You know what you have to do.' He snapped the phone shut and walked out the door, slamming it shut behind him.

Kenneth stood alone in the empty house and started to shake. He was a strong, proud man who had seen much sorrow in his life, but now, for the first time in many years, he felt like crying.

He heard the Hummer start up outside and roar down the gravel driveway. Maxwell came into the empty house. 'Are you all right, sir?'

'Of course. Do you have the walkie-talkie?'

Maxwell handed Kenneth the radio and he pushed the transmit switch. Doctor answered. 'It is Kenneth Ngwenya here. Please let me know when my son leaves.'

'Affirmative, sir. I will let you know when both vehicles leave, over,' Doctor replied.

Kenneth wasn't sure he had heard correctly. 'Please repeat . . . did you say *both* vehicles, over?'

'Yes sir, there was Mr Ngwenya's Hummer and a *bakkie* with four other men in it, over.'

Kenneth thanked the guard and told him to call when both vehicles had left the property. 'I'm worried, Maxwell.'

'What would the other men be doing here?'

The sun had set and it was gloomy in the house. Kenneth and Maxwell stood there, not knowing what to do. Kenneth suddenly realised that there was probably no bedding left in the house, although there was still a staff compound out the back of the farmhouse where the cook, maid and gardener lived, and there was a bigger compound elsewhere on the property where the labourers and security staff lived with their families. Both men turned at the sound of a knock.

'Mister, mister . . .' A boy, probably no older than ten, stood on the doorstep, his skinny chest heaving under his grubby white singlet. He was barefoot. 'Bad men,' he said in Ndebele. He was panting from the exertion of running. 'They are at the rhino *boma* mister. They have guns.'

'Slow down, boy. How many men did you see?' Kenneth asked.

The boy held up three fingers.

'Did they arrive in a car?'

'A *bakkie,* mister. A black truck. They have tied up my father . . . he was the guard on duty, mister.'

'Three men or four men?' Kenneth asked. Doctor had said there were four men in the other vehicle.

'No, three, sir.'

'We have to try and stop them,' Kenneth said.

'I'll get the car.'

'No, Maxwell, they will hear us coming.' Kenneth turned back to the boy. 'How far is it to the *boma*?'

'Not far, mister. We can take the short cut, through the bush.'

Kenneth pressed the transmit switch again. 'Come in Doctor, this is Kenneth Ngwenya. This is an emergency. There are armed men at the rhino *boma* and they have tied up one of your men, over.'

Kenneth waited anxiously for the reply, but there was no answer. He tried again, calling Doctor and repeating his message. Kenneth looked to Maxwell, who shrugged and said, 'Perhaps they dropped off the fourth man, and he has control of the gatehouse?'

'That is what I fear. Come.' Kenneth motioned for the boy to lead them out into the darkening bush. 'We must hurry.'

Tate had drawn Paul away from the celebrations earlier in the afternoon and the two men had had a brief conversation before Tate had taken the Bryants' Hilux and driven off.

Natalie had wanted to question Tate herself, about Braedan's theory that his brother had actually been the one who had darted and dehorned the rhino at the ranch. However, when she had asked her grandfather where Tate had gone he had cheerfully replied that Tate was heading straight back to Kariba. Now that Paul and Pip were going back to the ranch, Paul was keener than ever for Tate to embark on a fully fledged study, though still in secret, of the wild rhino he had found at Makuti. Perhaps, her grandfather had said, more than one rhino had survived poaching and the efforts of the national parks rangers to relocate all the animals back in the 1980s.

Natalie didn't know how to broach the theory of Tate's involvement in the poaching, but she assumed her father would do so.

Braedan sidled up to her, a near-empty beer in his hand. 'I don't know about you, but I think the party's winding down and I could use another drink. Let's go.'

She looked around. He was right. Grandpa Paul and Grandma Pip were in cheerful spirits chatting with Sharon. Her father looked as dour as usual, although he was on to his third beer. She knew he wouldn't kick on much longer and the older people would probably be off to bed as soon as they'd had some supper. Natalie had had two glasses of sparkling wine and now that she knew her grandparents once more had a home she was feeling pleasantly relaxed. Braedan's offer sounded good, and he really was a fine-looking man.

Tate had, in his slightly dorkish and clumsy way, charmed her at Victoria Falls and she had been well on her way to sleeping with him before he had run out on her. Now here was his 'evil twin' asking her out for a drink with the confidence of a man unused to rejections from women.

Braedan was an arrogant man, but he knew what he wanted, and there was something very attractive in that. And if she was honest with herself she was also feeling a little bruised by the business with Tate. She knew he was tortured by his past, and she suspected his running out on her was linked to what had happened to her aunt, but it had been confronting for Natalie too, yet she had been prepared to deal with it.

She set down her glass on a garden wall. 'Take me somewhere where we're not the ones lowering the average age of the crowd.'

Braedan grinned. 'I know just the place. We'll stick out like geriatrics, but you'll love it. It's the worst place in Bulawayo.'

A shiver went down her spine. 'I like the sound of it already.'

Despite his relative good health, at eighty-five years old Kenneth could not run. So the boy took his arm and led him at a brisk walk. Maxwell had picked up a discarded pick handle which was resting against the wall of a garden shed. 'We need a gun,' Kenneth said.

'I know where there is one,' said the boy. 'My father has been looking after the AK-47 of a man who is on leave. It is under his bed, wrapped in a blanket. I am not supposed to know it's there, or to touch it.'

Kenneth ruffled the boy's head. 'I don't think you will get in trouble this time if you take us to it.'

The first of the nightbirds were tuning up for their evening chorus. A tiny scops owl called a shrill *brrr* and its mate answered back a few seconds later. The young boy led Kenneth on a narrow but well-worn path through grassland and thorn bush. Even though the two of them were taking it slow, Kenneth was puffing after a few minutes of exertion.

'Are you all right, sir?' Maxwell asked.

'I'm fine,' Kenneth snapped. 'I'm sorry, Maxwell.' He paused for a breath. 'Make sure, whatever happens, that the boy is not harmed.' Maxwell nodded.

The boy put a finger to his lips and pointed to a trio of circular pole and *dagga* huts with thatched roofs. A pale light glowed inside the nearest hut. 'That is my home,' he whispered. 'My mother is in Bulawayo. The rifle is inside this house.'

As they crept closer Kenneth could see, beyond the staff houses, the silhouette of the high tin roof that sheltered the *boma* from the sun and rain, the secure pens in which it looked like four of the ranch's thirteen rhino were currently being accommodated. Kenneth recalled that a number of rhino were always kept in the *boma*, either because they were undergoing health checks or had arrived from somewhere else, and it was these captive animals that visitors paid to come and visit. They tended to be animals that were well habituated to humans and not averse to being stroked and petted by strangers. Kenneth had visited the pens himself a few times over the years and he could remember the layout.

The staff houses blocked them from view from the *boma* and Kenneth, Maxwell and the boy filed into the small chalet. The boy got down on his knees and rummaged under an unmade bed. He dragged out a cardboard box and then pulled out the rifle, which was still swaddled in blankets. Kenneth took it from him, removed the magazine, checked it was loaded with bullets, then replaced it and cocked it. He had never fired a shot in anger during the liberation war, but he had trained in the bush with the freedom fighters and had fired the AK on rifle ranges.

They left the hut and cautiously moved closer to the *boma*. Kenneth raised a hand and when they heard a voice they dropped to their knees in the long grass. 'That is my son,' Kenneth whispered to Maxwell. Kenneth stood and was about to call out and signal their presence – after all, he knew Emmerson would not harm him. A burst of gunfire tore through the night. The bright muzzle flash of the weapon bounced off the roof and walls, illuminating the inside of the *boma*.

'Stop!' Kenneth yelled, though his voice was croaky. He turned to Maxwell. 'Take the boy away from here, back to the farmhouse and the car.'

'But, sir –'

'Do as I say. If my son is involved in this he will not harm me. I have to stop him.'

Kenneth called again as Maxwell grabbed the boy by the arm and started back down the gentle hill through the grass towards the staff quarters. Kenneth's words were drowned out by another fusillade and he struggled on, stumbling on the uneven ground.

'Stop!' Kenneth reached the mown grass clearing at the edge

of the enclosures and saw his son's Hummer and the other *bakkie* parked in full view. 'Stop!' he croaked again.

The rhinos that lived were keening a high-pitched cry. It was a sound he'd never heard and he wouldn't have expected such a squeaky, frightened noise to come from such big creatures. Although he had his back to him, Kenneth recognised Emmerson's broad shoulders immediately. 'Emmerson!'

His son turned and looked at him, his face betraying no emotion. 'Get on with it, Fortune,' Emmerson said to a man standing next to him.

Kenneth forced himself to shuffle forward and watched, in horror, as one of Emmerson's men, similarly dressed in black, raised an AK-47 to his shoulder and slid the barrel between two of the heavy wooden railway sleepers that formed part of the pen's fence. The man pulled the trigger and he and Emmerson were lit up by strobing flashes of man-made lightning.

When the firing stopped, Kenneth heard a chopping noise from the furthest of the pens. He imagined it was a rhino's horn being hacked off. 'Emmerson, please . . .'

Emmerson ignored his father's pleas and the gunman calmly stood again and removed the empty magazine from his rifle. He carried a canvas bag slung over his shoulder, into which he dropped the banana-shaped magazine and fished for a new one.

Kenneth raised his weapon and pointed it at the man. 'Stop. Put down your weapon.'

Fortune looked at him, and then at Emmerson, who strode towards Kenneth. 'Give me the gun, Father.'

'No.' The tip of the barrel was wavering. Kenneth was not as strong as he had been in his youth. 'Stay where you are, Emmerson. Tell your dog to put down his weapon.'

'Who are you calling a dog, old man?' Fortune spat back. He pulled a full magazine from his bag.

'I will shoot!' Kenneth said.

Emmerson moved between his father and Fortune. 'Give me the rifle, Father. There is nothing you can do here. I told you I am taking over this place.'

'Yes,' Kenneth said, spittle flying from his lips. He was shaking with rage from the betrayal unfolding so casually before his eyes. 'And this is how you will *manage* this precious place. By killing, killing, killing. I didn't want to believe what they said about you, Emmerson. I didn't think you could be involved in such a thing.'

'Don't worry,' Emmerson said. 'I won't be killing the other rhinos any time soon. It's all about supply and demand, Father. There's a high demand at the moment and I have orders to meet. In time, though, I'll dehorn the rhinos humanely and take control of the market. But right now I don't have the time, the drugs or the inclination to let these animals live. If I'd been given control of this place, as I should have been, this wouldn't have happened. No, the blame for this slaughter rests with you and Thandi.'

'No!' Emmerson continued walking towards him, but Kenneth pointed the rifle at the ground and pulled the trigger. Three rounds sent up fountains of dirt no more than two metres in front of his son.

Emmerson stopped, but laughed out loud. 'You won't kill me.' Emmerson turned to his man, who had now reloaded and cocked his weapon. 'Kill the next one.'

Fortune looked unsure, craning his head to keep an eye on the older man. The surviving rhino, a young one, with barely a few centimetres of horn, squealed in panicked fear.

'I am not going to let you kill that animal,' Kenneth said through gritted teeth. He stepped to one side, to take aim at Fortune, but Emmerson moved as well and advanced on him again, arms wide, as if to protect the killer, who walked to the final pen. The rhino bleated and screamed. Fortune peered over the top of the *boma* railings and shook his head with disdain.

Two other men climbed over the adjoining pens, each stained with blood and hefting a cut-off rhino horn. They paused to watch the standoff, though none of them seemed concerned by the wide-eyed old man with the gun.

Emmerson was nearly on him. Kenneth raised the barrel and pulled the trigger again, and while the rounds sailed high into the night sky, his son stopped again. Kenneth lowered the weapon once more. 'Enough, Emmerson . . . just . . . go. At least leave the young one.' Tears welled from his eyes. He knew he couldn't kill his son and he suddenly felt defeated.

Emmerson turned side-on, looked back to his man again and said: 'Kill it.' Fortune raised his rifle again and propped it on the second railing of the fourth pen.

Kenneth saw the opening. With Emmerson still turned away watching his attack dog, Kenneth had a clear shot. He raised the rifle, took aim at the centre of Fortune's back and pulled the trigger.

For a moment none of them moved. Perhaps they all assumed the gunman had pulled the trigger, but the man's body was slammed against the fence posts and as he slid to the ground they saw the blood spreading on his back, and vomit coming from his mouth as he rolled. Fortune's body shook violently as he died.

Emmerson turned on his father.

'You stupid old fool. What have you done?'

'I have tried to do the right thing. You won't get away from here, Emmerson. It is time for you to pay for your sins.'

'Henry, Nicholas, get the AK,' Emmerson yelled to his other two men, but neither man moved. They edged away, back towards the parked *bakkie*. Emerson turned to his father. 'What are you going to do now, *Kenneth*? Kill me too?'

As much as he hated the killing of the animals, and as hard as he tried not to think about what he had just done, Kenneth was most hurt by his son's words. What had he done to his son that he would say such a thing? Emmerson had crowned the insult by referring to him in the most derogatory manner, by using his first name. The AK felt like a lead bar in his hand. It swayed and dipped as the tears blurred his focus.

Emmerson walked away from his father, to where Fortune lay. He picked up the fallen man's AK, which was still cocked and ready. He looked in the pen at the frightened, squealing rhino calf. He raised the rifle to his shoulder.

'That is a valuable animal, Emmerson,' his father called in a quavering voice. Kenneth swung the rifle so that it was pointing at his son. Perhaps he could appeal to his son's greed if not to his sense of right and wrong. 'Let it live, please.'

'I know it's valuable . . . Believe me, I know,' Emmerson said without looking back. He took aim through the wooden slats of the fence.

'That rhino, it belongs to the people of Zimbabwe, not to you,' Kenneth said.

Kenneth shifted his aim and fired. The bullet whizzed past Emmerson's head and ricocheted harmlessly off the brick wall at the rear of the pens. 'I will not miss next time.'

Emmerson turned and stared at him and, while doing so, brought his rifle around to bear. 'You are serious, aren't you?'

'It's not only me who will testify against you now, Emmerson. There is Maxwell, and a boy. They have escaped and they will tell the police that you and your men were here. It's over for you. It is time for you to confess your sins and pay your penance.'

Emmerson laughed. 'You just shot a man in cold blood and

you plead for the life of a dumb animal? And don't be stupid. There isn't a judge in this country I can't buy. I'll give you the ultimatum now. Hand over control of the community trust and I will cover up your role in the death of this man. I'll say he's a poacher that I shot.'

'I cannot do that. I will not do that.'

Father and son faced each other now, each with a rifle pointed at the other.

'What do you want us to do, boss?' one of Emmerson's henchmen called from the shadows.

'Take the horns to the front gate. Meet our other man there and if he doesn't already have the boy and Maxwell with him, then don't leave the ranch until you've found them. By the time we finish persuading them, neither will be game enough to run to the police.'

'Yes, boss.' Henry and Nicholas picked up the freshly hacked horns, loaded them into the black *bakkie* and drove off.

It was just the two of them now. 'I have decided you are right, Father.'

'*My son* . . .' Kenneth sighed, almost overcome with relief. He lowered his rifle and took a step towards Emmerson.

'You said the rhino belonged to Zimbabwe,' Emmerson said, smiling.

'Yes, Emmerson, it does.'

'I am Zimbabwe.'

Emmerson took aim at his father's heart and pulled the trigger.

CHAPTER 33

Braedan weaved his way between the swaying, drunken bodies with two glasses in his hand. He grinned and she smiled back at him.

He handed her the glass of cane and Coke and she took a sip. It was her third. She was beyond tipsy now. The fiery cane spirit burned the back of her throat, the cola barely smoothing its path. It sent a jolt out to her fingertips. The speakers were thumping to the point of distortion.

'Come on, let's dance!' Braedan had to yell over the noise, and before she could think of a reason not to, he'd taken her glass back from her and set it down on the table. He grabbed her by the wrist and pulled her into the throng of sweating, gyrating bodies. She laughed. It was like being twenty, back at university again; even the music was the same. Duran Duran, she thought, but couldn't be sure. The crowd was loving it, though, and the strobing lights just added to her high.

Braedan was completely uninhibited on the dance floor and she laughed again at his moves, which pre-dated even the music. He was, literally, the centre of attention on the dance floor after his ostentatious entry and the ridiculous moves he was performing. She felt her cheeks flush with more than the booze. She didn't like standing out in a crowd, but he stood there, with his hand out now, and she thought, *Screw it. Why not?*

Natalie strode across the floor and he took her in his arms then flicked her away, twirling her in the centre of the crowd. Natalie shrieked with joy and hoped to hell his head wasn't spinning as much as hers. The next thing she knew she was falling and being caught by one muscled arm, then lent backwards and spun around again.

Braedan pulled her back to vertical, thankfully, and held her close. She couldn't resist the temptation to hook one leg up over his thigh, and when she threw back her head she felt his lips on her neck.

Her heart stopped, but when she tried to say something she found herself being twirled around again. When she caught his eye he just winked her. The song reached a crescendo and Braedan ended with a final dip that left her tummy behind. The crowd around them broke into spontaneous applause.

Natalie felt lightheaded and knew it wasn't only because of the spirits. The DJ changed the pace and slid into 'You Sexy Thing'. It was more kitsch from her childhood, but at least it was a bit slower. Unconsciously she touched the place on her neck where his lips had brushed her skin. He took her in his arms again and held her close, swaying to the music. 'What was that?' she said into his ear.

She was aware of him closing the gap between them even more and when her belly brushed him she felt the hardness.

'What was what?'

'This kiss . . . on the neck?'

'A prelude to this . . .'

He held her eyes and she felt her body meld to his as he kissed her.

She'd had a chance, she knew, to pull back, to stop him, but she didn't want to. Quite the opposite, in fact. She wanted to be dragged out to the dance floor, shaken from her normally shy, comfortable self. It had been too long since she'd been held by a man and let herself fall over the edge. She kissed him back, hard and deep, as the other dancers moved around them, not caring who was staring or what they might be saying or thinking. For now, there was just him, and the surprising softness of his lips, the tantalising strength of him elsewhere, and his hand on her arse, in public. She ground against him.

They left their drinks and Braedan found a crumpled bill for the barman, who handed him his jacket. Braedan took her hand and led her outside. They kissed again in the street and she let him lean her up against the nightclub's brick wall.

She didn't know what this was. Was it a first date? She knew him well already. He was the man who had saved her life as a child and he was still as handsome as the day he had scooped her up and carried her to safety.

He was a knight in shining armour, but he was also the bad boy on the motorcycle who had stolen her aunt away from his highly principled brother. God, Natalie thought, it was happening all over again. She *had* felt a connection to Tate at Victoria Falls, but his behaviour the next morning and the revelation that he may have poached a rhino horn – for whatever screwed-up reason – had made her rethink her feelings towards him. Braedan was a rolling stone, divorced and broke, a soldier of little fortune, but his arms were tanned and muscled and beautiful in his tight white T-shirt and she felt like jelly in their embrace.

His stubble grazed her chin and she broke the kiss and licked his cheek to feel the sandpaper roughness on her tongue. That elicited a little groan from him and she liked the feeling of power that gave her. She saw the wild, animal desire in his eyes and knew it was mirrored in her own.

'Where can we go?' she whispered, surprising herself with her brazenness.

'Fuck, it's a madhouse at my mom's,' he said.

'What about out to the ranch?'

He looked uncertain. 'Too far. I want you. Now.'

She shivered, then took a breath. 'I don't . . . I mean, I want you to know, I'm not normally like this, on a first date.' She tried to sound more relaxed by forcing a laugh. 'Not that I've actually been on a first date in a while, but . . .'

He kissed her again, then whispered in her ear, 'I don't care. I just want you.'

God, she thought she might just catch fire from the inside out. 'I don't care,' he said again. 'Let's just get on the bike and ride.'

She clung to him as they rode through the darkened streets, the lights either stolen or out from lack of power, and then out into the countryside towards the ranch, where grasslands swayed white-gold under a moon that was riding high. She felt the warmth of him through his back, and the vibrations up through the leather seat of the bike. She kissed the back of his neck and he gunned the engine faster, as impatient as she was.

After about twenty minutes Braedan eased off the throttle and turned left onto a rough dirt track. He slowed, but the ride was so bumpy she had to cling tighter to him. Over Braedan's shoulder Natalie could see a small kopje about three hundred metres ahead. She was sure he'd be able to feel her heart pounding through his back. Braedan gunned the engine a little as the track climbed to the top of the small hill. The high ground gave a commanding view over the open veldt. Braedan stopped the bike and kicked it up on its stand. Natalie climbed off first and looked around. There were a few stone blocks lying around.

'What is this place?' Natalie asked, trying to sound casual. She was breathing faster. She wasn't sure she could go through with this now.

Braedan swung his long leg over the motorcycle. 'It's the site of one of the forts built by Selous during' the Matabele Rebellion. Romantic, huh?'

'This country's known so much bloodshed, it –'

Braedan closed the gap between them, pulled her close and kissed her again. He moved a hand to her breast and it was her turn to groan as he found her nipple, pinching it through the fabric of her shirt. She moved her hand down and traced his hardness through his jeans. He looked around and she read his mind.

She eased herself away from him and, walking backwards, retraced her steps to the motorcycle. 'I've wanted to do this since I saw Kelly McGillis and Tom Cruise in *Top Gun*.'

'I feel the need,' he said.

She laughed, and straddled the bike facing backwards, leaning her elbows on the handlebars. He got on the rear of the seat, facing her. As they leaned into each other to kiss he undid her belt, unbuttoned her jeans and unzipped them. 'Uh-huh,' she murmured as he pulled them down.

Natalie felt the cooling leather under the bare skin of her bottom, the cool night air on her. She gripped the handlebars to stop from falling as she kicked off her high heels and Braedan pulled her pants off completely. He looked down at her and opened her, with his callused thumb, grazing it across her clitoris. She closed her eyes, arched her neck back and let her hair cascade down over the front of the bike. As he played with her she felt herself swelling, and her arousal quickly building.

Braedan slid forward, along the seat, and unzipped. She had a moment of panic but when she sat up and looked at him he was pulling a condom from his wallet. He winked at her. Of course he had one, she thought. She reached up and locked her hand behind his neck.

Braedan kicked out the highway pegs with his boots, hooked the heels of his riding boots on them and Natalie lifted herself a little, hanging from the muscled body above her. She lifted her legs and hooked them behind his thighs as he entered her. She was almost off the bike and he was perched, supporting himself with his hands on the handlebars, muscles straining. He pushed himself up into her, as deep as he could, and she savoured the feeling of being filled. He paused, staring at her, and her whole body was tensed and quivering as he began to move his hips, sliding her bum back and forth along the leather seat.

Just as Natalie could feel her orgasm building again Braedan eased out of her, perhaps unable to sustain the effort of bracing himself on the handlebars. He sat back on the seat and simply beckoned to her with a wave of his finger and a flick of his head. She wanted to slap him but her need for him was greater. She slid along the seat and climbed up onto his lap. It was her turn now to stand on the pegs and she lowered herself down on him. She felt his fingernails run up her back as she moved up and down. She felt vulnerable and exposed out here, nearly naked in the African night. Braedan was as self-assured and arrogant while making love as he was the rest of the time, but God she needed him right now.

Natalie felt her body tense around him just as Braedan raised himself up off the bike to meet her last thrust. She clung to him and buried her face in his neck.

'That was great,' he whispered.

'Come in,' Thandi Ngwenya said in answer to the knock at her office door.

Her media adviser, Matthew, opened it and stood there, as though afraid to cross the threshold. 'Minister, there are some men here to see you . . .'

Thandi glanced down at the computer printout of her schedule. There was a mountain of paperwork on her desk to get through and she had to leave soon to accept an aid donation from the British Council on behalf of a charity that employed HIV-positive women in a craft workshop. 'Ah, but I don't have any appointments listed, Matthew.'

Matthew's Adam's apple bobbed. 'It is the police, Minister.'

A man in a shiny grey suit pushed past Matthew, followed by a similarly dressed colleague. Both were heavy set and the first had a shaved head. He carried a document in his hand. 'We are CIO. I am Agent Makoni and this is Agent Bitai. Minister Thandi Ngwenya, we have a warrant for your arrest.'

Thandi sighed. 'What charge this time?' She had been arrested three times during her candidacy as an opposition MP on a variety of trumped-up allegations. Harassment by the police and the CIO had been a fact of life for opponents of the Mugabe government but she had assumed that it would have ceased now that she was a member of the GNU.

'Conspiracy to commit treason.'

'That's preposterous. Get out of my office immediately!'

'There is a police car downstairs, Minister,' the bald-headed man, Bitai, said, for the first time addressing her by her title. 'I am sure you don't wish to be led out of here in handcuffs.'

'Let me see the warrant.' Thandi read the document and saw that it was legitimate, even though the charge was rubbish. She looked over the top of her reading glasses at the two thugs. 'You do know that one day soon there will be a complete change of government.'

Makoni shrugged. 'I serve the government of the day.'

'No, young man, you serve the strongest man in the government, and that is not the same thing. Exactly what am I alleged to have done that is so treasonous?'

'You have been consorting with foreigners who would over-throw the government.'

'Have I? Do you have any names of these people?' Thandi asked, momentarily confused.

'An Australian national, George Bryant, and a former Rhodesian soldier, Braedan Quilter-Phipps.'

Knowing George was in the country and coming to meet her had set her heart beating like a young girl's again, and though she hoped it hadn't shown, the sight of him after all these years had nearly taken her breath away. Just seeing him had brought back so many memories, both fond and painful. Their love had been doomed from the very start. Their backgrounds, their race, their politics and their destinies were so far apart that nothing could ever have come of it, but that hadn't stopped her burning for him. There had been many times over the years when she had wondered, what if? Temba, the freedom fighter she'd met in Mozambique and married after independence in 1980, had later hit her and slept with his female staff and prostitutes until he had died of AIDS. Thandi had tried to make Temba use a condom when she became aware of the growing problem but he had refused. It was when she forced the issue by refusing to have sex with him unless he protected himself that he began physically abusing her. In time, he had tired of her protests. Miraculously, she had not been infected by the disease that was the scourge of her country, and the rest of Africa. She had shed no tears when he died but she cherished the children he had given her. If she'd eloped with George she would never have been able to join the struggle for independence, or rise through the party ranks. She'd sacrificed love for her country, and she would never know whether she'd made the right choices.

Thandi had checked up on George when ZANU–PF had come to power and in a way she had been relieved to learn that he had emigrated to Australia. She'd read of the trauma his daughter had gone through but it wasn't until some years later that she had learned her brother had been involved in the raid on the Bryant family farm. Thandi also knew that Emmerson had shot down the Viscount aircraft carrying George's sister, Hope. Thandi had actually cried, alone in her tent in the training camp in Mozambique, when she'd read a newspaper report of Hope's death. She remembered Hope as a sweet, inquisitive child, who had discovered Thandi and George's secret, but kept it.

There was so much she had wanted to talk about with George when she had seen him again, and yet so much more that they could never share. She had been both grateful and disappointed that the short notice of the meeting had left her genuinely unable to reshuffle her schedule to spend more time with him. George would probably fly back to Australia, now that she had secured a deal to give her father and Paul and Philippa Bryant control of Kiabejane ranch, and Thandi imagined she would never see her former lover again.

'Quilter-Phipps?' Thandi said to Agent Makoni. 'I don't know that name.'

'He is an associate of Bryant, a mercenary who has been working as security at Kiabejane ranch in Matabeleland. He is wanted in connection with the murder, last night, of your father.'

Thandi dropped the paper onto her desk. She looked up at Makoni again, her mouth agape. What had the man just said? Tiny pinpricks of bright light appeared at the periphery of her vision and the room felt as if it was swaying around her. 'What?'

Makoni looked confused now. 'Minister? You haven't heard? My God . . .' He sounded almost sympathetic.

'Did you say . . . did you say my father had been murdered?'

'Minister, I am sorry. I assumed you had been informed already, because . . .'

It was too much to process, but the terrible truth was out there, circling her like a man-eating lion. 'Because my brother told you all this.'

'I'm afraid I cannot divulge any more information,' Makoni said.

Thandi tried to stand, but she couldn't make her legs work, and she dropped back into her chair. 'I don't understand . . . You tell me my father is dead and that I am accused of conspiring with a suspect in the killing. This is ridiculous.'

'I am sorry, Minister, for your loss, but I have my orders. We are to escort you to your home and keep you under house arrest, pending a full investigation. I expect there are things you need to organise as well, given the circumstances. Let us take you home.'

Thandi looked up at the men and they loomed like giants over her. Her head was spinning and tears began to well in her eyes. Her precious father . . . Makoni reached out a hand and, not ungently, took her by the forearm. She wanted to shrug it off, to order him out of her office, and ordinarily she would have. However, she knew who had ordered this sham of an investigation and why he had done it.

And if Emmerson had done what she was sure he had done, then her whole world had just fallen apart.

Tate was on his way back to Kariba when he got the call from Paul Bryant telling him Kenneth Ngwenya had been killed and the future of the ranch was once more in jeopardy.

'I'm in Gweru, Paul,' he said into his cell phone. 'I stayed the night with some friends who are still running a dairy farm near here. Where are you now?'

'I'm at your mother's but soon I'll be heading out to the ranch, to the security office. The police are there,' Paul said. 'The security guards called me, but they're playing dumb, Tate. They say they can't remember what the poachers who tied them up looked like. I'm betting that Emmerson's behind this.'

'You think he killed his own father?'

'I wouldn't put it past him. Four rhinos were killed last night, too, Tate. It's a bloody disaster. I also spoke to Kenneth's driver. He didn't actually see the killing, but he has confirmed that Kenneth was confronting Emmerson before the shots were fired.'

'My God. That settles it, I'm coming back to Bulawayo now.'

'Put foot, I need you here as soon as you can make it.'

Emmerson Ngwenya and his three remaining men, Henry, Nicholas and Simba, shared the driving as they travelled through the night and arrived in Harare in time for breakfast with Nguyen van Tran at the Deli Café in the Borrowdale Village shopping centre, not far from the Vietnamese embassy in Avondale.

Emmerson rubbed his face. He'd slept part of the way but was still exhausted. He had nothing to fear from the diplomat, and having extra muscle with him might only attract more attention, so he dismissed the trio of hired guns to get their own breakfast. All three were former comrades who had fought with him during the liberation war. They were tough, ruthless men, driven by their pursuit of the dollar, and Emmerson knew he could count on their loyalty.

He felt a little lightheaded as he walked past the shoppers in the mall. He had killed his own father. But his father had been a weak man, who had needed his wife to prop up his convictions. Emmerson had cherished his mother and been devastated when she died. She was a true heroine of the struggle, unlike his *mtengisi* father. His father pandered to whites, like the Bryants, who had been responsible for sending Emmerson to the hell of the juvenile prison. Emmerson forced himself to suppress the memory of the terrible, shameful things that had been done to him there, and that he had been forced to do.

Nguyen, dressed in chinos and an Armani shirt, stood when he saw Emmerson approaching, and extended a hand. Emmerson shook it, noticing the expensive watch and the chunky ring on the man's right hand. Nguyen was a communist comrade from a country not as poor as Zimbabwe, but not much better off, yet he sported the trappings of a wealthy businessman. And he was about to get wealthier. So, too, was Emmerson.

'I was not expecting to hear from you,' Nguyen said.

'You thought we would no longer have a deal?'

Nguyen leaned back in his seat as he sipped his coffee. 'Let us just say that you have had some, ah, problems delivering in the past. There was the unfortunate business of you being intercepted by the police near Victoria Falls, and when I heard your father had taken over the ranch you spoke of, I assumed there would be nothing coming from that venture. So, it was good to get your call last night. Will there be trouble?'

'There will be no more trouble from now on. My father is no longer in control of the ranch – I am,' Emmerson said. He was famished and had ordered bacon and eggs. 'We now have a reliable supply for the foreseeable future.'

'Good, I am pleased. You have something for me?'

Emmerson nodded. 'I will leave the bag under the table when I go.'

Nguyen slid across a copy of the *Herald*. The front-page story was the allegation that MDC politicians were being investigated on corruption charges. Emmerson smiled to himself and wondered how his sister was feeling right now. The story in tomorrow's government-run press would be of the investigation into Thandi's links with some reactionary mercenaries. Emmerson took the paper and allowed the fat envelope hidden inside to slide into his lap. He then transferred it into his pocket. He didn't need to count the money, as he knew the Vietnamese man was now relying on him more than ever for future supplies.

CHAPTER 34

What seemed like a lifetime ago, but what was only twelve hours earlier, Braedan, Natalie, George, Paul and Pip had stood by the rhino *bomas* and watched as the ambulance left with Kenneth Ngwenya's body. Paul had put an arm around Pip's shoulders as she wiped the tears from her eyes.

Natalie had felt like crying as well. There were half-a-dozen farm workers in one of the pens and they were chanting in unison as they heaved together to pull the dead rhino out into the open.

Even the other animals at the ranch had seemed to be aware of the senseless killings that had taken place. Gerry, a semi-tame giraffe with a head knobbled by calcium growths, had wandered over to the *boma* while the police forensics people were photographing Kenneth's body in situ. The animal had hovered on the periphery of the human activity, but it had seemed particularly interested in craning its neck to look into the rhino *boma*. Pip had started sobbing again. 'Look at old Gerry,' she'd said, nodding to the giraffe. 'He knows there's been a tragedy here.'

'What are you going to do, Dad?' George asked Paul now as they sat glumly around Sharon's breakfast table, moving food around their plates. Once they'd taken Kenneth's body away, there hadn't seemed to be a lot of point staying at the ranch.

With Kenneth dead the future of Kiabejane was once more in limbo. They'd quietly made their way back to Sharon Quilter-Phipps' house, shocked by the viciousness of what had taken place and collectively worrying about what further trauma the next day would bring.

Paul gave Pip a squeeze and Natalie thought that for the first time her grandfather looked all of his ninety-two years. 'I don't think there's much point moving our stuff back to the ranch.'

'I'll try Thandi's office again later to see if they have any more news,' George said.

It seemed there was no one left for them to turn to for help. Thandi Ngwenya had been arrested that same morning.

'Tate will be here soon,' Paul said.

'Isn't he part of the problem?' George asked, looking at Braedan, who said nothing.

'All right, all right,' Paul said. 'George, I don't know where you got this harebrained idea that Tate cut the horn off one of my rhinos and sold it, but I can guess.' He looked at Braedan. 'I don't think for a moment that your brother would do anything illegal when it came to wildlife – at least not without getting me in on the act. But even if Tate did immobilise one of them and pinch a horn, I still need him here today.'

'Why, Grandpa?' Natalie wasn't a hundred per cent sure she wanted to see Tate, especially after what had happened between her and Braedan last night. Oddly, she felt a little guilty, despite the fact that it had been the best sex she'd had in years. She felt embarrassed at the thought that Tate might somehow guess or, worse, that Braedan might let his brother know. She thought of what had happened with Aunty Hope and felt her cheeks start to colour.

Paul looked meaningfully at Pip before answering. 'Because

we've got a hell of a lot of rhinos to dart today and Tate's the only person other than me who's qualified to do that.'

'Why do you want to dart them?' Braedan asked.

Grandma Pip blew her nose and seemed to finally compose herself. 'Because, Braedan, we're moving the rhinos. Today. As soon as possible before Emmerson Ngwenya takes over the ranch. We've found out he's gone to Harare on business.'

'The business of selling rhino horns, probably,' Paul cut in.

'You're going to move nine rhinos?' Her father sounded typically pessimistic.

'Where to?' Braedan asked. 'Are you taking them to one of the other conservancies?'

Paul looked around to make sure there was no one else in earshot. 'No. Even though that's what Tate's been suggesting for a long time, I don't think it's a good idea. The writing's on the wall. If thugs like Emmerson Ngwenya can take over Kiabejane, then the reality is that until Mugabe dies there is no farm or private game reserve in the country that will be safe from poachers.'

'So where will you take them?' Natalie asked. 'Botswana?'

Paul shook his head. 'As much as I'd like to get them out of the country, we'd never be able to organise the permits and these *are* Zimbabwean rhinos. Also, there isn't time to organise their release in a national park, where there would at least be a few rangers to protect them.'

'So what are you going to do, Dad? Surely you're not just going to let them loose?' George asked.

'That, my boy,' Paul said, 'is exactly what we're going to do. We're going to dart the remaining rhinos, load them into vehicles and drive them to the other side of the country, up near Kariba, and we're going to release them all into the wilds of the Charara Safari Area without anyone knowing.'

George banged his fist on the table. 'That's crazy. You're going to set your rhinos free in a hunting area, where they'll have no armed guards, no protection and no one to even keep track of them.'

'That's it, don't you see?' Pip said. 'Tate found that there is at least one wild rhino that has lived in that part of the country for God knows how long – maybe forty years or more – without ever being discovered. Because no one even considered there could still be a rhino up near Lake Kariba, no poachers ever bothered to look for them there.'

'And,' Paul continued, 'who knows . . . if one survived perhaps there are others there. This wild one might even be a good mate for one of our cows.'

'Or he might kill a couple of your bulls if he sees them as competition,' George said.

Paul nodded slowly. 'That's quite true, George, and your mother and I discussed all of this late into the night last night. Look, these animals would have been released into the wild eventually anyway and territorial fights are always an issue with black rhino, but what's the option? If we leave them here or move them to another farm they'll be dead inside a year. All of them.'

'I still think it's crazy.'

'This whole country is crazy, Dad,' Natalie said.

Paul cleared his throat and Natalie saw the old sparkle in his eyes. 'I've called everyone I know in Bulawayo with a three-tonne truck and five are on their way as we speak. I can expect two more later this afternoon, and with our two that gives us nine – one per animal. I'll get one of the dart guns and the M99 and we'll dart and load as many as we can before Tate gets here. When he arrives we'll split us and the labour into two teams and do the rest. I hope to have them all loaded by last light today.'

'I can do some darting, too,' Braedan said.

'You can?' Paul adjusted his glasses. 'Are you qualified to do game capture?'

Braedan shrugged. 'I don't have a piece of paper, but Tate taught me how to prepare the darts and use the dart gun.'

Paul turned to Pip. 'What do you reckon, love?'

Pip frowned. Natalie knew she didn't particularly like the brasher of the two Quilter-Phipps boys and she suddenly felt nervous that her grandmother had guessed what had gone on last night. 'It's a risk, Paul, but time's more important than anything else now.'

'All right, that settles it. I've only got two guns anyway, so Tate can take over from Braedan when he gets here, but if you can get a couple of them down, young fella, then that'll put us ahead of the game.'

'Yes, sir,' Braedan said, and Natalie liked the way he showed her grandfather respect.

'Let's get going then,' Paul said, standing up from the table.

By the time Tate arrived at the ranch three rhinos had already been darted and loaded into the trucks that would take them across the country to Makuti.

Tate took directions from the security guard on the gate and made his way along the dirt road past the big dam and the bird hide towards an open grassy *vlei* where he could see a lorry, two *bakkies* and a motorcycle parked in the distance.

He was by no means convinced of the merits of Paul's scheme – in fact, he considered it harebrained in the extreme – but he also conceded the point that the rhinos faced a grim future wherever they went. He might not have agreed with the old man, but Tate was privately looking forward to seeing Natalie again.

She'd been on his mind a good deal lately. It had been a very long time since he'd been so close to a woman, even if he had behaved so clumsily. Of course he felt urges now and then, but mostly his work kept him too busy to think about sex. Women were always around in the research camps, and he knew some were attracted to him, but when he thought of striking up a relationship with any of them, it always seemed so difficult, logistically.

Perhaps that's my problem, he thought as he drove up to where the capture party was doing its work. *I think too much.* His brother always had a girl hanging off his arm, and Tate wondered if his marriage had fallen apart because Braedan had been unfaithful. He told everyone who would listen about Lara leaving him for a doctor, but Lara had once told Tate that she loved Braedan more than anything else in the world. By contrast, Tate had once overheard one of Braedan's rugby mates telling of how Braedan had bedded the wife of an opposing team's captain on an away trip to Gweru. Tate wondered if Lara had been driven into the arms of another man by Braedan's infidelities. Despite his brother's bad-boy reputation, Tate had to admit to being a little envious of him. He wished, sometimes, that he could be comfortable with having sex with a woman and then walking away.

He could see Natalie in the distance. Again, the practicalities began clogging his mind, blocking up the emotions. She had a life in Australia and a seemingly good career as a journalist. She would be flying home soon and there was little he could offer in terms of money or employment that would tempt her to stay in Zimbabwe. Tate had an offer of some work in Botswana, but it would be poorly paid and would take him out into the bush for weeks on end. It was no place to try to start a relationship.

Tate gripped the steering wheel tight when he saw the block-like silhouette of his twin brother sidle up to Natalie and put an arm around her shoulders. 'I don't believe it.'

Tate exhaled a long breath and forced his arms and hands to relax. He'd been right not to follow his foolish heart and try to get closer to Natalie again. She'd fallen for the ignorant brute and Tate was old enough and wise enough to accept that this was the way of the world.

Tate pulled up next to Paul Bryant, who was working at the back of a pickup, preparing darts on the folded-down tailgate. He looked up from his work and waved to Tate. Braedan and Natalie stood near a motor-cycle, and Tate noted Braedan had taken his arm off Natalie's shoulders. *And so you should feel guilty, you bastard,* Tate thought. Natalie gave a little wave as Tate stopped the *bakkie* and got out. He acknowledged her with a curt nod and blanked his brother out.

'Paul, howzit.'

'Tate! Glad you could join us. We've got three loaded already and your brother here's proved a bit of a dab hand with the dart gun and the M99,' Paul said.

'He's not qualified to dart rhino. Paul, this is a very serious business and it's not something that should be undertaken by amateurs. You know yourself M99 is lethal if it's not administered properly.'

'Don't get huffy with me, Tate,' Paul said, standing up straight to ease the muscles in his back. 'We don't have time for sibling rivalry. There's too much work to be done.'

'Paul,' Tate said, his tone conciliatory, 'have you thought about what's going to happen to the rhinos once they're released? You can't just let them go wild.'

Paul slid a rubber ring onto the end of a dart he'd been preparing, then looked at Tate over the top of his glasses. 'Yes, I can, Tate, and that's what I'm doing. But we're also fixing radio transmitters into the horns of the animals that don't already have them. Someone, sometime, with the right gear, will be able to find them later on if they've a mind to.'

Natalie walked over and said hello to Tate, interrupting the conversation. 'Grandpa, Braedan was just saying that maybe we should think about setting up some sort of temporary *boma* for the rhinos when we get to the area where they're going to be released.'

Tate answered before Paul could. 'Well, Braedan doesn't know what he's talking about. We want to minimise the stress these animals go through. If they were in *bomas* here it might make sense to move them to another *boma* – relatively familiar surrounds and conditions. But they're not. These rhino have been living free. Moving them into an enclosure would put them under some stress and we'll be moving them to a wild area where there are no facilities.' He looked over at his brother and shook his head. 'And there's no such thing as a temporary *boma* for rhinos. No, translocating from the field to the field is as good a way as any of introducing rhino to a different area. Ideally we might pick an area that has no rhino in it already, to avoid territorial fights, but I think the benefits of giving the old bull at Makuti some girls to mate with outweigh the risks of him killing one of the males.'

'Time is a-wasting,' Paul proclaimed. He whistled and a team of fifteen African guards and labourers roused themselves from the shade of an acacia where they had been sitting. 'Tate, you go for Chengetai next. She's an old female. Watch her – she's been darted plenty of times in her life so she'll know what you're up to. She can be a bit of a handful. We'll go for Gomo, her young toy boy.'

Tate nodded. He was familiar with most of the ranch's rhino. '*Gomo*' was a Shona word for hill or mountain and the three-year-old male was already growing quickly enough to match his name.

Pip spoke to the African men in rapid Ndebele and they divided themselves into two groups. 'Braedan, you can come with Paul and me and the first group of men, and Natalie, you go with George and Tate and the second group.'

Tate noticed Natalie look to Braedan for some sort of confirmation. His brother just winked at her. Tate quietly seethed, but Natalie was not his to lose, so he said nothing.

'Right, let's go,' he said to George and Natalie, then ordered his group of men to climb on the back of a three-tonne truck fitted with a winch and carrying a steel-framed wooden crate. The crate was about three metres long, two metres high and a metre and a half wide.

Tate, Natalie and George got into the double cab *bakkie*. 'Where is Chengetai, Elias?' Tate said to the ranch's senior field guide, who climbed into the front passenger seat next to Tate. Elias's green uniform was already crusted with white-ringed sweat stains. He and his men had been hard at work for several hours capturing and loading rhino.

Elias pointed ahead and off to the left and Tate put the truck in gear and set off. He imagined the men were not overly happy at seeing all the rhinos being loaded; the smarter ones would realise that the ranch was ending its days as a rhino-breeding outpost.

Tate looked in the rear-view mirror and saw George Bryant's typically unfriendly eyes glance away. Natalie was very quiet. He wondered what was on their minds.

'There,' said Elias, pointing through the windscreen.

Tate pulled a small pair of binoculars from the centre console. 'That's Chengetai.'

'What does her name mean?' Natalie asked.

'"To take care",' her father answered. 'Let's just hope she doesn't take care of us.'

Tate told Elias to get behind the wheel, but knew he didn't have to give the old field guide any more instruction. 'Natalie, you can come up in the back if you like and hand me a second dart if I miss.'

'OK.'

Tate got out and then vaulted up into the bed of the pickup. He extended a hand and lifted Natalie up. She was slim and when she bent over to tie up a shoelace he couldn't help but notice her pink underpants showing above her green bush trousers. The skin of her lower back looked smooth and soft. He wanted to touch it. Elias started driving and Tate grabbed Natalie's hand to stop her falling over.

'Thanks,' she said. She stood next to him and held on to the roll bar.

'Tate, you didn't dart the rhino on the ranch whose horn went missing, did you?'

He looked at her, into her eyes. 'No.'

'It's just that . . . I remember you talking about sustainable harvesting of rhino horn when we were at Victoria Falls.'

'I did, but there is no way I would have done that to Paul, not for my own gain. If you ask me, I think it's exactly what he should do here. He should dehorn all these rhinos and sell the horns direct to the Vietnamese or the Chinese or whoever wants them, but we all know that's not possible. As well as being against the law it would cut out Emmerson Ngwenya and we now know what he's capable of.'

'Why should I believe you?' she asked.

'I don't care if you believe me or not. It means nothing to me. I'm not trying to impress you, Natalie.' He looked into her eyes and couldn't read them. She bit her lower lip.

Elias reached out of the driver's side window, tapped on the roof and pointed. Tate saw old Chengetai. She raised her head and sniffed the air. She had seen human beings in their vehicles nearly every day of the sixteen years of her life – rangers, researchers, tourists – but she sensed this was no ordinary day and no ordinary vehicle.

Tate loaded a dart into the stock of the gun, tapped it home and screwed the cap closed. He adjusted the air pressure and leaned across the cab of the truck. Behind them the three-tonner trundled along at a sedate pace. 'Try and keep her out of the thick stuff,' Tate called down to Elias.

They bounced along the rough ground and Natalie picked up a spare dart, ready to hand it to Tate if he missed. 'Be careful with it,' he said to her, 'just a drop of the stuff inside that dart is enough to kill a human.'

Chengetai tossed her head again, then started to run.

'Faster! Don't lose her,' Tate called.

Natalie swayed beside him, gripping the roll bar with one hand and holding the dart in the other. Tate hoped she didn't fall and stab him with it. She grinned at him like she was having the time of her life and her smile cut through his thick-walled defences. God, he still wanted her. And it wasn't just because his brother was taking her from him.

Chengetai ran across the grassy plain towards a wall of thorn bush. Elias had to get Tate in position for a shot before the rhino led them into the trees. Not only would it be harder to keep pace with her and get a good shot, but it would be a mission to get the bigger truck in there and to load her. They might end up having to walk her out, in a semi-drugged state, or clear a path for the truck. The first option was risky and the second meant hours of hard work.

Tate leaned around to yell through the driver's window. 'Put foot, Elias!'

Natalie gave an involuntary whoop of excitement as the truck crested a small rise and became airborne. Tate bent his knees to brace for the impact as the Hilux slammed back to earth. He stayed on his feet, but Natalie lost her grip on the roll bar and her arms flailed as she started to fall. Tate reached out with his left arm and hooked it around her waist. Elias swerved to miss a stout shrub and Natalie fell sideways into Tate.

'I've got you.'

She laughed and looked up into his eyes and for an instant he kidded himself that anything was possible, but then she straightened and Tate had to focus all his thoughts on the capture as Elias yelled and pointed to one o'clock. 'There she is, *baas*!'

Tate tapped on the roof of the *bakkie* to signal he had seen her. He brought the stock of the dart gun to his shoulder and leaned his body across the roof of the cab, legs spread and braced. He registered Natalie's arm around him, presumably because she thought it would help steady him, but didn't look back to acknowledge the gesture. Tate's concentration was focused, as much as possible given the bouncing of the truck, on Chengetai's left hindquarter.

As the truck closed on the galloping rhino Tate pulled the trigger and the dart found its mark, the bright pink fluffy bouncing against the animal's skin as she continued her mad charge.

Natalie patted him on the back. 'Good shot!' But when he straightened and turned to her, she was looking straight ahead again. Elias kept pace with the rhino, though he had to swerve to avoid a deep, washed-out creek. Tate knew this was the time of maximum danger for the rhino, in case she fell into such an obstacle and broke a leg.

When they veered back onto the rhino's course Tate was pleased to see Chengetai had slowed her run to the classic high-stepping walk that indicated the opiate was working its magic. Elias slowed the vehicle and they all watched until, finally, Chengetai stopped, swayed a little, then sat down on the ground.

'Everybody out, but watch her . . .'

Tate led the way, jumping over the side of the *bakkie*. When he got to the rhino the first thing he did was wrap a long length of cloth around her eyes to blindfold her. 'She's not unconscious,' Tate said to Natalie, 'and covering her eyes will stop her from becoming panicked.'

Elias was talking loudly in Ndebele into a handheld radio. 'The lorry's on its way *baas*,' he said to Tate. 'Three minutes.'

'Good.' Tate opened the plastic toolbox he'd brought with him from the *bakkie* and took out a syringe and laid it ready in the opened lid. 'OK, nose rope and leg rope.'

The African men had worked on countless rhino captures and one was already dragging Chengetai's left rear leg out from under her and tying a stout rope around it. Elias helped Tate and Natalie lift the animal's massive head so they could tie a second rope around her snout, just behind the second horn.

Chengetai tossed her head suddenly. Elias dodged quickly to the left and narrowly escaped having his shoulder opened by the sharp tip of the rhino's horn.

The three-tonne lorry appeared and the driver cautiously negotiated his way around ant hills and fallen logs to get as close as he could to the prone rhino and her captors. Tate gave the thumbs-up and the driver got out and operated the small crane on the back of the vehicle, swinging out the steel-reinforced transport crate. Three of the capture team swung the crate around as it neared the ground, pointing the rear towards where Chengetai lay so that its opening was only about ten metres from the drugged rhino.

'Good work,' Tate said to the men. 'Natalie, you can climb up on the back of the truck, so you can lean on the open top of the crate. Take the electric prod from my toolbox and reach in and give Chengetai a zap on her bum if I tell you to. OK?'

Natalie nodded. She found the prod, gave it a couple of tests and climbed onto the truck. Tate had one man take the nose rope and pass it in through the rear of the crate and out a hole at the front. The man took up the slack, and when everyone was in position Tate took the syringe of Naltrexone and jabbed the drug into the rhino. Chengetai became more alert instantly. Tate gave her a slap on the rump and, still somewhat groggy, she got to her feet. 'Take up the slack on the ropes!'

The man on the nose rope, together with a colleague who had joined him, heaved hard, one of them putting a foot against the grate. Chengetai tried to fight the force that pulled her head up and forward, then, as Tate had hoped she would, she charged forward, sensing the men in front of her. 'Keep control of her,' Tate told the others. Chengetai hopped a step as her left leg was hampered by the efforts of Tate and his men. 'Heave!'

Tate looked up and saw Natalie sitting on the edge of the crate. He would have preferred her standing safely on the truck and looking on while they worked but saw, too late to do anything about it, that there was a gap of a metre or more between the three-tonner and the crate, and she couldn't stand on the flatbed and reach over to see into the crate. 'Careful up there!'

She smiled, enjoying the spectacle. 'I'm fine.' She brandished the cattle prod and gave him a wink.

The men on the nose rope continued to pull, but Chengetai baulked when she came to the entrance of the crate. Tate let go of the leg rope and went to Chengetai's rump. He grabbed hold of her curled-up tail, pulled it straight then leant over, placed it between his teeth and bit down hard. Natalie laughed, but the rhino snorted and whined, and when the nose-rope crew redoubled its efforts she stomped halfway into the container.

'Now, Natalie!' Tate yelled up to her. 'Zap her on the rear.'

Natalie leaned over, pressed the prod into Chengetai's hindquarter and pushed the button activating the zap of electricity. Chengetai surged forward to escape the pain and lowered her head and slammed into the far end of the crate. The impact knocked over one of the rope crew, who had been pressing a foot against the outside of the crate. Chengetai threw back her head and backed up a couple of paces and the second man on the nose rope yelped as the coarse hemp was dragged through his bare palms.

'Get hold of that bloody rope! Close the back!' Men were pushing and slapping Chengetai's butt as the big rhino, temporarily free of the tension from the nose rope, tried furiously to back out of the crate. Two other workers were trying to slide down the trapdoor at the rear of the crate, but Chengetai had moved half a metre of her rear end past the entrance to her temporary gaol. 'Zap her again, Natalie!'

Natalie leaned into the crate, her belly bent over the steel frame of the container above the wooden walls. Tate could see the rhino bucking and rocking inside and the end of the electric prod waving about as Natalie tried to make contact with the panicked animal. 'I can't reach her, Tate!'

Tate used his shoulder to heave against Chengetai's rear and with the help of the others managed to push the rhino inside just enough for him to be able to give the command to drop the door. The men jumped back as the heavy barrier slid down its rails into place. Suddenly freed of the tension on her rear leg

Chengetai charged forward again and slammed her head into the far end of the box.

'Tate!'

Tate, his face covered in sweat and his clothes filthy from heaving against the rhino, looked up but couldn't see Natalie. 'Shit.'

'Tate!'

Tate scrambled up onto the truck and to the rim of the crate. Natalie screamed as she scrambled to get to her feet. She had fallen into the crate and was crouched at the rear. The rhino heard her scream and started to back up. Natalie reached out and hit Chengetai with a zap from the cattle prod, which made the rhino jump on the spot and thrash about in the impossible task of turning around. Even though she couldn't charge forward, Tate knew the rhino could easily crush Natalie to death by backing into her.

Tate leaned into the crate and reached for Natalie. 'Grab my hand.'

She reached up and locked onto his hand and Tate heaved as hard as he could. Natalie's boots slipped on the crate's wooden walls but couldn't find purchase. Her hand was slippery with perspiration and she slipped from Tate's grip, and screamed.

Chengetai was bustling backwards and Tate knew that unless he tried something else Natalie would be jammed against the rear of the crate. He jumped over the rim of the crate and landed, legs astride, on the rhino's back. Chengetai hopped on the spot like a bucking bronco as Tate reached again for Natalie. She took both his hands and managed to get her foot onto one of the metal framing ribs that ran parallel to the ground. Tate rode the jumping rhino and got a hand under Natalie's bottom to steady her. When she was able to grab the rim of the crate Tate half-slid and half-fell off Chengetai's back. He landed on the floor of the crate and reached up in time to get a hand under Natalie's foot and heave her up, giving her the boost she needed to get out.

Tate yelled and slapped Chengetai's bottom so hard it stung his palms. He looked up and saw Elias standing on the back of the truck leaning in. He had Tate's toolbox in one hand. 'I don't know how to load the dart gun, *baas*!'

'The dart! Throw me a dart!'

Natalie grabbed the box and opened it. She found the spare dart Tate had made up earlier.

Tate looked for the electric prod but Natalie had dropped it and Chengetai had stomped on it and destroyed it. The rhino kicked back and Tate dodged to one side and nearly lost his balance. He started to climb, but Chengetai reversed at full speed and smashed her body into the rear of the crate. Tate yelled in pain as he felt his left leg being crushed against the timber of the rear door. The whole crate shook with the impact and it was only the fact that his leg had been to one side of a steel reinforcing tube that had stopped his bone from being pulverised. Nevertheless his leg buckled under him when he dropped to the ground.

Chengetai continue to push back, slowly but steadily. Her mad panic had subsided to a crushing, killing force. Tate felt his chest being squashed against unyielding timbers and, as much as he slapped and yelled, Chengetai would not move forward. The African crew screamed from outside and banged on the crate. A third man went to help the crew on the nose rope, but Chengetai could not be stopped or controlled.

'Tate!'

He looked up and managed to get his right hand up in time. The left side of his body, including his arm, was now pinned by the rhino's bulk. Natalie hefted the dart, point up, and Tate prayed it wouldn't start tumbling. If the needle pierced his skin the M99 would kill him before anyone could get to him to administer the antidote – that was if the rhino didn't finish him off first.

Tate caught the dart, reversed it in his hand and jabbed it into Chengetai's thick skin with all his remaining might. The rhino continued to push home even as the dart took effect and Tate felt a stabbing, searing pain in his left side.

'Get him out!'

Hands were reaching over the rim of the crate now. Tate grabbed hold and felt himself being lifted off his feet as Chengetai finally succumbed to the drug and the heaves of the men on the nose rope. Tate gritted his teeth and moaned at the intense pain in his side. Once out of the crate he sank to his knees on the hard surface of the truck's bed.

'Oh, God, Tate,' said Natalie, 'you saved my life. Are you all right?'

He winced as she put an arm around him. 'I'm . . . OK. I think I've got a couple of cracked ribs.'

'Oh, I'm sorry.' Natalie released her hold on him. 'I didn't mean to make it worse.'

'No,' Tate breathed, biting back the pain. 'It's OK. You didn't make it worse, Natalie . . . you couldn't.'

'Oh God, Tate . . .' Tears started welling in her eyes as he looked at her.

Instinctively, and despite the pain in his ribs, he reached for her and drew her to him again. 'I would have died if anything had happened to you.'

CHAPTER 35

Braedan had gone by the time Tate and Natalie got Chengetai back to the assembly point at the *boma* where the other rhinos had been killed.

'Where is he?' Tate asked.

'I sent him on ahead, in the first group of five vehicles,' Paul said.

'Damn,' Tate said.

'What's wrong, apart from your ribs?' Paul asked.

Philippa was strapping Tate's bare chest with surgical tape as they spoke. 'I needed to talk to him about something . . . about some accusations he's made.'

Paul waved a hand as though swatting a fly. 'I've no time for this, Tate. I sent Braedan ahead because I know he's a smooth talker and he's got plenty of cash on him. If we're going to get trouble at any roadblocks between here and Kariba I want him to try and smooth the way. Also, if he gets caught, he's going to call me on the cell phone and we'll take a different route with the rest of the rhinos.'

'That's a good plan,' Tate conceded.

Emmerson Ngwenya's hulking, bald-headed man, Simba, pressed the buzzer on the intercom outside the walled mansion in Willowmead Lane and identified himself to the man who responded. The gate rolled open slowly and Simba drove up the paved driveway to the house. Henry was in the front passenger seat and Nicholas sat beside their ministerial boss in the back of the Hummer.

The place was a single-storey, whitewashed affair with a Mediterranean-style terracotta roof. Emmerson had bought it from an Indian family who had left two years earlier, finally giving up on the country's plummeting economy. One man's loss, Emmerson thought as he followed Simba to the front door.

He liked this house and he could see himself living in it one day. Perhaps he would install a mistress here in the interim. It only had three bedrooms, and they were small given the size of the house and the property, but everything else about the place spoke wealth. It had a tennis court, a pool, a bar and separate billiards room with a full-size table; it even had a gym. Emmerson walked through the grand entrance, his feet tapping on the polished parquetry floor, then out through double French doors to a paved verandah. All the house's rooms were linked by a covered walkway whose roof was supported by pillars that gave the place the feel of a Roman villa. A place for a modern-day emperor to repose, Emmerson smiled to himself.

Two of the bedrooms faced onto the pool and outside one of them sat a bored-looking CIO man reading a newspaper. The man looked up then jumped to his feet. Emmerson loved the feeling of power that money and fear purchased.

'My sister?' Emmerson asked, not bothering with pleasantries.

'She is inside, Comrade Minister. Safe. But plenty angry.' Emmerson smiled. He wouldn't have liked to be the man tasked with keeping Thandi quiet and in one spot.

'Let me in.'

The man reached into his pocket and pulled out a key. He

unlocked the door and Emmerson walked into the room. Thandi was lying on top of the bed, fully clothed, reading a South African women's magazine. She pretended to continue to read for a few seconds then peered over the top of her reading glasses at him. 'I wondered how long it would be before you came, brother.'

He grinned. 'I hope you are comfortable. Do you like my house?'

'I don't like anything you have bought with the proceeds of crime. You and your kind have bled this country dry, Emmerson.'

He shrugged. 'I would have thought that your time here would have given you the chance to realise it is not wise to make unfounded allegations in public, Thandi.'

'I knew it was you behind these trumped-up charges. I'm not guilty of treason, and you know it.'

'You think I don't know about you and George Bryant?' said Emmerson casually. 'You think I am stupid? I knew you were his slut when you were younger, and I knew he used to visit you in Mozambique.'

Her eyes widened at his remarks, but she said nothing. He knew he had her. Emmerson had told some senior ZANU cadres, back in the early seventies, that he suspected his sister of being a spy for the Rhodesian security forces, and let them know that she had been sleeping with a *mukiwa*, a white boy. He'd heard, later, that she had suffered during her time in the camps in Mozambique.

Thandi stayed silent. Emmerson moved closer to her bed and had the satisfaction of seeing her cringe away from him, ever so slightly. She was putting on a show of defiance, but she, too, feared him.

'You shamed us all by sleeping with George. I spent my war

trying to atone for your disgraceful rutting, Thandi. It was me who raided the Bryants' ranch and kidnapped the child. I would have killed her if I'd had the chance, to repay the sorrow those meddling whites caused me. I killed Hope Bryant as well.'

Thandi glared at him for a few seconds, then turned her face away from him, ashamed of his boasting.

He kneeled beside the bed and grabbed a handful of her hair, yanking her head around so he could fix her again with his stare. He spoke softly now. 'Yes, sister, she lived after the crash and I bayoneted her through the heart. This is the only way to rid our country of the people who you plot with.' He could see the turmoil in her face. But Emmerson knew he needed more to ensure his sister's silence. He sat down on the bed beside her and the springs creaked. He would have to get them oiled. He let go of her hair and she slithered out of his reach. 'Amazing, when you think of it. Your daughter, my niece, is now the same age that you were when you were in the camp, learning your lessons . . .'

Thandi rolled over and glared at him, the defiance back in her eyes. 'If you touch my daughters, I will kill you.'

He shook his head. 'They are my family, too, Thandi. I would never touch them in that way. Others, however, might not be so kind, so forgiving of lies and treachery. And if it did come to that, to the children being punished for the sins of the parent, then you would already be dead, sister. I can only keep you here for so long. You know that, and I know that. You probably have your puppet masters in England and America on the internet organising petitions for your release as we speak. I know that even if I get you to court you will probably get off. But we both know that you betrayed your country once before, by sleeping with George, and that he is still in this country. Africa is a dangerous continent and anything could happen to him. Anything could happen to you, too, Thandi.'

'What do you want from me, you bastard?' She spat the words at him.

'Your silence, that is all. It is a terrible thing that our father has died, killed by poachers. But it paves the way for me to take over the rhino-breeding program and you, dear sister, will support me in my claim to the land, and together we will grieve in public for a true hero of the struggle for freedom.'

'Our father would be ashamed of you. You murdered him, didn't you?'

Emmerson stood. 'Talk like that will keep you here much longer than needs be, Thandi.' He walked to the doors. 'Think of your children. Think of the white man you whored yourself to all those years ago.' He turned his back on her and locked the bedroom door behind him.

She talked tough, his sister the politician, but she was still a woman. He knew how to keep her in her place, and he was sure she would do what was required.

Emmerson smiled. He was feeling pleased with himself now, after a few worrying days and weeks. The inside pocket of his tailored black suit coat bulged with an envelope containing $100,000 in cash – the proceeds from the sale of three adult rhino horns and the stubby protrusion of the calf to Nguyen. A ranch stocked with rhinos waited for him in Bulawayo, and an up-and-coming young *Kwaito* pop star would be looking for him in the audience of her gig tonight. He had booked a suite at the Miekles and she would be in the hot tub with him, drinking French champagne by midnight. He would have to ask her if she had a friend. He felt strong. He walked along the corridor to where Simba was sitting on a chair.

The driver put down the newspaper he'd been reading on a side table. 'Where to, sir?' Simba asked.

Emmerson was about to answer when his phone buzzed in

his pocket. He answered it and clenched his fist as he listened to the man speak. 'What do you mean, all the rhinos are being moved?' The tinny voice on the end of the phone gave him some more details about where the animals were being taken. 'It will take us about three hours to get there, maybe longer. This cannot be allowed to happen. I have paid you too much.' Emmerson looked back through the French doors at Thandi as the man on the other end of the line made more excuses. His sister was lying on her side, in the foetal position, immobile.

'I don't care,' he told the caller. 'Delay them. I'm on my way.' He ended the call and felt like crushing the phone to pieces or throwing it at someone.

'Sir?' Simba asked tentatively, sensing Emmerson's sudden change of mood.

Emmerson checked his watch. 'Makuti. Kariba Road, now!'

Natalie had tried to sleep as they drove through the African night. But it was so different to night-time in Australia. Here the night blanketed the country. It was as if Zimbabwe had gone back in time, to the days before electricity – which was partly true, thanks to power cuts and failures – but it was more than that. The country of her birth was entombed in darkness and as much as most of the population prayed for someone to open the door and let the light back in, many people had given up hope. And many people had died.

She had been too confused, and still too charged from the events of the days before, for any sleep to come to her as Tate had driven them through the night. Their route had taken them east from Bulawayo, through Gweru and Kadoma. At Chegutu they'd headed due north on a tar road towards Murombedzi, and Chinhoyi, where they had rejoined the main road to Kariba, bypassing Harare.

They'd been travelling most of the night but they still had a few hours ahead of them. She could see that every time Tate leaned across to change gear he winced at the pain in his ribs. And that was her fault.

'I really am sorry, about falling into the crate. I feel like such a fool.'

He glanced at her, then back at the road, and she saw the beginnings of a small grin curl his lips. It was a rare enough occurrence for her to be surprised. 'What are you laughing at?'

He kept looking straight ahead. 'I wasn't laughing.'

'Well, grinning then. It wasn't that funny, was it?'

'I was just going to say, I know how you mean about feeling foolish.'

'What do you –' She was confused, but when he looked over at her again she realised what he was talking about. The embarrassing night in the Victoria Falls Safari Lodge. 'Tate, you don't need to feel foolish about that.'

He didn't look at her and she thought she could see his cheeks colouring.

'I feel so stupid, but . . .' he glanced at her now, taking his eyes off the road for a moment, 'it was just that you do remind me so much, physically, of Hope. I know I need to let go, but I might not ever be able to forgive myself for letting her go.'

Natalie shifted across the wide bench seat until she was sitting next to him.

He glanced at her. 'What are you doing?'

'Steady, tiger. I just thought I'd help you change gears. It seems to be hurting you.'

'Go to fourth,' he said. He stomped on the clutch and Natalie grabbed the gear stick and brought it down, across and down some more. Tate let out the clutch and pumped the accelerator to build up some more revs as they tackled a hill.

'How was that?'

'Perfect,' he said.

Natalie sat for a while with her hands in her lap, then tentatively reached over and laid her right hand on Tate's left thigh. He kept looking straight ahead, but she saw the small smile return, and it made her feel good, but then she thought about the predicament she'd landed herself in. From having no man in her life she now had two – twin brothers who hated each other.

Thandi Ngwenya turned her head to peek over her shoulder once her brother had stopped talking. She saw the CIO man had settled into his chair again, with his back to her, and was once more reading the paper.

The house she was imprisoned in looked ostentatious, but she had discovered its finishings were cheap. The panes of glass on the French doors were thin and she had heard Emmerson talking on his cell phone. He'd said something about rhinos being moved and that he was on his way to Makuti, which was near Kariba in the north of the country, near the Zambian border.

She put the pieces together as best as she could. The only rhinos – live ones at least – that Emmerson was interested in were the ones he had planned to take charge of on the Bryant ranch. George would still be in the country, from what she remembered of his plans. With her father's death, old Paul Bryant would know that his rhinos were doomed. Would he move his own rhinos to Makuti or Kariba to keep them from falling into Emmerson's hands? That seemed unlikely. Perhaps he was going to truck the rhinos across the border into Zambia – there were road crossings across the dam wall, and at Chirundu, downriver from the dam. If it were a covert operation, Paul could even put the rhinos on a boat and cross the lake. It sounded crazy, but Emmerson had sounded incensed. She didn't have a phone number for Paul Bryant, but George had left her his business card, which she had placed in her handbag.

Thandi sized up the secret policeman outside. CIO men, she knew from her own experience, were thugs and bullies, but there was no requirement for them to be fit, like soldiers, or adept in any particular skills, like proper spies. They were enforcers more than killers, and if they did kill it was with a gun or with a car. Zimbabwe's recent history was littered with examples of opponents of the regime who had been forced off the road or had their cars rammed by heavy trucks. Morgan Tsvangirai's wife had been killed when the car she and her husband were driving in was forced off the road by a lorry. The subsequent investigation had declared it an accident, but the Mugabe faction had enough form for serious questions to be raised.

Thandi's fears gave her courage. She knew that Emmerson would not trust her to keep her mouth shut, whatever she promised him. When she defected to the MDC she had done so in full knowledge that other members of parliament and party organisers – even ordinary MDC voters – had been beaten and burned and killed by the president's nationwide network of henchmen. She had visited the victims in hospital – seen the broken bones and the angry blistered burns made by cigarettes on flesh. She had read of the district chairpersons who'd been bludgeoned to death or beheaded. She had fielded her fair share of threats of death and violence from those still loyal to Mugabe but she supposed, perversely, that as Emmerson's sister and the daughter of Kenneth Ngwenya she might have been afforded some tacit, lingering protection. She had been too well connected to disappear or to wind up in hospital, she had thought. Thandi now knew that she'd been wrong to harbour such foolish notions. Her brother was going to kill her, and probably make it look like an accident.

The backside of the man guarding her was too big for the chair he sat on. He was overweight, but bulk was not to be underestimated and big men were not always slow. Thandi had been trained in unarmed combat in Mozambique decades ago; she hadn't used those skills in a long time, but she hadn't forgotten them either. She planned her attack, then reached for the pen with which she had been doing the magazine crossword.

Checking the guard was still engrossed in his paper, she raised the pen to her mouth and started to moan loudly. 'Help . . . help, me . . .'

She knelt on the floor beside the bed and glanced back over her shoulder. The man had risen from his chair and had his face pressed against the glass.

'Help me . . . I feel ill . . .'

The agent frowned, but made no move to open the door. This was one of the oldest prison ruses in the book, and Thandi knew she would have to up the ante if she was to convince the man to come in and check on her. She turned away from him again, steeled herself, then thrust the pen down her throat. She gagged, and pushed harder. Her lunch of *sadza ne nyama* – thickened mealie-meal porridge with a gravy of stringy beef – erupted over the bedspread. Thandi let herself slump to the floor, on her side.

She listened to the door being opened. Thandi was immediately encouraged by the fact that the man had not called for help. That probably meant he was alone. In her peripheral vision, through her lidded eyes, she saw him take the precaution of unbuttoning his suit jacket. There was a pistol stuffed into his belt.

Thandi groaned.

'What is wrong with you?' She moaned again and the man reached down for her, grasping her by the wrist. '*Ah*, this is disgusting. Get up, woman.'

Thandi made herself go limp and gave him minimal assistance. She wanted him using all his strength to lift her. Only when he had both hands on her left arm, heaving her up, did she suddenly find her feet. She lashed out with her right hand; fingers curled back to the second knuckle and punched as hard and as fast as she could into the man's throat. He gasped and let go of her, but Thandi was already balanced on both feet. As he straightened and staggered back she raised her knee into his groin and at the same time grabbed the pistol from his belt.

The fat man crumpled to his knees and Thandi jammed the pistol into the back of his neck. 'Do not move.' She lifted the back of his suit jacket and found his handcuffs. 'Into the bathroom.' The man stood and shuffled, still short of breath, to the ensuite, where Thandi ordered him to handcuff himself to the stout downpipe.

'You can't do this to me,' the man squeaked.

'Really? I am a government minister and you arrested me on the orders of a criminal. We'll see who can do what to whom when I get back to Harare.' She searched the man's jacket pockets and found his car keys. 'Where is my handbag?'

The man sneered at her.

'You need to learn to respect your elders, and women,' she said. Thandi raised the pistol and brought it down on the side of his head, cuffing him hard enough to break the skin but not to knock him out.

'On the kitchen table, inside . . . Minister.'

'Much better.' Thandi caught her breath, then rinsed her mouth while the man knelt at her feet. As she left she locked the door and went in search of her handbag, cell phone and George Bryant's card. She hoped she could get to him before Emmerson did.

Finally, they were approaching the rendezvous point, a tobacco farm not far from the main road, just north of the town of Karoi. The farm had been taken from a white family and had gone to ruin under its new owner, a senior government bureaucrat. However, the enterprising grandson of an old air force friend of Paul's had leased some land off the owner and had got the farm back on its feet.

Natalie eased her cramped, tired body down from the cab and walked to where the men and her grandmother were clustered around a fire burning in an old forty-four gallon fuel drum. A young white couple tended a *braai* made from another cut-down barrel just beyond the ring of light cast by the fire.

'Hello my girl,' Grandma Pip said. Her face was bright in the glowing light of the flames, but there was no mirth there.

Braedan stood to one side of the group, smoking. He nodded at Natalie and she returned the silent greeting. 'How's everything going?' she asked her grandfather.

'We've made good time,' Grandpa Paul said. 'Braedan smoothed his way through a few roadblocks, and one of his group had to stop to change a flat tyre, but we're all present and accounted for. Not far now.'

There was enough time for the late arrivals to down a reviving cup of coffee and a *boerewors* roll prepared by the young farmer, Ross, and his girlfriend, Claire. Natalie thought the roll was the best thing she'd eaten in years.

Natalie looked at Tate and saw that he was staring at his twin brother. Braedan looked back at him, saying nothing. Tate set his cup down, squared up and walked towards Braedan.

'What's up, *boet*?' Braedan said.

Natalie watched and gradually other heads turned. Even the other drivers, who might not have known of the enmity between the two brothers, couldn't have missed the tension as Tate stopped just three paces short of Braedan. Natalie was struck by how different the two were, despite their physical similarities. Braedan had the look of a soldier still, confident and muscled, loose fists by his side. Tate had his arms folded.

'What have you been saying about me?' Tate said.

Braedan shrugged.

'Answer me. Or aren't you man enough to say it in front of everyone here.'

'Be quiet, Tate, you're making a scene.'

'You're a bully, Braedan, you always were,' Tate said, his voice rising.

Braedan snorted a laugh. 'A *bully*? Newsflash, man, we left boarding school years ago. One of us grew up.'

'You told the others I drugged a rhino and took its horn – sold it to help Mom out.'

Braedan said nothing.

'How could you say something like that, how could you –'

'Out of my way.' Braedan sidestepped but when Tate went to block him he reached out and palmed him in the chest.

Natalie put her hand to her mouth, hoping Braedan wouldn't hurt his gentler brother, but then gasped when Tate fired a fast, sharp uppercut into Braedan's chin that knocked the big man's head back and set him staggering.

'No!' Natalie yelled.

Braedan looked as shocked as any of the onlookers, but his reflexes were fast. He neatly dodged Tate's next wild punch and retaliated with a jab into his brother's belly. Tate grunted and took a half-step back, then danced lightly to the left.

Braedan wheeled and raised his right leg in a furious kick-boxing move that connected with Tate's hip and knocked him to the ground. Braedan yelled a primal war cry and dived on top of his brother.

'Dad, stop them,' Natalie called, but George just sipped his coffee and shook his head.

'They've probably been wanting to do this for thirty years. Leave them to it,' Grandpa Paul said, but Pip came to Natalie's side and chastised her husband and son, telling them to break up the fight.

Braedan was putting punch after punch into Tate, who seemed to be done in already, but just when Natalie was about to go in herself and break up the fight Tate saw an opening and brought his knee up into Braedan's groin. Braedan yelped and Tate rolled from under him. Braedan got to his knees but Tate knocked him to the ground with a swinging punch.

Tate shifted his weight from foot to foot, fists clenched and up. 'Get up.'

Braedan coughed and spat blood and started to get to his feet.

'Enough!' Paul yelled, pushing his way between the two men. Despite his age and his obvious frailty the old man clearly meant business. He put a hand on each of their chests. 'Enough. We have to move these rhinos. You two can settle your differences after the job's done. I don't want to hear any more rumours about who did what. Understood?'

The brothers glared at each other, nostrils flaring, teeth clenched, but each eventually nodded.

'OK, everyone mount up and let's get going!' The drivers and crew said goodbye to the farmers and climbed into their rigs. Blue-black exhaust spouted as engines turned over.

'*Sah*,' Elias called to Paul from the truck he and Braedan had been driving. 'We have a problem. The engine, it is buggered!'

CHAPTER 36

Braedan got out of the truck, opened the engine bay and was head down inside the compartment when an impatient Paul Bryant walked up to him. 'What's wrong?'

'Could be dirty fuel. I've just drained a span of water out of the fuel filter. Elias, crank the engine again!' Braedan yelled.

Elias turned the key again and the engine sparked to life.

'There you go, all fixed,' Braedan said.

Paul waited for Braedan to close up and get down. As Braedan was wiping his hands dry on his shirt, Paul leaned in close to him. 'Son, if you darted that rhino and sold its horn, that's a terrible crime.'

'Paul, I didn't . . . how could –'

'Enough, enough.' Paul patted his arm. 'We all knew how tough your mother was doing it. I can't condone what you've done, even if it was for a good reason. You could have come to Pip and me and asked us for money. We've been supporting your mother off and on for the last few years anyway. We could have managed a little more.'

'No, wait . . .' Braedan began.

'No, don't say anything. You don't have to confess. The rhino's alive and there are many people who would say that what you did is what we should have been doing all along – harvesting horn and selling it. But I'm not one of those people. You saved Natalie's life all those years ago, Braedan.'

'I was just doing my job, sir.'

Paul shook his head. 'No, it was above and beyond that, and this family owes you for that. I won't go to the police, Braedan, but I need to know two things. Firstly, are you with us?'

'I am,' Braedan said.

'And secondly, do you really think we would have believed that your brother darted the rhino?'

Braedan shook his head. 'No, sir.'

Paul clapped him on the arm. 'Good man. We have work to do, so let's go.'

Tate and Natalie had taken the lead in the convoy for only Tate knew the exact location of the turn-off on to the old national parks access track that led deep into the Charara Safari Area, where he had found the last surviving black rhino.

Tate rubbed his jaw and gingerly fingered the cut under his eye. Natalie sat close to him, changing gears when he gave the command. 'That fight must have killed you, with your sore ribs.'

He looked at her and gave a small smile. 'Almost.'

Tate had to concentrate on the track, which had rarely been used by vehicles over the years and was badly washed away in places.

'How far in will we go?' Natalie asked.

'We need to get at least five kilometres from the road, maybe even further if the track holds out. I walked it for ten kilometres and it gets worse and worse. Bottom line is we need to get these rhinos as far away from people as possible.'

'Do you really think this is a good idea, Tate?'

'No.'

He studied the track. He'd been quiet after the fight and she wondered if he was retreating into his shell again. As much as she had feared for him, part of her had been secretly proud and excited by the way he had confronted his brother and thrown the first punch. But the fight had ended without resolution and the tension was still there between the brothers.

She'd watched her grandfather approach Braedan afterwards, and she thought that if he had made peace with Braedan, then perhaps she should too. But if, as Tate believed, Braedan had stolen the live rhino's horn to care for his mother, did that justify the crime? At least Braedan had done *something* to alleviate Sharon's poverty. Tate espoused radical ideas, but he didn't *do* anything. She shifted slightly away from Tate. Two could play at that game.

The portable radio her grandfather had given her squawked on the dashboard. 'Paul to Natalie, over?'

Natalie picked it up and pressed the transmit switch. 'Go ahead, Grandpa.'

'Natalie, Braedan's truck has broken down again. Your grandmother and I are going to wait with him, but you carry on. Tell Tate we'll be there eventually. If worse comes to worse you can release your rhino then come back and we'll try and move Braedan's from his truck onto yours, over.'

'Roger, Grandpa.' Natalie looked at Tate, who nodded to show he had heard and understood the message.

The sky was just starting to lighten in the east and Natalie yawned and stretched in the cab of the truck. She wondered what would happen to her grandparents when the rhinos had been released. She imagined they would have to leave the country for Australia. They had nowhere to live in Zimbabwe and they would face the wrath of Emmerson Ngwenya and whoever else wanted to get their hands on the rhinos. She would help them pack, quickly, then take them back to Australia and write her book. She had a dramatic story to tell now, something that could have come straight out of a novel.

The Quilter-Phipps brothers would exist as characters in a book and memories only. She knew in her heart of hearts that Braedan would be disastrous for a long-term relationship, and Tate was so closed off that he was unknowable. Back in Australia she would bemoan the lack of single men and go back to trawling through online dating websites, in the knowledge that she had left two handsome men behind in Africa. Her mood sank.

The truck bucked and rolled as Tate aimed for the least eroded sections. Natalie could only imagine what Chengetai was making of the sickening motion. They came to the crest of a hill and Tate veered off to the left, onto a large clearing. 'This is it,' he said.

Natalie and Tate got out, and as the rising sun started turning the hills around them from purple to a glowing red-gold, she couldn't help but be uplifted by the moment. For the first time she could appreciate the grandeur and the wildness of the place her grandfather had chosen to release the rhinos. There was nothing here but rolling hills covered in trees and bush: miles and miles of African wilderness. There was no guarantee the rhinos would be safe here or anywhere else in the Zambezi Valley, but there was an awful lot of Africa here for them to get lost in.

And that was the idea. The plan to kidnap and release the rhinos in a different part of the country was so mad that it just might work, Natalie thought. There had to be a change of regime sometime and the overwhelming majority of people in Zimbabwe who simply wanted to go to work, feed and educate their children, and live in peace under the rule of law would surely, one day, be able to elect a government which respected that. If that day came, then her grandparents' rhinos could be 'rediscovered' and the proper resources put in place to either monitor them in their new home or move them to other parts of the country where they might be better able to live and breed.

At least that was the theory.

Makuti stopped and sniffed the air.

There was danger about and his first instinct had been to run. On the faint morning breeze he'd caught the oily, smoky smell of vehicle exhausts. Humans. It had happened every now and then over the years, when speculative poachers ranged deeper and deeper in the wilderness where he lived. Usually Makuti would move on and by the time he returned there were just the old cooking fires and occasionally the stinking corpse of an elephant left as evidence of the two-legged ones' foray into his domain.

But this was different. There were too many smells on the wind. There were vehicles and humans and . . . It had been more than twenty years since Makuti had smelled another rhino, and maybe twenty-five since he'd smelled a female in heat, but there were some things that could not be erased. He sniffed again.

He had lived this long, by himself, in isolation in the hills above Kariba because he had honed his senses and his instincts. In his youth he had sought out other bulls to fight, and had rutted as he pleased, but these days he was cautious. But he had not smelled a female in so long.

Makuti took three paces, head high. It was unmistakable. But when he sniffed again there was a different scent. It was also a rhino, but not female. He grunted and shook his head. He couldn't interpret this sudden influx of strangers. In his small brain the primal urges that ruled the world battled for supremacy.

Fear.

Aggression.

Procreation.

If it had been anything else on the wind he would have run, but this was not the time to flee, to show fear. This was the time to fight . . . and to find that female.

'You should go, Mr Bryant,' Braedan said.

'Nonsense,' Paul said. 'We'll wait here with you. If we have to, we'll jolly well push this truck, or let the rhino out here. We don't want to be seen by passing cars.'

Elias turned the key again and the starter whirred, but the engine refused to catch. Braedan wiped his oily hands on his shirt and straightened his back. 'I just don't know if I'm going to be able to get it started. Tate's in position and already getting ready to let his one go. Don't you want to be there, to see it happen?'

Paul hesitated. Braedan was right. He and Pip did want to be there for the release of every one of the rhinos, including the young male, Gomo, who was jostling restlessly in his crate on the back of their truck right now.

'All right, Braedan,' Paul said, making his decision. 'George and Pip and I will get up to where Tate is, release our rhinos, and then head back down here. If you're still stuck, we'll offload yours, dart it again, load it into one of the other trucks and take it further in to the bush. I just hope like hell no one sees you from the road and comes to take a look.'

Tate sat on a rock and stared out over the wilderness of acacia-covered hill and valleys, but Natalie noticed his eyes kept coming back to one particular point, a steep-sided peak in the middle distance. He squinted as though he was trying to focus on something.

'What are you thinking about?' Natalie asked him.

'The past.'

She shivered. Dawn and the hour before it were the coldest times in the bush, she remembered from her childhood. She remembered freezing in her nightdress as Emmerson Ngwenya dragged her across thorn-studded ground. She reached out and put a hand on Tate's shoulder, and was encouraged when he didn't move away from her, though he kept staring at the far-off hill.

Chengetai sniffed and huffed in her crate. Natalie saw the animal's frozen breath rising like exhaust from the crate, which had been lowered to the ground in preparation for the release. They were just waiting on the others to join them. Tate had said, in his annoyed voice, that it was partly for sentimental reasons that Paul and Pip wanted to be there, but he'd added that with cranky old Chengetai it would be good to have two dart guns loaded and ready in case she did something crazy.

'Sometimes it's best to leave the past alone,' Natalie said. 'I've discovered that while working on this book.'

He shook his head. 'No. It never goes away. It's part of who we are. If it doesn't define us, it shapes us. Or rather, our memories of the past shape us.'

She stood beside him and said nothing for a while, just rested her hand on him. She knew she couldn't push him. 'It's so beautiful here,' she said at last. 'I'd forgotten how much I love the bush. I'm a bit envious of you, Tate Quilter-Phipps. I reckon I could live here. You must wake up every morning thinking how lucky you are.'

He pointed straight out, towards the hill he'd been looking at. 'I nearly died up on that hill. I didn't think I was lucky when Hope left me for Braedan. When I met her at the airport she told me what had happened, and I turned her away. I was about to shoot myself when a rhino trotted up and plucked up the courage to walk past me, to confront its fears and get on with its life.'

'Wow.'

'Yes. Wow. You know, I've wondered, these last few days, if it could be the same animal I saw around here at the waterholes. There were very few rhino in this area back in 1979, so that one had to have been a survivor of note already. To think of the terrible things it escaped, and how it adapted. It was up on that hill that I got the radio call telling me that Hope's plane had crashed and I knew right then, Natalie, that I was wrong and that I'd been a total idiot. I had no right to judge Hope – I don't have the right to judge anyone. She was human. She'd come here to apologise to me. She didn't hide anything from me, and I turned her away. And the rest . . . well, you know the story. I've pretended to hate Braedan ever since then, but it was me I loathed.'

She squeezed his shoulder. 'But you're human, too, Tate. None of us gets an instruction book for life and love. We all get it wrong sometimes. And sometimes our actions hurt others.'

They were silent a long time and Natalie didn't know whether to stay or to go. Then Tate lifted a hand and rested it on hers. 'Meeting you, seeing you, has brought it all back.'

'I'm so sorry, Tate . . .'

'No, no. It's a good thing. I needed to let Hope go, and it's time for me to stop living in the past. It's like this business with the rhinos. I don't know if it's right or stupid to release them here, but we have to give them the best chance we can to get on with their lives, to be free and to find their own way.'

Natalie's heart was pounding. He squeezed her hand and she wanted so much to avoid telling him what she knew she must. 'Tate . . . there's something I have to tell you.'

He craned his neck to look up at her, into his eyes, and she felt it then, pure and simple. He had opened himself, as much as he could, to her, and it was time for her to do the same. 'It's about Braedan . . .'

He kept his hand in hers. 'You slept with him?'

Natalie swallowed hard and could feel the tears welling, but she didn't want his pity. She was an adult and so was he, and she had done what she did because it was what she needed at the time. She'd missed the intimacy, the touch, the feel of another person, and that's why she'd gone with Braedan on the motorcycle. But being here with Tate she knew that wasn't enough. She wanted more than just sex. Natalie nodded.

For a few long, agonising seconds his face was set in stone, and Natalie held her breath. The corners of his mouth started to crinkle and she was suddenly reminded of Braedan. 'That's understandable,' he said.

She didn't know what to say.

'He's a very handsome man,' Tate said, his grin spreading across his face.

Natalie burst out laughing, and when the tension had left her body she moved in front of him, blocking his view of the far-off hill, and extended both her hands to him. 'It's not Braedan I want to spend time with, Tate.'

'I've got nothing to offer you, Natalie.'

She looked over her shoulder, at the view. 'You've got this.'

Natalie turned back to him and Tate slowly raised his hands and reached for her. Then they heard the gunfire.

CHAPTER 37

'Tate, we have to go,' Natalie said, striding from their lookout spot back to the track.

'Wait,' he said. 'We have to release these rhinos. If they're poachers down there shooting, these animals will be killed like sitting ducks.'

Natalie stopped and stared at him. 'I cannot believe this. My family are down the bottom of that hill where the shots are coming from, Tate.'

'But –'

She shook her head and raised her hand. 'Christ, I was wrong about you.' She turned and jogged down the road.

Tate looked at the knot of other drivers who had gathered around them. Chengetai's crate was the only one on the ground, ready to go.

The noise of the firing assaulted Chengetai's sensitive ears and she squealed with alarm. If her small brain registered anything about the din, it was to link it with the smells of blood and death at the *boma*.

Chengetai knew enough to flee. She bolted from her cage as soon as the sliding door was raised. She was confused and disorientated. The trees and smells around her were different and the stony ground was loose under her feet, so unlike the sandveld on which she'd been raised. But the important thing was she was free.

She ran, crashing headlong through thorn bush and flattening small trees. Unused to the steepness of the hills in her new environment, Chengetai's pace slowed when she moved through a valley and tackled the opposing slope. As she huffed and puffed she caught a scent on the wind. It was another rhino. She had lived in close proximity to others of her species all her life – much nearer than if she had grown up in the wild, where she would have only come across others at times of mating and, generally, would have avoided contact with strangers.

But Chengetai was a breeder. Eight times over the years she had given birth to calves, though each of them had been taken away from her to be hand-reared and eventually moved away.

Chengetai stopped, raised her head and sniffed the slight morning breeze. He was close, and coming towards her. As it happened, she was in oestrus and, despite the unfamiliarity of her surroundings, Chengetai knew very well what her big body was made for. She plodded uphill towards him.

Tate ran down the track after Natalie. He carried a panga he'd taken from one of the drivers before dismissing the men and telling them again to abandon their vehicles and run off and hide in the bush. They could drive no further in the direction they'd been heading and if they turned around they would walk straight into an ambush.

Chengetai was the only animal Tate had released. The three animals being carried by Braedan, Pip and Paul, and George Bryant were still somewhere down the hill. The remaining five rhinos were still in their crates, at the release spot but still not freed. Tate could hardly bear to look at them as he ran past them. If the people shooting were poachers then these animals were destined for slaughter.

But the sound of the second volley of gunfire had flicked a switch in his brain. Natalie was foolishly running towards the danger, but she cared more for the safety of her family than herself. For most of his life Tate had been far happier in the company of wildlife than mixing with people. He hadn't suddenly developed a passion for all human kind – just Natalie Bryant. He realised that if Chengetai and the other rhinos on the hilltop survived but something happened to Natalie, then this time he truly would take his life.

Tate slowed his pace down the washed-away track when he heard raised voices in the distance. It sounded like orders being issued in Shona. His command of the language was excellent, but the speakers were far away. He was afraid for Natalie, but not for himself. He felt a raging hatred rise up inside him for the men who would kill defenceless animals and the people who tried to protect them. He gripped the machete tighter in his fist.

He half-ran, half-slid down the steep hill, trying to watch his footfalls and the path ahead and the bush on either side. He detected a blur of movement in the trees to his right, but he was too slow to get into cover himself. Tate stopped, the weapon half-raised in his hand.

'Don't move.' Braedan emerged from the cover of the trees and raised Paul Bryant's .303 rifle to his shoulder and took aim at his brother.

'You bastard,' Tate said.

'Look in the mirror, brother.'

Natalie was sitting on the ground with her hands tied behind her back with duct tape. Her knee was bleeding through the rip in her trousers from where she had fallen, and her right cheek smarted from the stinging blow of the man's hand. She looked at Emmerson Ngwenya with undisguised hatred.

'Nice to see you again, by the way,' he said to her.

Natalie felt foolish and helpless. As she'd run down the hill she'd heard more gunfire, but before she could run off into the bushes, a man had emerged from the side of the track and grabbed her. He'd been armed with an assault rifle and when she'd tried to shrug off his hand he had hit her, knocking her to the ground.

She'd been half-dragged, half-frogmarched to where the other three trucks, driven by her father, grandfather and Braedan, were parked. Blood dripped from the rhino crate on the back of Braedan's vehicle and Natalie had seen the fallen outline of the slain beast. The animals on the other trucks snorted and stamped in alarm.

Natalie had tried to run to her grandmother, who'd been kneeling beside Grandpa Paul, who looked deathly white and was lying on his side. 'I think he's having another heart attack, or a stroke,' her grandmother had said. The terror was plain in her face.

Emmerson had bound Natalie while one of his henchmen covered her with his rifle. When he was finished he had pushed her to the ground, between her father and her grandmother, who was checking Grandpa Paul's pulse. Paul looked bewildered and when he saw Natalie he opened his mouth to speak but no words came out.

'My father needs a doctor, can't you see that?' George said. Natalie's father also had his hands tied behind his back.

'Where's Braedan?' Natalie whispered to her grandmother. Emmerson had not bound the older woman's hands, presumably because he didn't consider her a threat.

'He disappeared into the bush just as this lot arrived,' Pip muttered. 'I think he might be one of them. There are two others, also with guns. Emmerson sent them off into the bush to look for something, or someone, just before you arrived. And that bastard Elias . . .'

'Shut up!' Emmerson strode over to Pip and shoved the end of the barrel of his AK-47 into her temple, hard enough to almost topple her over onto her prone husband. 'No talking unless I tell you to.'

'Hah! You're pathetic, Emmerson, you two-faced bastard,' Pip spat back.

Emmerson raised his free hand.

'No!' Natalie yelled.

He looked down at her and grinned.

'It's no wonder your grandmother is angry and calls me two-faced,' he said.

Natalie looked up at the back of the truck Braedan had been driving and saw a man climbing up over the top of the rhino crate and down the outside. She hadn't seen him at first. It was Elias, the chief game scout at Kiabejane, and he carried a hacked-off rhino horn, which he took to Emmerson and handed over.

'Good work.'

Natalie could hardly believe that one of her grandparents' most trusted employees had betrayed them. 'You . . . you're the one who darted the rhino on the ranch and –'

'No,' Grandma Pip said.

Natalie looked at her.

'Go on,' Emmerson said, grinning down at them. 'Tell them, old lady, who really did poach the rhino horn from the ranch.'

George and Natalie looked at Philippa, who now cradled her husband's head in her lap. His breathing was laboured and his eyes were half-closed. He was still terribly pale, Natalie thought. She watched her grandmother, who closed her eyes for a few moments before beginning to speak, unable to look at any of them.

'I did it.'

'What?' George said. 'Mom . . . why . . . how . . .'

'It's all right, George.' She opened her eyes and looked up at Emmerson. 'I've been wanting to tell you all since I did it. I was so ashamed. But this . . . person here came to me with a proposition.'

Emmerson smiled and nodded.

'He said to me, weeks ago, that if I could supply him with a rhino horn, from a live or dead animal, it didn't matter, he would give me thirty thousand US dollars and he would ensure that the ranch stayed in our names. He told me . . . swore to me . . . that would be the end of it. He needed one rhino horn to get some people off his back and Paul and I needed the money. George, Natalie, I'm so sorry . . .'

Natalie was as astounded as her father.

'But Mom,' George said, 'I could have sent you money.'

Pip shook her head. 'I'd never ask you for money, George. The ranch is hopelessly in debt. Our electricity bills are thousands of US dollars a month now and we've got virtually no income. I needed the money to pay our staff.' She looked at Elias, who had the grace to turn away, not meeting her eyes. 'I shot the rhino with a dart gun and Elias helped me saw the horn off. Then Elias went behind my back, after I told Emmerson I wouldn't deal with him again. After he double-crossed me . . .'

Emmerson laughed. 'Don't try and lecture me about morals, old woman. You broke the law.'

'Yes, and you used the fact that we couldn't account for the missing rhino horn against us, as an excuse to take over the ranch. I tried to help you, Emmerson, after what happened to you when you were a boy. I tried to make amends, and I broke the law for you and you betrayed us.'

Emmerson spat on the ground. 'You got my father arrested, you got me thrown into juvenile gaol because your daughter lied. You think you could have made it up to me and my mother by bringing us a basket of eggs now and then? I care nothing for your white guilt. You don't belong in this country and you don't deserve to own our land.'

George looked from Emmerson back to his mother. 'What does he mean?'

Pip took a deep breath, then shook her head. 'It's nothing, George. Leave it.'

But Emmerson filled the void. 'Your sister told me at your wedding that you were sleeping with Thandi. I was shocked, angry. I did nothing to hurt Hope, but when the police came she said nothing, she betrayed me.'

George looked at the man whose life had always been filled with hatred. 'Then why didn't you say something to the police, tell them that was why you were so angry?'

'I did,' Emmerson said. 'And they called me a stinking lying *kaffir* and they beat me until I confessed that I had wanted to hurt Hope, to have sex with her.'

George looked at Philippa. 'Mom . . .'

She raised a hand. 'I knew, George. I'm your mother, after all, and it was obvious, the way you two looked at each other . . . how much time you spent at Patricia's place in the township. I wondered if Hope knew but I chose not to force the issue at the wedding. I felt guilty – yes, Emmerson, white guilt – about what happened to you in prison. It's one of the reasons I agreed to break the law for you.'

'But Grandma,' Natalie asked, since it was all coming out,

'what happened to the money? We thought Tate or Braedan might have stolen the rhino horn and sold it to help their mother.'

Pip sniffed and shook her head, then wiped her eye with a finger. Paul coughed. 'I couldn't take the money in the end, not for us. I paid the staff the three months' wages they were owed, and I transferred the rest of the money to Sharon's bank account and sent her an email from a phoney address.' She looked into her husband's face. 'My darling, do you understand what I'm saying? Can you hear me?'

Paul blinked his eyes twice, and his head moved a fraction in a nod. He reached up, his hand shaking, and took her hand in his and squeezed it.

Her grandmother was crying and her father was staring out blankly over the hills. Natalie turned to look at Emmerson Ngwenya again and saw he was staring at her, smiling. 'You kidnapped me,' she said.

His grin broadened. 'Yes, and I would have taken you across the border into Botswana if my sell-out brother hadn't shot me.'

George snapped his head around. 'You . . . you killed Winston?'

Ngwenya laughed. 'No. That is very funny. You know, the great irony is that he was killed by Braedan Quilter-Phipps, the great hero who rescued the little girl.'

'The man who found me . . . the African man who picked me up,' Natalie said, looking at her father, 'Braedan shot him.'

George sighed heavily. 'I picked up the bodies that day. There was a cover-up at the highest levels of the military. It was a mistake of war that Braedan entered an area where a group of Selous Scouts led by Winston Ngwenya was already on the trail of the terrs. When I challenged the official version I was told not to discuss what I'd seen with anyone. I couldn't look

Braedan in the eye afterwards and, ultimately, that's why I left the air force and why we moved to Australia. I felt I let Winston down by being too cowardly to stand up for the truth.' George lowered his head between his knees.

'Pah, he was my brother, yes, but he was a traitor who wanted to be a white man's dog rather than a patriot.' Emmerson spat again.

Tate didn't know why he should trust Braedan, but he did. Braedan had told him that he had been urinating in the bush when Emmerson Ngwenya and his henchmen had pulled off the road in a black Hummer. Ngwenya and three other men, all of them armed with AK-47s, had spilled from the truck and surrounded the Bryants.

He'd come looking for reinforcements, only to find that Tate had dismissed all the other drivers and told them to make for the main road, and that none of them had been armed. Braedan had talked quickly, and only just convinced Tate to follow him back into the bush when two armed men had rounded a bend, moving in tactical bounds along the track. One would stop by a tree and cover the road ahead while the other moved forward.

Braedan had held a finger to his lips, then placed his mouth next to Tate's ear and said: 'We'll come back for them. They're out looking for you and me.' Braedan had led Tate back downhill, through the bush, until at last they were behind a granite boulder, looking over the clearing where the other three trucks were parked and Emmerson Ngwenya and another man were guarding Paul, Pip, Natalie and George with their rifles. Elias stood to one side, watching.

Braedan raised his rifle to his shoulder and aimed at Emmerson. He whispered to Tate as he adjusted his stance, resting the rifle on the rock. 'When I drop him, I'm moving. I hope Elias and the other guy will scatter, but if he decides to stand and fight he'll aim at me. If I go down, pick up the rifle and kill Ngwenya, all right, *boet*?'

Tate took a deep breath. 'All right.'

Braedan glanced at him and winked. As he looked back down the sights at Emmerson Ngwenya the black man's words drifted across the hundred metres between them.

'*You know, the great irony is that he was killed by Braedan Quilter-Phipps, the great hero who rescued the little girl*,' Ngwenya was saying.

Braedan pulled the rifle tighter into his shoulder.

Now Natalie spoke: '*The man who found me . . . the African man who picked me up . . . Braedan shot him.*'

'*I picked up the bodies that day. There was a cover-up at the highest levels of the military . . .*' George Bryant continued talking but the damage had been done.

Tate looked again at Braedan and saw his brother blink a couple of times and lick his lips. He wouldn't have thought Braedan, of all people, would hesitate to shoot a man.

'Braedan,' Tate whispered. 'Take the shot.'

Braedan looked away from his target, at Tate. 'Did you just hear that?'

'It doesn't matter,' Tate hissed. 'Natalie – we've got to get to her.'

Braedan stared at him. 'I killed a Selous Scout. One of our own guys. And they gave me the Silver Cross for it. I've lived a lie for thirty years, Tate. I was so full of myself. I took Hope because I thought I deserved her more than you.'

Tate saw his brother's face start to crumble. His hands were shaking on the rifle. Braedan looked back to the vignette in the clearing below them, then screwed his eyes tight.

'It's all right,' Tate said gently, 'it was an accident, Braedan, you couldn't have known. Those scouts always dressed as terrs, yes? Someone else is to blame.'

Even though his eyes were still closed, a tear squeezed out as Braedan shook his head. 'He was surrendering to me, Tate. Even if I did think he was a terr, I shouldn't have shot him, man.'

'Enough,' Emmerson Ngwenya boomed from the clearing. 'Enough talking.' He closed the distance between him and Natalie, stood behind her and pressed the barrel of his rifle into the back of her neck. 'You, I will keep alive for a while, so you can see your family taken from you, and so I can use you later.'

'No!' Natalie yelled.

'Fuck,' Tate said. Braedan was a mess. He reached over and grabbed the rifle his brother was holding. Braedan opened his eyes and stared at him blankly, his eyes red and brimming as he released his grip. Tate worked the bolt and raised the rifle to his shoulder. There was no time to find a supporting firing position.

'Simba,' Emmerson said to his armed henchman, 'kill the son first, then the old people.'

As Simba raised his AK-47 Elias darted from behind Emmerson, where he'd been cowering, and moved between the gunman and the Bryants. Elias raised his hands. 'No, please don't shoot them.' Elias looked down at Pip. 'Mrs Bryant, I never meant for anyone to be harmed.'

'Kill him,' Emmerson said to Simba. Simba fired and felled Elias with a single shot between his eyes. Pip screamed and Simba shifted his aim to George.

'Daddy!' Natalie cried.

Tate took a breath and steeled himself for what he knew he needed to do. He took aim and fired at the man who had just shot Elias. The round caught the murderer in the chest and he pitched backwards, where he lay screaming in the dust.

Emmerson swung around, still with his arm around Natalie, and fired a wild, one-handed burst of automatic gunfire. George cried out in pain.

Tate worked the bolt of the vintage rifle as he started to climb over the granite boulder. He was raising the rifle for a second shot, on the move, when he was knocked off his feet by a rugby tackle from his left flank. Bullets whizzed over his head, harmlessly, but Tate was more worried about his crazy brother. 'Braedan, what the fuck?'

'Give me the rifle.'

'No,' Tate said. 'I can do this.' Tate gripped the weapon, but Braedan had both hands on it as well. The hardness was back in his eyes, the tears gone as quickly as they'd appeared. He flicked the butt of the rifle viciously towards Tate who, unprepared for the move, couldn't move his face out of the way in time. The rifle smashed into his cheek and he yelped in pain.

Braedan wrenched the rifle from Tate's weakened grip. He yelled a wild war cry as he vaulted the rock and ran down the hill through the bush. In the clearing Emmerson was dragging Natalie in front of him, by her hair, using her as a human shield. If Braedan had a place to stop and aim, and perhaps the fork of a tree to rest the .303 in, he might have been able to take Emmerson out with a head shot, but it was too risky on the move.

Tate, scrambling after Braedan, could see Natalie being dragged back towards the Hummer. She was yelling in agony as Emmerson pulled at her hair. George was on the ground, bleeding, but he half-raised a hand, indicating he was still alive.

Emmerson turned and fired a wild burst of bullets at Paul and Philippa, and Tate marvelled at the way the old lady threw her body over her husband's. The rounds seemed to miss them, though.

The trucks carrying the rhinos – two alive and one dead and already dehorned – were parked in a line, and the rough track leading up the hill to where Tate had released Chengetai was too narrow and sunken for the three-tonners to turn around with ease. Emmerson saw this and, as he dragged Natalie back towards his Hummer, he fired a burst of three bullets into the fuel tank of the vehicle carrying the dead rhino. Diesel fuel gushed out. Tate stopped by Pip and Paul and helped the frail Pip drag her husband behind the middle vehicle, out of Emmerson's line of sight.

'Ngwenya!' Braedan yelled. 'Stop! Let her go and I'll let you live.' Braedan had taken cover behind another truck.

'Drop your rifle or I'll kill her now!' Emmerson called back.

'Braedan,' Tate said, from a tree he was leaning against, panting.

'I don't have a clear shot. He's holding Natalie too close.'

'No, listen,' Tate said in a low voice, 'sirens.'

'The bloody cavalry, *ek se*?' Braedan grinned.

Tate smiled. 'I hope so. Throw down your rifle.'

Braedan looked at Tate and nodded, but then ducked as two other AK-47s started firing at them from further up the hill.

Natalie heard the sirens, too, but they were a long way off. When the new storm of gunfire swept the clearing Emmerson pushed her in the small of her back, sending her sprawling face first onto the front passenger seat of the Hummer.

With her hands still bound behind her it was a struggle for Natalie to right herself in the seat. By the time she had done so Emmerson was in the driver's position and had the truck in gear. He reversed the wide vehicle down the track at a scary speed, heedless of the ruts and bumps that shook her from side to side. Unrestrained by a seatbelt, Natalie cracked her head on the side window as the rear wheels left the ground in a washout.

Once out of the firing line, Emmerson turned the vehicle in a fast but sickening three-point turn and started to gather speed on the short drive back towards the main road. Emmerson drove with his left hand and kept his right on the pistol grip of the AK-47. He had the rifle cradled across his body, pointing at her. He looked at her and smiled, then started to laugh out loud.

Oh God, Natalie said to herself, the maniac was going to get away. She was going to die, just as horribly as her aunt had.

CHAPTER 38

Bullets brought up mini geysers of dirt as Tate crawled furiously across the open ground to where Simba lay dead. He snatched up the fallen man's AK-47 and turned his head at the sound of a moan of pain.

George Bryant was still alive, but his chest was soaked in blood. Tate slithered across and drew a breath at the ghastliness of the man's wound. Pink frothy bubbles of blood were forming around the wound and when George tried to speak a gargling noise came from his mouth. Tate knew a sucking chest wound when he saw one. He'd seen an anti-poaching scout die the same way.

A bullet whizzed close by his head as Tate slung the AK, put one of George's hands around his neck and heaved himself upright, lifting George in a fireman's carry. George gave a strangled cry of pure pain.

Braedan sidestepped out from behind the truck he was using for cover and screamed at the top of his lungs as he fired another round at the two men who were shooting at them from the bush. The distraction worked for a moment, and as the other gunmen concentrated their fire on Braedan who was keeping their heads down with shots aimed in their direction, Tate was able to carry George to the relative safety of the middle vehicle, where he laid him beside his father, Paul. Philippa looked up at him. 'Tate, go get Natalie.'

Tate climbed up into the cab of the truck, attracting his share of the erratic gunfire as well. He rummaged around under a seat and in the glove compartment until he found a small first aid kit. He hurriedly climbed down and tossed the kit to Philippa. 'Yes. I will,' he said to her.

Tate lifted the AK, set the selector to fire, and fired two blind shots at where he thought the gunfire was coming from.

'Over here,' Braedan called.

Tate sprinted to the next vehicle, where Braedan was crouching. There was a lull in the fire from the other two men. 'They're moving,' Braedan said. 'Trying to circle us. You've got to go get Natalie, quickly. He'll be driving at walking pace for a while, on the track. If you get behind him, shoot out his tyres. Try and get him as he's getting out of the car.'

'Braedan, I'm no good at this stuff, you –'

'I've got to nail these other guys, Tate. Listen to me,' he laid his hand on his brother's hand, 'there are the rest of them to think about as well, Paul and Pip and George. Those two gooks out there will kill them for sport if I leave, and you couldn't beat them.'

Tate nodded. He knew his brother wasn't being arrogant or unkind, just telling the truth. He was thinking like a soldier again, as if he was back in the war. Braedan's eyes were as hard and sharp as flint. He was in his element.

'I'll be right behind you, hey, as soon as I flatten these two. Then I'll come help you get Natalie. Just make sure you stop him from getting away. Go, brother,' Braedan said.

Tate looked into his reflection. 'I was wrong about you, Braedan.'

'Me, too,' he said. 'I don't know how I thought you could have dehorned that rhino, even to help Mom.'

Tate shook his head. 'No, about everything, I mean. You're a good man.'

Braedan smiled. '*Ja*, but you're the better man. You deserve her. Go.'

Before Tate could say another word Braedan was gone, opening the breech and ramming another clip of five rounds into the .303 as he ran, his movements fluid and natural as any other predator as he melted into the bush.

Tate heard the gunfire continuing behind him as he ran down the hill as fast as he could.

Makuti knew, instinctively, that he needed to protect the new female presence in his realm. He was made for this – fornicating and fighting. He heard the distant bangs, and the low growl of the machine.

All his life he had run from humans. They had hunted him and their wars had nearly killed him, several times. He was angry now, and he would, finally, defend his territory. He smashed through the young trees, their thorns and branches barely scratching his thick hide.

Emmerson could see the black ribbon of tar, the narrow road from Makuti, to the left, and Kariba, to his right.

His plan had been to turn left, but he saw the flashing blue lights rounding one of the tight bends. He cursed. From Makuti he could have headed towards Chirundu and the lower Zambezi Valley, where a man could get lost in the bush for a while. Now, however, he would have to turn towards the lake-side town of Kariba, a dead end option by land. It would be impossible for him to cross the dam wall by road into Zambia, but perhaps he could abandon the Hummer somewhere on the lake shore and commandeer a boat to cross the border, or head up river.

The last section of the track was through a creek. It wasn't flowing, but it was a steep-sided gully. He slowed the Hummer to crawling pace. The police Land Rovers were visible now, and speeding ahead of them, now that it had cleared the bends, was a black BMW. The car looked familiar.

'They are too late,' Emmerson said as he wrestled with the steering wheel one-handed, his other hand still clamped on the rifle.

Natalie looked at him and he could see the despair in her eyes. She knew he was right and her terror aroused him. He would make it. He was Emmerson Ngwenya. He would find a way through this and he would use her on the boat and throw her body overboard afterwards. Emmerson was also confident his men Nicholas and Henry would kill the other whites before they disappeared into the bush.

The Hummer passed through the muddy creek bed and began to climb. Emmerson floored the accelerator. The wheels spun for a moment, then gained traction as the front tyres found level ground and bit in. As the horizon came into view through the narrow windscreen, so, too, did a black rhino. It lowered its head and charged.

Emmerson, shocked by the sight of the animal and unsure what to do, took his foot off the accelerator. A solid tonne of rhinoceros smashed into the front grille, buckling the bonnet and sending a jet of steam high into the air from the shattered radiator. Emmerson rammed the gearstick into first and pumped the gas pedal. The rhino danced to one side, then circled. As the vehicle started to move forward Emmerson felt the rear of the solid truck being knocked askew as the rhino rammed into the passenger door behind him.

Emmerson saw the rhino back off and then it started to gallop alongside him, trying to head him off. He didn't think he could push it aside or even kill it if he rammed it, and the temperature gauge was climbing. Emmerson stuck the AK-47 out the window and pulled the trigger. Most of his wild burst went wide of his target, but he was sure he saw two bullets hit the blurred grey flank.

Instead of scaring the rhino off, though, it only enraged the animal further. It charged and smashed into the vehicle once more, shattering a headlight and the front bumper. It lowered its head and pushed again.

Emmerson tried to accelerate, but the rhino must have caused greater damage to the front of the engine than just holing the radiator. When he took his foot off the brake the Hummer started to move backwards, such was the force of the rhino's push. It backed up and rammed the vehicle again. Emmerson knew he would have to escape on foot, but that meant killing the rhino first. Given the length of the bonnet and the position of the rhino, there was not enough room to get a good shot in. As the rhino backed up for its next charge it drifted further out of his field of view, towards the passenger side.

Emmerson opened the driver's side door and got out. He edged slowly forward, bringing the rifle to bear in his shoulder. As he neared the right front edge of the vehicle, the rhino put up its head. A couple of inches closer and he would have it clearly in his sights. The rhino turned, almost on the spot, and started to run away from the vehicle. A perfect shot, Emmerson thought as he squeezed the trigger.

As the first two bullets left the barrel Emmerson was pitched forward. Natalie Bryant was on top of him, her body flailing without the benefit of her hands to cushion her fall or protect her. He threw her off and lashed back at her with the butt of the rifle, striking her on the face.

Natalie got herself to her knees and shuffled towards the rear of the truck. Emmerson heard the wail of the sirens clearly. The black BMW had pulled over on the edge of the tar road and a police Land Rover was easing onto the rough track.

Emmerson looked down at Natalie, crawling away from him in fear of her life. He saw the police and wondered if he could talk his way out of this one. The door of the BMW opened and he recognised his sister Thandi immediately. If she had the police on side he was finished.

His mother was right. The whites cared nothing for them. Philippa Bryant pretended to the world she was a do-gooder, but her misguided acts had landed his father in gaol, and her coddling of his older brother had caused him to sell out his own people. His mother had known best when she'd told him that all settlers must, in the end, die, if Zimbabwe was to be free. He raised the rifle to his shoulder.

Tate crested a rise in the track and, at last, caught sight of the black Hummer. It had stopped on the far side of a dry creek bed. He saw Emmerson Ngwenya standing beside the open driver's door, with a rifle pointed down at the ground. There was no sign of Natalie.

Tate didn't think twice. He lifted the AK, aimed quickly and fired two rounds at the corrupt minister. Emmerson ducked and turned around. He loosed off a burst of fire, but Tate was already running down the hill. Emmerson leaned on the roof of the four-by-four, steadying his rifle. Tate kept running. He had to get to Natalie. He readied himself for the tearing impact of the bullet. There was no turning away now, no running, no hiding. He would save her or he would die trying.

Tate looked at Emmerson and fancied he could see the hate in his expression from a hundred metres. Then something caught his eye.

From the bush, on the side of the track, came a blur of grey tailed by a cloud of disrupted leaves, twigs and dirt as the rhino burst from the bush. The creature lowered his head and charged into the open door of the Hummer. As it slammed closed it crushed Emmerson Ngwenya and the rifle fell from his hand. He screamed in agony, but the rhino kept its head against the door, scrabbling for purchase in the dirt with its big front feet.

When the rhino finally eased off and took a step back, Emmerson fell to the ground, his organs pulverised. The rhino lowered its head to the bleeding man and hooked him with its long, wickedly sharp front horn. The rhino lifted Emmerson off the ground then tossed him aside.

Tate kept running. He could see police in field uniforms disembarking from a Land Rover, and a woman in a business suit was following in their wake. As Tate ran closer he saw the rhino clearly. It was a big, old male, his hide scarred and ear mauled from past battles and his ribs starting to show. This was not one of the Bryants' sleek, pampered, overfed animals. This was the same bull he'd seen, the one whose presence had led them here from the other side of the country.

'Tate!' Natalie called.

He saw her now as she awkwardly made it to her feet and stumbled towards the rear of the Hummer. Tate sprinted towards her, but the rhino, which had started to amble back into the bush after losing interest in Emmerson Ngwenya's body, suddenly turned.

'Get in the truck!' Tate yelled.

Natalie paused, then looked back over her shoulder. She saw the rhino, its head up and full of the arrogance that comes with victory. Natalie backed along the vehicle and reached for the rear door handle. 'It's locked!' She started to run, towards Tate and away from the rhino.

Makuti lowered his head for another charge.

'Into the trees!' Tate shouted. But even as he said the words he knew it was impossible for Natalie to outrun or out-dodge a black rhino in full charge, and totally impossible for her to get up off the ground to a safe height without the use of her hands. As these thoughts came to him he was raising the rifle to his shoulder.

'Tate!' Natalie screamed, looking over her shoulder at the charging tonne of muscle, hide and bone, his horn lowered like a knight's lance.

Tate drew a breath and pulled the trigger. Makuti had turned and was just coming on broadside to Tate. At less than a hundred metres he couldn't miss. He held the pressure and raked the grand old animal's side. Tiny puffs of dust and flowering dark holes told him at least half-a-dozen of the rounds had found their mark, ripping through the tough skin and shredding the rhino's vital organs. It was the way the poachers did it. No finesse, no precision, no care.

Tate sprinted again, even as he saw the rhino's faltering steps. Natalie tripped and fell in the animal's path and Tate dropped the rifle, the magazine now empty, and reached for her. Makuti hit the ground, raising a cloud, and blew blood and dying breath out of his wide nostrils as his momentum ploughed grass and dirt.

Tate wrapped his arms around Natalie. The rhino had come to rest with its lower jaw almost on her heels. With his last ounce of strength Makuti gave a final dismissive toss of his head that would have skewered Natalie if Tate hadn't picked her up off the ground and crushed her to his chest.

Natalie buried her head in Tate's bush shirt, her breath coming in racking sobs, as he fumbled for the tape on her wrists and unwrapped them. Tate looked down at the dead rhino as Natalie shook her hands free of the remnants of her bindings. She placed her hands around his neck, looked up into his eyes and kissed him.

From the distance, back up the hill, where the other rhinos were still in their crates, they heard gunfire.

Charara Safari Area, Zimbabwe, 2011

Braedan's grave was in the cemetery in Bulawayo, in the company of friends who'd died during the war, so they hadn't erected a memorial on the hill in the middle of the bush, in sight of Lake Kariba.

On their second annual visit to the cemetery, George and Thandi also took the time to visit the grave of Sergeant Winston Ndlovu. They stayed a while, pulling the weeds out and tidying it as best they could. Afterwards they walked hand in hand back to the car and went for a cup of tea in town at a nice new café full of business-people and tourists.

George surprised Thandi in the café by asking her to marry him. George's divorce from Susannah had come through, and they'd been lovers, again, for more than a year, but as a high-profile government minister Thandi couldn't live openly with a married man.

'Thandi,' he said nervously, 'I can understand if you don't want to . . . for political reasons. But I've decided to stay on in Zimbabwe. It's where I'm from and I want to see if I can help and . . .'

She reached out across the table and took his hand. 'Of course I want to, George. Yes.' She leaned across and they kissed, and

George ordered champagne. He could tell people in the café recognised Thandi – she was being tipped as a possible future prime minister of Zimbabwe – and the whispers turned to murmurs, but he didn't care.

When he told his mother that evening over dinner she was delighted, but a little sad too. 'I just wish your father could have been here for the wedding,' she said. 'All we ever wanted for you and Hope was a happy life in a peaceful country.' She raised her glass. 'To happiness and peace.'

George thought of all the sorrow in their lives, and their country, and he wondered if peace and happiness could ever really be possible. Thandi smiled at him, and he thought they just might be.

Two days later he, Thandi and Philippa drove to Makuti. Tate was waiting for them on the main road, with a white Land Rover Defender that had been a gift from a rhino-conservation charity overseas. When George pulled over he helped his mother get out of the car and into the passenger seat of the Land Rover. George and Thandi, both of them dismissing Tate's offer of a hand, climbed into the rear of the pickup and sat on the wheel wells as Tate negotiated the rough track to the top of the hill.

George's father had never really recovered from the stroke he'd suffered on the day of the gunfight with Emmerson Ngwenya and his cronies, and he'd passed away, peacefully, in hospital a month later. In some ways, George thought, it was probably for the best. Kiabejane was gone and Paul and Philippa Bryant had done well not to face prosecution for illegally moving so many of the state's rhinos from one part of Zimbabwe to another, and losing two – one dead and one illegally released – in the process.

Without Thandi Ngwenya's evidence, against her brother and in favour of the participants in Paul's audacious scheme, they probably all would have been locked up. The late Emmerson Ngwenya had been abandoned by his influential government friends, including the President, in the days after the shootout, and other witnesses, a chauffeur and a young boy, had come forward to corroborate Thandi's suspicions that Emmerson had murdered their father.

Thandi had saved George's life.

The police had put a dressing on George's gunshot wound and loaded him into Thandi's BMW. It was only thanks to her negotiating the winding road to Kariba at high speed that George had made it to hospital before he bled out. A doctor stabilised him and George was rushed to the airport for a flight to Johannesburg and the emergency surgery that had saved his life. Thandi had begged to travel with him to South Africa, but without her passport she hadn't been allowed. She'd caught a commercial flight and rushed to his bedside as soon as she could extricate herself from the investigation that followed the killings at Makuti.

Thandi had also been instrumental in helping Philippa explain to the parks and wildlife authorities that the Bryants had only shipped their rhinos across the country illegally because they feared Emmerson would have killed them all. The surviving animals had been fed and watered, checked by a vet, and then turned around and driven back to Kiabejane.

Tate had changed for the better, George thought, in the past year. He looked fit and tanned and the mane of wavy professorial hair had been trimmed into an edgier, more rugged cut. He was also a more personable human being, though still quite reserved around people he didn't know. Tate smiled as he chatted to Philippa in the cab, and George was pleased to see his mother return the grin, plus a wink and a hand laid on Tate's as he changed gears. George had wondered if the trip to Kariba might be too taxing for her, emotionally and physically, but he reminded himself that she was probably tougher than the lot of them. Nothing had been said of Philippa's involvement in the illegal dehorning of the rhino and the investigators had assumed that Elias had been reporting directly to Emmerson Ngwenya.

While the Bryants' name had been cleared, there was no stopping the handover of Kiabejane to the local community. What was confirmed, however, as soon as the dust from the investigations had settled, was the appointment of Minister Thandi Ngwenya as chairperson of the Kiabejane management trust in the place of her late father.

Pip had decided to move into a retirement home in Bulawayo, much to George's relief, although she regularly organised bus trips for her fellow residents to travel out to the ranch, where she would sit for hours, while the other elderly people went on game drives, talking to and stroking the rhinos in the *boma* and then tending to Paul's grave on a hill overlooking their favourite dam on the property.

The climb to the top of the hill was slow and bouncy, but George felt good being out in the bush again, with the sun on his back. He squeezed Thandi's hand. Natalie knew about the divorce proceedings, and had met Thandi socially several times. She'd seen her parents drift apart into their separate worlds, but she was mature enough not to take sides. George hoped she'd be happy with his news. He got on well with Thandi's daughters, who seemed only to have bad memories of their late father.

Halfway up, at the spot none of them could forget, Tate stopped the truck and helped Pip out while George and Thandi climbed down from the back. They followed Tate, single file, a short way into the bush to the boulder with the view that looked out over the hills to the lake. George had been in the back of Thandi's BMW, being driven down the narrow winding road to Kariba, when Tate and a party of policemen had cautiously advanced up the hill.

The first of Ngwenya's henchmen they had come across was lying on his back with his throat cut. Braedan had evidently ambushed him and killed him first, but something had gone wrong for him afterwards. The police investigators theorised that he had begun sneaking up on the second gunman, having successfully outflanked him, but before he was close enough to get a clear shot at him, the man had spotted Braedan and opened fire on him, hitting him in the gut. The blood trails, the detectives said, showed Braedan had advanced on the man, courageous to the last, and taken another two shots to his arm and leg, but had managed to fire back and hit the other man in the shoulder. The two men were locked together in an obscene, bloody embrace, and in the process Braedan appeared to have killed the final gunman with his bare hands, strangling him before dying himself.

They paused by the rock and Tate looked at George. 'You wanted to say something?'

George nodded. He felt a little self-conscious, not being given to public displays of emotion, but he also knew he needed to say this. 'I didn't like Braedan Quilter-Phipps, for a long time. In fact, I hated him. I channelled my hatred for the war, and for my friend Winston's death, into my feelings for your brother.'

George swallowed hard, and Thandi moved next to him and took his hand. 'It was small of me to see Winston's death as anything other than a tragic accident of war, but perhaps I was envious of the glory that was bestowed upon a young man who, for all he knew, had saved the life of my child. I was wrong.

'Braedan was as much a victim of the war and its aftermath as any of us, yet he had the courage to carry on, despite what life threw at him. Others, me included, were happier to complain and turn our backs.' George looked at his mother and she nodded to him. 'Braedan saved our lives that day. No, more than that. He laid down his life for us.'

There was a movement behind them and George turned.

'Sorry,' Natalie said. 'I wasn't going to come, but I decided in the end I should come back here, for his sake.'

'Grandpa!' said the fair-haired little boy in her arms. Natalie dropped him down and Tate smiled as his son ran to George's leg and tugged on his trousers. Natalie followed the boy and greeted George, Thandi and her grandmother, and kissed each of them in turn. In his hand the boy held a photo, printed on plain paper. 'Rhino, Grandpa . . . rhino.'

George bent and scooped his grandson up into his arms. 'Hello, my boy, what's this you've got here?' George took the picture in his free hand and held it away so he could see it without his glasses. Thandi tickled the little boy while she craned her head around him to see the image.

'Tate took it two days ago, Dad, just before dawn,' Natalie said. 'We've been dying to tell you and Grandma, but Tate made me wait.'

'Let me see,' Pip said, moving closer. George showed her the photo and she peered at it, moving his hand so it was just a few centimetres from her eyes. 'My goodness, that looks like Chengetai.' She placed a hand over her mouth.

'You're right, it is her,' Tate said. 'And the calf behind her looks to be about one year old. It has to be Makuti's. They must have mated just before I had to kill him.'

George looked at Tate and saw the grin. The autopsy done on Makuti had shown that the old rhino was almost dead from the wounds inflicted by Emmerson Ngwenya before Tate delivered the coup de grâce to him, saving Natalie's life in the process.

'What's going to happen to them now that you've finally found her? Does this mean my daughter won't have to live the life of a poor researcher in a tent any more?'

'I'd miss the bush if we had to leave, Dad,' Natalie said, hooking her arm through Tate's.

'Parks and wildlife have decided to leave Chengetai and her calf here, and possibly release another male and female here from Kiabejane. If that happens we'll probably get funding to stay on, monitoring them all,' Tate said.

'Well, if it makes you happy, then good for you,' George said.

'I'm sorry, Dad,' Natalie said, 'I interrupted you before.'

George shook his head, then looked at his grandson in his arms. 'No, there's nothing more to be said. Just make sure Braedan here knows his uncle died a hero.'

ACKNOWLEDGEMENTS

As I write this, the future of the rhino in Zimbabwe is by no means certain. The same goes for democracy. However, while travelling in Zimbabwe, researching and writing this book and some of the previous ones, the thing that has struck me time and again, through the years of privation and ruin, is the underlying conviction of the people of that country that things will change for the better one day. There is no lack of will, but sadly no lack of obstructions either.

Several people inside and outside of Zimbabwe helped me a great deal with this book and I'd like to thank: Rowan Calder of Sirtrack Tracking Solutions for his information on radio tracking devices; Neville Rosenfeld and Georgina Winch for information about the Bulawayo/Plumtree area; Dr Peter Buss, Senior Manager of the Kruger National Park Veterinary Unit in South Africa, for telling and showing me how to dart animals; Peter Petter-Bowyer, author of *Winds of Destruction*, a history of the Rhodesian Air Force, for details of helicopter call signs and airfield locations; Dave Munro and Ian Puller for information about the Rhodesian African Rifles; Wally van Welie of Aviation Adventures in Hazyview, South Africa, for taking me up in a microlight; and Michele Hofmeyr, manager of the Kruger National Park plant nursery, for facts about endangered plants, and for once again finding people for me to interview.

Taku Scrutton, Ross and Margie Milne, Julia Salnicki, Neil Johns, Tracey Hawthorne, Jim Welsh and Elizabeth Reese all read all or part of the manuscript and provided invaluable feedback and corrections on places, language and culture in Zimbabwe and the former Rhodesia. I thank you all for your time.

My friends inside Zimbabwe – Dennis, Liz, Don, Vicky, Sally, Scotty, Doug, Helen, and Colin – all make travelling and staying in that country a pleasure, even when times are tough. I hope we'll all see happier times there soon.

Two civilian Air Rhodesia Viscount passenger aircraft en-route from Kariba to Salisbury (now Harare) were downed during the Rhodesian Bush War by ZIPRA forces armed with Soviet-made SA-7 surface to air missiles. The Viscount *Hunyani* was downed in September 1978 and the *Umniati* in February 1979. Although I've changed the date, I drew heavily on the details of the *Hunyani* tragedy when writing the scene of the Viscount crash in this book. Of the fifty-six crew and passengers on board the *Hunyani*, eighteen survived the forced landing in a cotton field, although ten of these passengers, including seven women and two children, were subsequently murdered by ZIPRA forces that arrived shortly after the crash. All fifty-nine people on board the Viscount *Umniati* died when their aircraft crashed. I drew much of my information on this section from Rob Rickards's memorial website, *Viscounts in Africa – The Air Rhodesia Story*.

My prime research source for background on the Selous Scouts was the book *Pamwe Chete* by the unit's former commanding officer, Lieutenant Colonel Ron Reid-Daly. Friendly-fire incidents, where scouts dressed as enemy combatants were mistakenly killed by Rhodesian Security Forces, did happen.

I've probably distorted history a bit by having Braedan's Rhodesian Light Infantry Fire Force stick in Matabeleland in 1979, but other than that I've tried to stay as true as possible to the military tactics, techniques and procedures of the time.

As with some of my previous books, several fine people donated (in some cases, staggering) amounts of money to various charity auctions to have their names used as characters in the book. I'd like to publicly thank Fred Quilter for paying for his grandsons Tate and Braedan Quilter-Phipps to appear, via his donation to the Save Foundation (NSW), a charity dedicated to rhino conservation; and Sue Chipchase and Bev Poor for their contributions to Painted Dog Conservation INC for the respective inclusions of Victoria Reagan and Nicholas Duncan. Farina Khan's character was named in recognition of her support for The Grey Man, an NGO which rescues child prostitutes in South East Asia.

Thanks, as always, to my wonderful unpaid editors, my wife, Nicola, mother, Kathy, and mother-in-law, Sheila. I couldn't be doing any of this without you three.

My friends at Macmillan allow me to live a dream life and I hope no one ever pinches me and wakes me up from it. Thanks to Publishing Director Cate Paterson, Publisher James Fraser, Commissioning Editor Alex Nahlous, Senior Editor Emma Rafferty, Copy Editor Julia Stiles, and Publicist Louise Cornegé. Thanks, too, to my agent Isobel Dixon for her fantastic work in getting me known further afield.

And last, but not least, if you've made it this far, thank you.

www.tonypark.net
www.tonyparkblog.blogspot.com